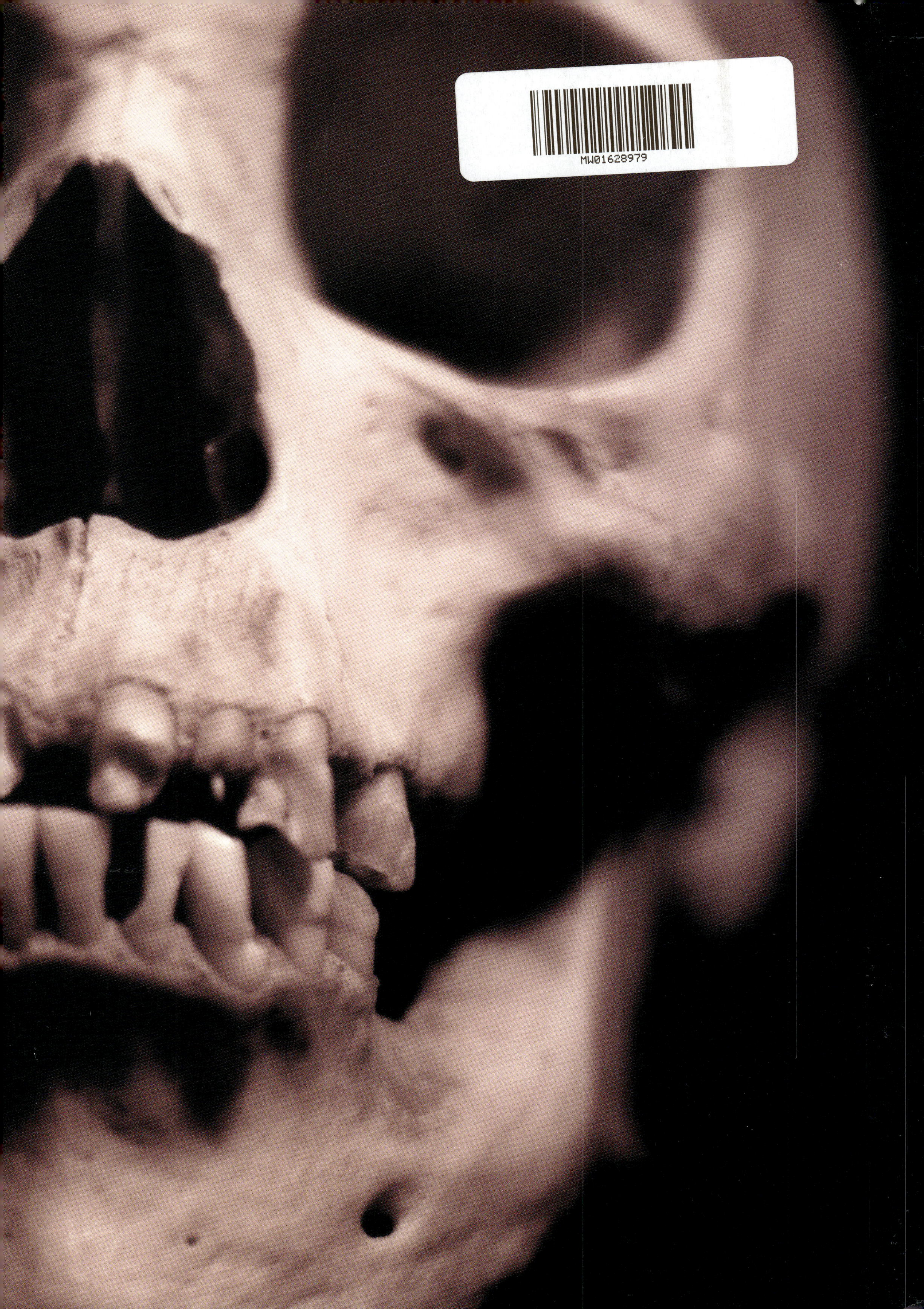

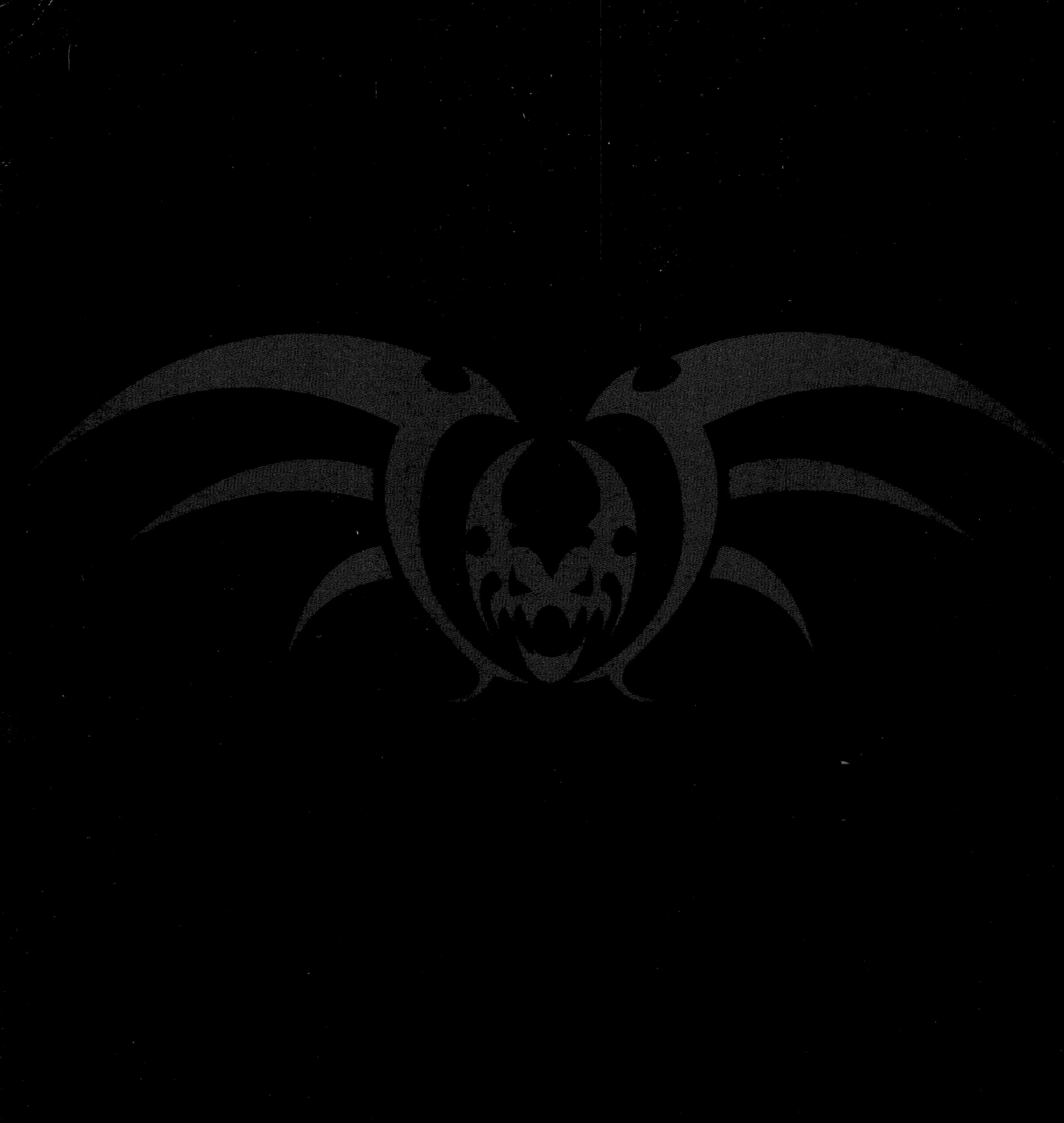

American Gothic

The Artwork of Carlos Batts

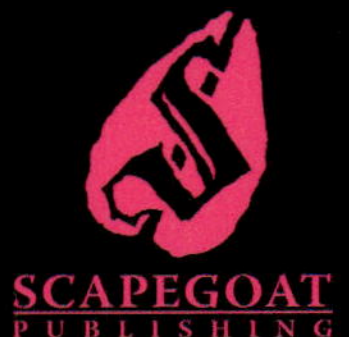

SCAPEGOAT
PUBLISHING

Published by Scapegoat Publishing (a division of Reptilian Inc.)
403 South Broadway
Baltimore, Maryland 21231
410.327.6853
www.reptilianrecords.com
www.adversaryrecordings.com
www.scapegoatpublishing.com

Editor Roger Gastman
Art Direction Tony Smyrski (www.crashcontentcreative.com)
Copy Editor Simon Steinhardt
Production Assistant JasonVaughn
Introduction Steve Lemons
Foreword John Gilmore
Batts Logo Design Nathan Carlisle

Photography Print and Drum Scans
provided by Chrome & "R"
8016 Melrose Avenue
Los Angeles, CA 90046
323.651.5173
www.chromeandr.com

Thank You to
My Wife, my Muse, my Everything: Lillian, my Mom and Dad, Antoine, Kyron, Eca, Laura, my friend and publisher Chris X, and Roger Gastman, for his support and persistence.

All my friends: Mike Timpson, Chris Haston, Anthony Trifiletti, Mark Sponagule, Jeff Siegel, Matthias Reuss, Steve Lemons, John Gilmore, Darryll Wharton, Andre Owens, Mikaya & Precious, Nathan Carlisle, Jason Vaughn, Allen Savage, Olga & Antonio, Seaton Lin, Kevin & Shari, Jay Taylor, Tom Monteleone, Alfred, Eddie Donaldson, Dave Naz & Barb, Nico B., Stanley Key, Tony Acosta, Rich & Shawna, Steve Diet Goedde, Patrick Hoelck, Rick Castro, Estevan Oriol, Gus, Mitch, Brian, Shayan, El Evil, Scott Phillips, Pat Rogers, Joe McCloud, George Pitts, Amy & Doug, Abby Ehman, Keck, Mike DHUNDEE, Nelly, Scott Ewen, Rick Berry, Ellen Datlow, Ben R., Danzig, Chip, Christopher J., Ryan Rapuy, Danny Boy, Kelly @ 3rd Rail, Derek, Todd, Wafe, Axis, Shephard, GIANT, Rich Coleman, Emilia Serrano, Suzanne K., Mu & Jackson, Tony, Jorge, Richard @ Chrome & R, Chris @ FROMEX, Ron, Colin, Maria, & Juliet @Last Gasp, Eric, Lisa, Mark, Boris, Marina @ The Erotic Museum, David Anderson @ AFX Studio, The ROUGHHOUSE, Reptilian Records, Century Media Records, Roadrunner Records, Relapse Records, Metal Blade Records, Prosthetic Records, Abacus Records.

All the models that have contributed to my work, especially Sarah and Anna.

All the bands & musicians that have been the soundtrack to my life: Bad Brains, Public Enemy, Slayer, Minor Threat, Cro-Mags, Mos Def, Hatebreed, Company Flow, N.W.A., Guns & Roses, EPMD, Metallica, Tricky, Pig Destroyer, Beastie Boys, Fudge Tunnel, Godflesh, Helmet, Septic Death, Black Sabbath, Run DMC, Misfits, Mastodon, Dog Fashion Disco, Carcass, KRS-ONE, Agoraphobic Nosebleed, Bjork, Radiation 4, daybreak, Earth, Wind and Fire, Stevie Wonder, Al Green, Frankie Beverly & Maze, Baltimore Club Music, bad Drum & Bass and horrible Speed/Death Metal Bands.

Printed in Singapore

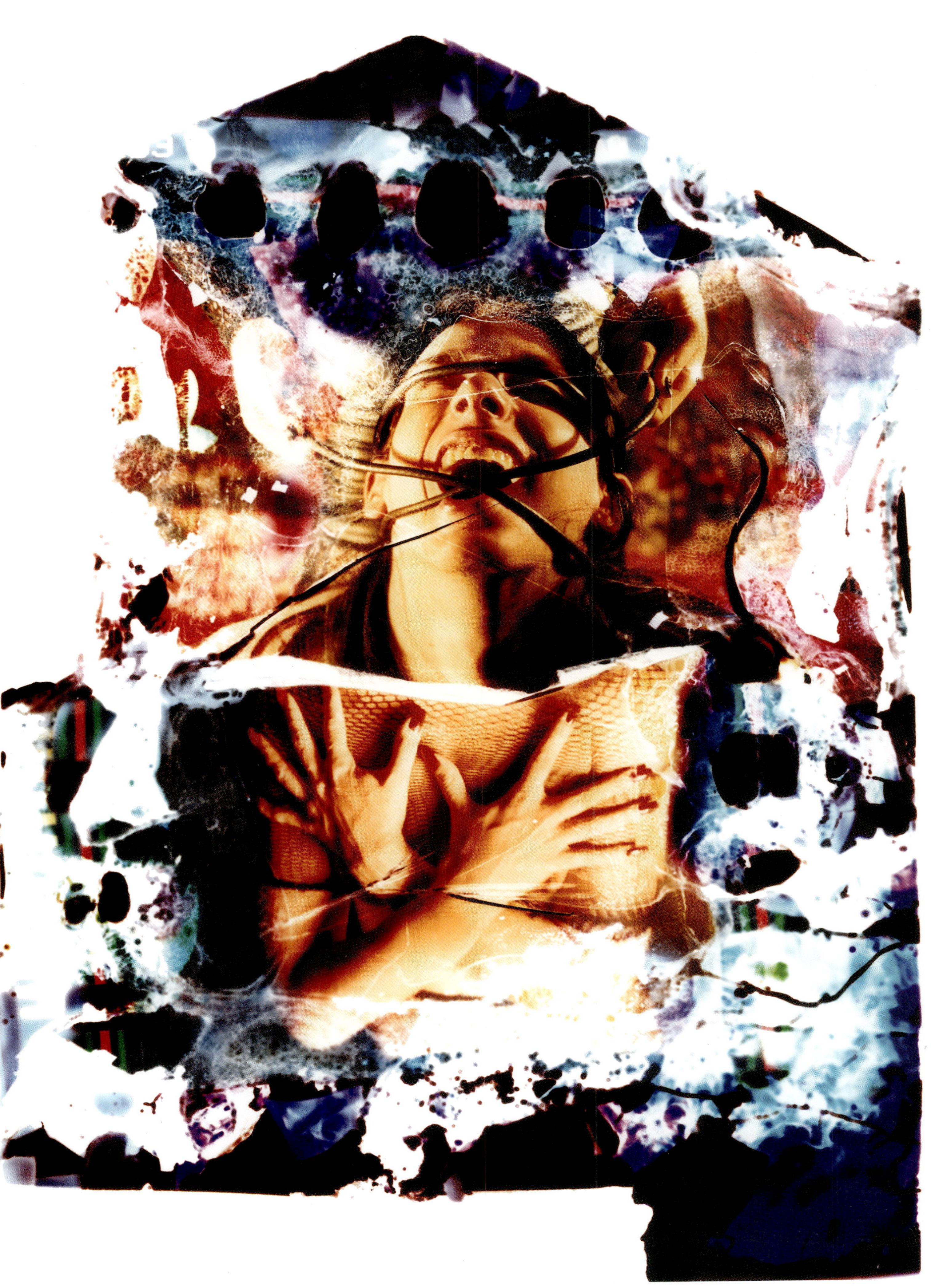

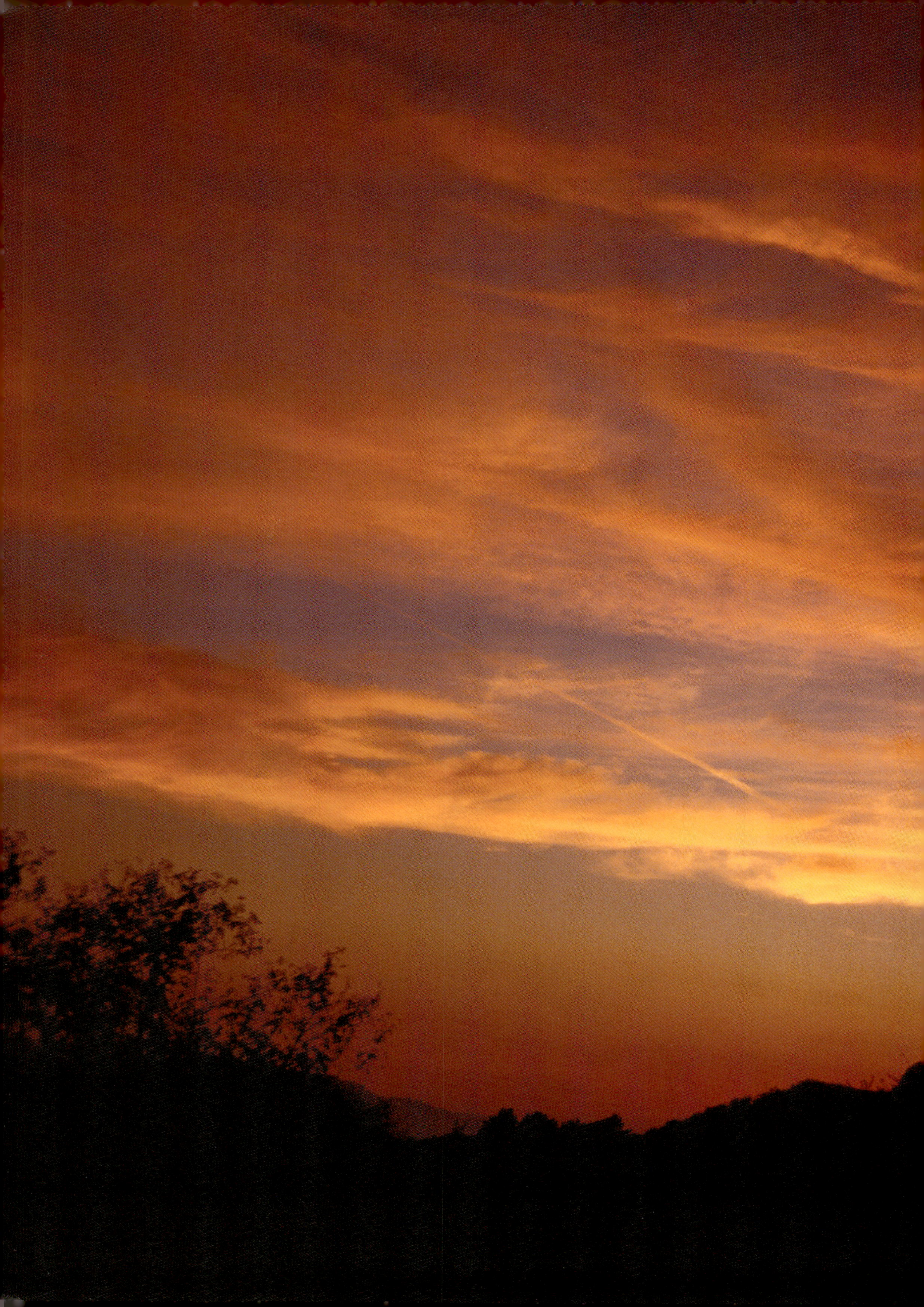

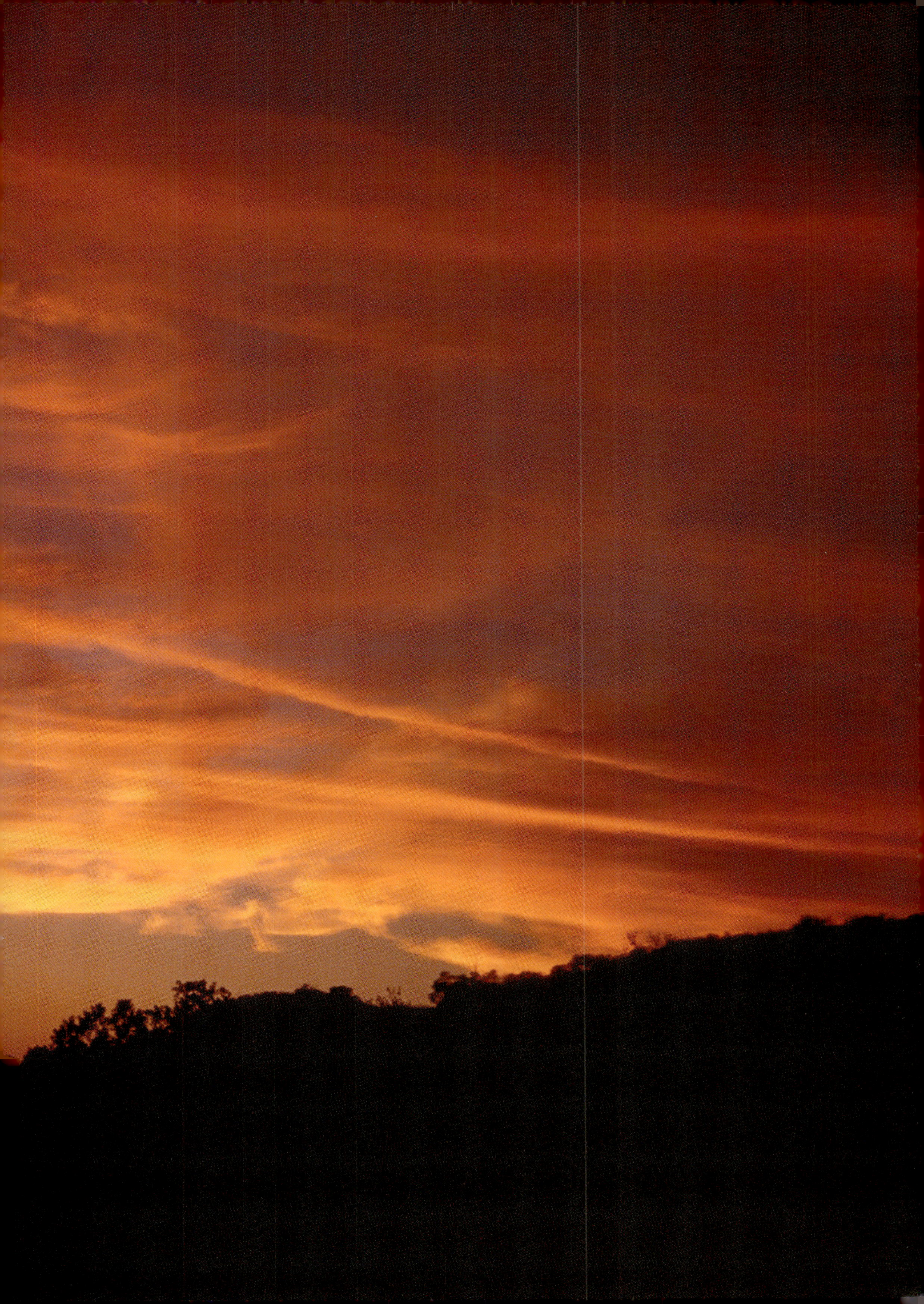

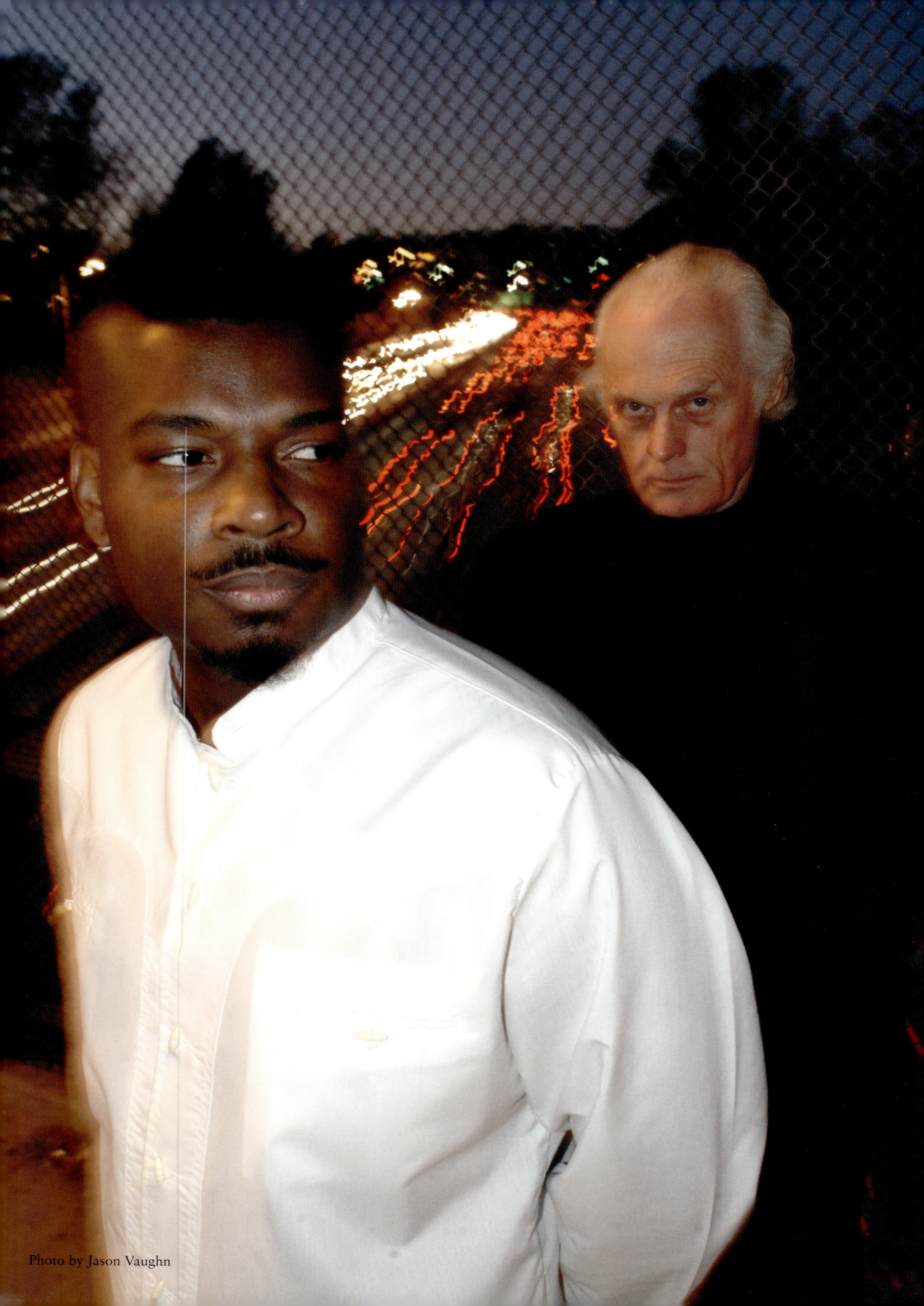
Photo by Jason Vaughn

FOREWORD

FALLING INTO A CHAMBER OF DARK MIRRORS

I am captivated, sucked into the breathing membranes of movement and color and dark, pulsing images. A glowing window lunges at me from a shamble of twisted hues and black motion. Like a stark eye, it beckons. I can climb through and I'm in a maze of props and sidewalks, broken into partial slots as crowded as stacks of sets from some old movie I was in so long ago, hunting the ghost of myself. I'm pulled amidst these convoluting, distorting façades, taken behind the screen and thrust of Carlos Batts's imagination. I'm hurled into the dark, overwhelmed, but then the suddenness of a scalding light knifes between bent barriers of color and shapes. I'm finding some potent revelation I've missed in all the years of my life: terror and sexuality fusing, melting like hot plastic or a lava lamp. Lust and love shred into one another, impulses torn like limbs from sockets and slung spinning into space. Magic and fear float and weave in an apparition of a sheet of tumbling, mismatched fabric like cascading dark water I've never seen before.

I collide with innumerable spurts of tortured mirrors, each reflection ringing a part of myself in recognition of what we've buried, beating beneath the surface. Art beyond the cusp of convention, shrieking originality and defiance, announces the arrival of the real artist: Carlos Batts, stepping off some limit of mind and falling at a hurtling pace through the special and terrible space of his renegade spirit. Chunks of twisted humanity leap and clutch like desperate lovers, pulling us into the work bodily; pulling us spiritually.

I say, "He can't know exactly what he's done," which is on target, for his art contains the purity of genius that doesn't ask, "What've I done?" It keeps going, diving deeper into what the poet Rainer Rilke called the *ding en such*—the thing in itself. Batts grabs it by the balls. His work ravages and stultifies the placid mediocrity of his contemporaries. He eats them for breakfast. Mixing color and splicing pictures from the contractile aperture of his soul, the scalpel of his craft slicing carefully like a pathologist, Batts rises above the *dinge* of nowadays art. He butchers lumps of experience, whacking at chunks of truth and squeezing them into our mind and spirit where they shake and quiver, wriggling like the legs of capsized bugs.

Batts emerges in *American Gothic* as the visual poet of our time. His visceral language rapes reality and sucks it into the dream. His penetration overwhelms. He rolls out heretofore-unknown shapes and hunks of the dead, or thriving things with haunted mouths and hungry eyes. And the ancient is alive in Batts's work beneath the wet, leaking colors and shapes, yet his futuristic reach is planetary – miles out in space.

I pinball or float through these overlapping layers of unnamed human history: mysterious, pulsing about me as if I'm swept in some vicious mudslide and swallowed in mankind's perversity as it dances in silent ascent from the grave.

I'm traveling in a symphony composed by a genius or madman. The milieu sinks me into its black depths, so rotted in spots I'm being consumed. I cry for help and a hand reaches. There are bones, voluptuous breasts, a lunar mouth, and the neck of a skeleton. Something is saving me from the terror I've carried all these years. Or am I being carted off for a sacrifice? No – I'm cuddled in a mush of soft flesh and paint, and, whether dead or alive, these nipples beat like red, bleeding hearts.

This astounding array of uncompromising art allows me to lose my footing in the day-to-day, and I rejoice. Lost in Carlos Batts's brutal funhouse of self-reflecting mirrors, I'm in the depths of art, prowling past the fangs and gags and the beams of lines, some heavy as jagged sticks of iron, past planks of color collapsing and thrusting abstractly like the pilings of a sinking pier. Love vomits forth in secret yearnings, forbidden and dangerous: bound heads, bound bodies, fear beyond order, and blind sexuality in chained resignation. Murderous impulses are probed in the dark holes of the soul.

I still say, "He can't know what he's done" to all who witness the power of his art. Like playing some twisted Devil's fiddle, Batts rushes me into this world of black mirrors, sticks and stacks of props, and discombobulated, leaking bodies, and I'm awhirl in a daze of seeing faces in the broken glass. Each face is mine. My spirit loosens from its threads and wires and I'm on the dark side of the moon, knowing the peace of completeness that true art affords.

The impact of great art is never manufactured as a message. The meaning is subliminal and integral to the textures, sticks and mortar, and assemblage and completion that comprise a masterpiece. With *American Gothic*, Carlos Batts reaches into our psyche as his artistic brilliance shoves its way to the front ranks as a major voice in our dark, passionate, troubled, and aching time.

John Gilmore
Los Angeles, California

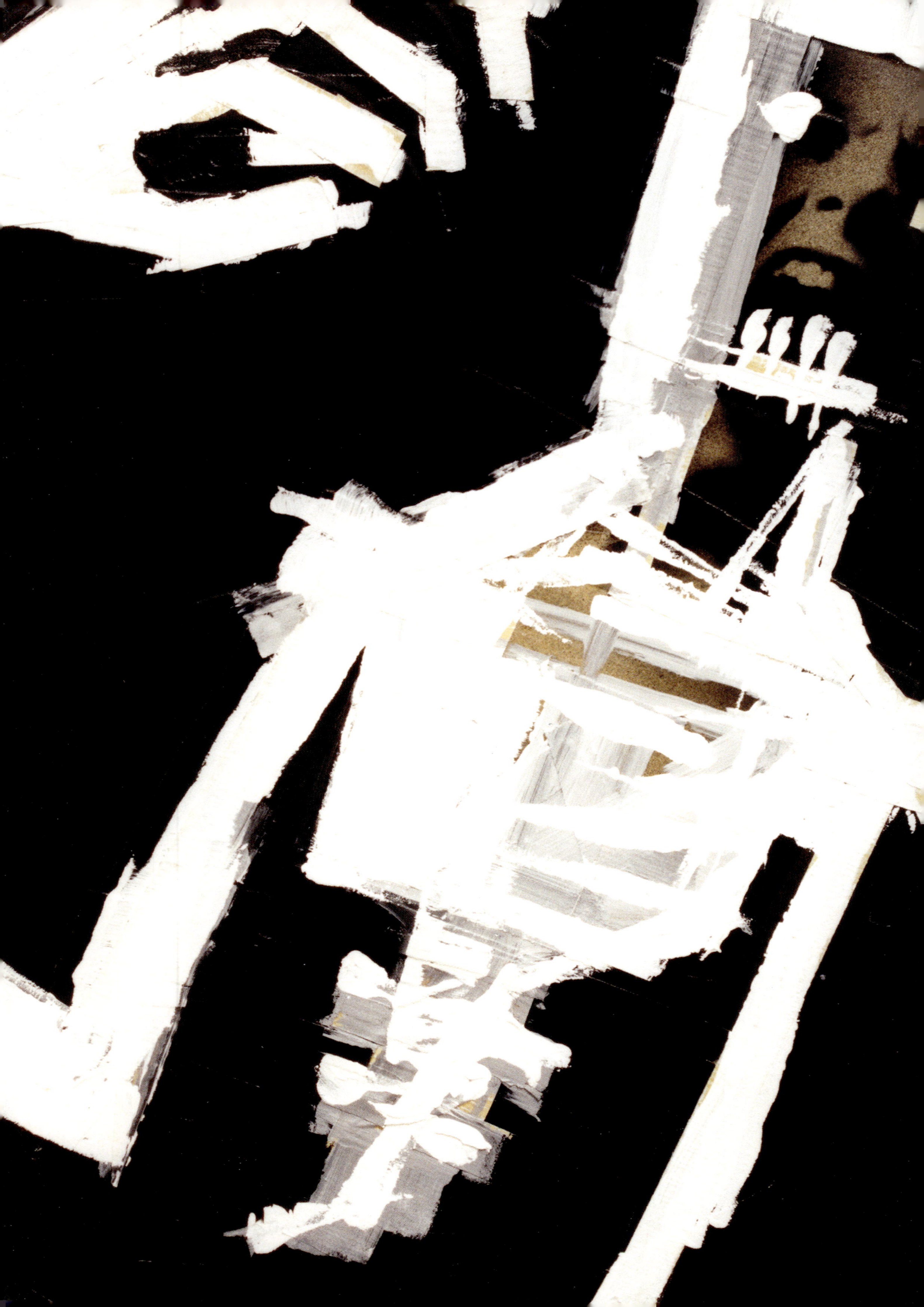

The bourgeoisie had
better watch out for me.
All throughout this so-called
nation, we don't want your
filthy money, we don't need
your innocent bloodshed.
We just wanna end your world.
Well my mind's made up.
Yes, it's time for you to pay,
better watch out for me.
I'm a member of the F.V.K.

Fearless Vampire Killers
Bad Brains

INTRODUCTION

CARLOS BATTS AND THE YELLOW BRICK ROAD TO AMERICAN GOTHIC

What, exactly, makes an artist? There's never a convincing answer to the oft-asked question, maybe because there are as many replies to that as there are artists. But even when we hone the subject of our inquiry down to one specific individual or one particular work of art, any analysis, no matter how protracted and in-depth, eventually leaves us feeling unsatisfied. Like some sort of cosmic recipe, you can enumerate the ingredients and even go through the process of preparation yourself, but the result will never quite equal the original. Such is the reason why biography is, in the end, a lie, though it may be brilliantly told. For example, no life story of Francis Bacon will ever quite bring you to fully understand *Three Studies for Figures at the Base of the Crucifixion*, though it might like to claim that is has.

And yet, we desperately want to crack open David Lynch's brain and see *Eraserhead* crawling around in there. The same goes for Octave Mirbeau and *The Torture Garden* or Hans Bellmer and his dolls. We might believe so-and-so was abused as a child, or so-and-so was tormented by their homosexuality. But then, witness the millions who've encountered the same experiences, all to wildly different ends. And what do we make of the rare artist and/or murderer whose formative years were generally tranquil? How did their lives come around to them splashing either the canvas or the bedroom wall with paint or blood?

This is the dilemma we have when faced with Carlos Batts's oeuvre, especially the work he reveals to us in *American Gothic*. Herein, with the energy and skill of a modern-day Romare Bearden or Ed Gein (take your pick), Batts slashes at his victims: his images. They're cut and rearranged like the ill-fated Black Dahlia (so eloquently eulogized in John Gilmore's *Severed*), and painted over with an astonishing array of mixed media – spray-paint, fingernail polish, watercolor, duct tape, acrylics, and so on. They've been scratched into, often right onto the negative itself, the "soul" of the photograph, over which Batts has appointed himself Chief Torturer. Like some psychopath obsessed with corpses, he's taken these bodies, so often of women, dismembered them, and reassembled them, like grisly puppets in the hands of a twisted puppeteer.

Unlike Batts's previous books *Wild Skin* and *Crazy Sexy Hollywood*, which offer his take on fetish and trashy Tinseltown erotica respectively, *American Gothic* was born of a different artistic desire. It's modeled, as the name suggests, on Grant Woods's famous 1930 portrait of an Iowan couple, in part meant to depict the rigidity and humorlessness of rural America.

"The title comes from the painting," Batts confirms. "At the time, the painting was a big deal because it was saying, 'This is what America is right now.' It's rural. Big country. Farmland. Manifest destiny. So the book is what I think of America now. This is my world. I live here. I breathe here. And this is the visceral planet that I've created."

Batts's America is a disjointed montage drawn from a feverish mix of sex, fetish, murder, and appetite for destruction. Is it too much to see an echo in this celluloid of imagery from the Abu Ghraib prison scandal, or even the beheading of western hostages by Iraqi insurgents? Of course, that's only part of the picture. There is also the monstrous exhibitionism and voyeurism of our age, seen through a schizophrenic Viewmaster with a broken lens. As much as Bacon's *Painting 1946* or his *Figure with Meat* captured the horror of modernity and contemporaneous history, Batts's photos reflect a time where we see things falling down and apart in front of us, whether the World Trade Center or the idea of America itself.

What about Batts's story brought him to this point of being lightning-struck by the zeitgeist? Well, therein lies the rub. His background is modest: Baltimore-born and raised by middle-class parents in a suburb relatively free of crime. By his own admission, he had a childhood that, if not perfect, at least was no better or worse than the norm. "I got to play with G.I. Joe, read comic books, and be a kid," he says. "My parents were strict when it came to manners. But it was never like, 'You can't watch or read this.' I don't think they knew I was watching porn or films like *I Spit on Your Grave*, but they knew I wasn't into drugs."

Batts went to grade school when there was still a budget for arts programs, which encouraged his talent at a young age. A great deal of his time was spent either copying or creating his own comic books. By the time he was in 5th Grade, he already knew what he was going to do with the rest of his life. He knew he was going to be an artist.

Like many teenage boys, his tastes grew morbid as he moved into his teens. Clive Barker was more interesting than Marvel Comics, and films like *The Texas Chainsaw Massacre, Scanners, Faces of Death*, and Italian horror director Lucio Fulci's *Zombie* made a lasting impression. Serial killers like Ted Bundy, Charles Manson, and Ed Gein became the subjects of intense fascination. Black Sabbath's *Paranoid* album, especially the song "Ironman," turned him on to heavy metal. Batts was so into animal skeletons that he would clean deer skulls he found, just so he could take them to school and show them off to his friends.

In some ways, his time in high school was much like any other American boy's, spent wrestling and playing football and lacrosse. But in 10th Grade, he took his first photography class, and though he'd been into painting most recently, he realized this would be his *metier*. He began shooting seriously, idolizing such great African-American photographers as Gordon Parks and James VanDerZee. He was also influenced by the works of Andres Serrano, Annie Leibovitz, Richard Avedon, Helmut Newton, and Robert Mapplethorpe, to name a few. It was during this time of growth that he first began experimenting with photomontage, mixed media, and negative manipulation, which, married to his outré subject matter, formed the basis of an aesthetic universe he still inhabits today.

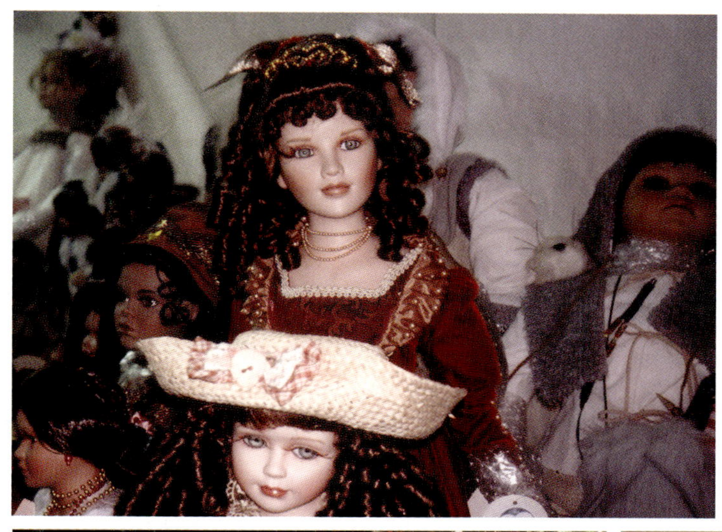
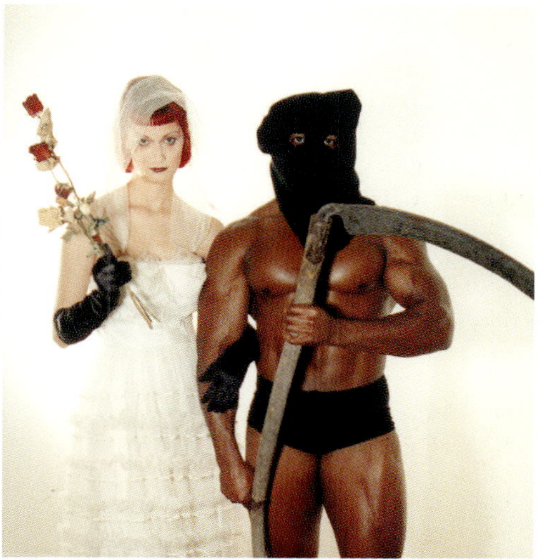
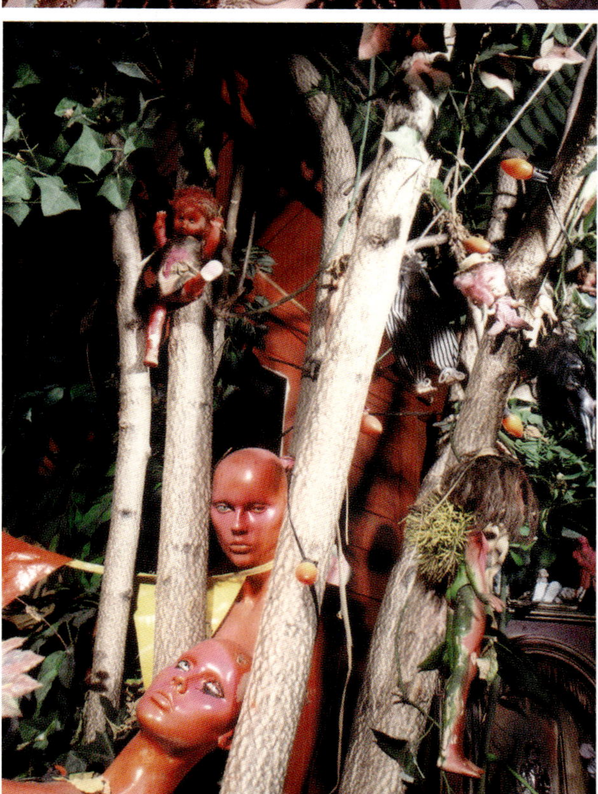
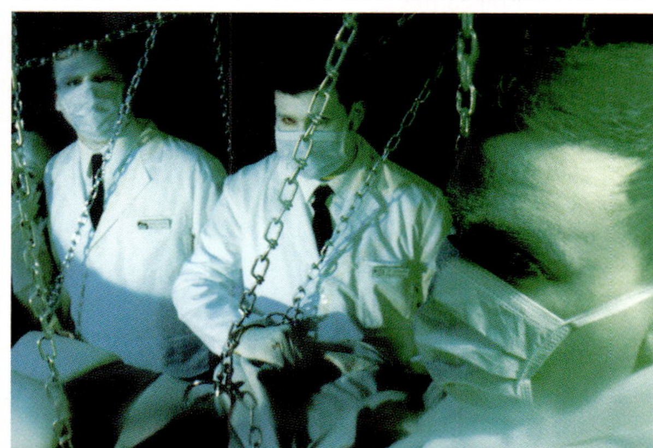
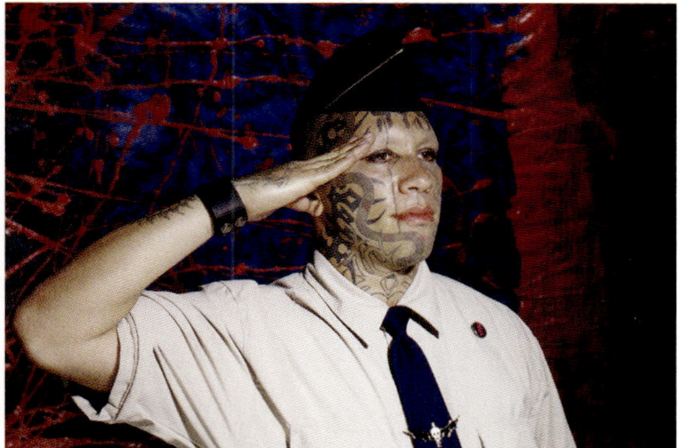
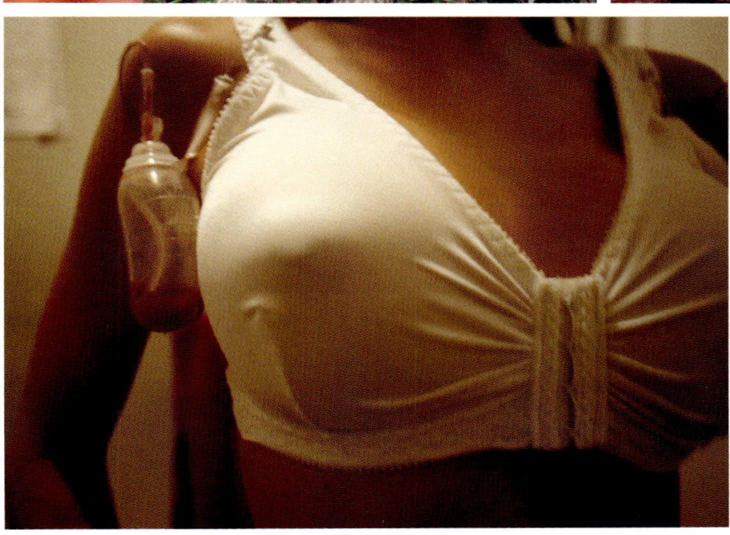
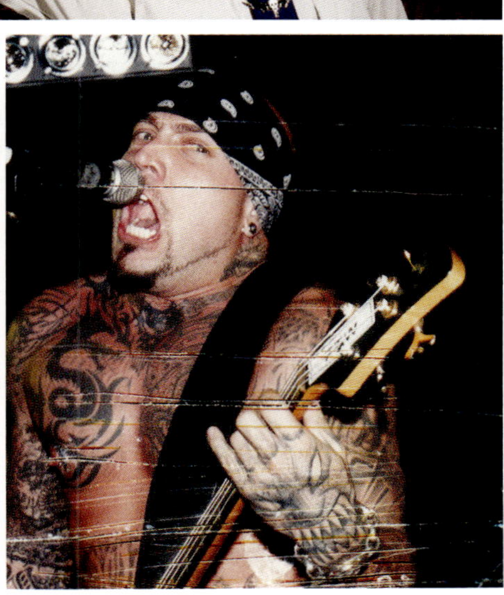

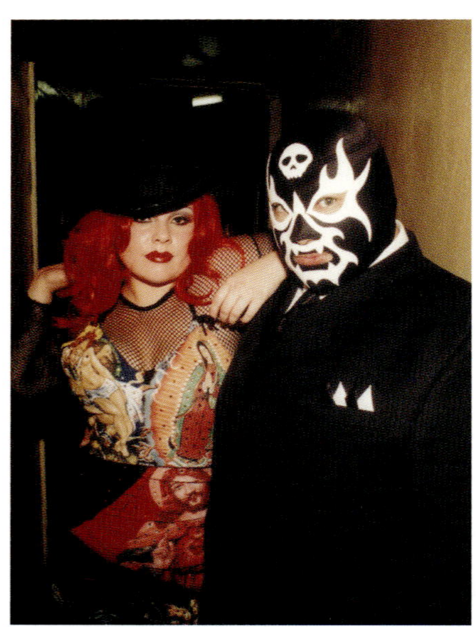
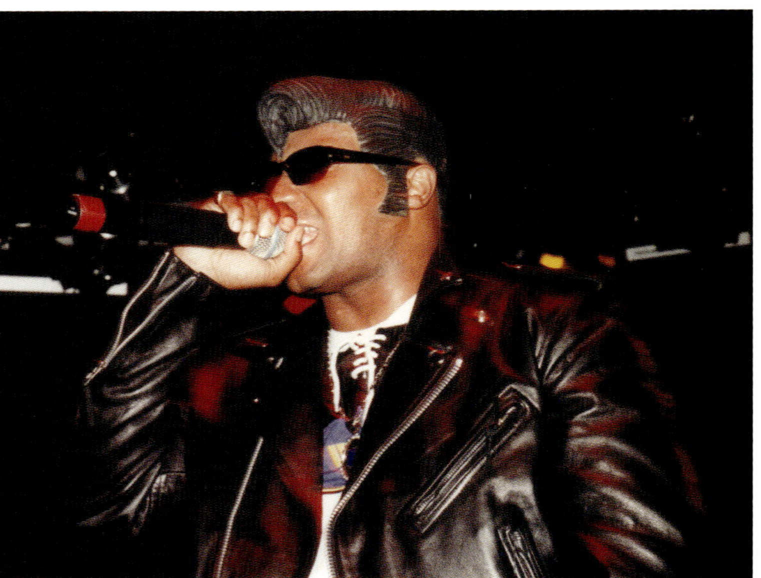
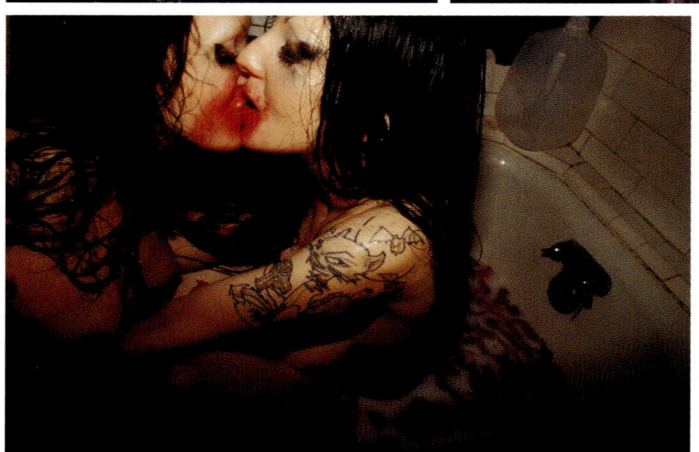
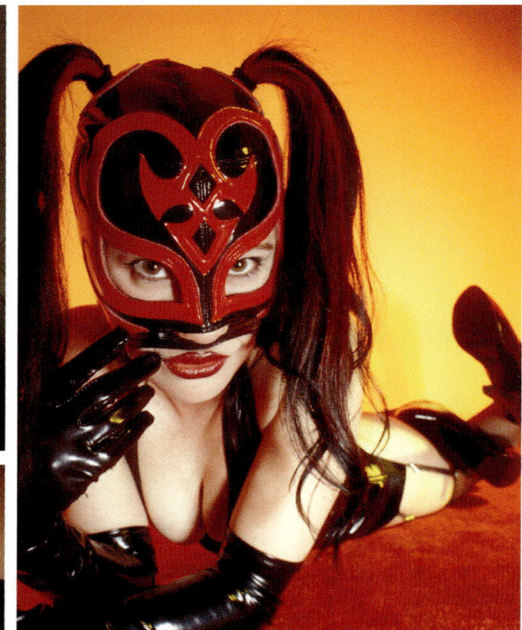
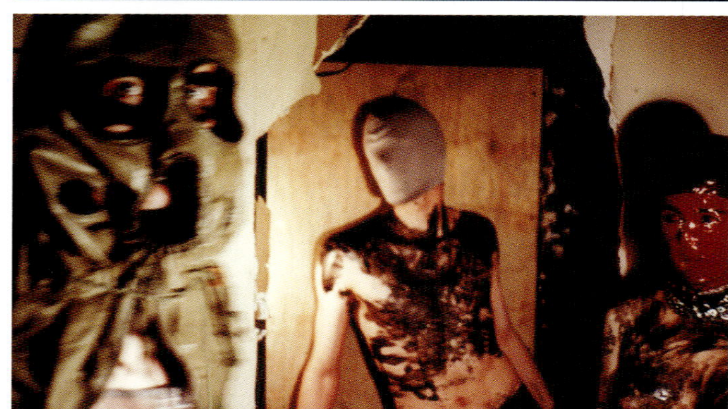
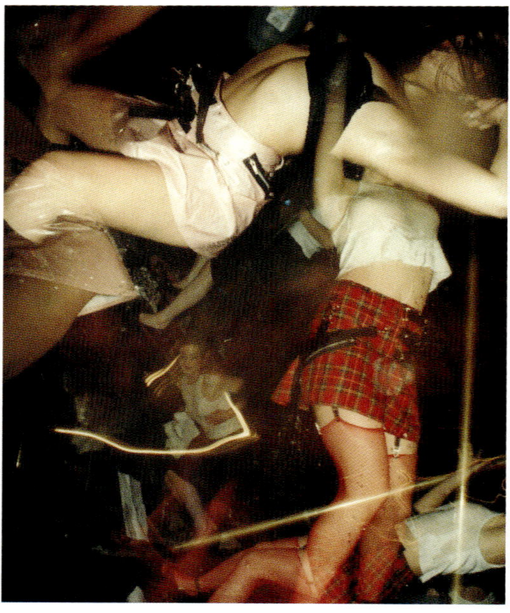
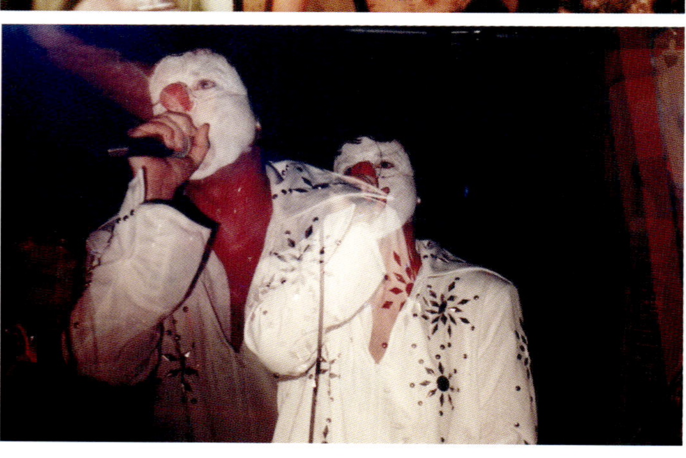

"I thought, I'm not going to be able to take a black-and-white photo better than Gordon Parks or Robert Mapplethorpe," says Batts. "So the pictures I was shooting then, I started painting on them. I just thought it was a cool idea. I remember that in the 11th Grade, I won an award and an honorable mention for a collage I did of Charles Manson. I took pictures of the TV while Manson was being interviewed by Geraldo. I painted the negatives, color Xeroxed it, taped it to fake wood paneling, squirted on blood red acrylic paint, and screwed Plexiglas onto it."

There were more awards, then graduation, followed by a stint at B.I.M., the Broadcast Institute of Maryland. After B.I.M., he worked for local TV stations and pursued his artistic vision in his free time, exhibiting at galleries in Baltimore and at horror conventions on the east coast. He shot his first book cover at the age of 19 for Dell Books, and, with $3,000 in his pocket, picked up and moved to Albuquerque, New Mexico, where a friend was attending college. What followed was a creative surge in his art.

His day job was at Albuquerque Downs racetrack, snapping the photo finishes; at night, he fell in with an artsy crowd, many of whose girlfriends ended up posing for him. He used body paint and masks to remove the element of race, leaving only the product of his imagination. "Using body paint and grease paint, it was like you weren't looking at a photograph of a white or black person. Instead, you were looking at a photo that was only in my head," he states.

After one year in Albuquerque, Batts returned home to Baltimore for a while and began shooting for skin mags, including *Hustler*, *Taboo*, *Oui*, *Legworld*, and *Nugget*, among others. There was money in it, as well as more mainstream editorial work for magazines such as *While You Were Sleeping*, *Vibe*, and *Sportswear International*. Perhaps inevitably, his commercial work prompted a move to Hollywood, where eager starlets were more than willing to strip for the camera. Batts paid the rent with this kind of work, while at the same time holding it in professional disdain. He stayed true to his vision of himself as a fine artist, and this vision bled into the commercial work, giving it a unique edge envied by other commercial shooters. Even when Batts dipped his toes briefly into video porn, with *Girl Trouble* and *Love Hurts 1 & 2*, they were more Dario Argento than Larry Flynt, despite the explicit sex involved.

It should be pointed out that, while in Hollywood, Batts also got to shoot stars and musical acts, such as Snoop Dogg, Andy Dick, Joe Rogan, Glenn Danzig, and the Dwarves. He showed and continues to show his work at a number of influential venues in Los Angeles, such as the Merry Karnowsky Gallery and Hollywood's Erotic Museum, where he also curates exhibits. During a trip to Italy with fellow artist Rick Berry, he made contacts that led to German publisher Edition Reuss, who put out *Wild Skin* and *Crazy Sexy Hollywood*. But Batts wanted to push past the erotic work that had won him so many plaudits and show the world the true Carlos Batts, the dark, twisted maestro of the macabre. So, he teamed up with Baltimore's Scapegoat Press to finally bring *American Gothic* to fruition.

"In this book, I'm focusing in on my art, my collages," explains Batts. "The celebrities I've photographed, they don't represent me. Nor do the girls. I wanted to go back to what was most important. There are so many bad street art books out there, which are all about pop culture. But it's time for me to break with that."

And yet, despite what we know about Batts, the book assaults us with an unexpected force, like the brutality we witness in Picasso, Bacon, and the German expressionists. The past is prologue, perhaps.
Still, nothing quite prepares us for the assorted demons Batts has chewed up and spat onto *American Gothic*'s pages. There's nothing to be done about it.
Thus are artists born.

Stephen Lemons

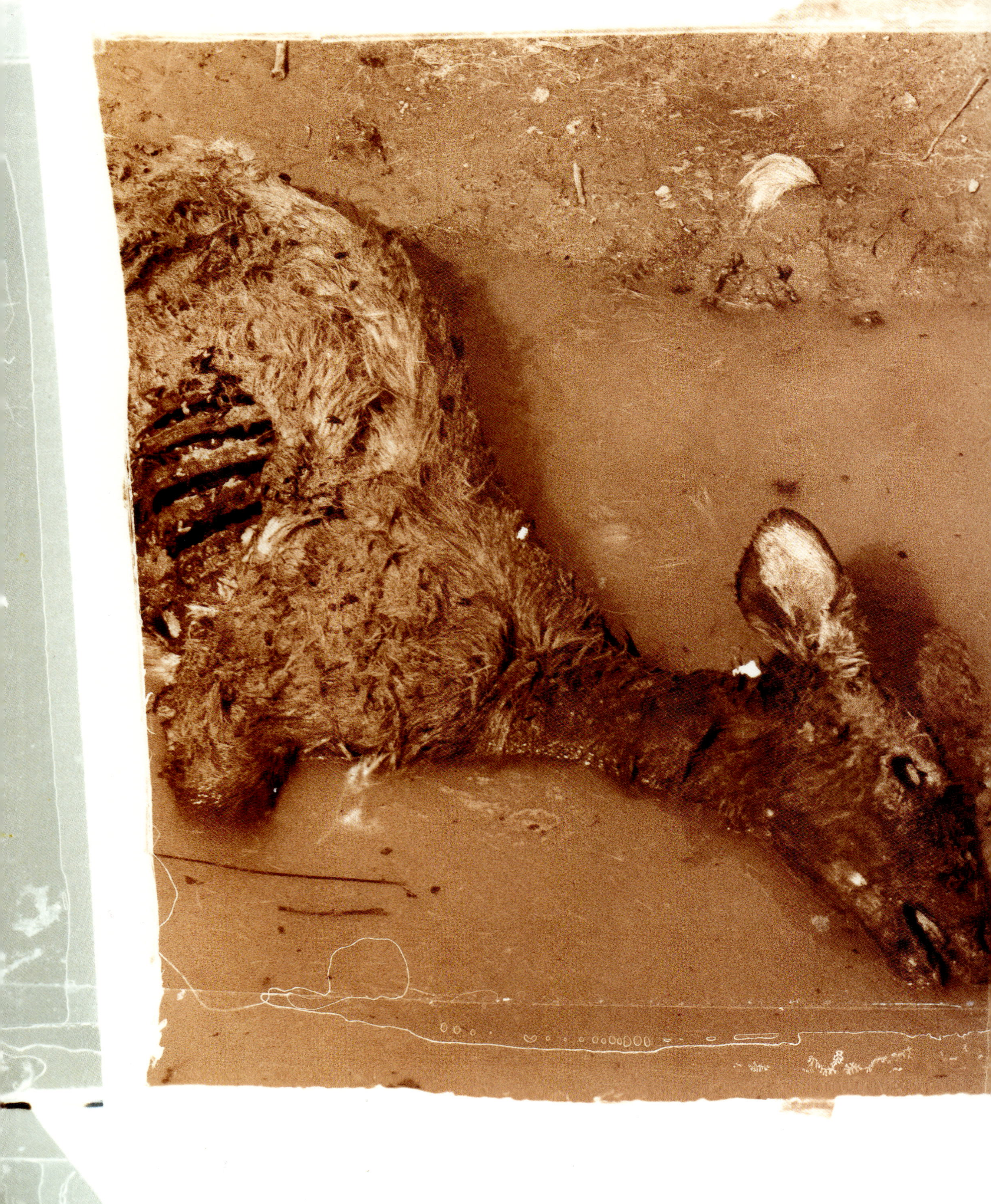

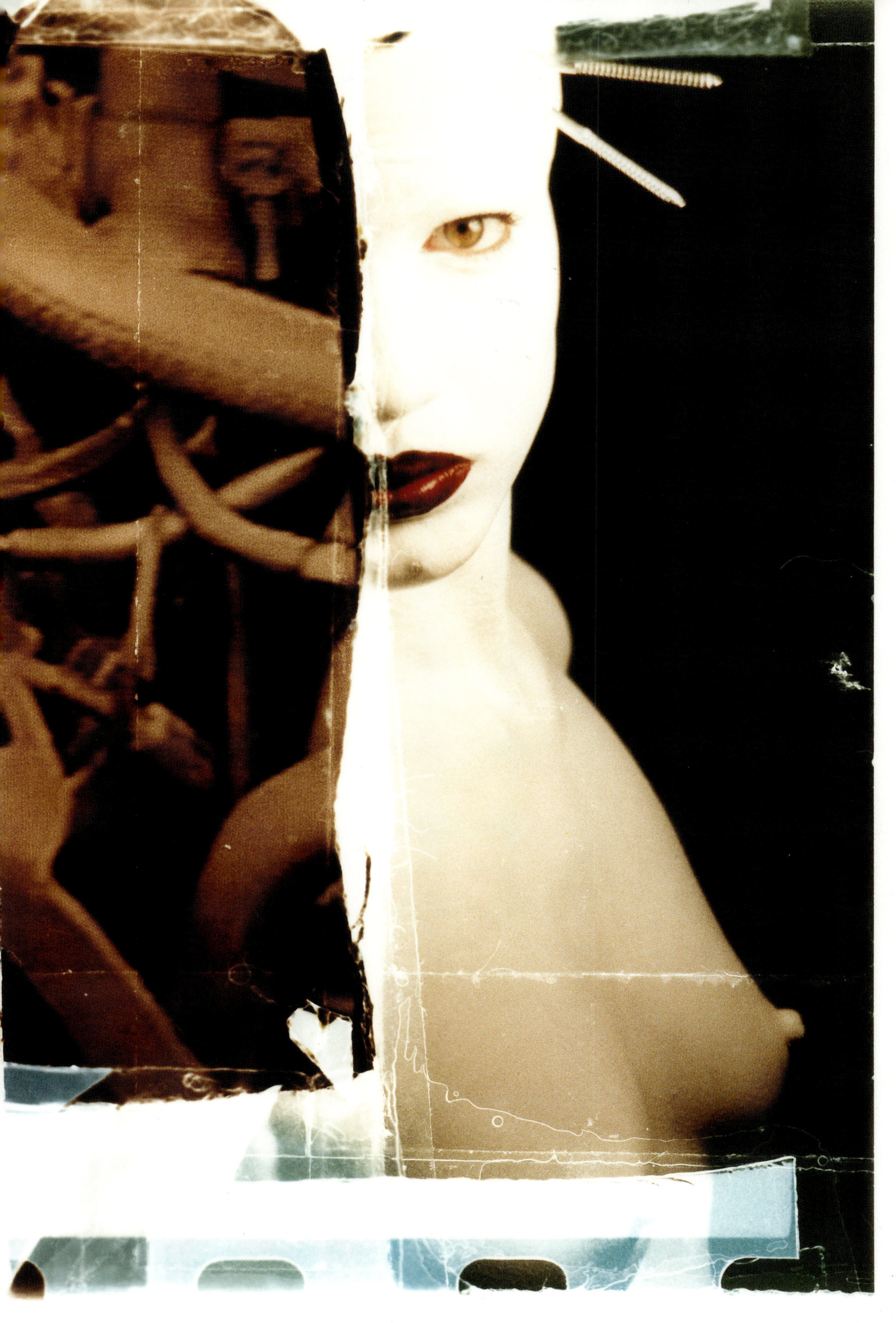

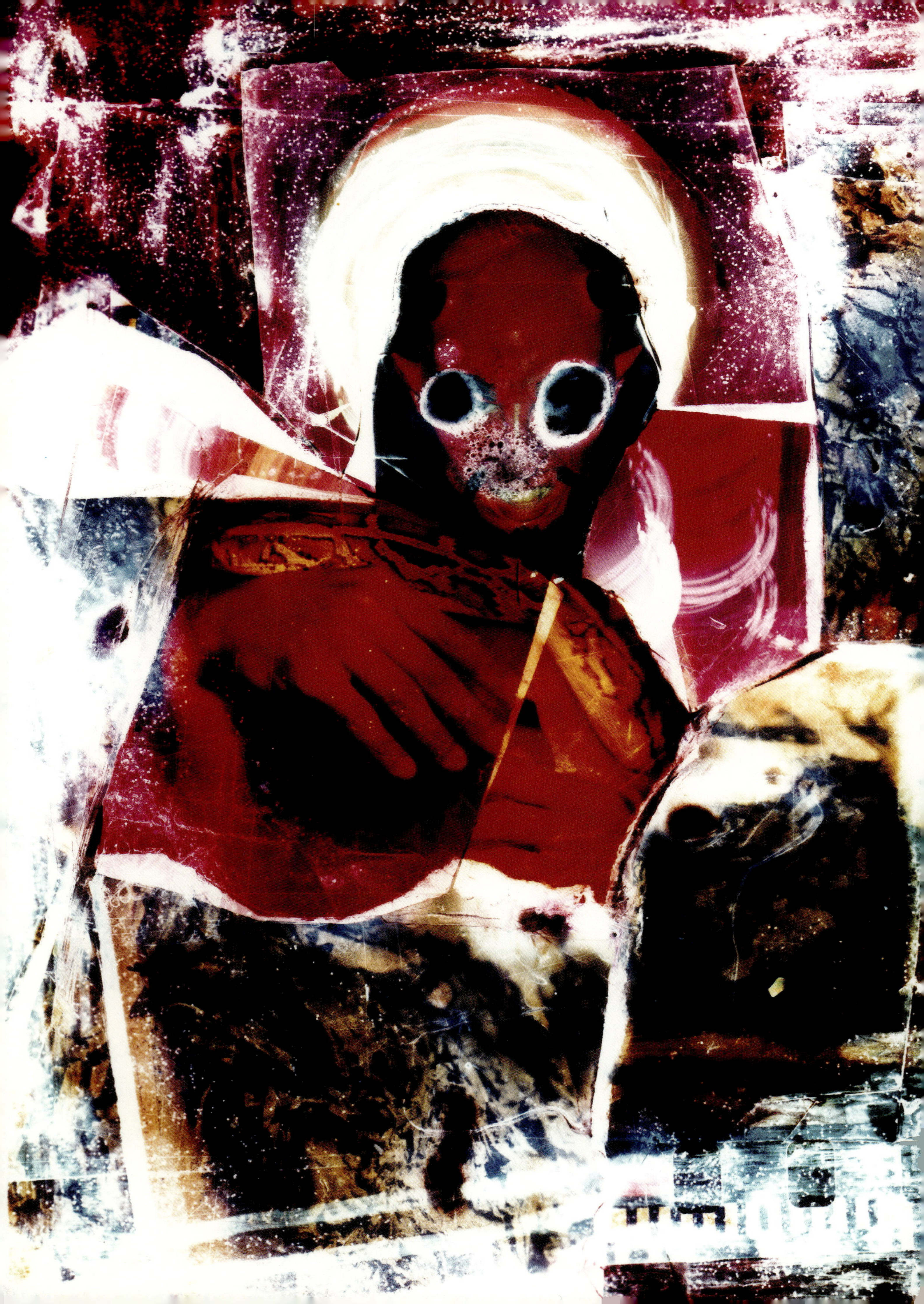

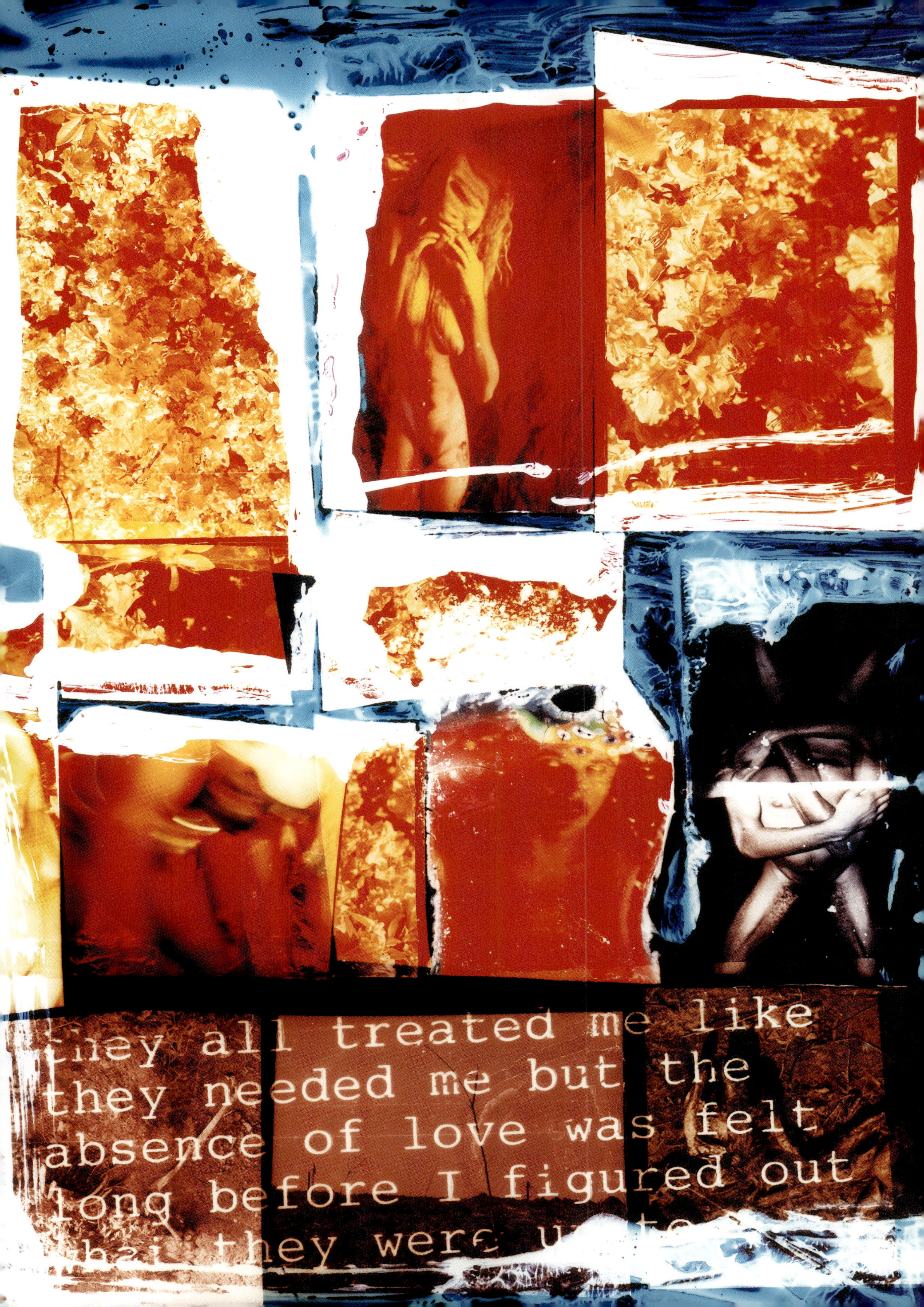
they all treated me like
they needed me but the
absence of love was felt
long before I figured out
they were

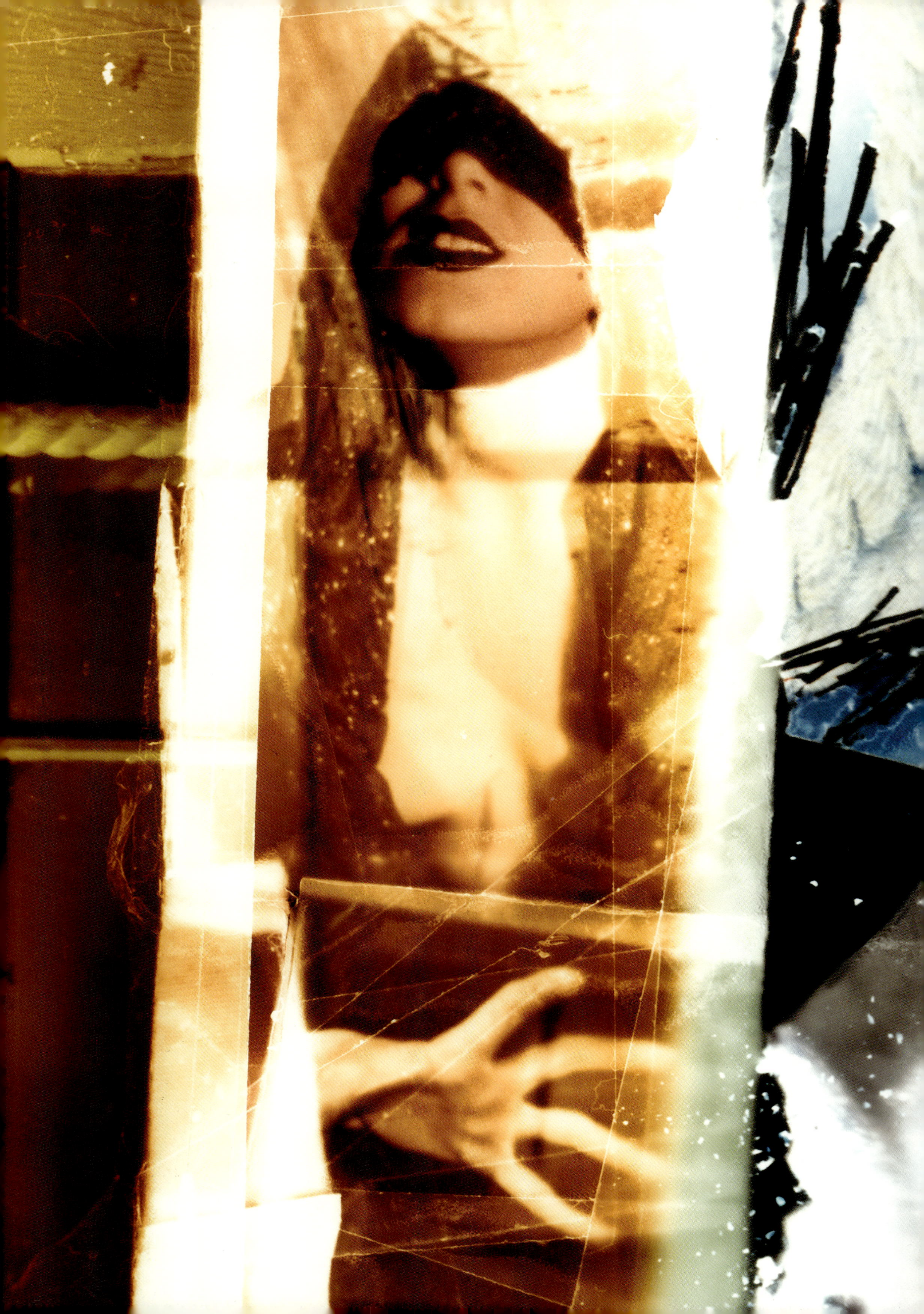

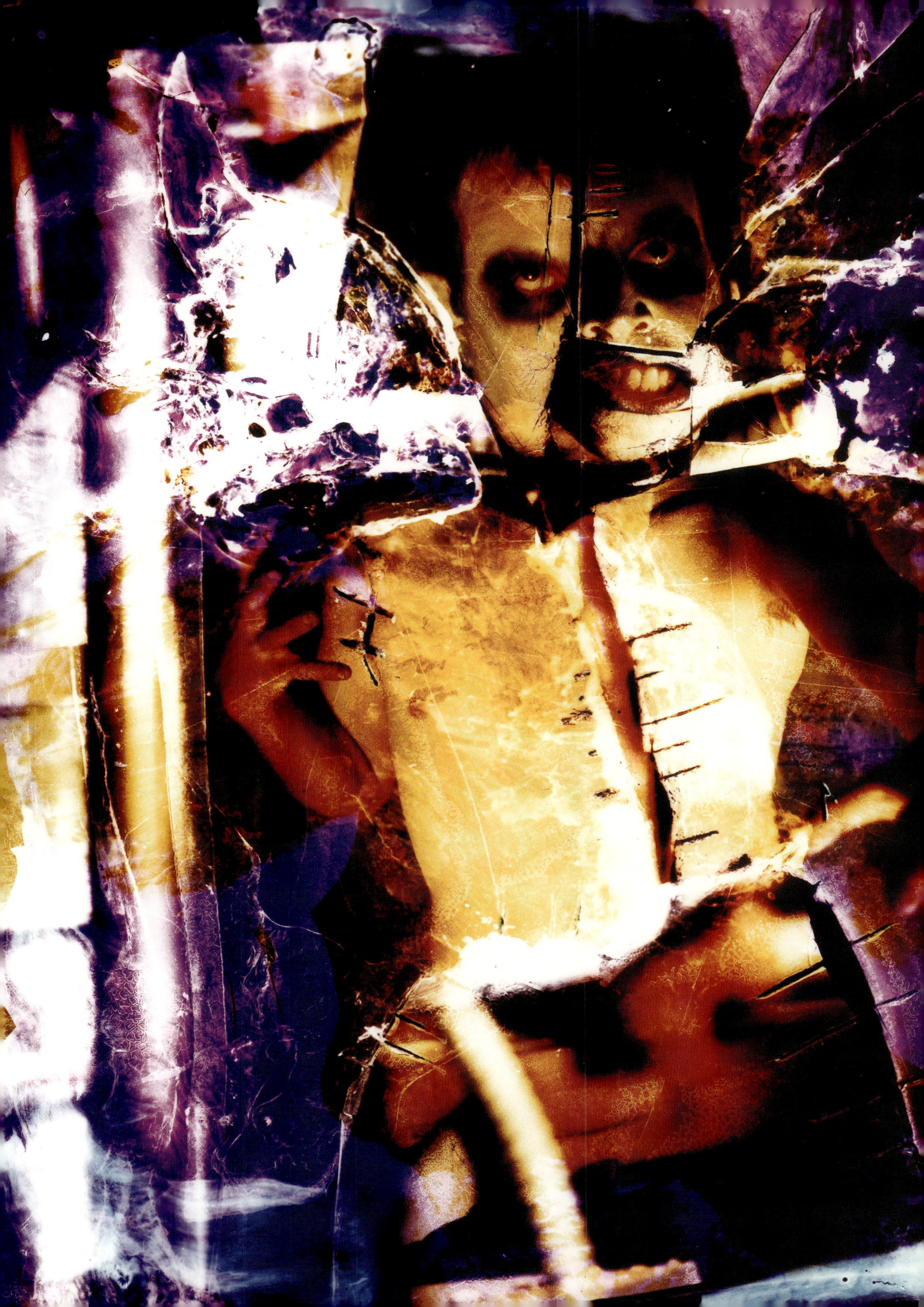

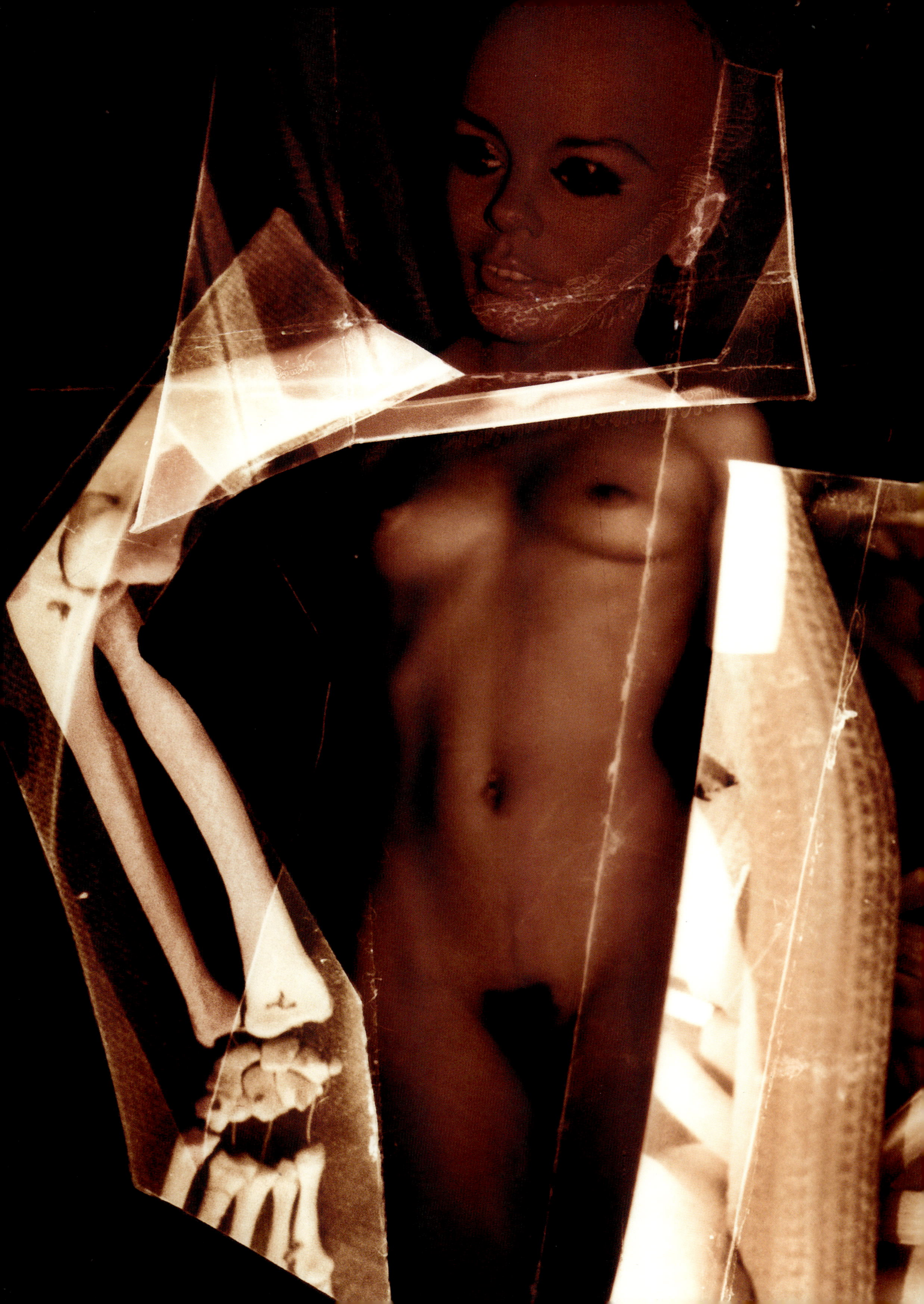

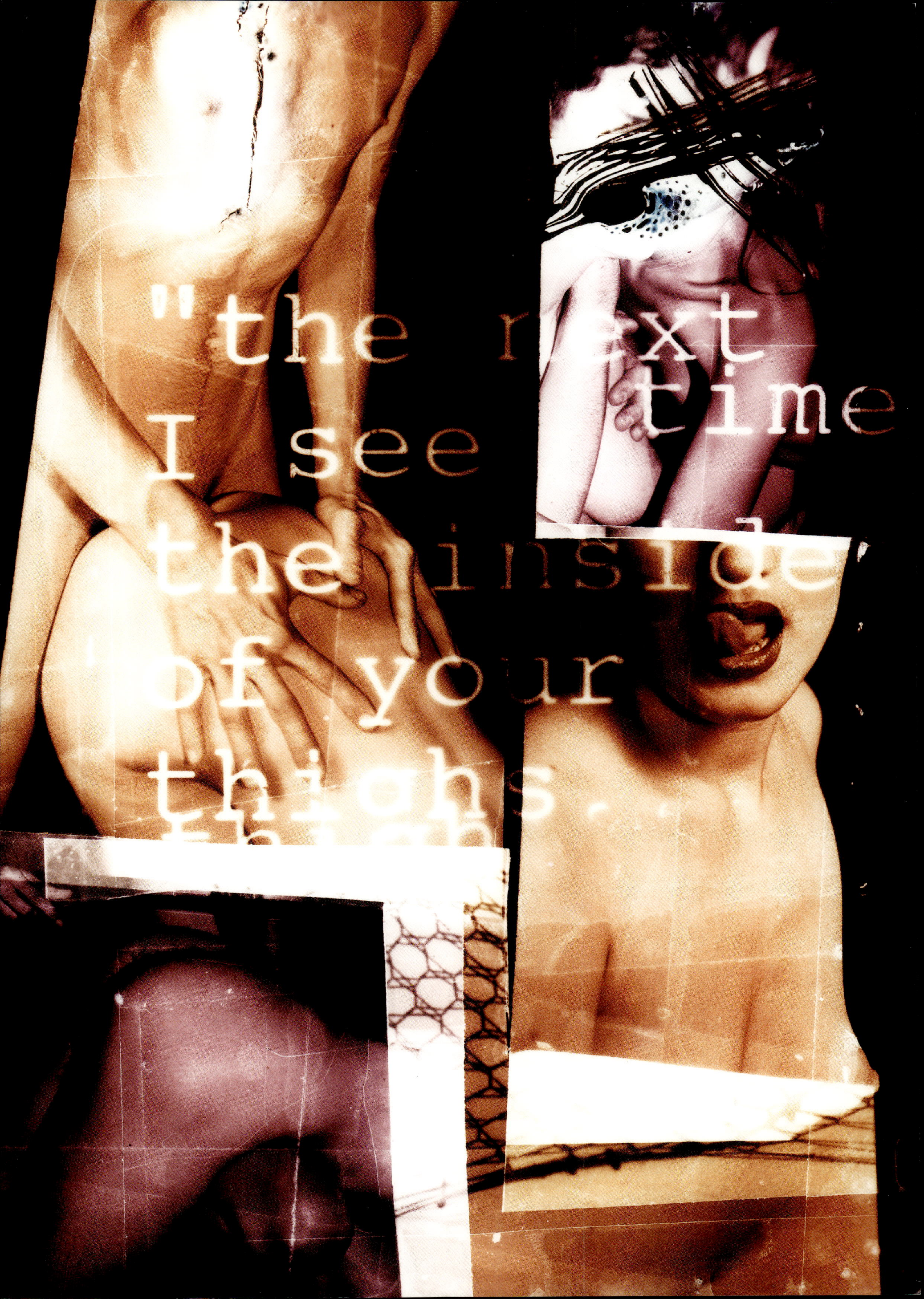

"the next time I see the inside of your thighs.

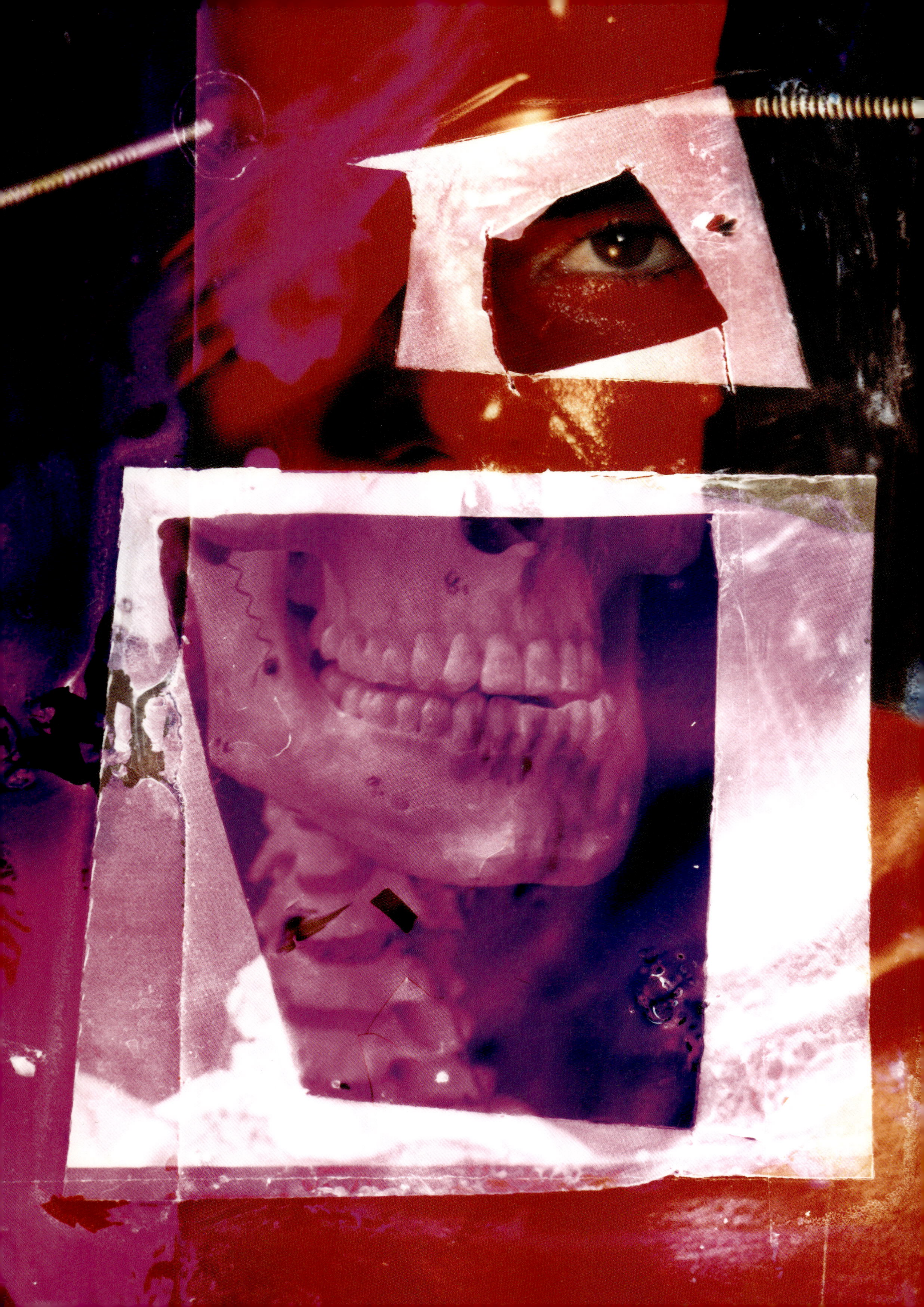

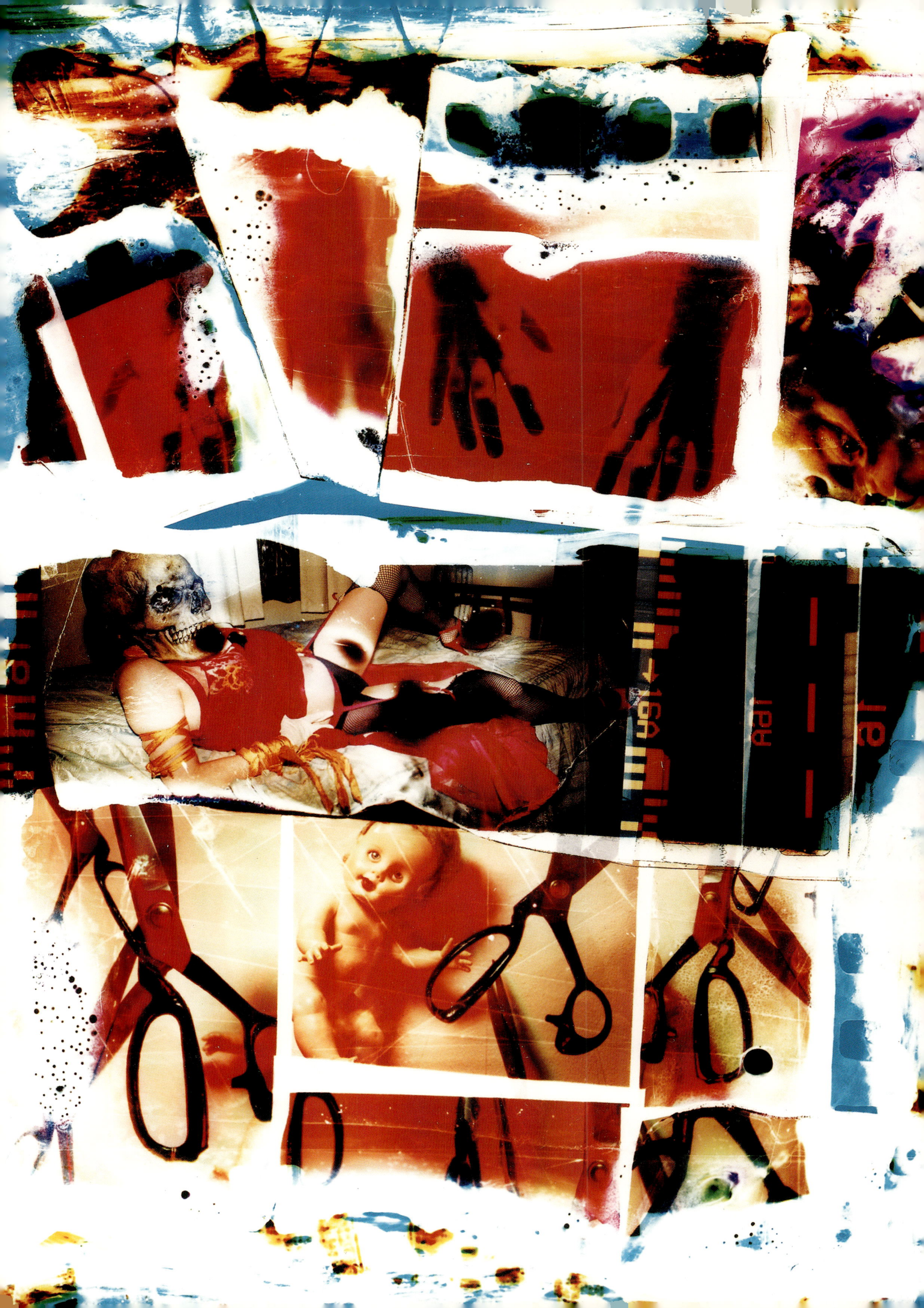

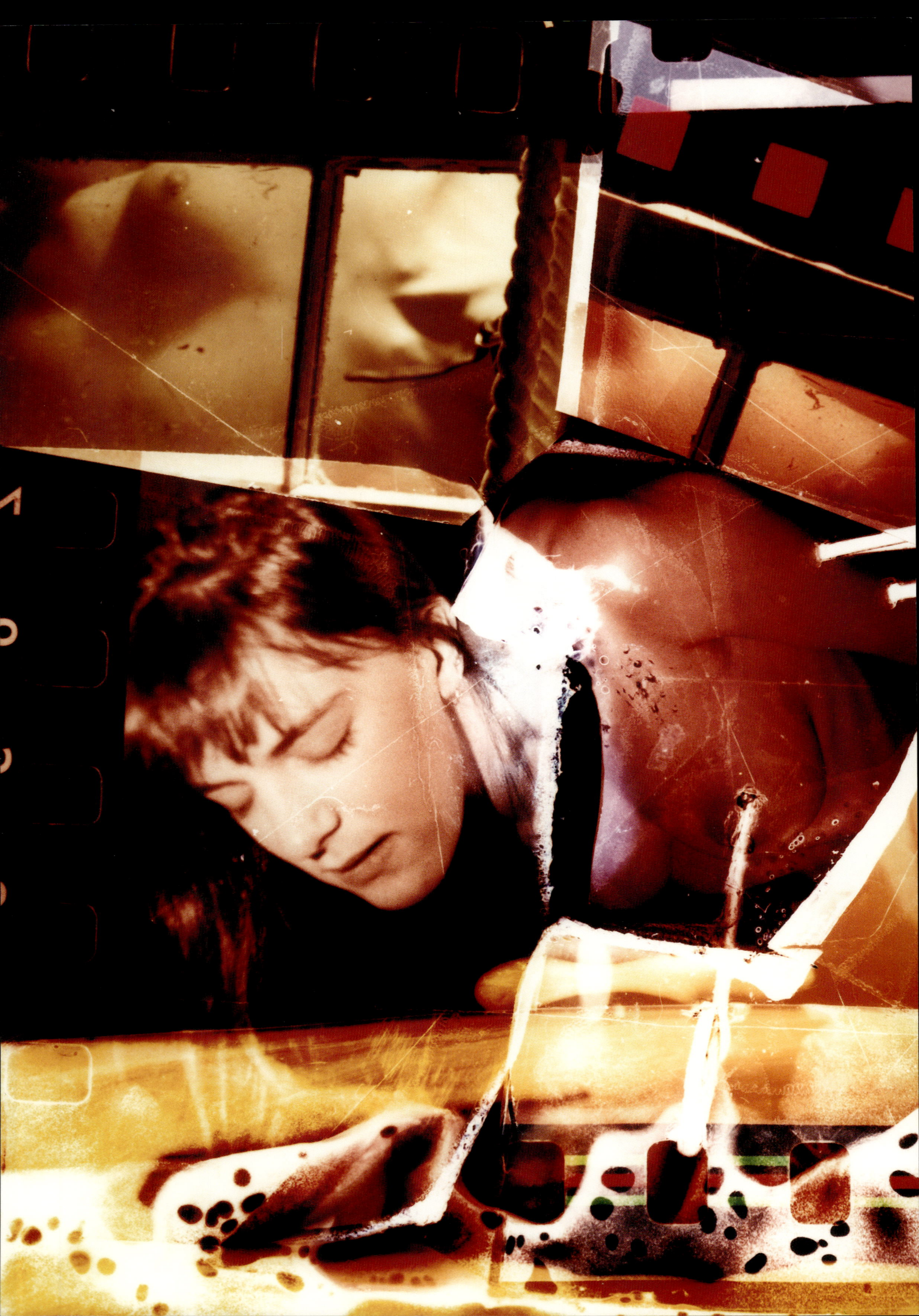

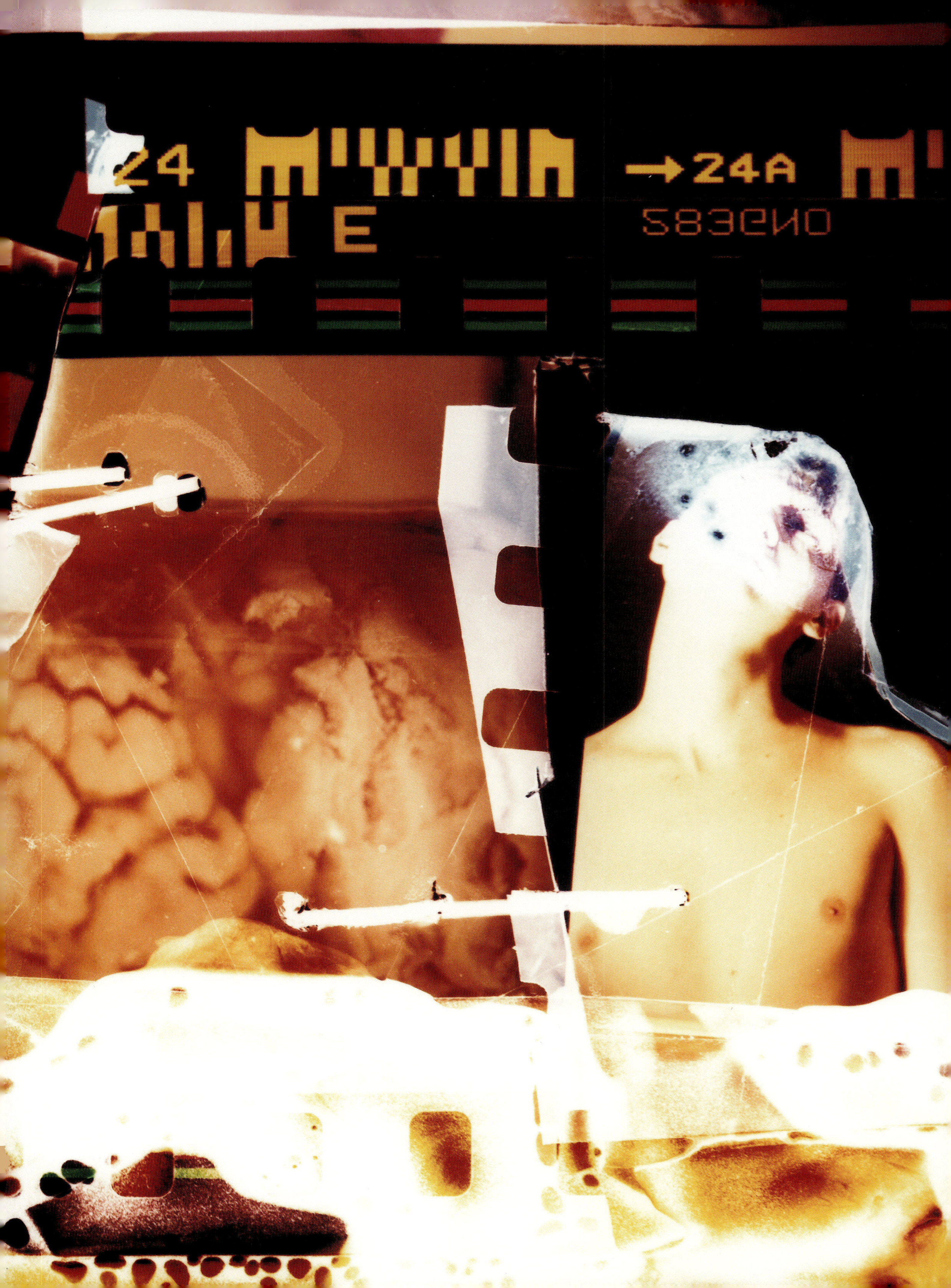

24
→24A

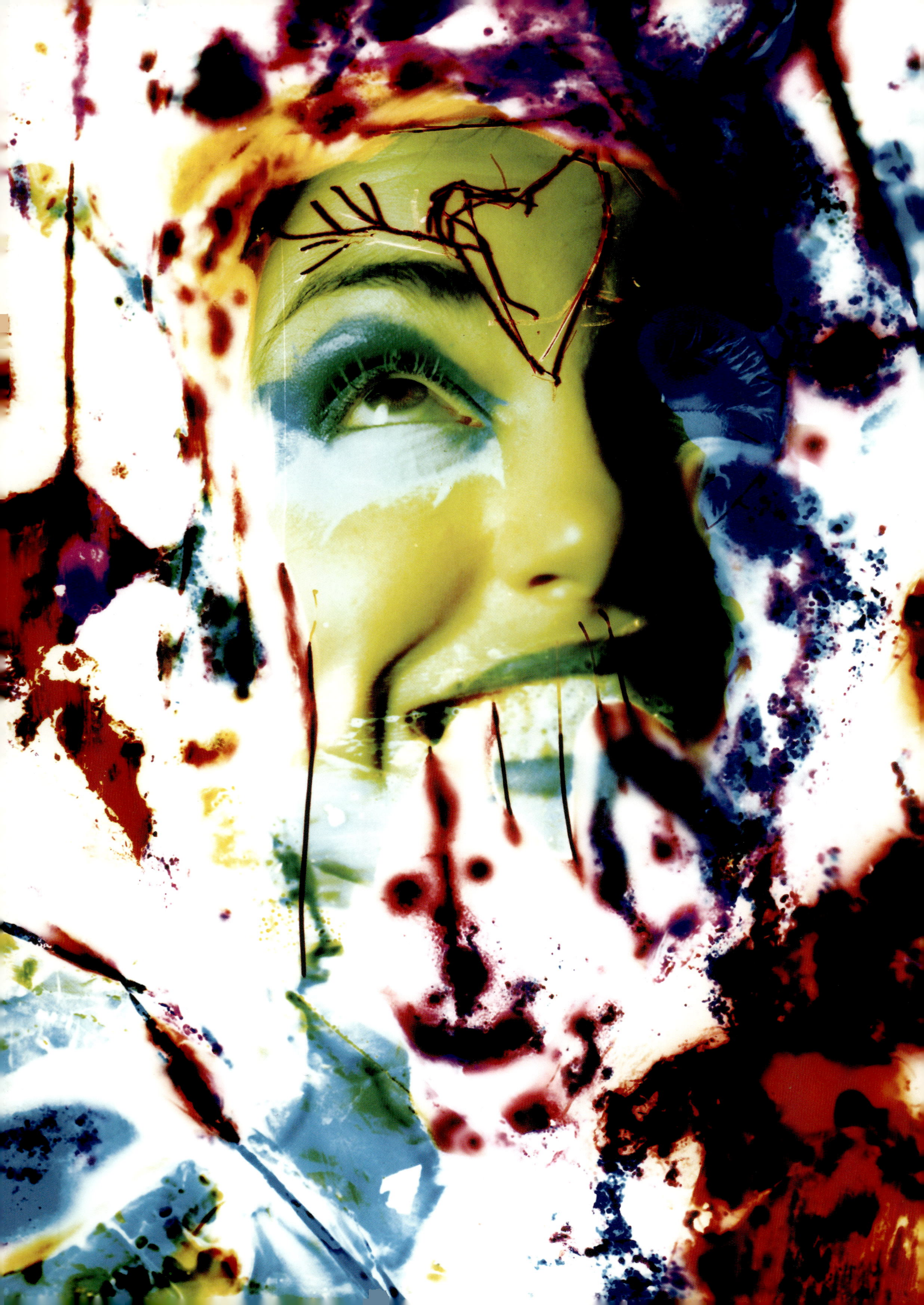

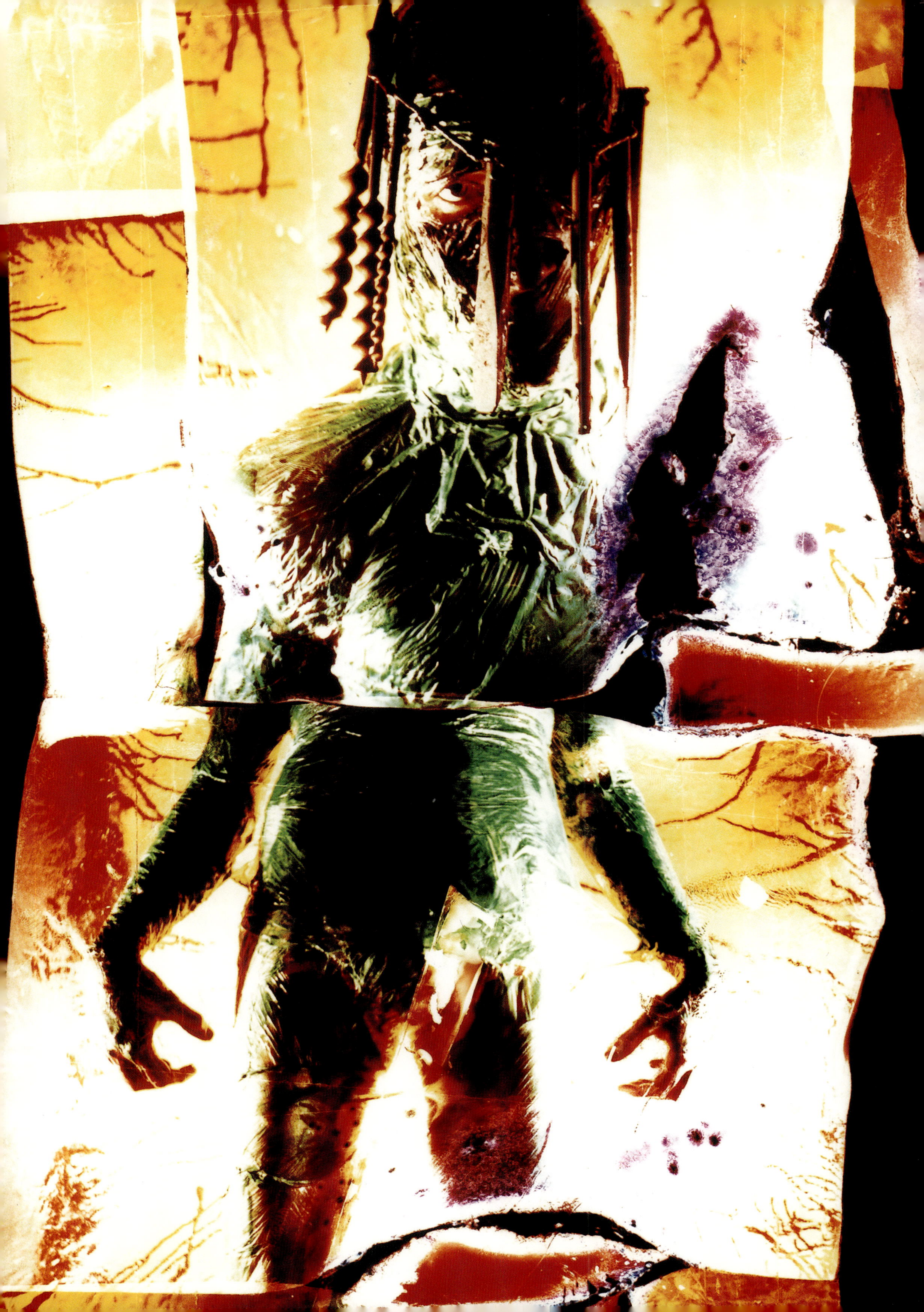

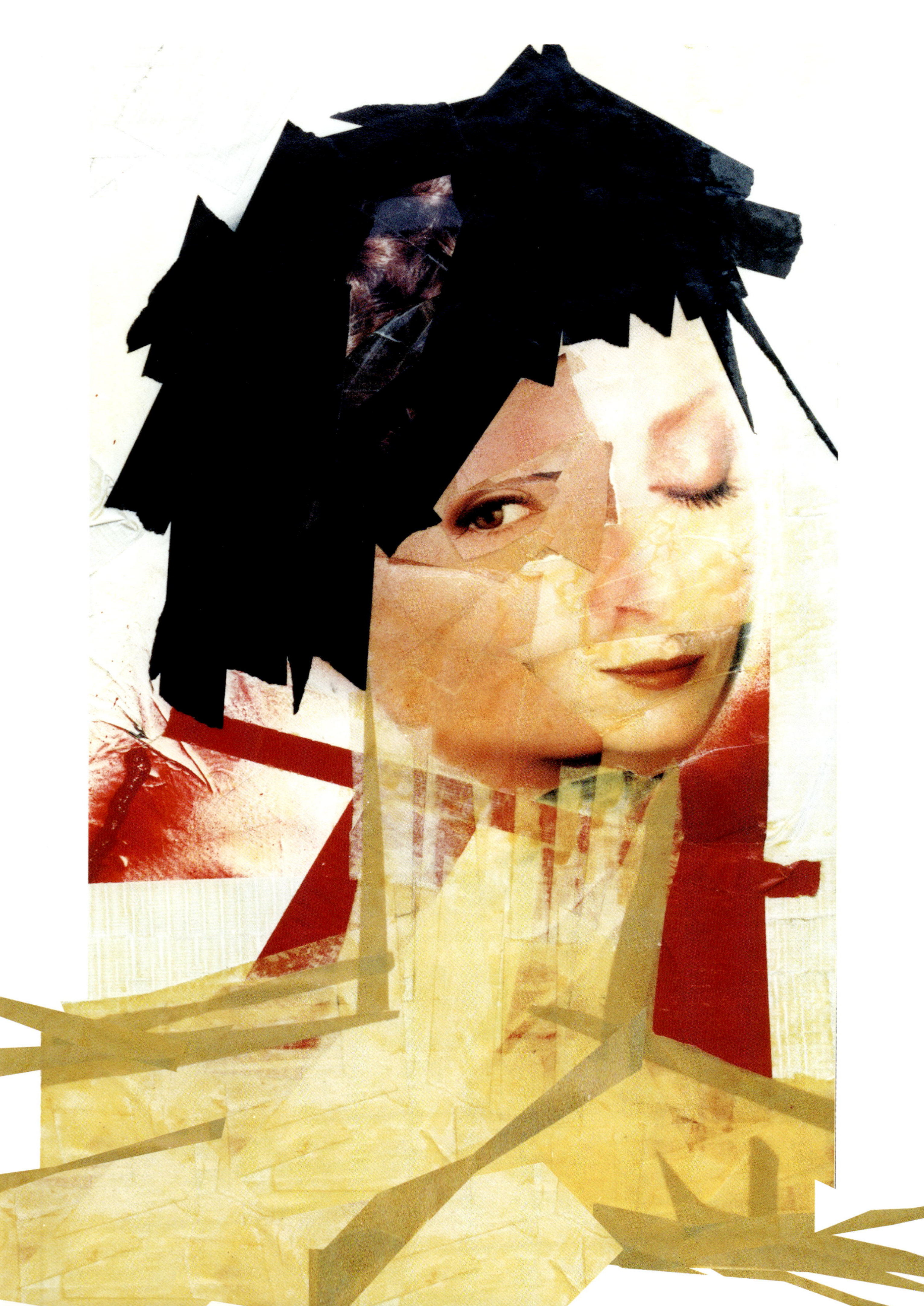

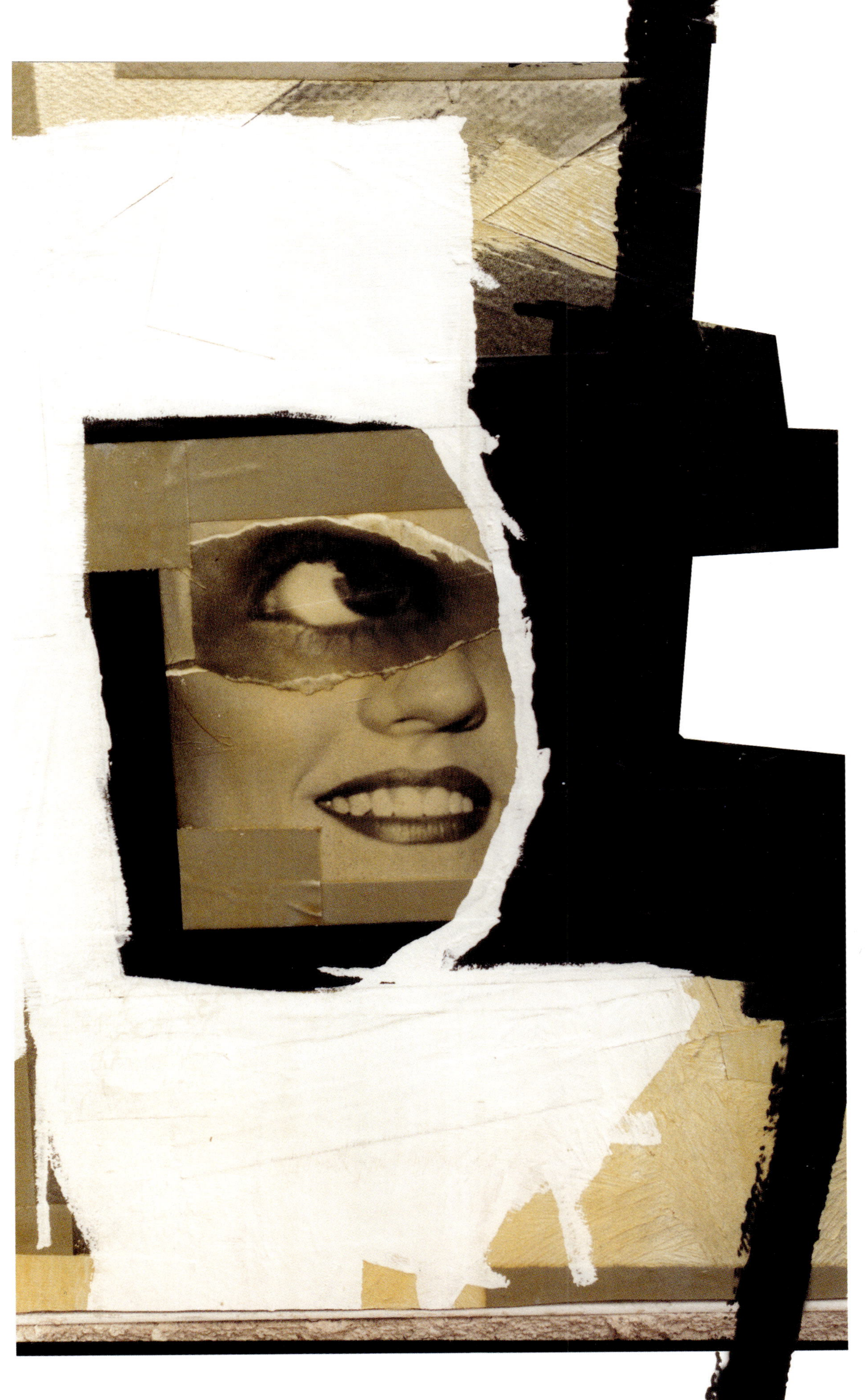

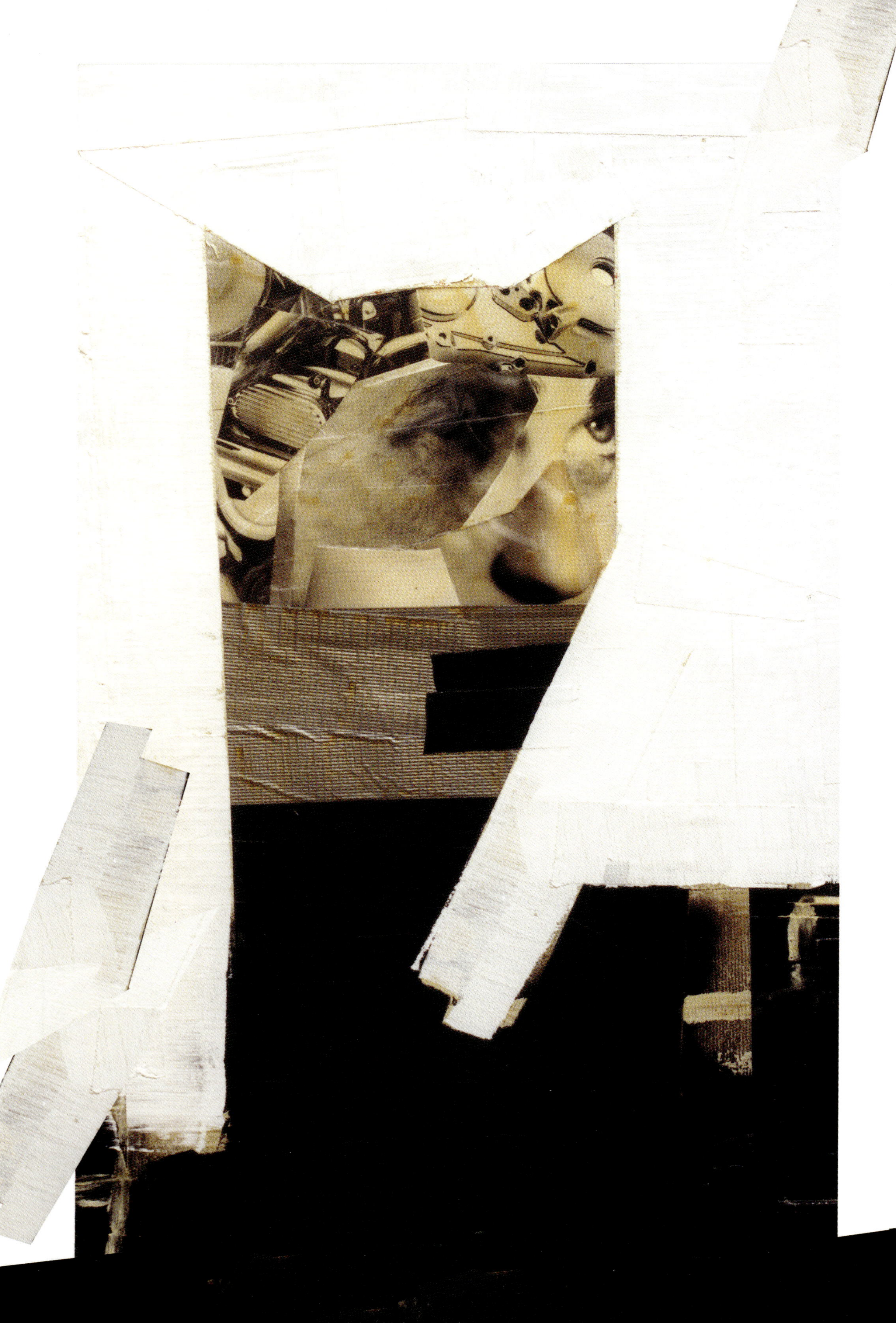

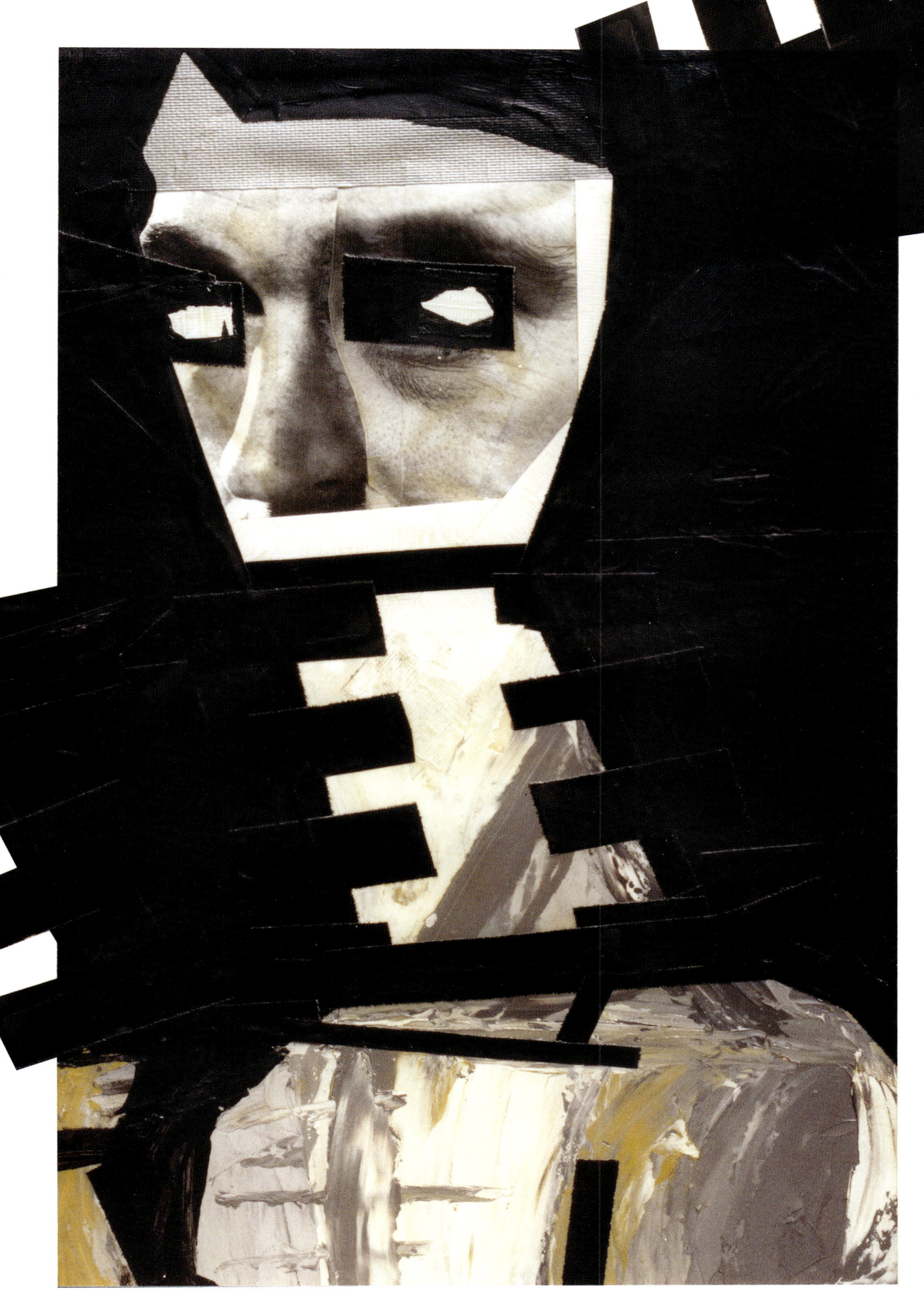

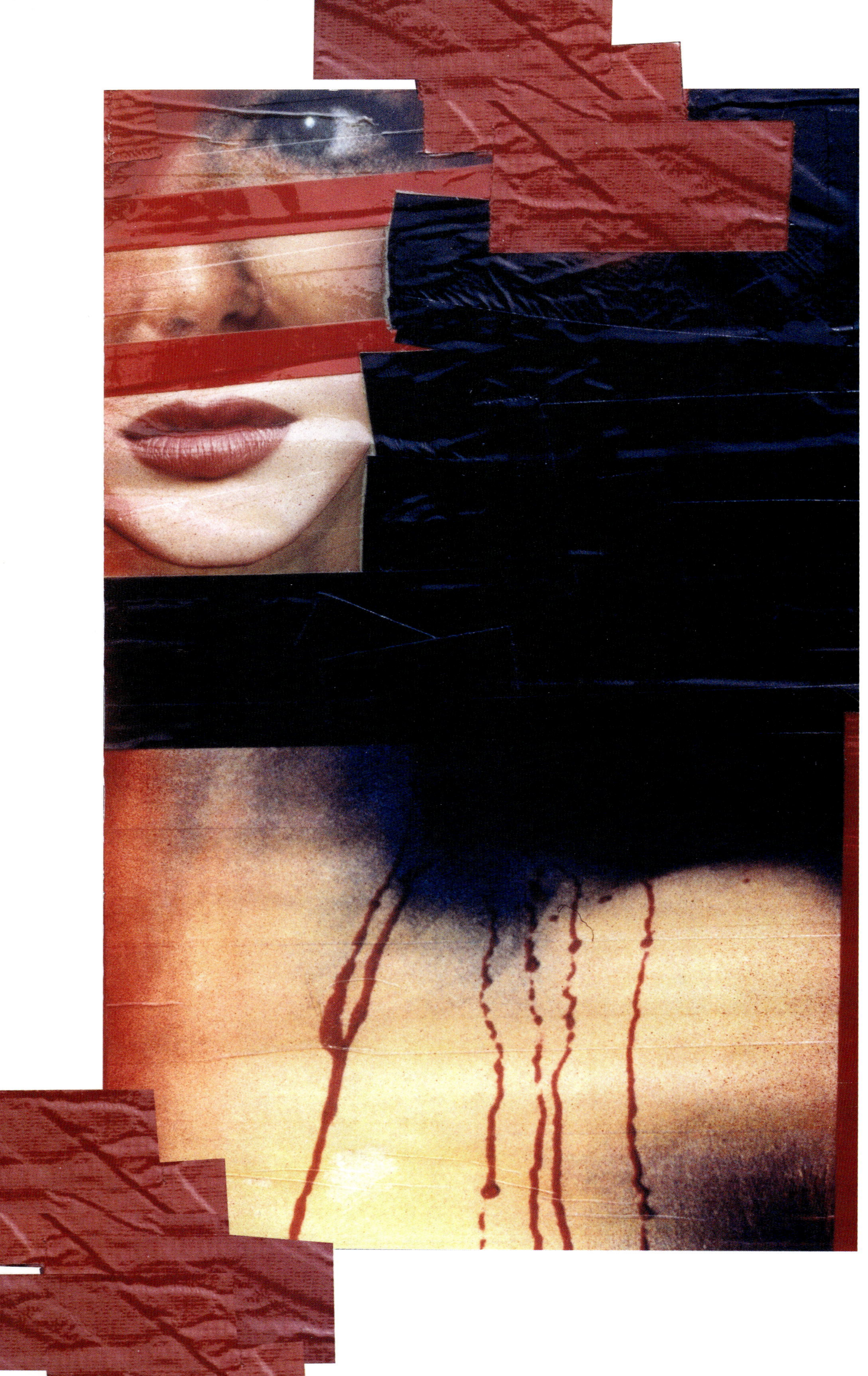

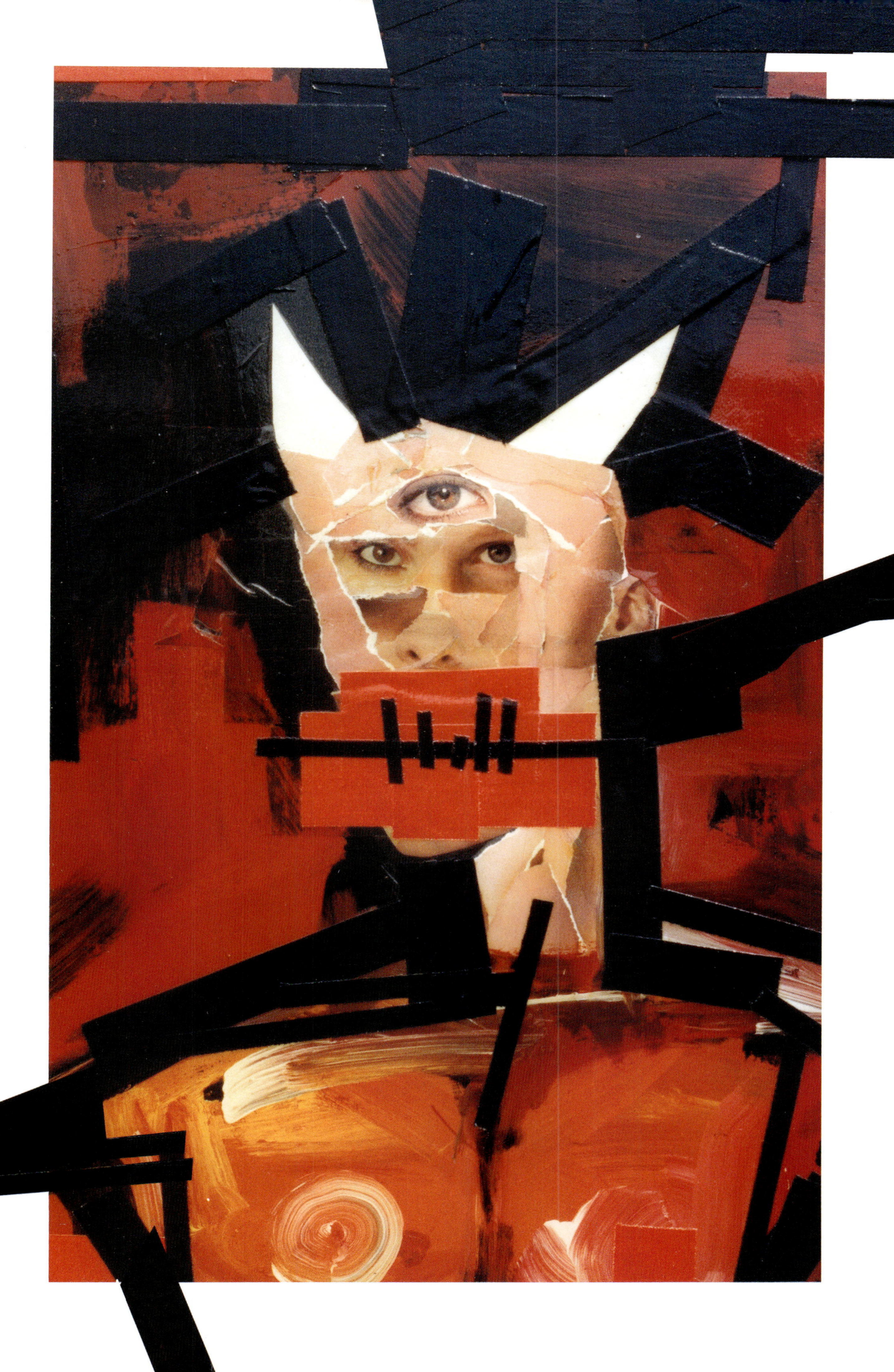

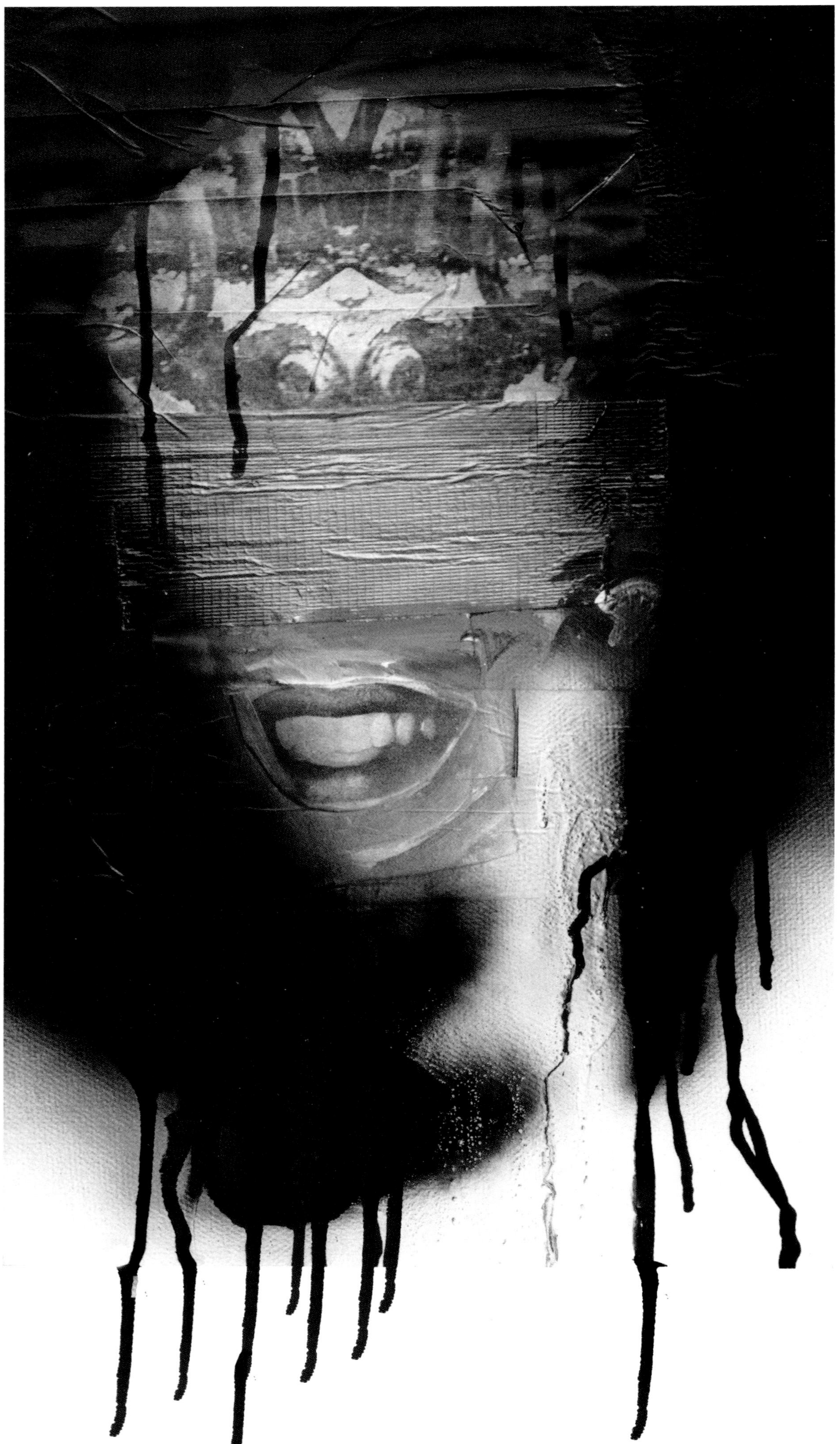

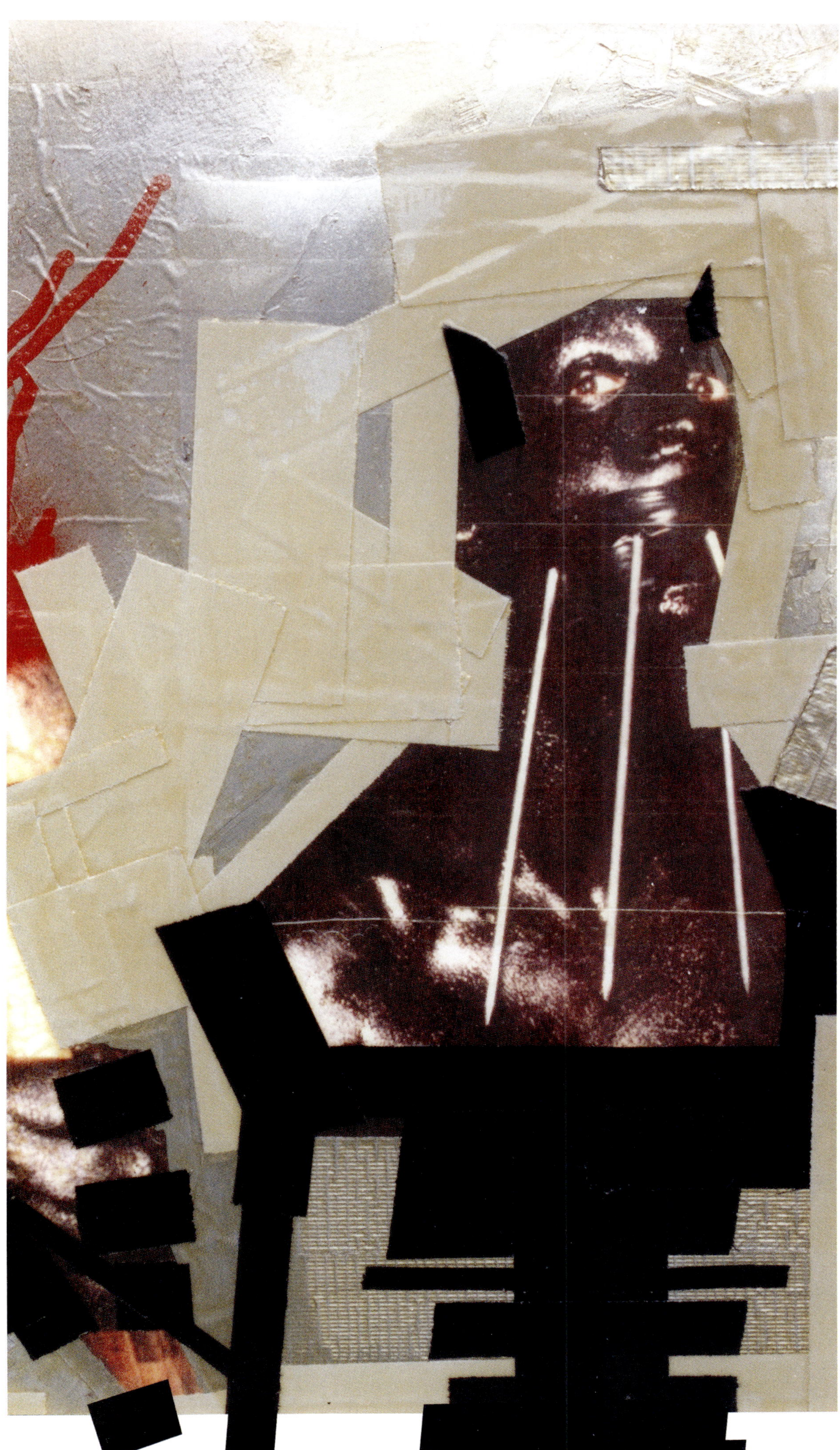

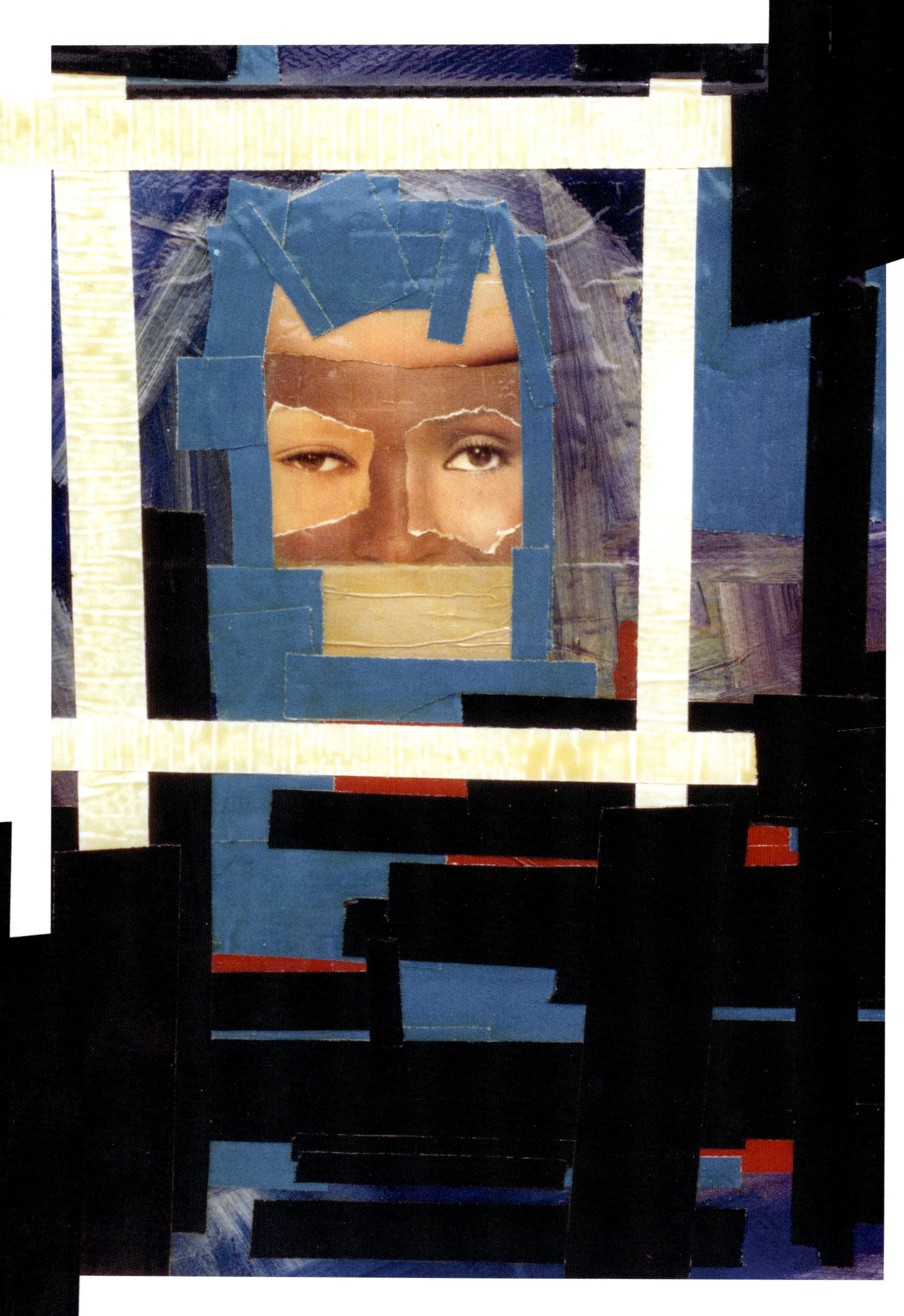

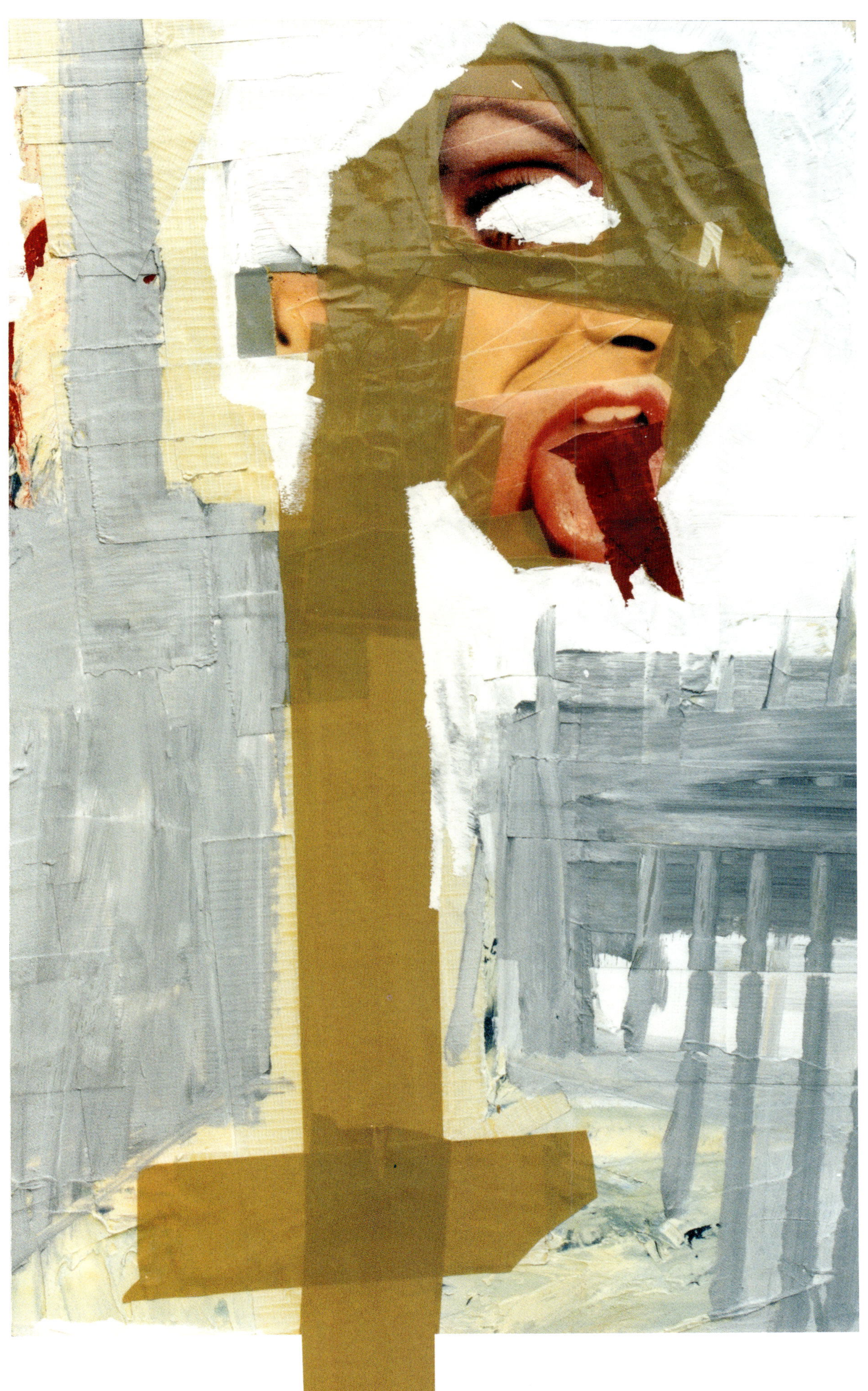

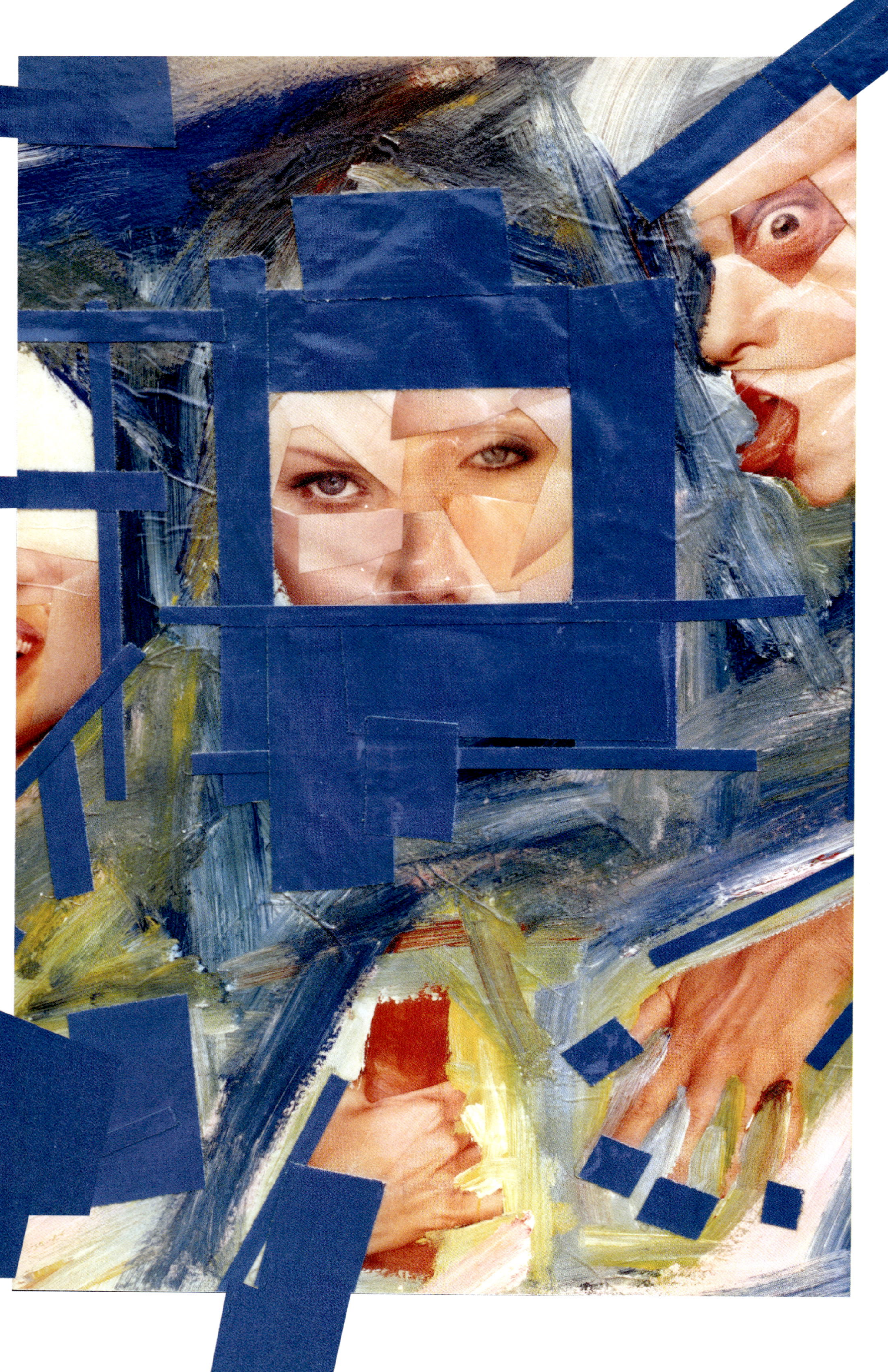

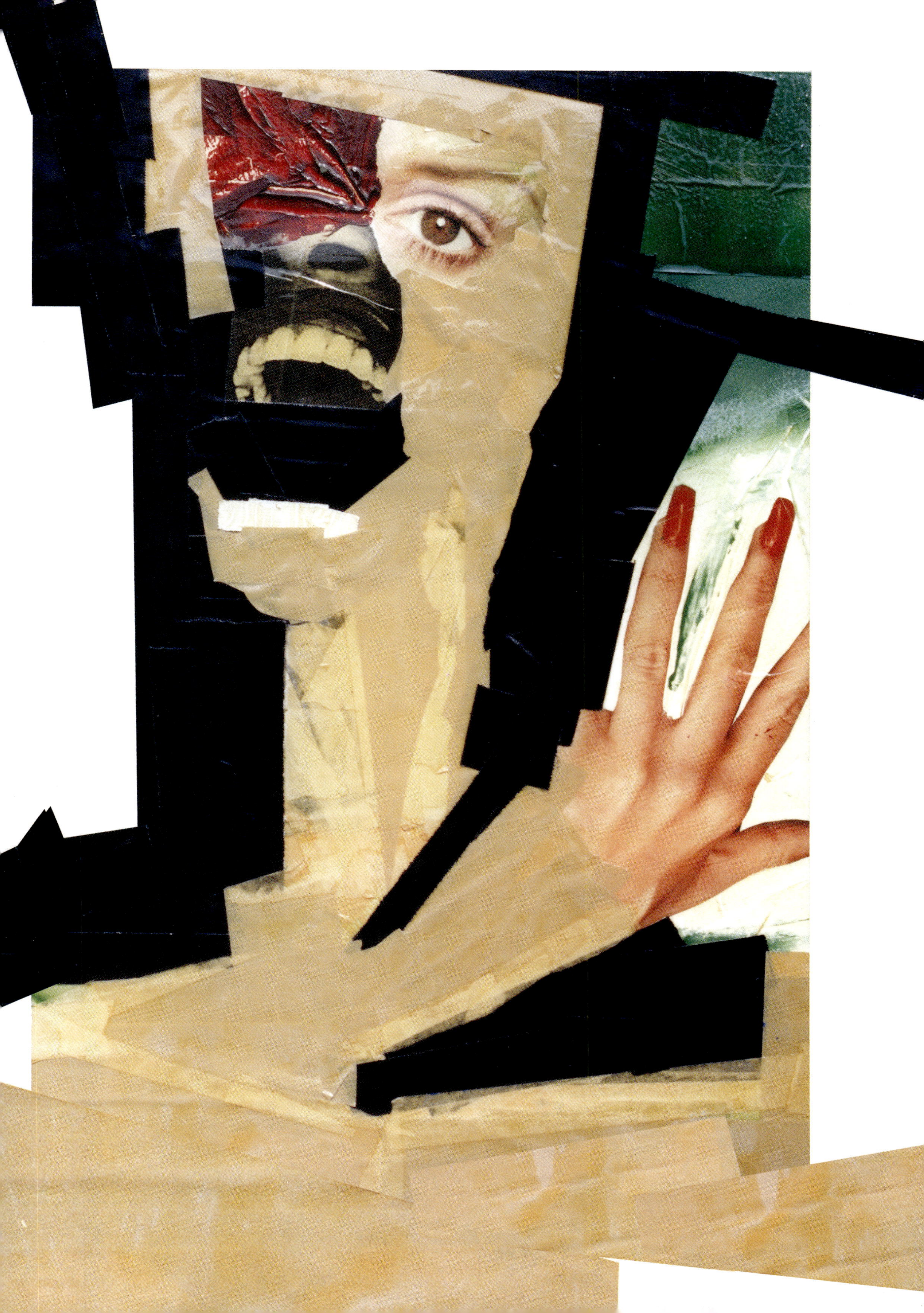

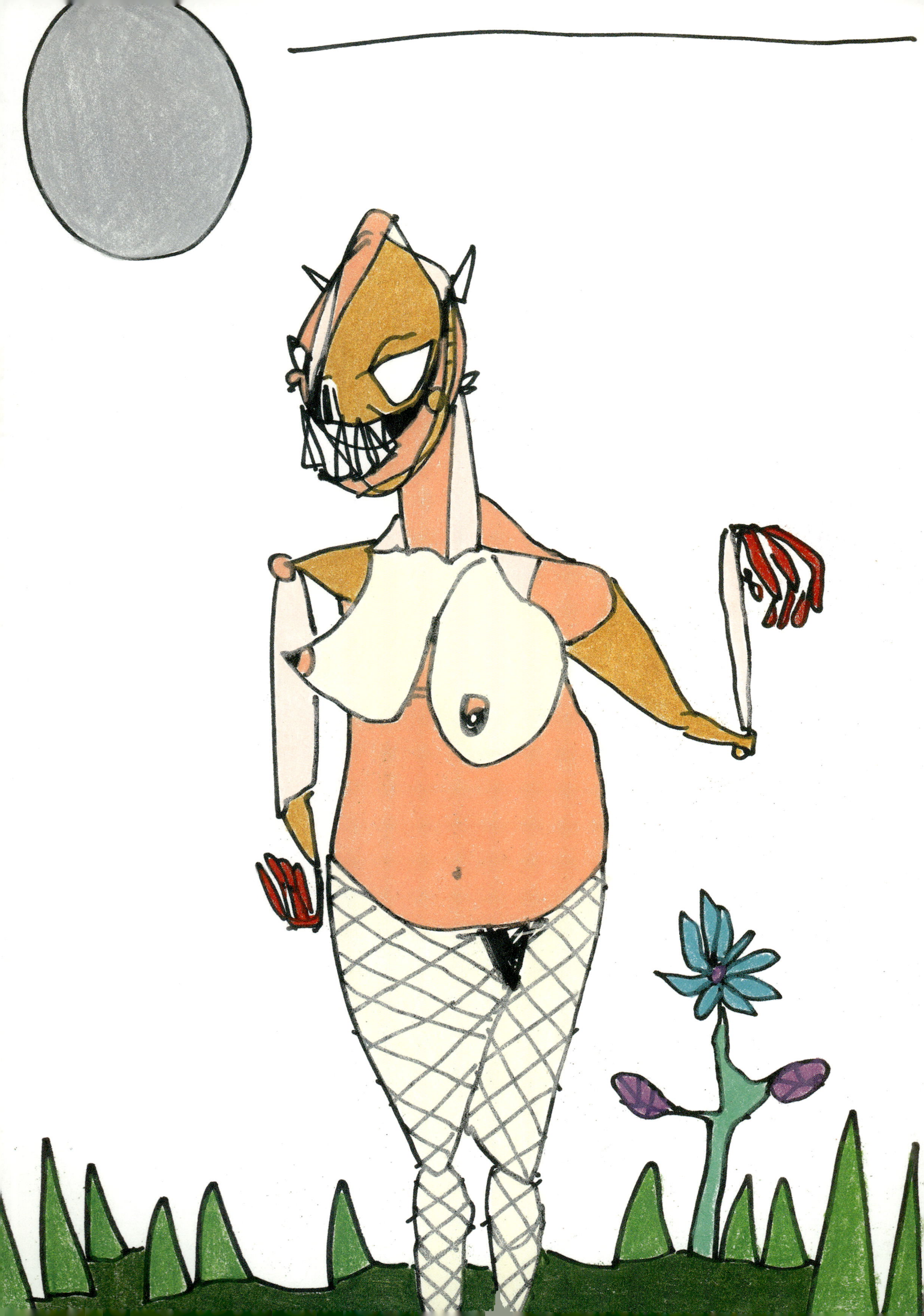

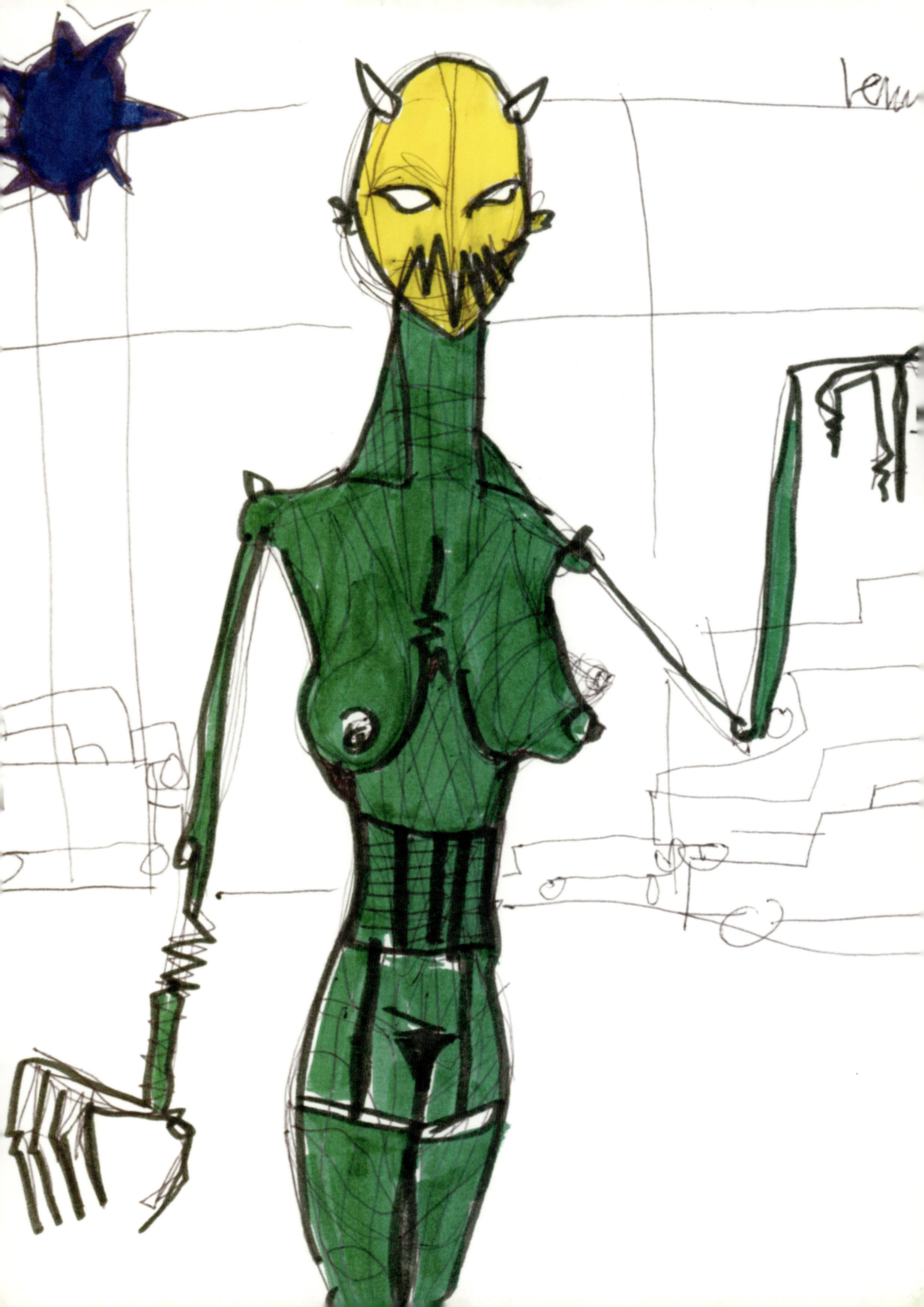

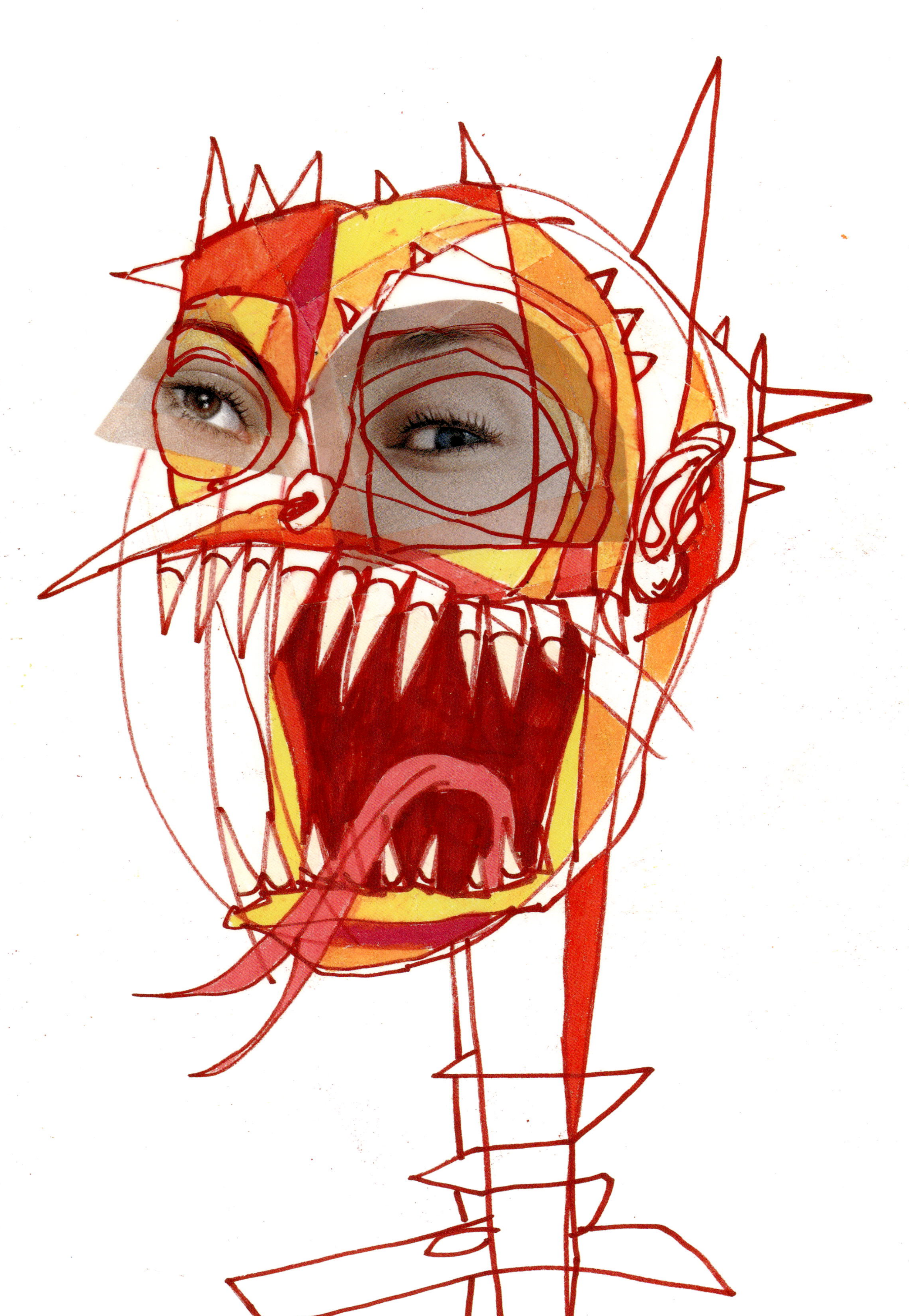

with a mouth full of blud he says
do you believe in love

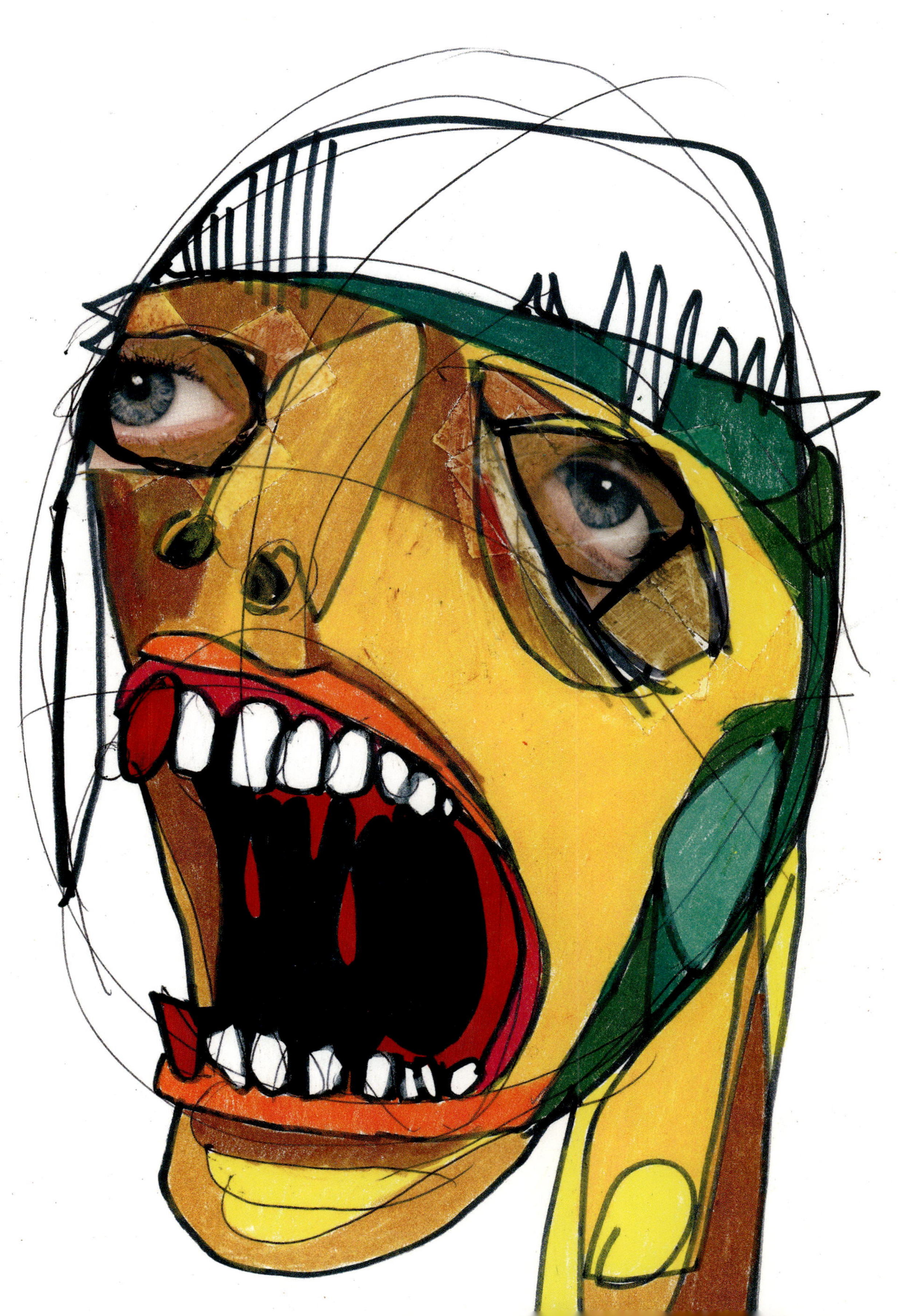

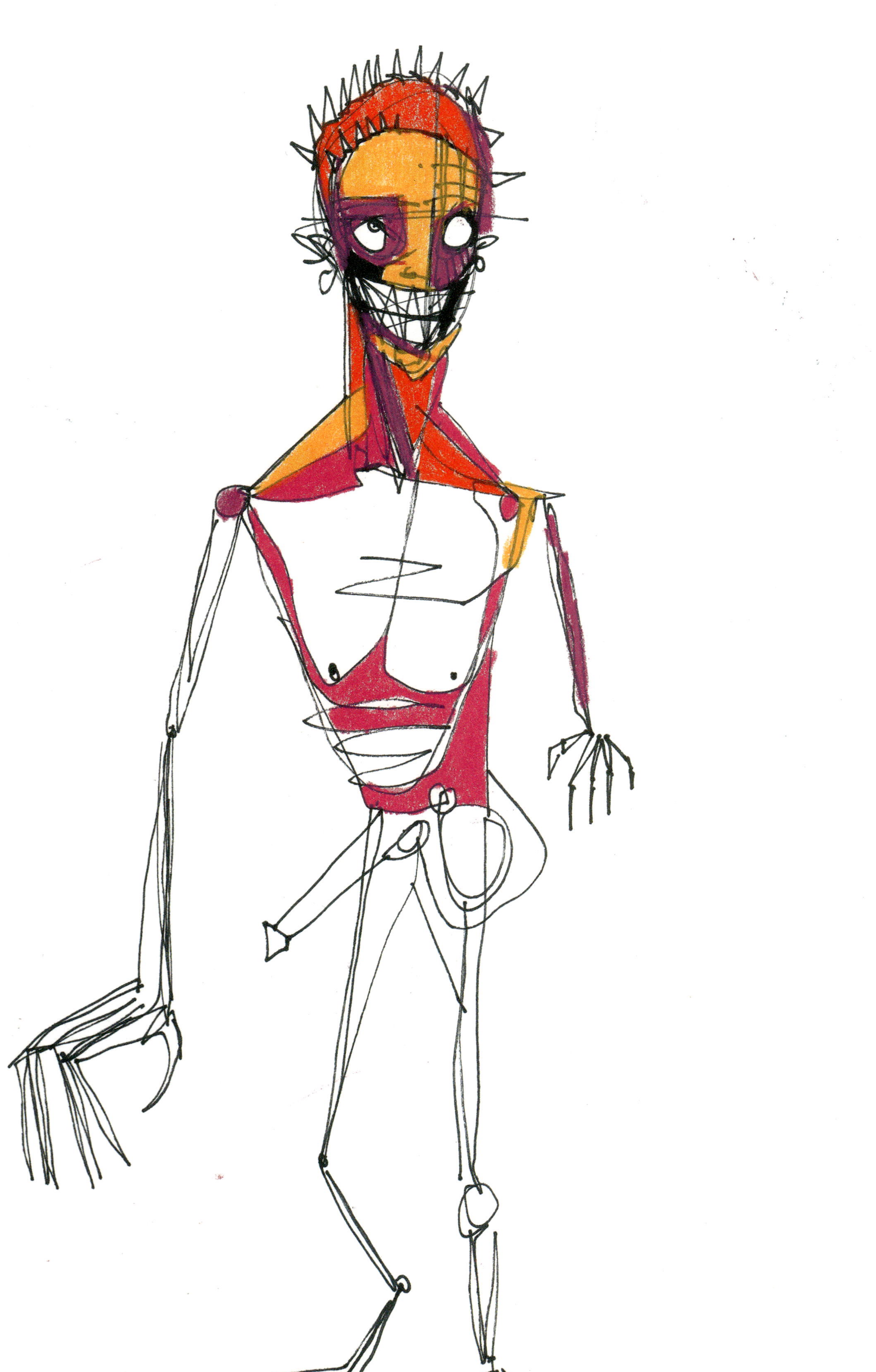

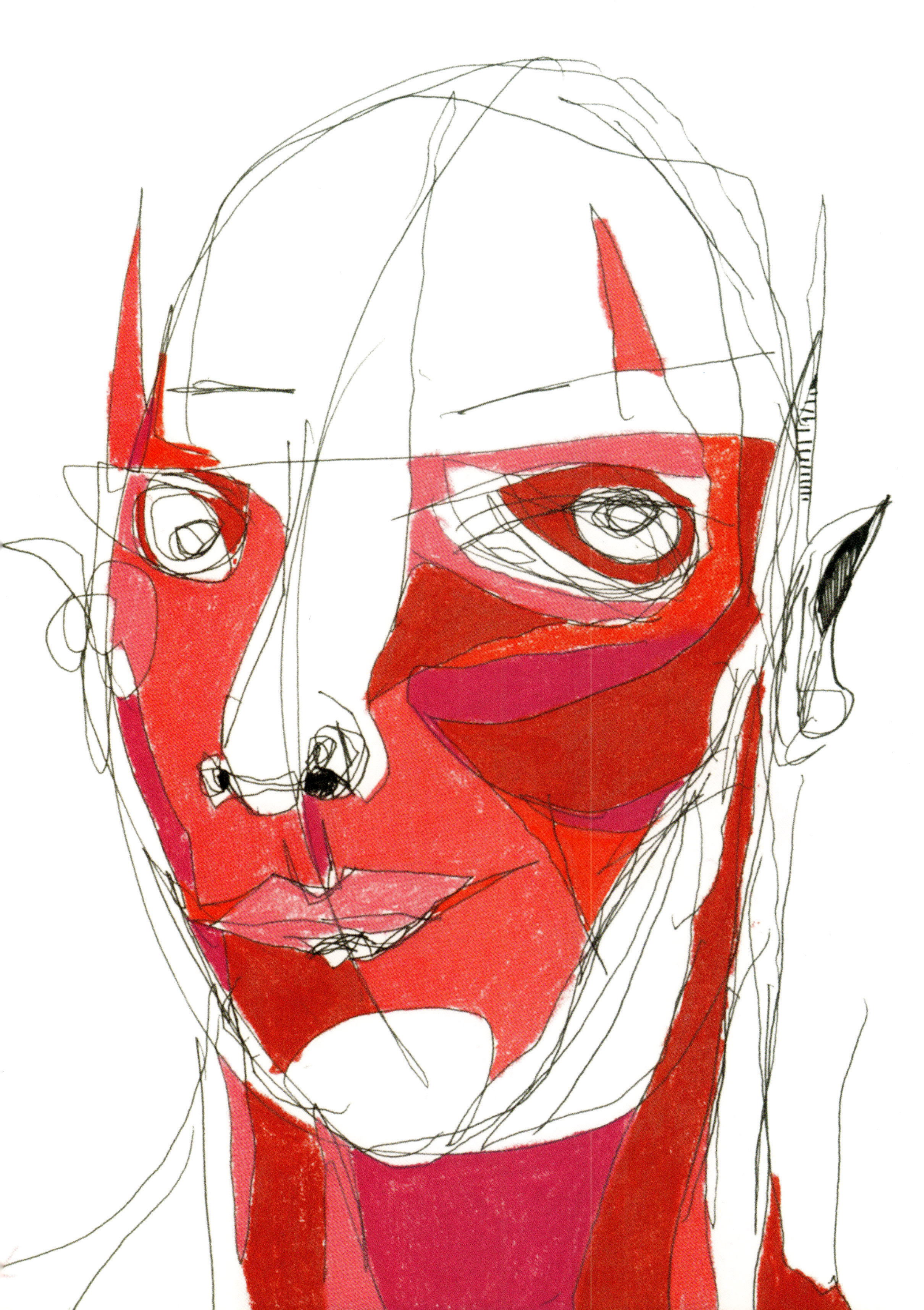

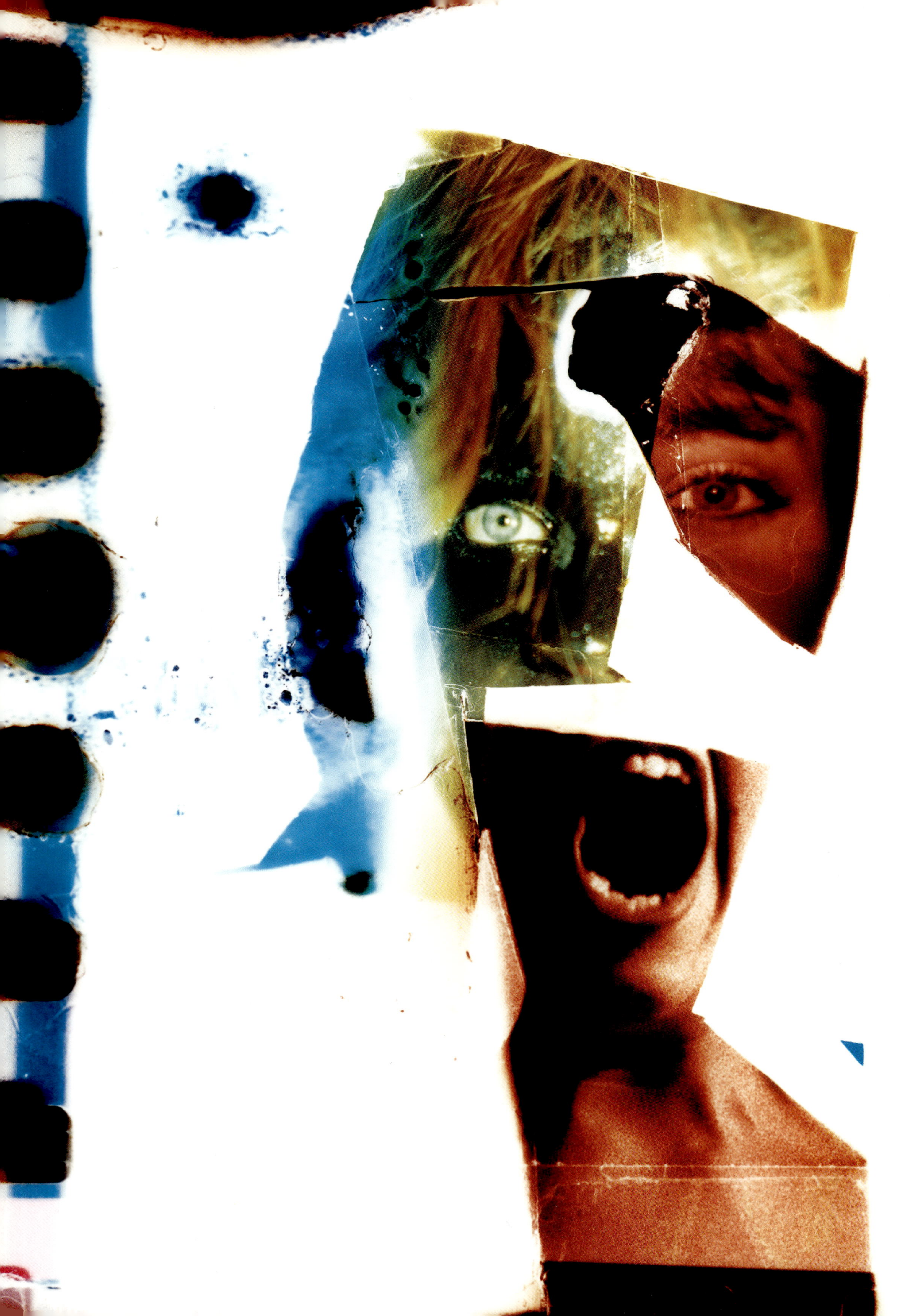

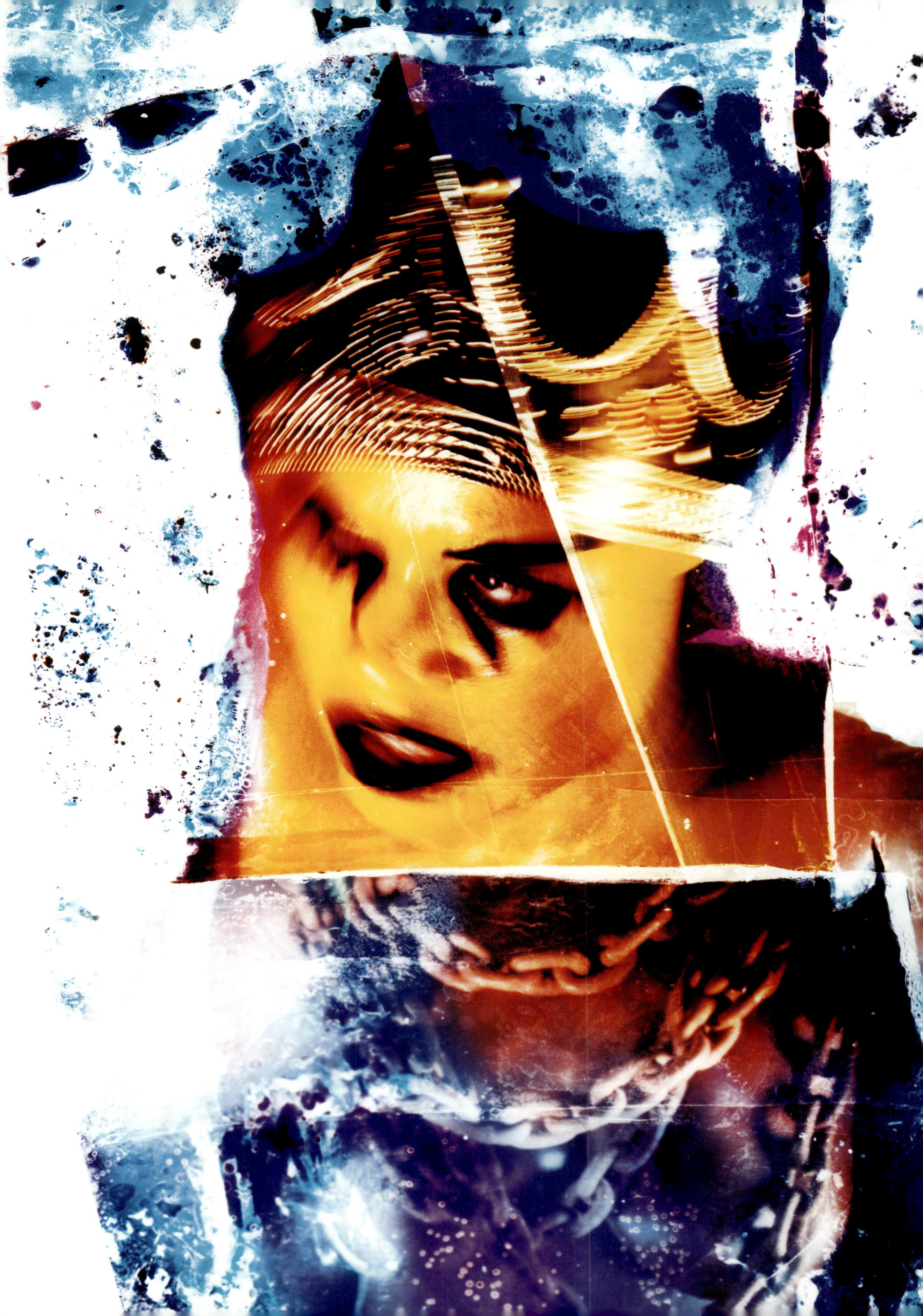

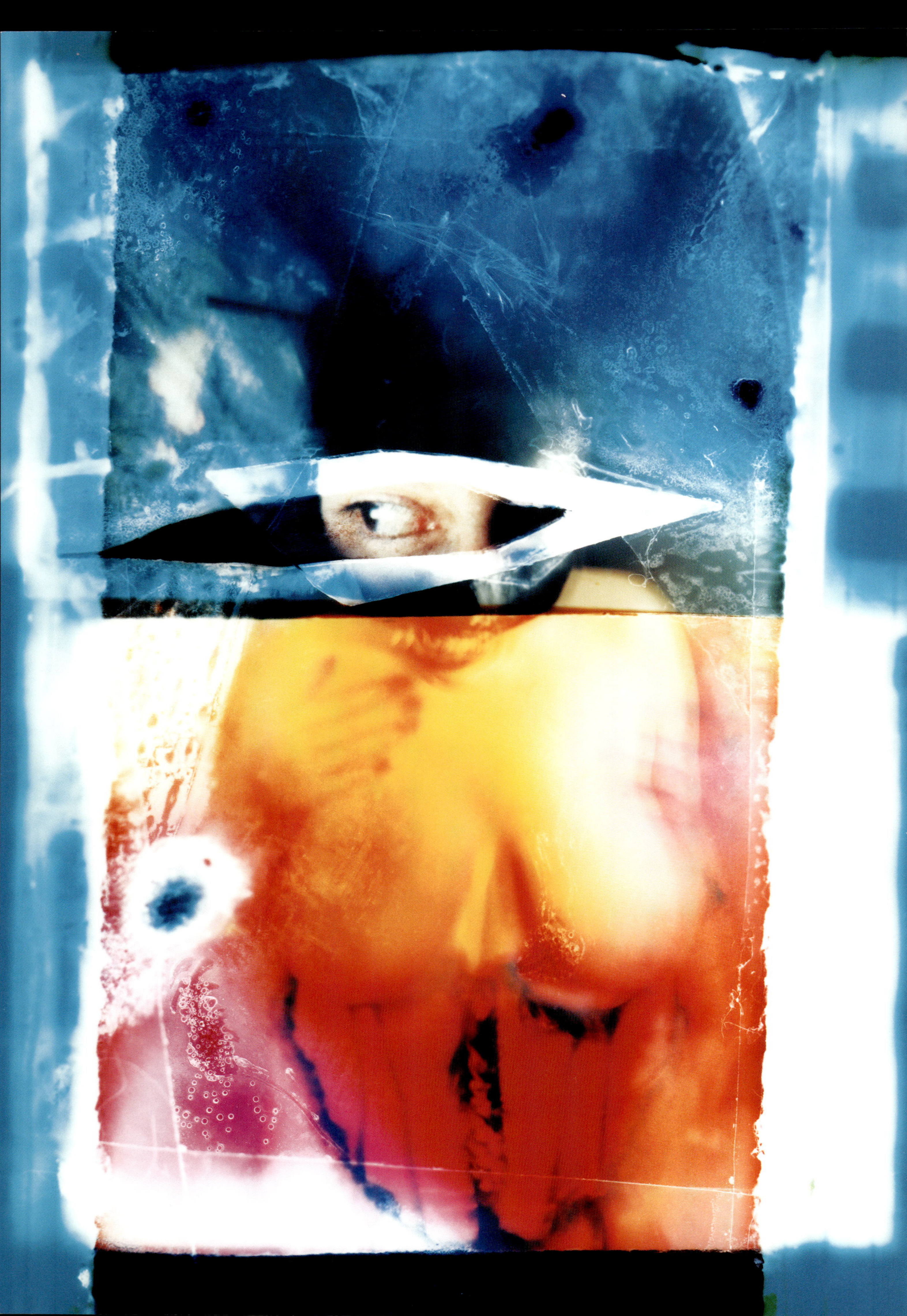

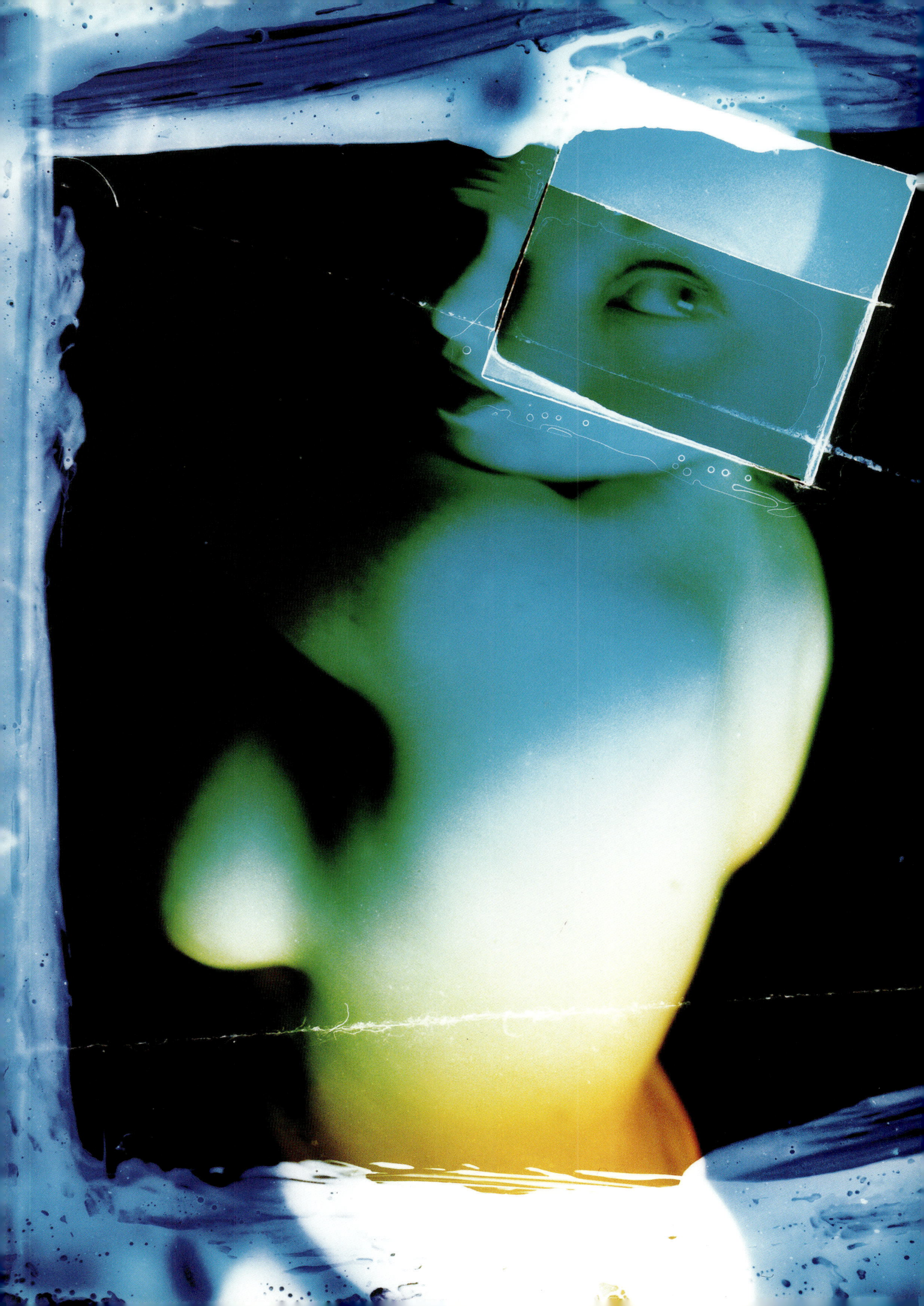

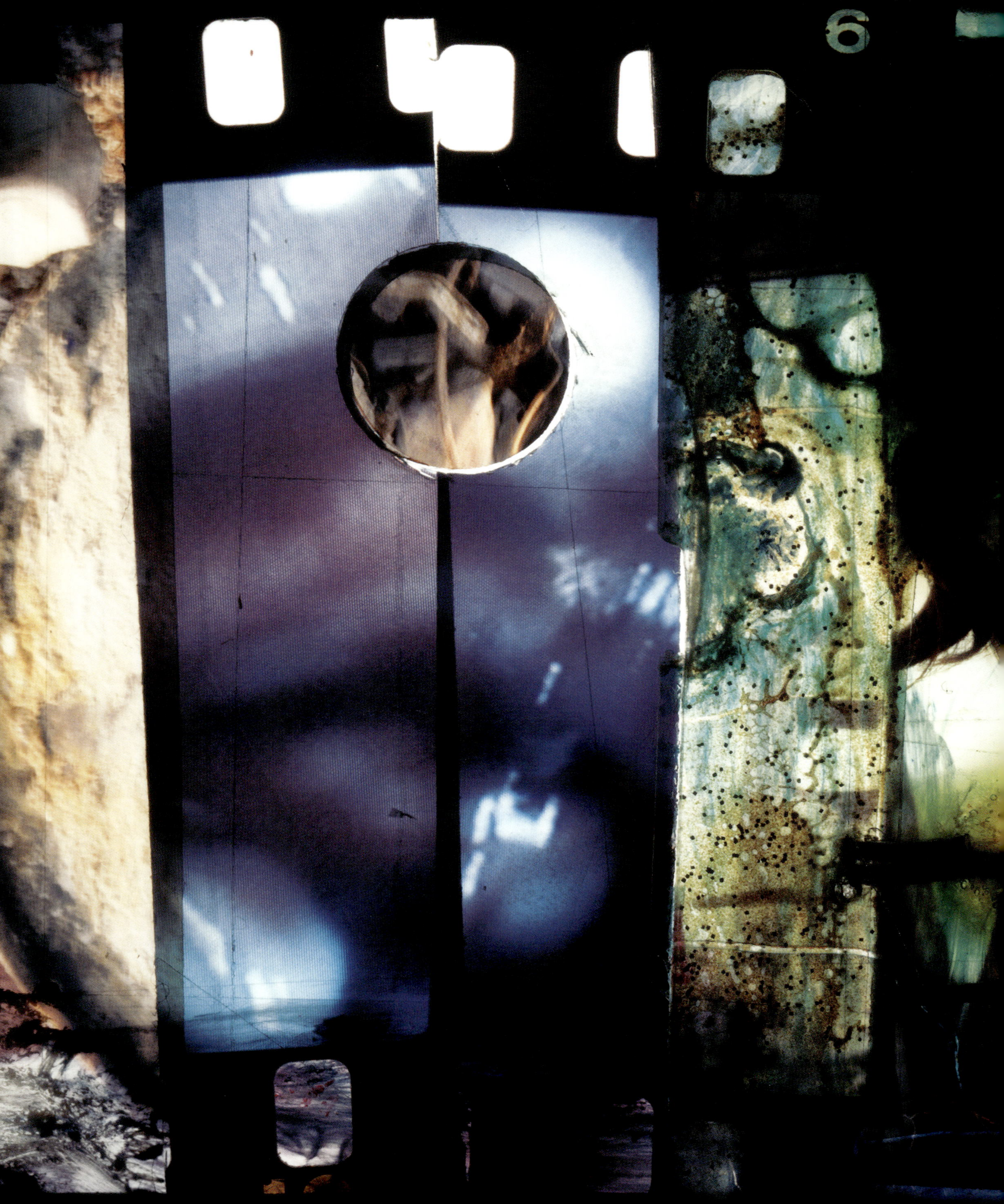
6

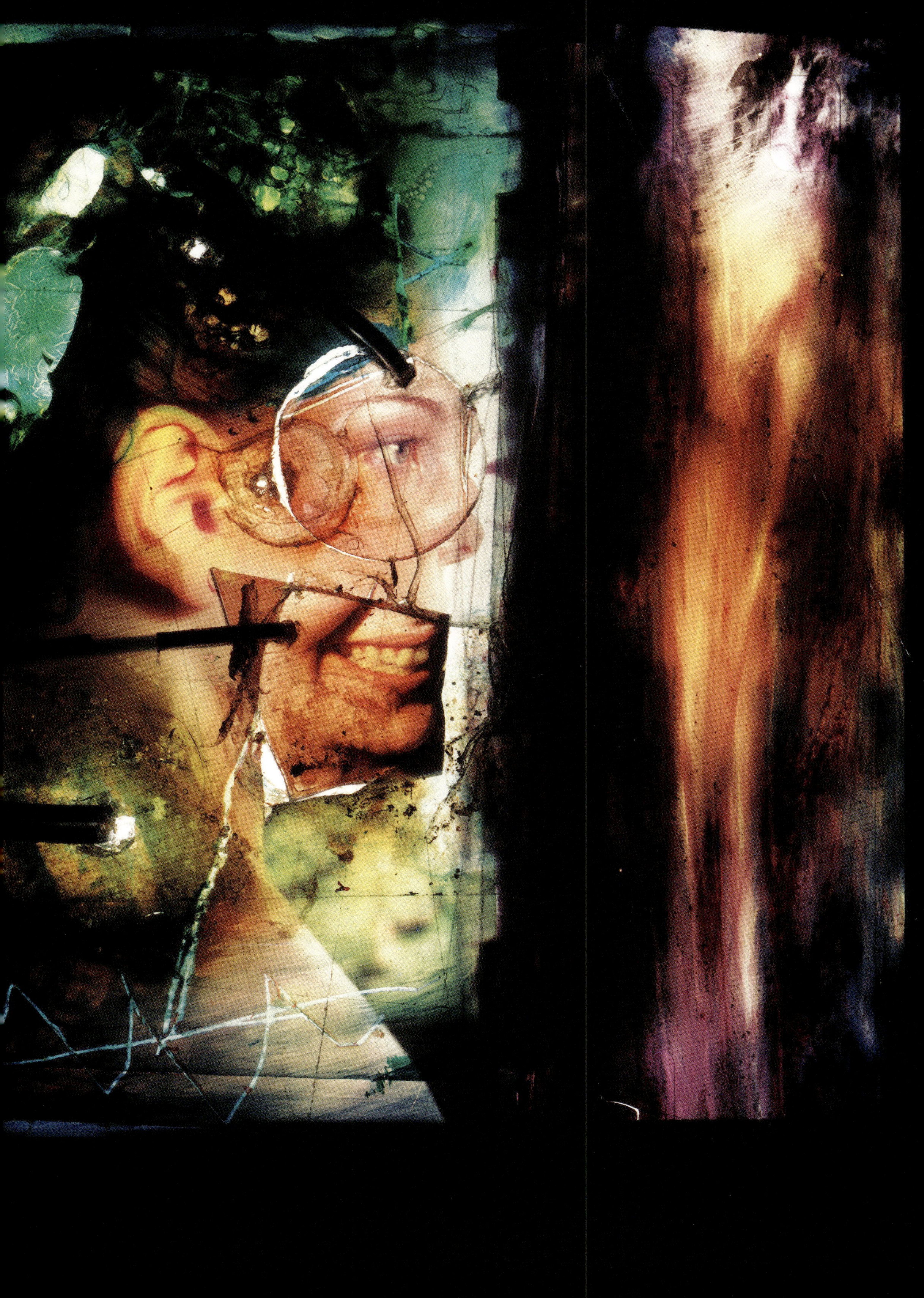

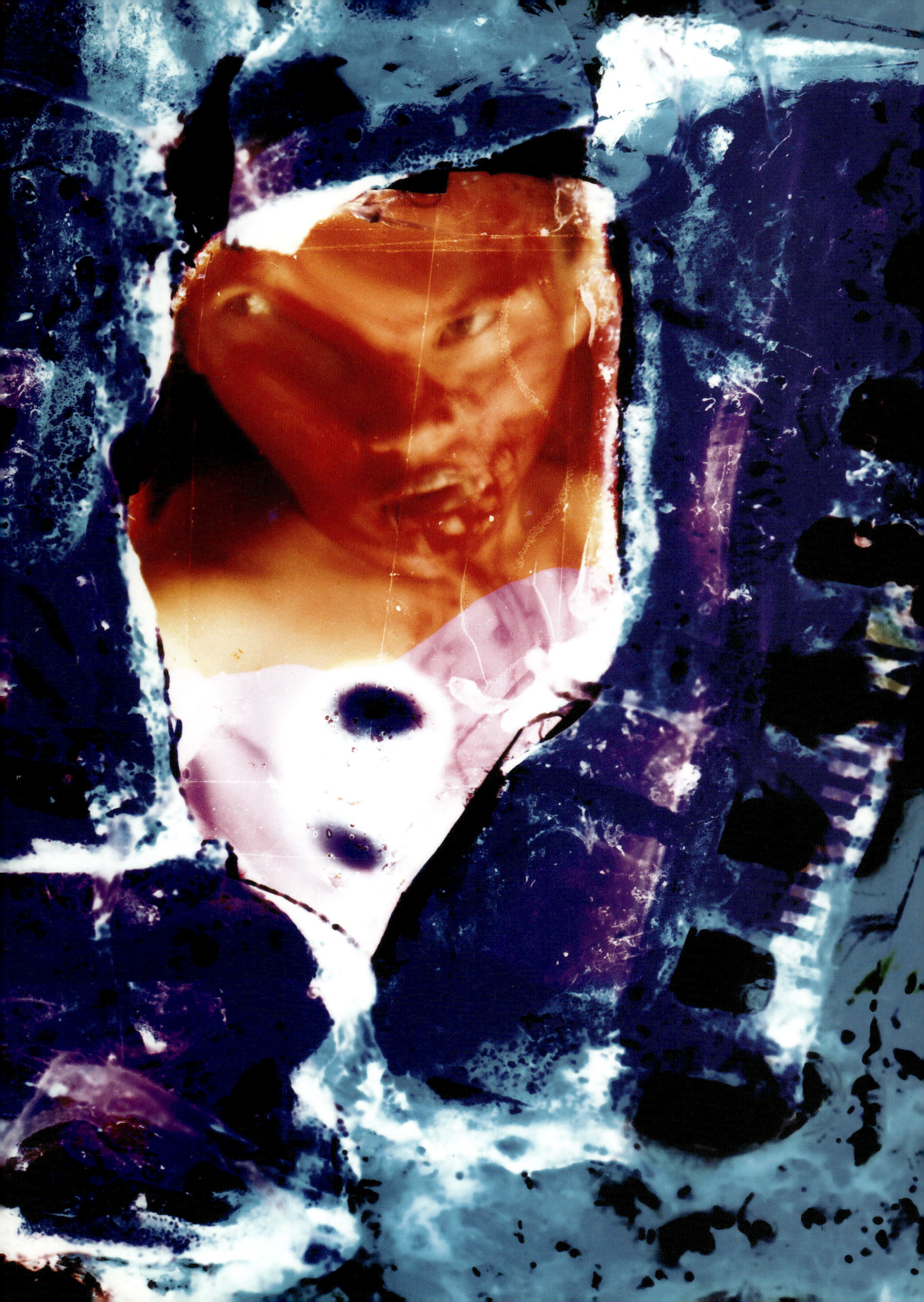

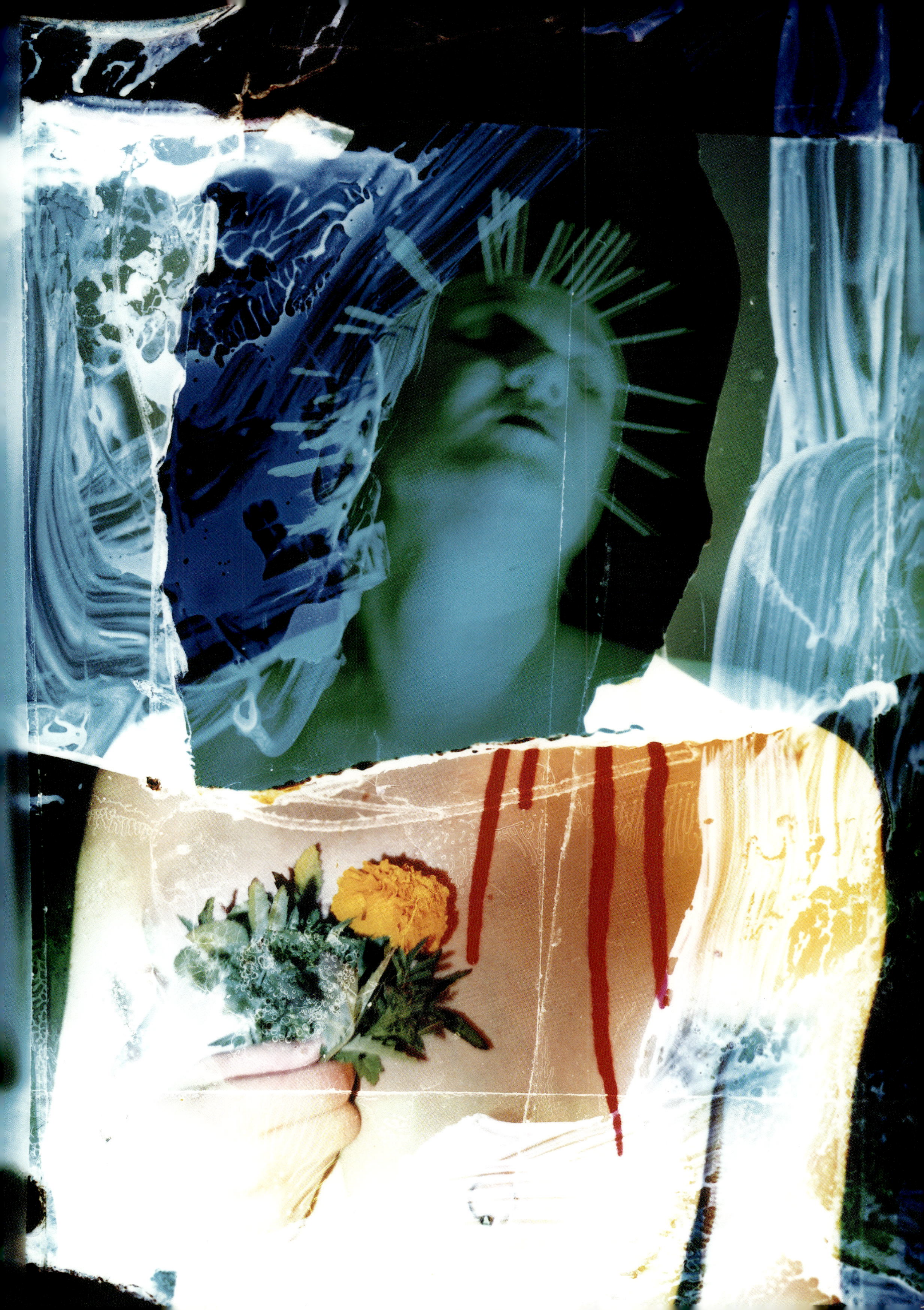

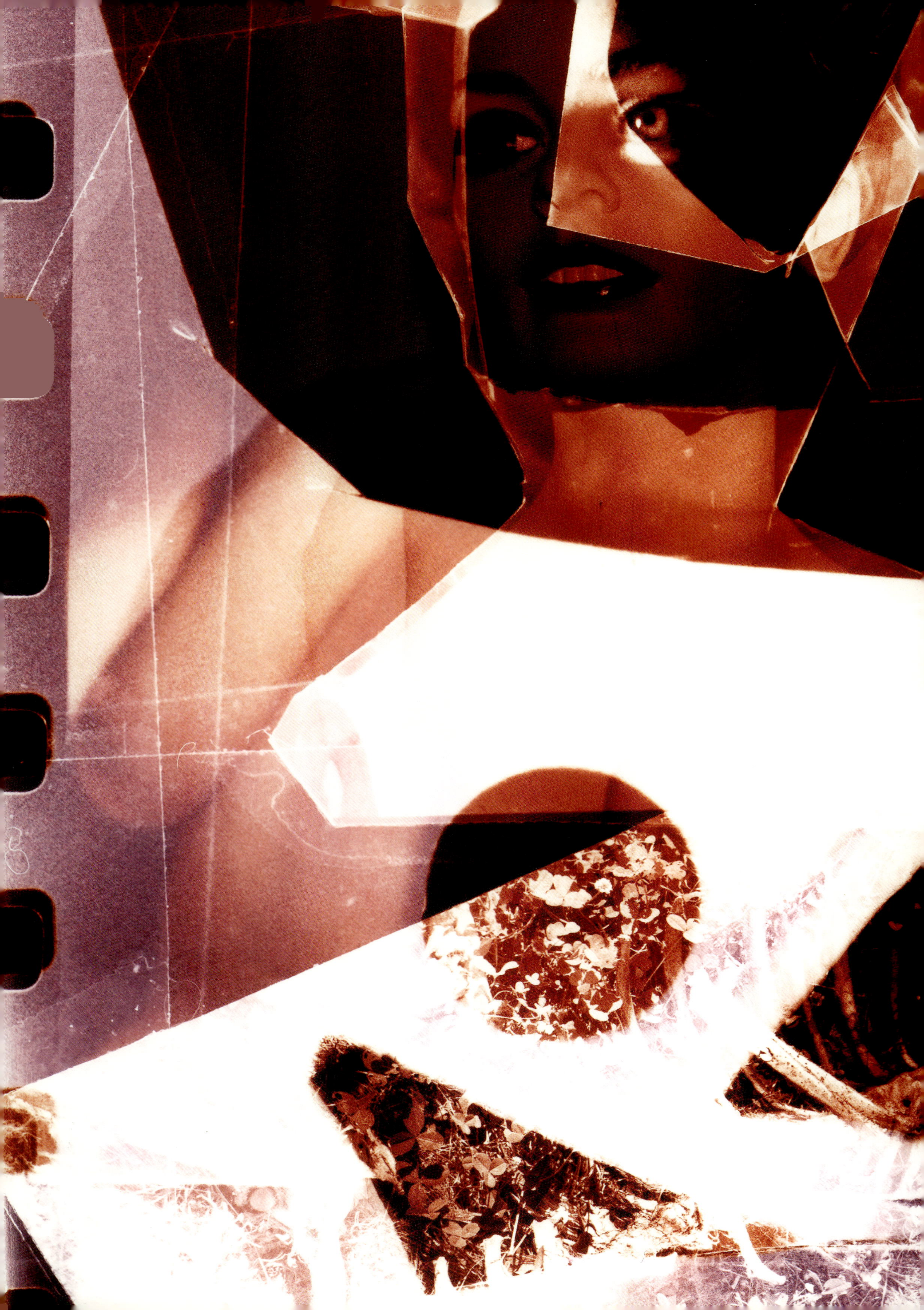

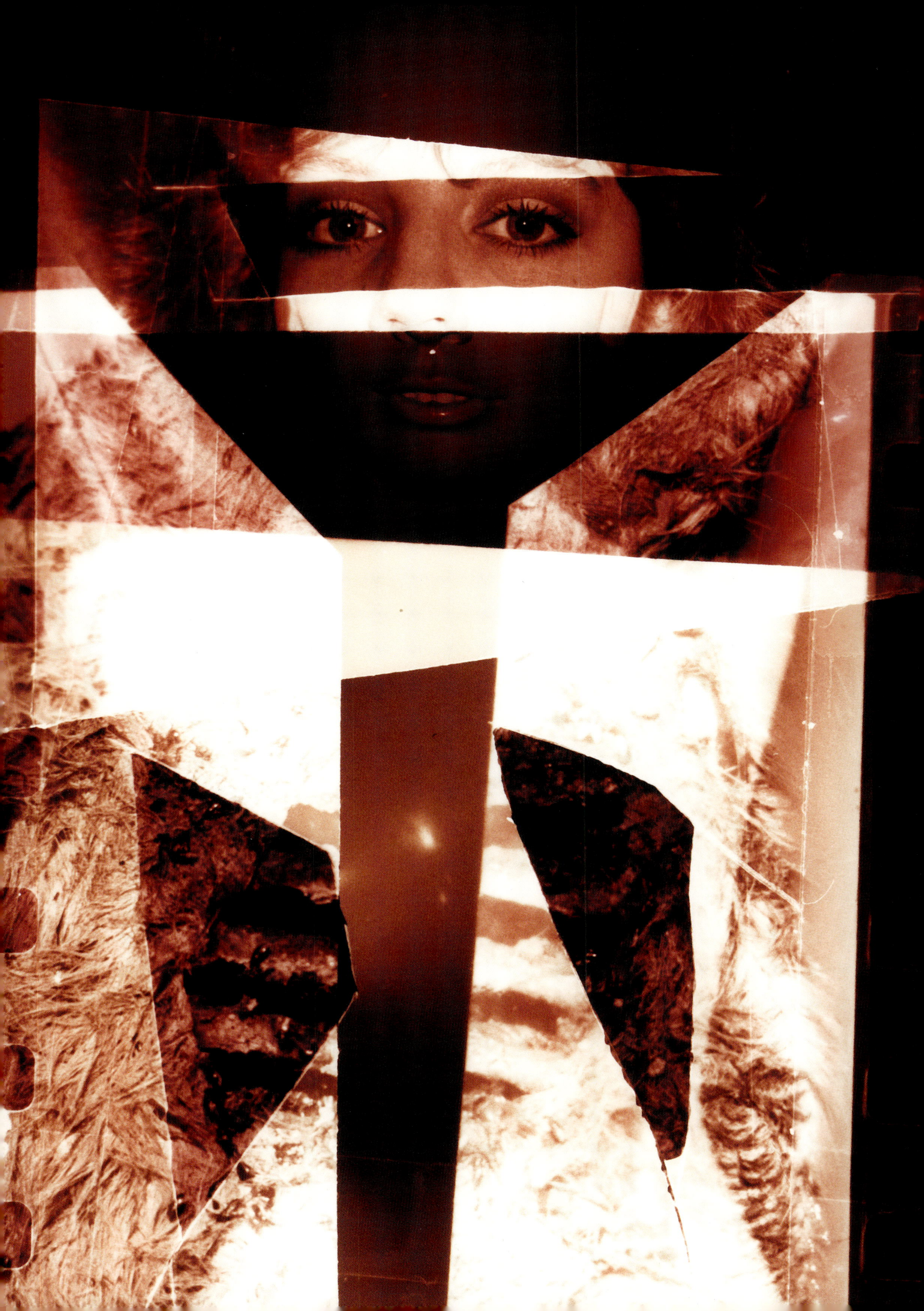

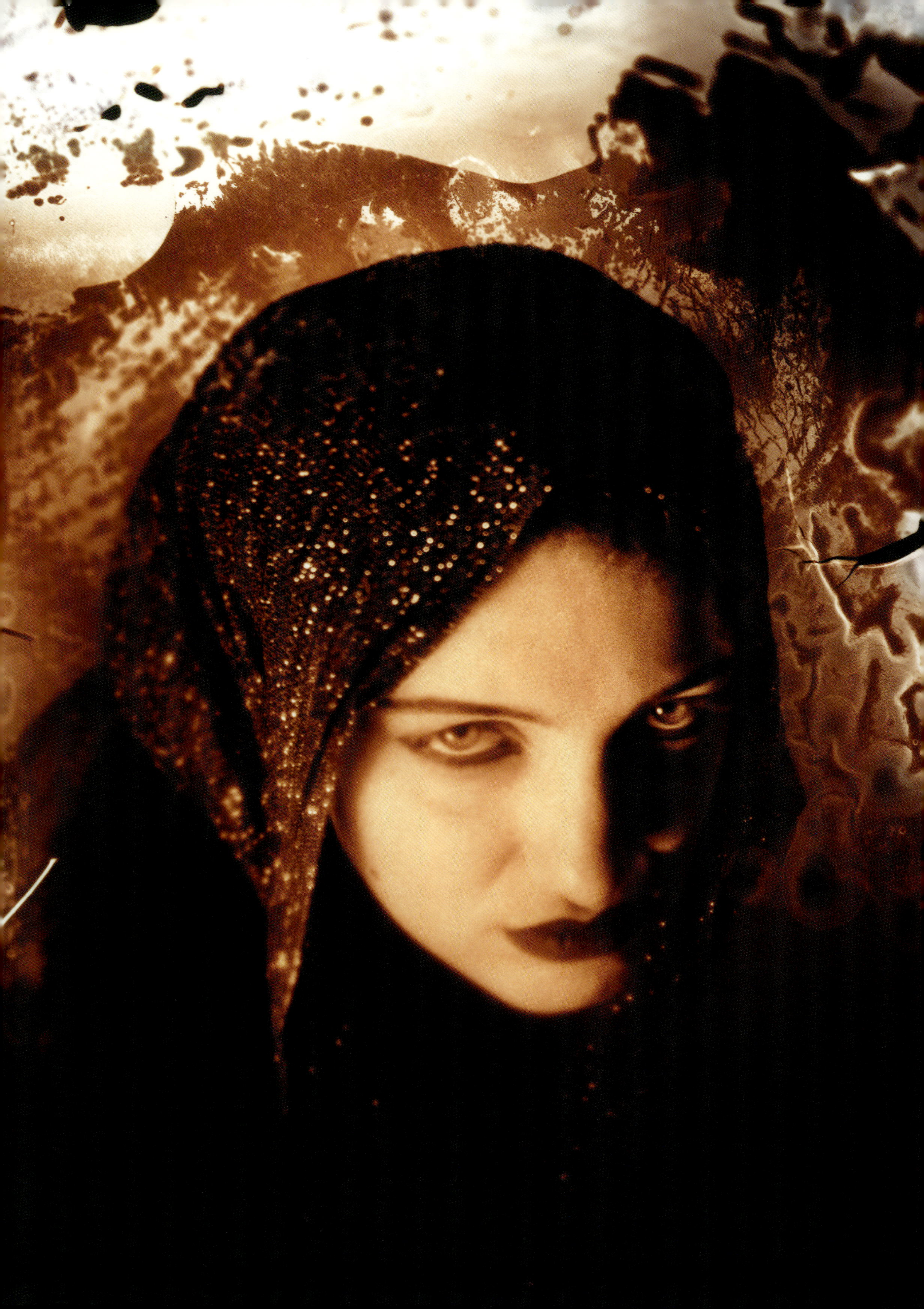

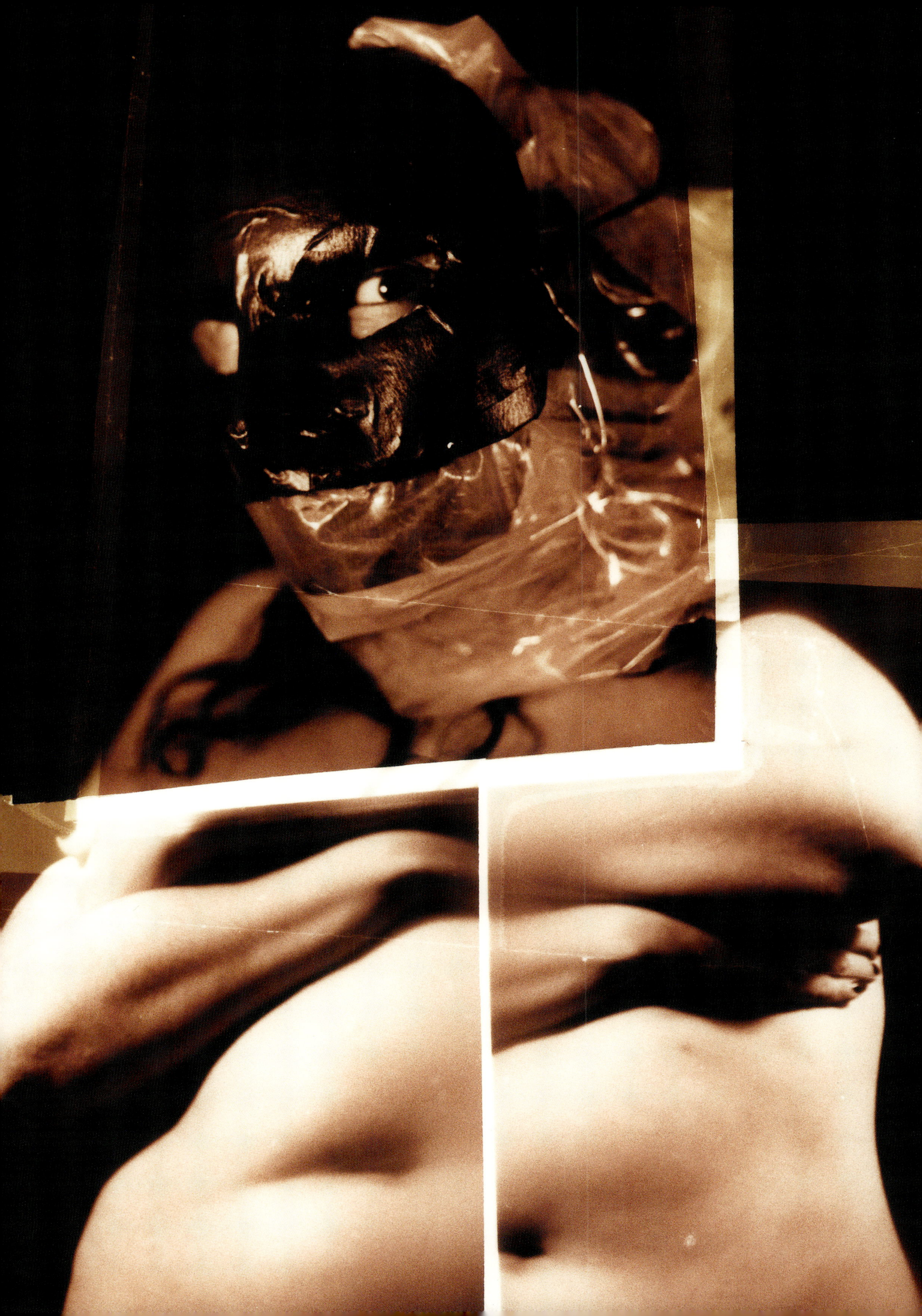

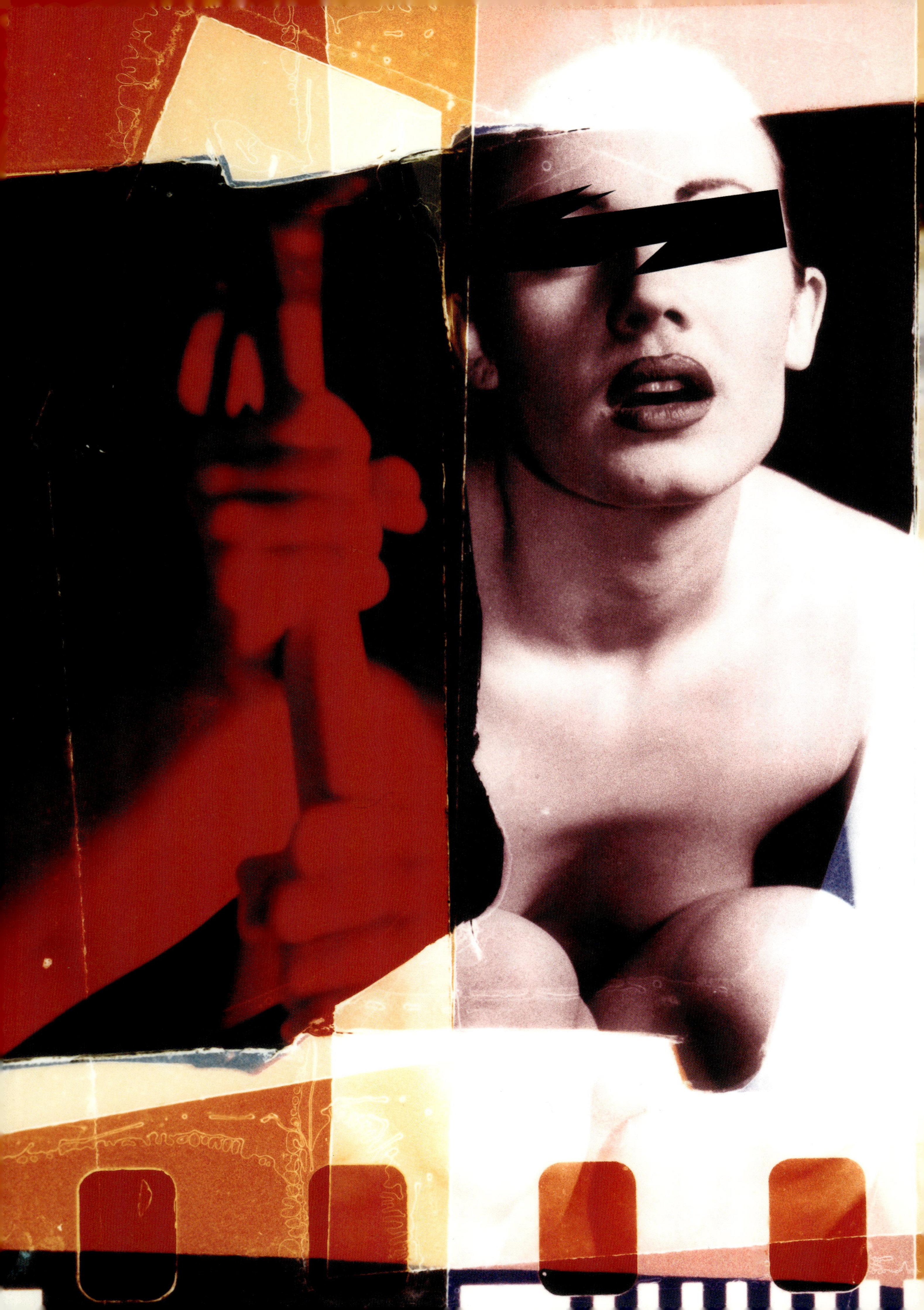

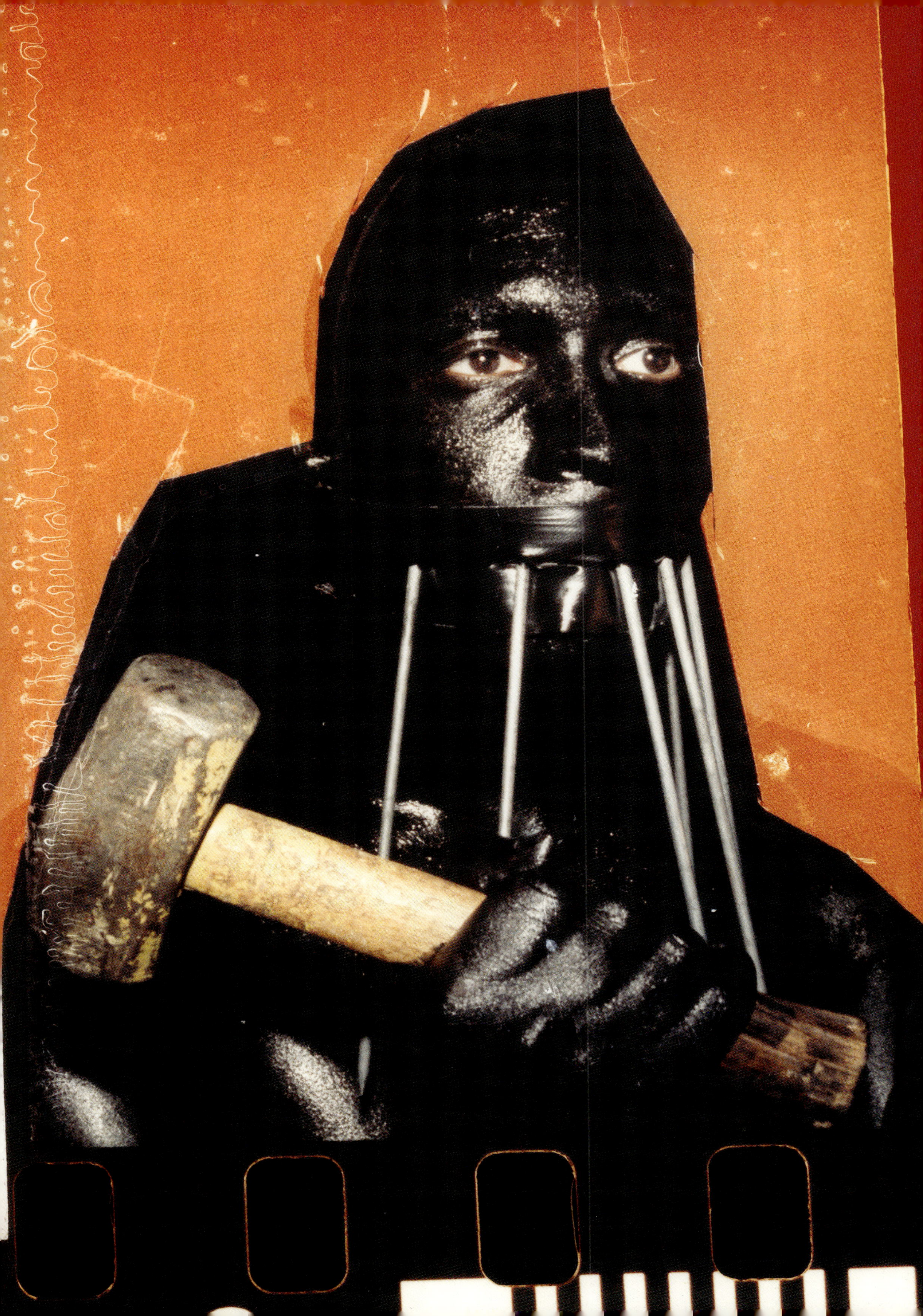

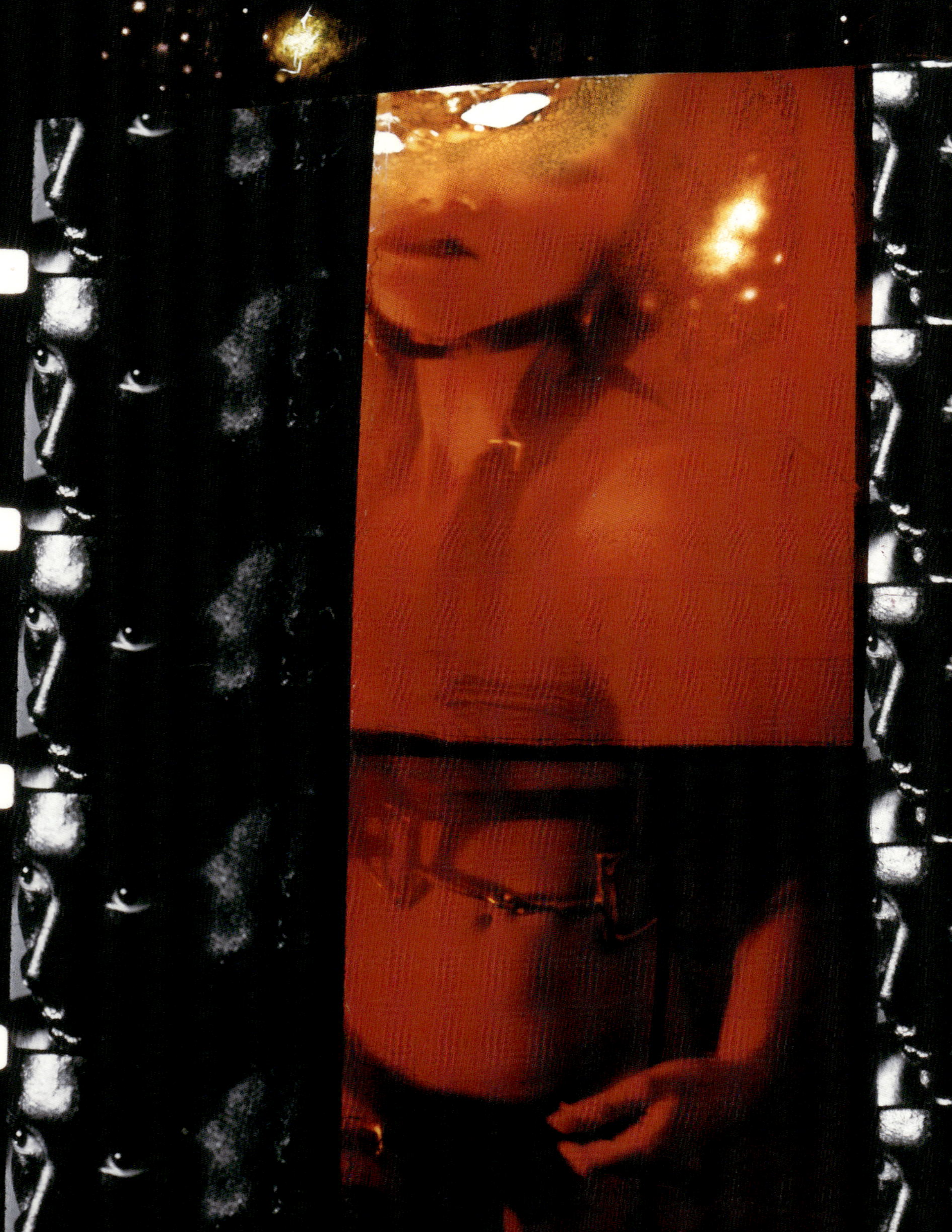
HOLLYWOOD

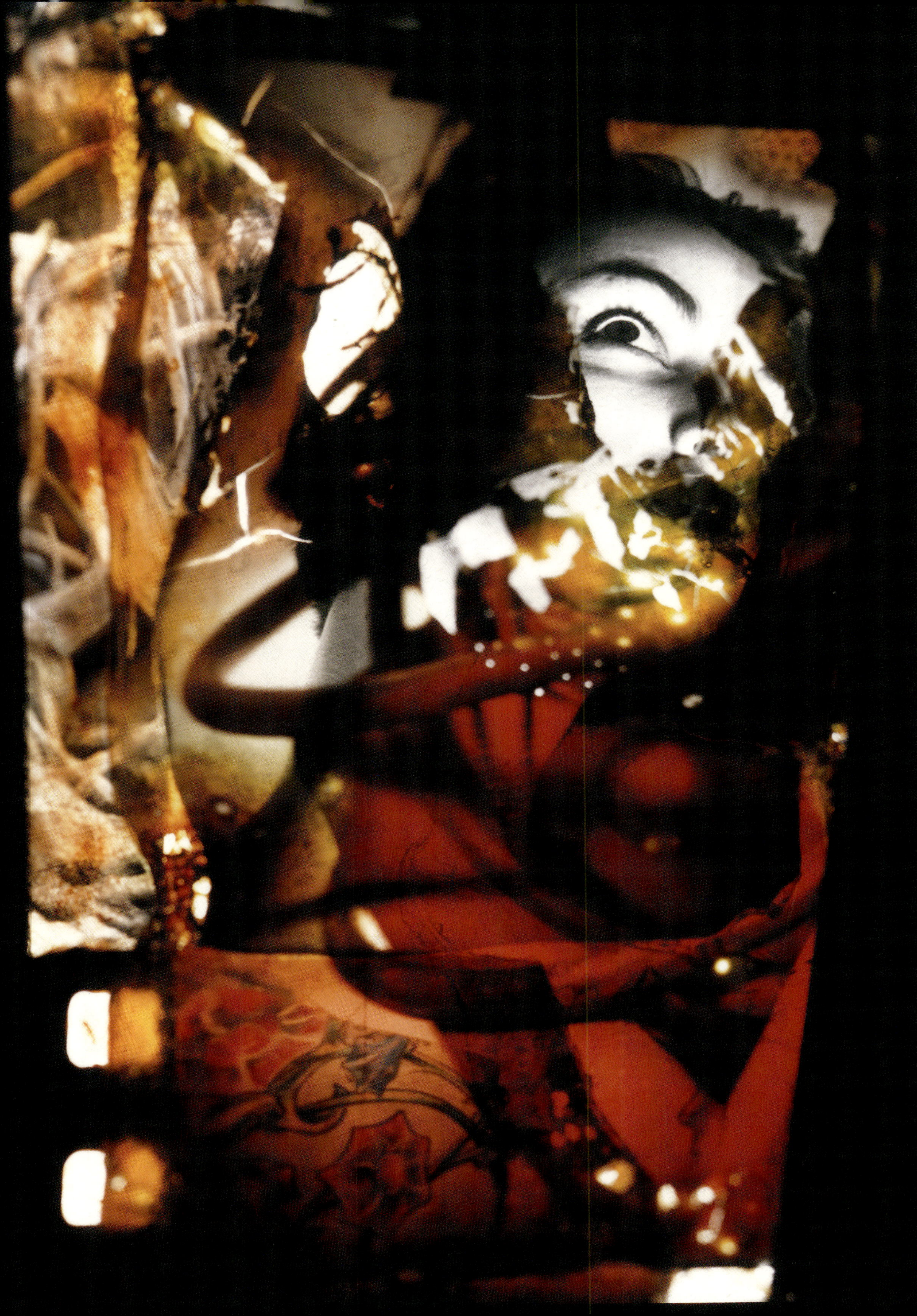

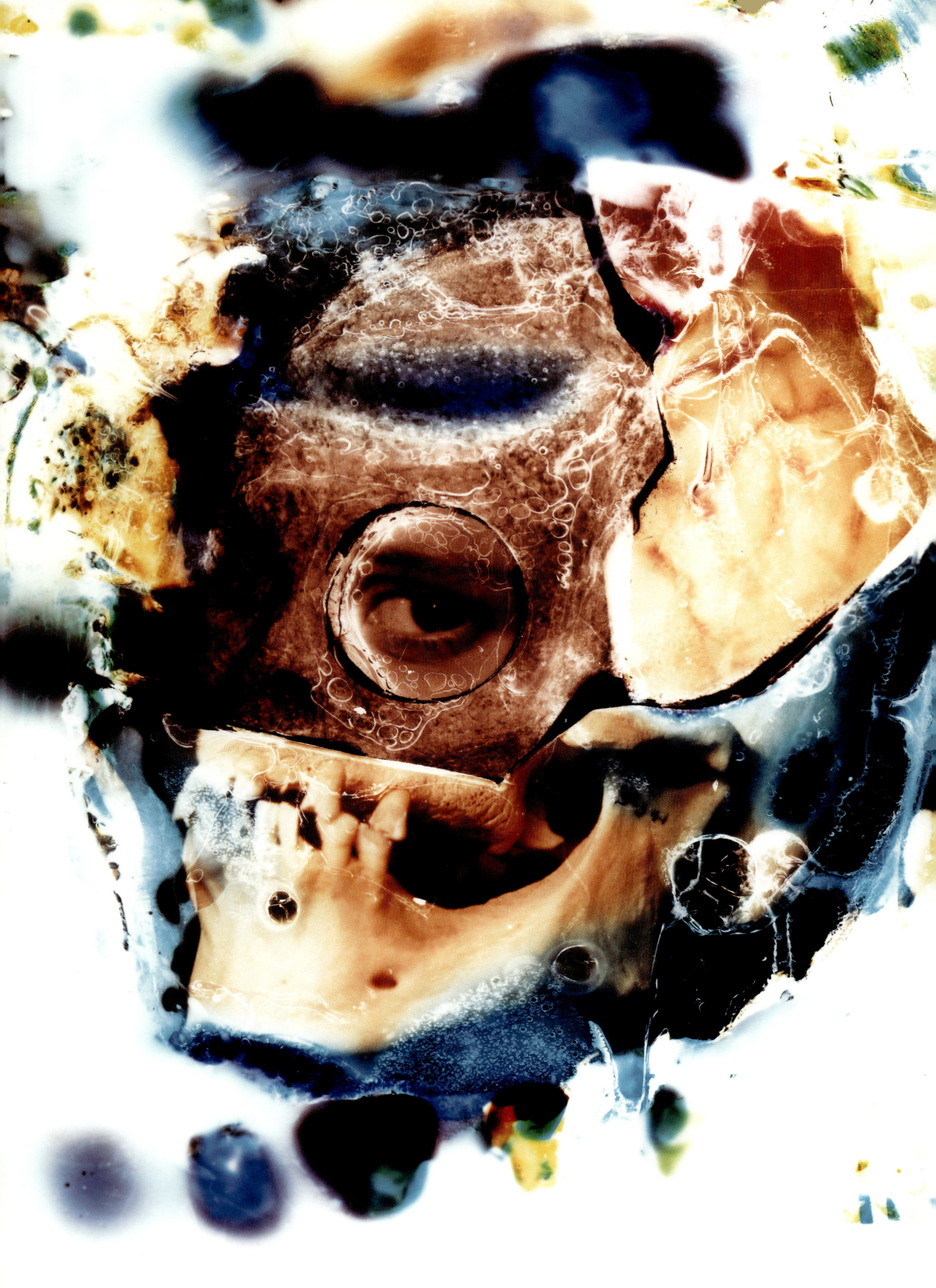

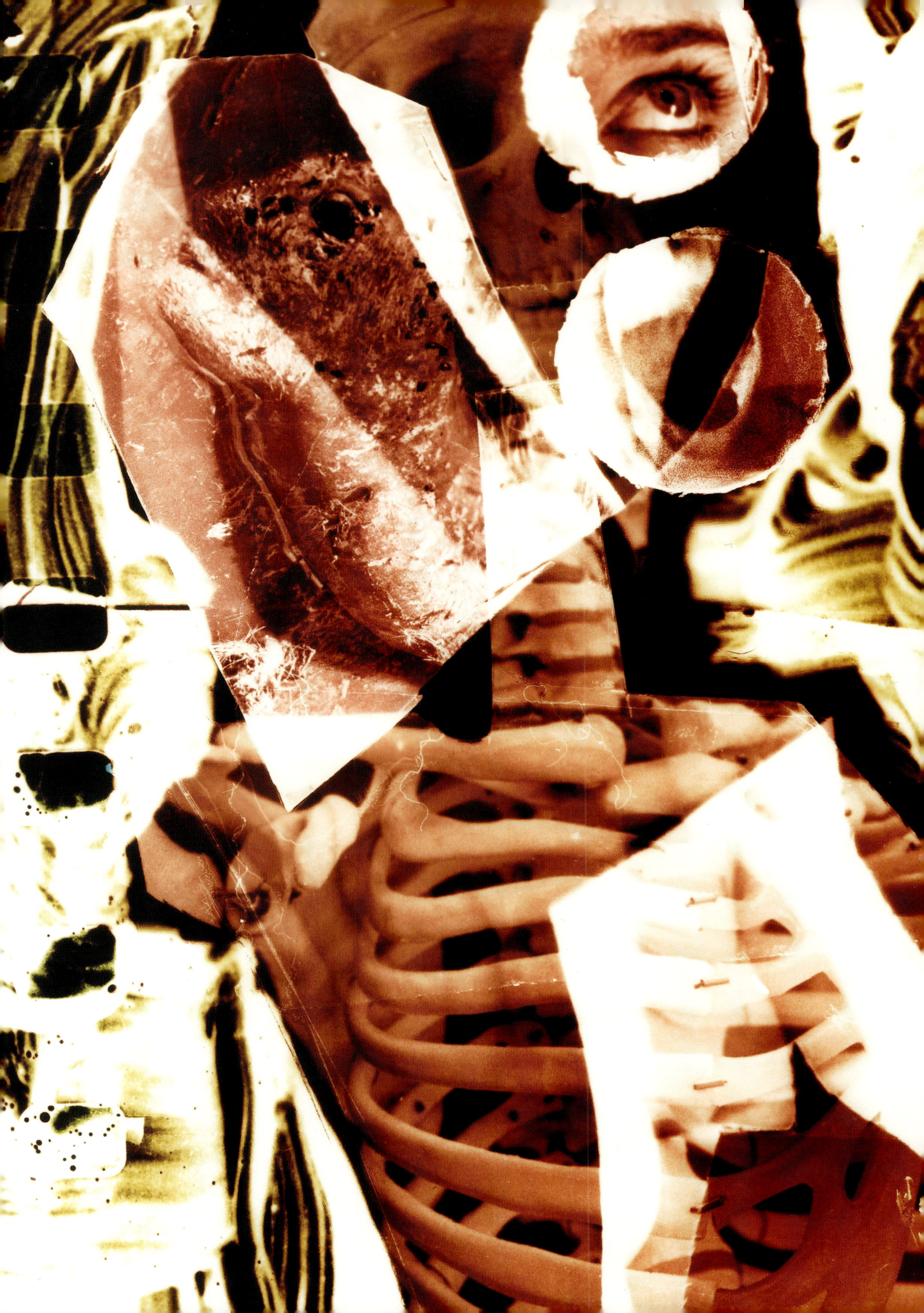

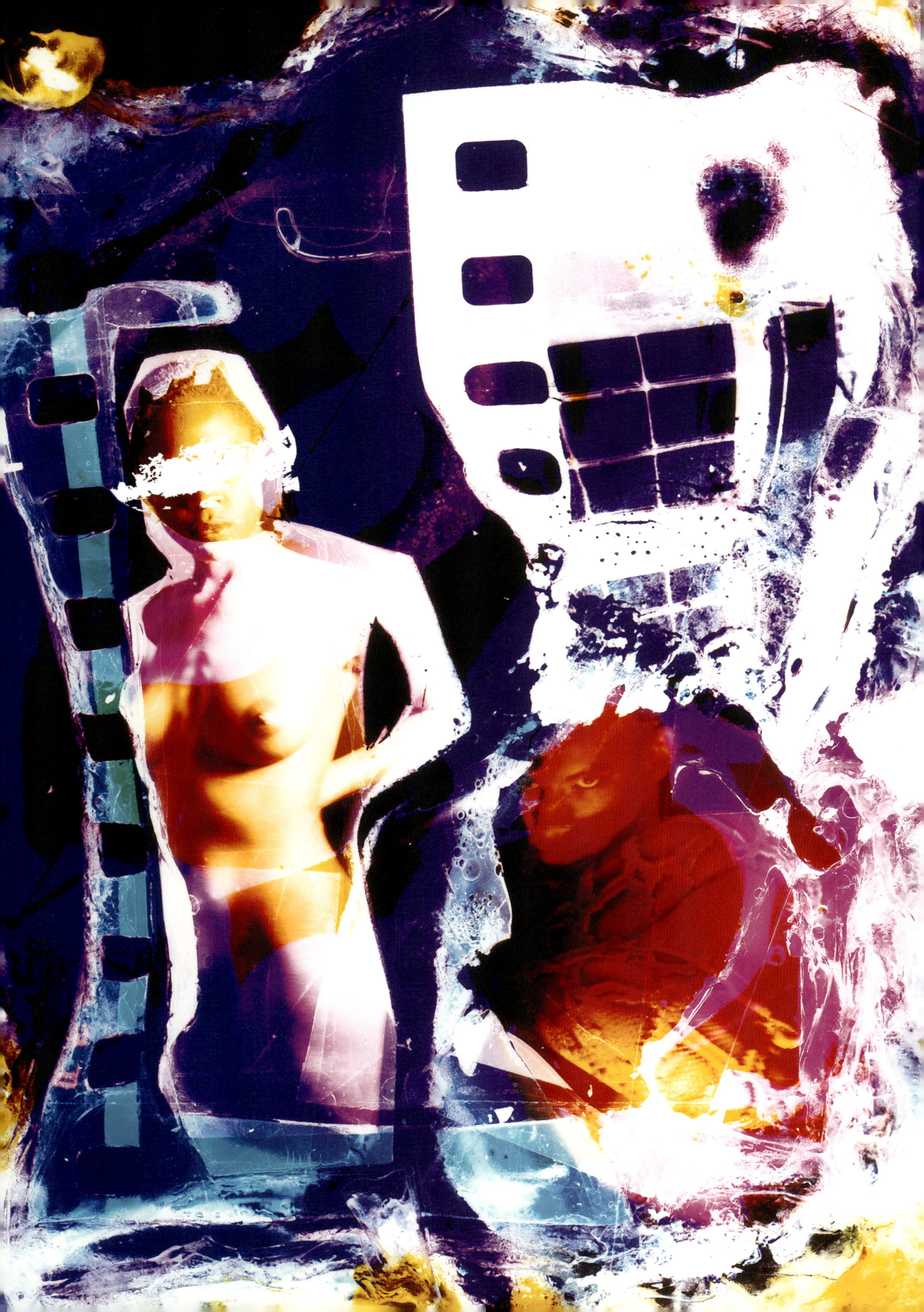

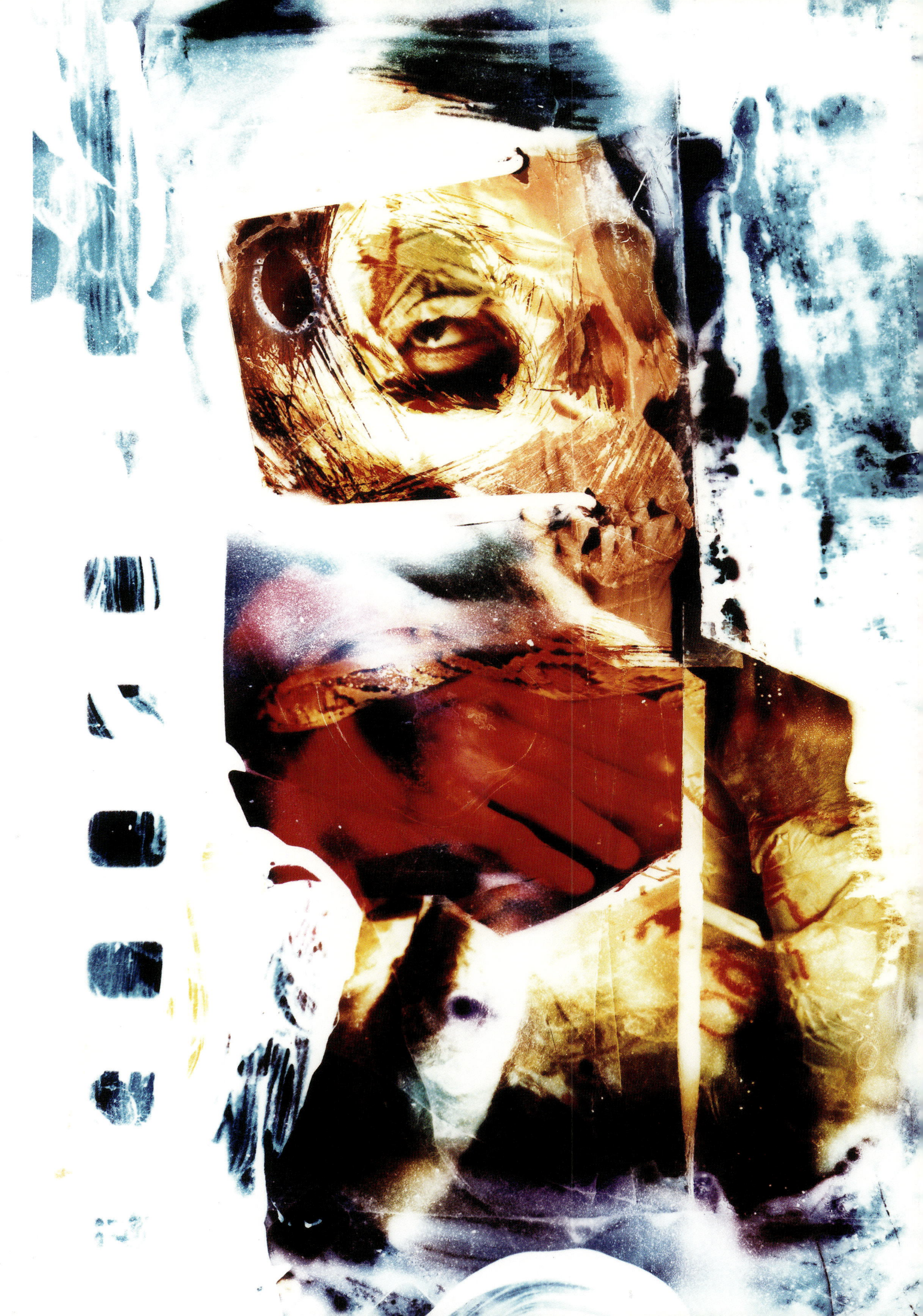

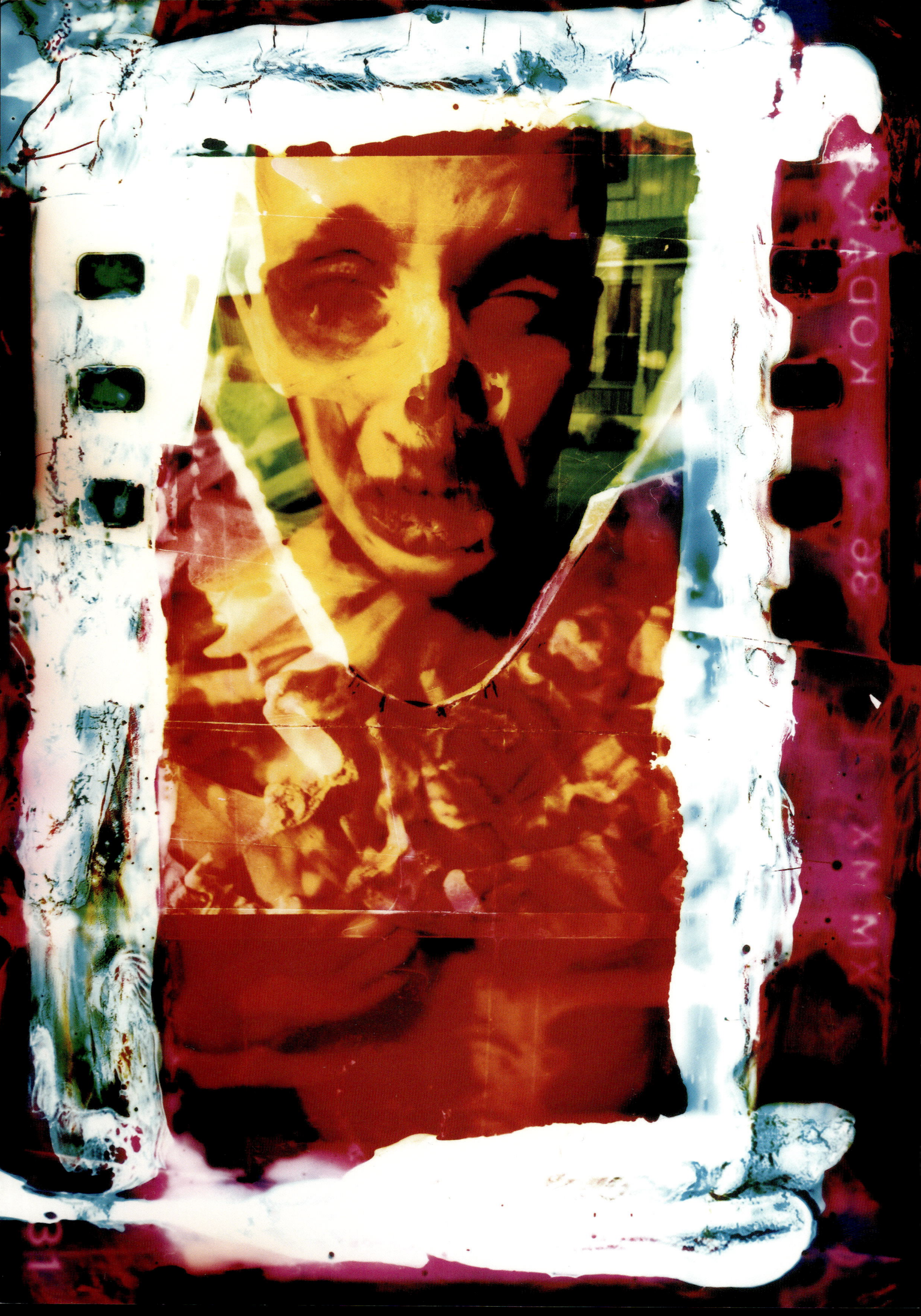

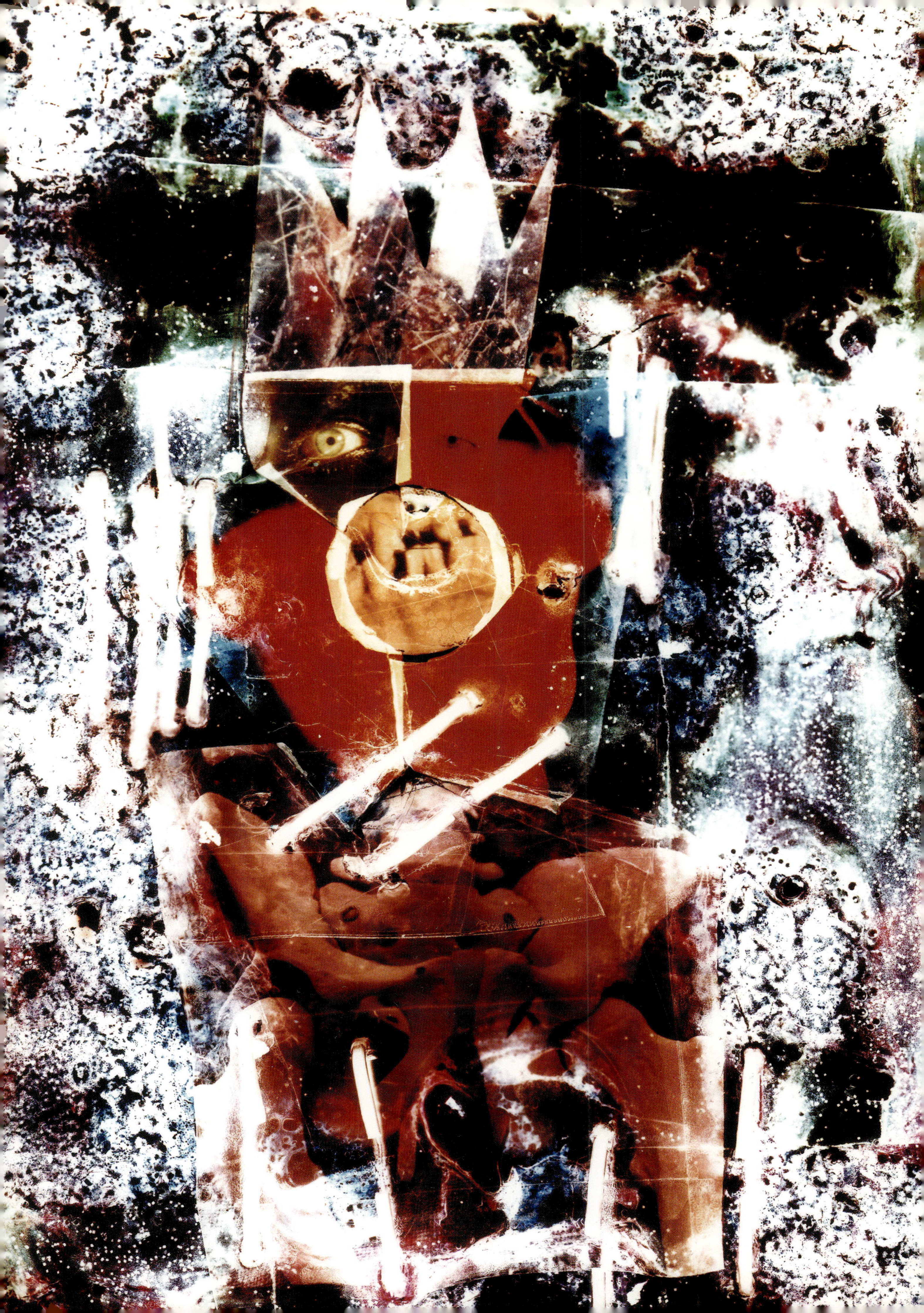

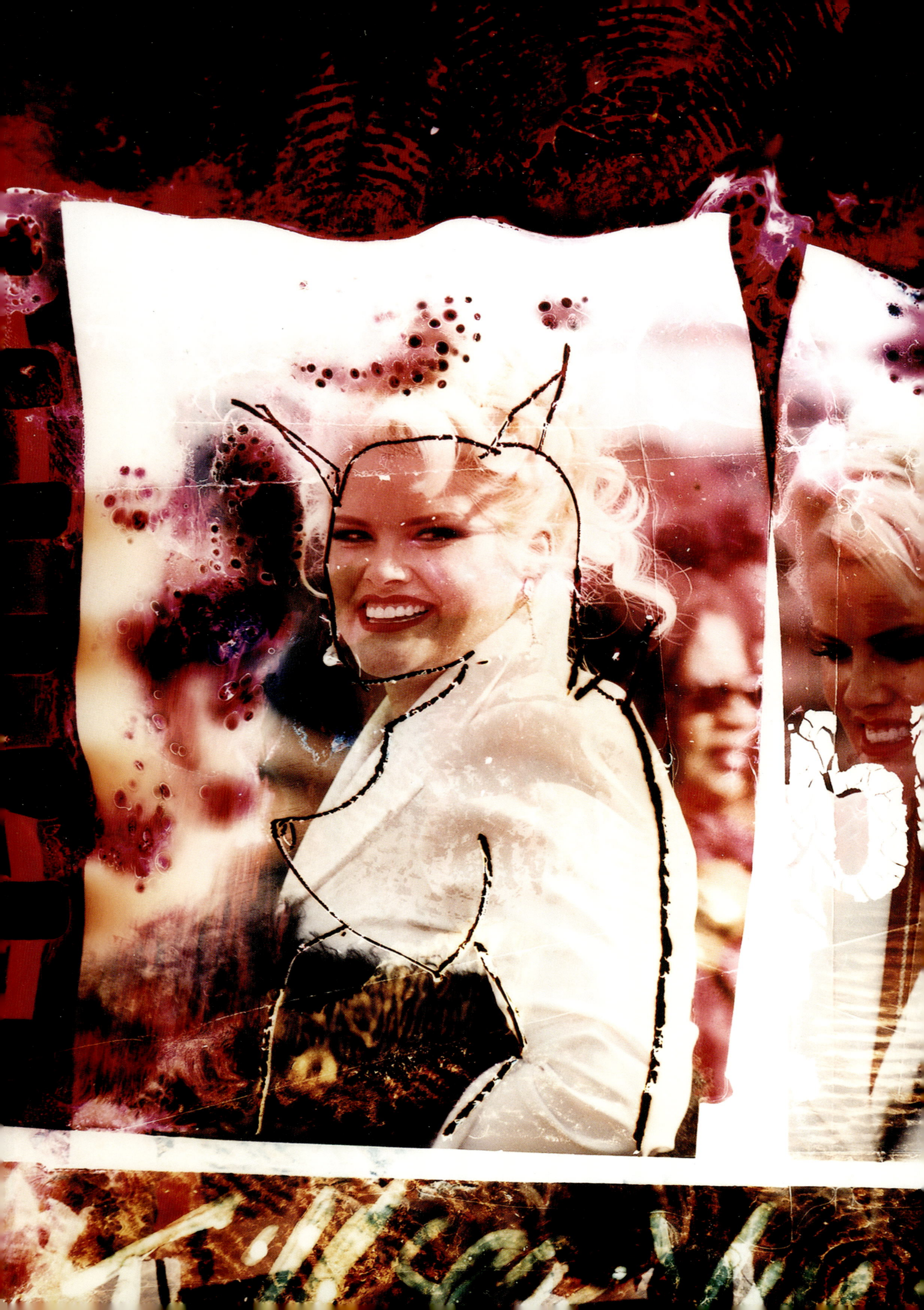

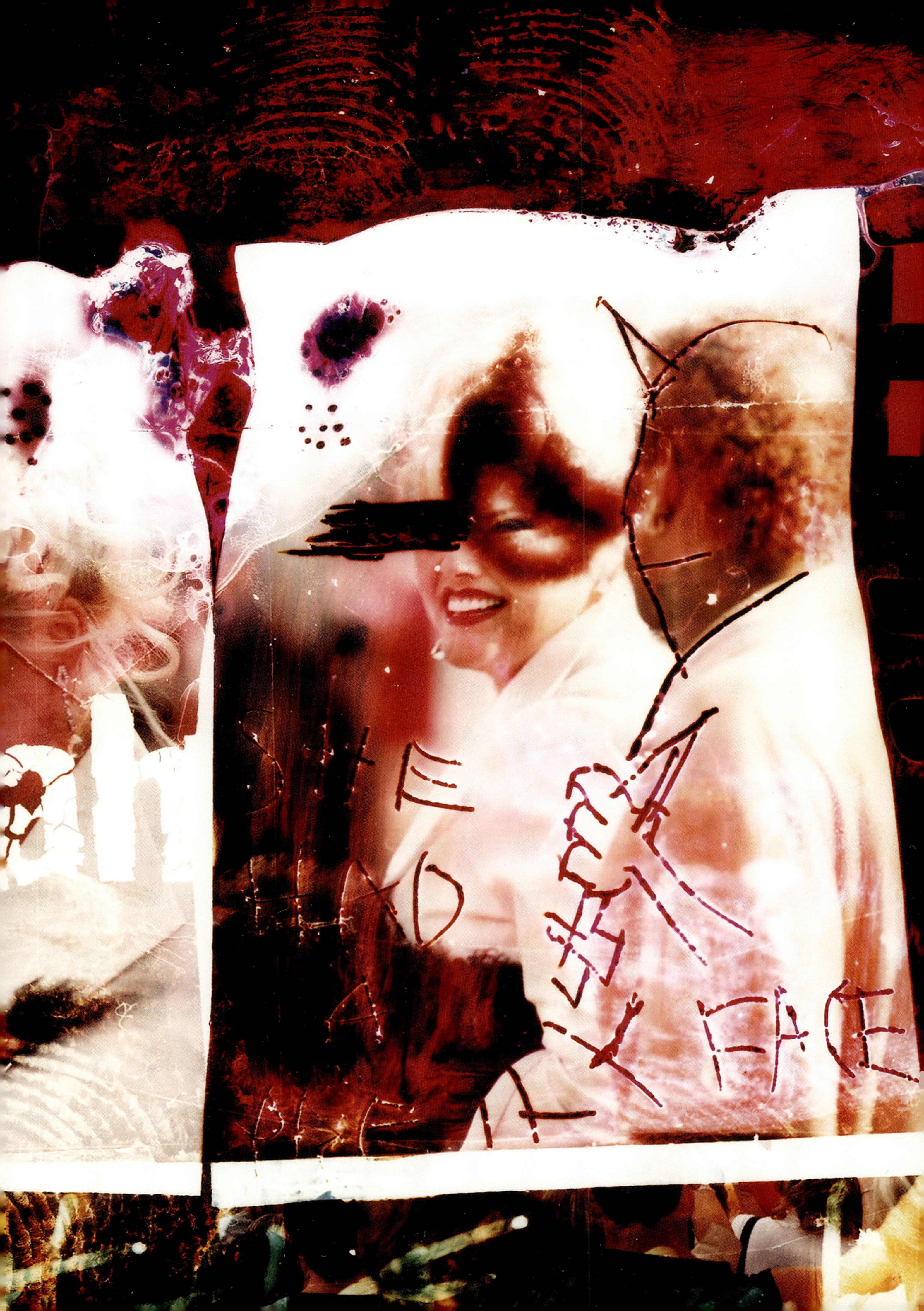
FACE

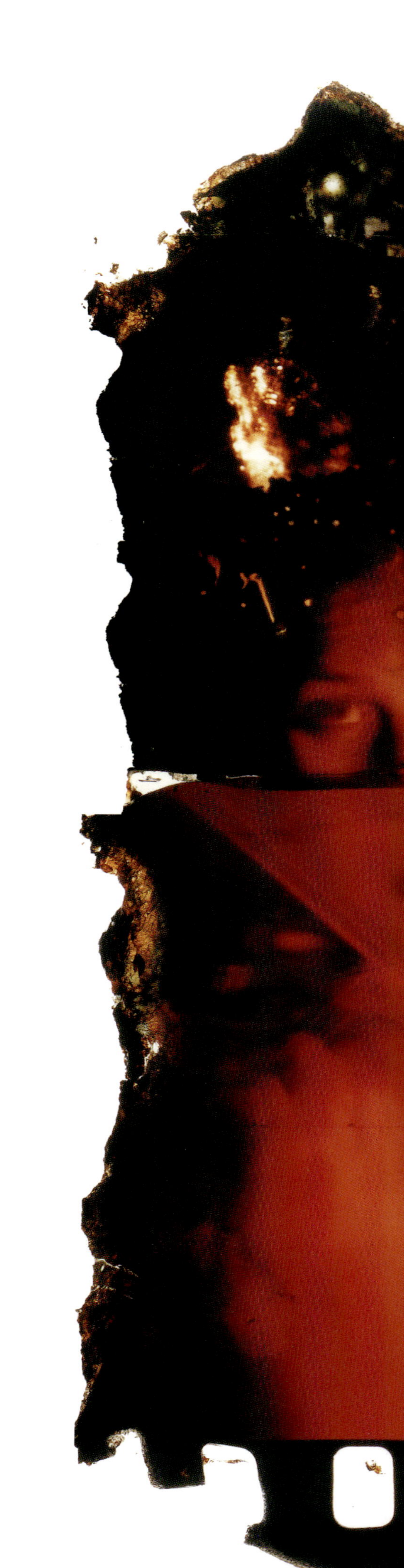

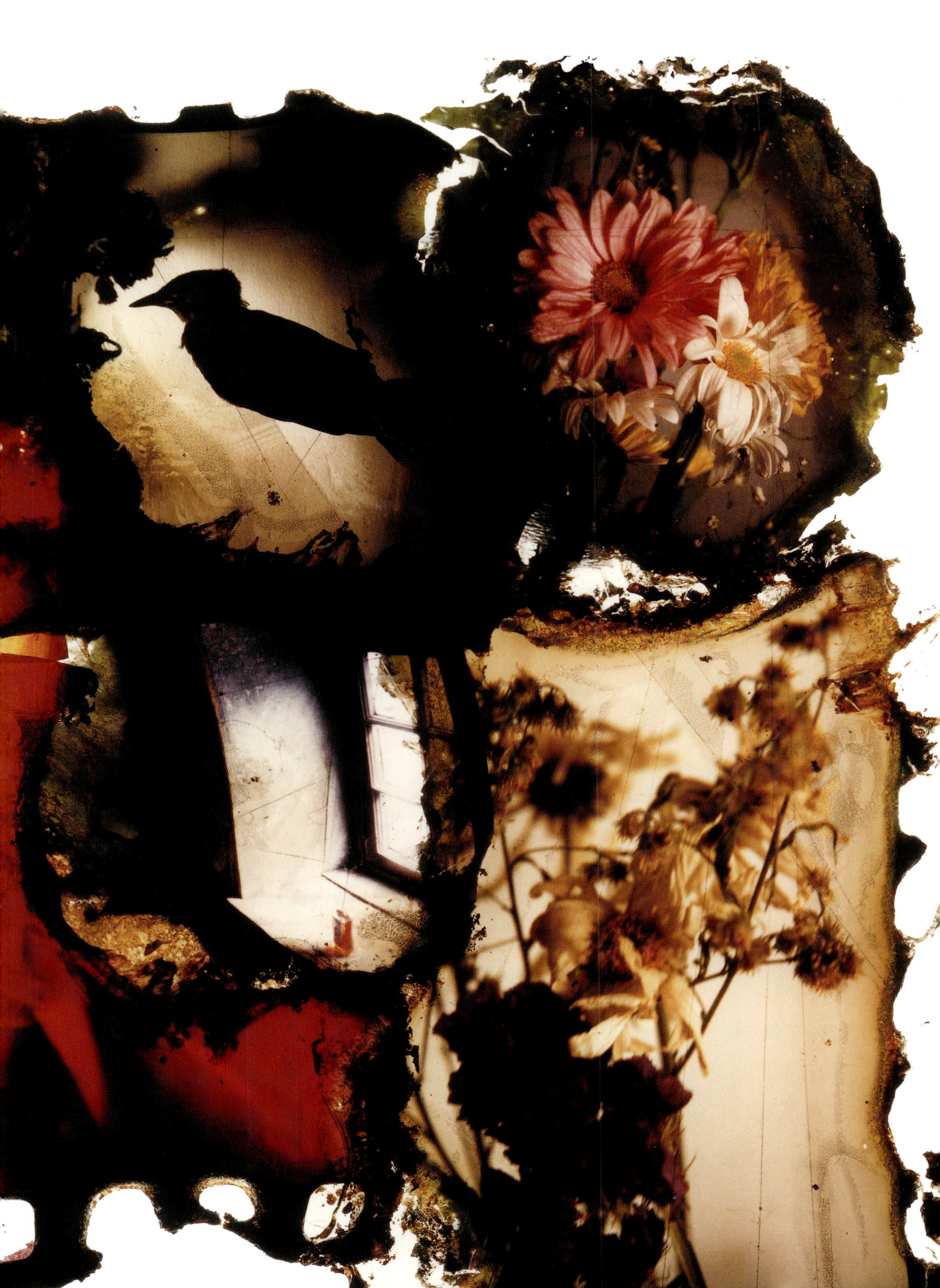

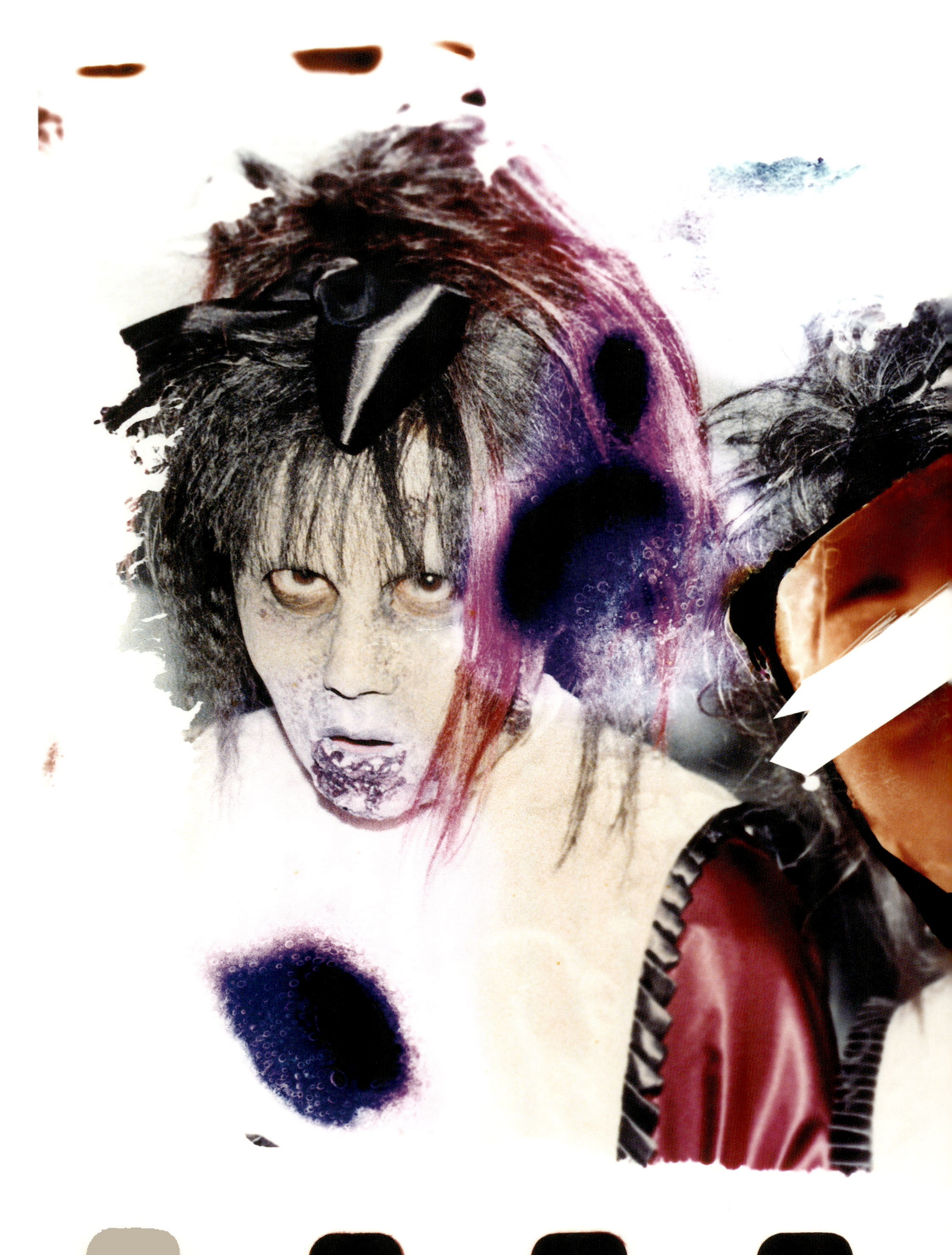

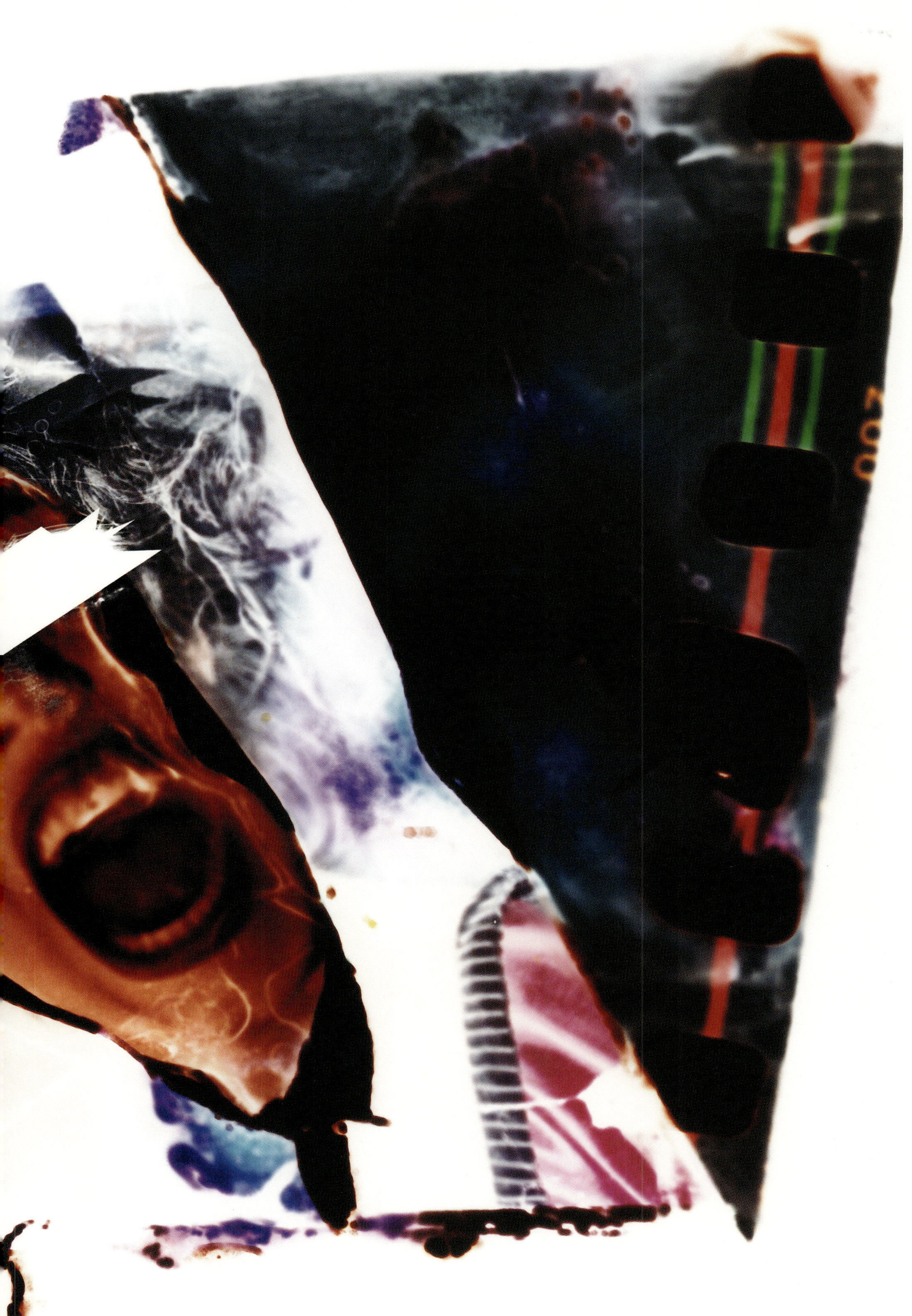

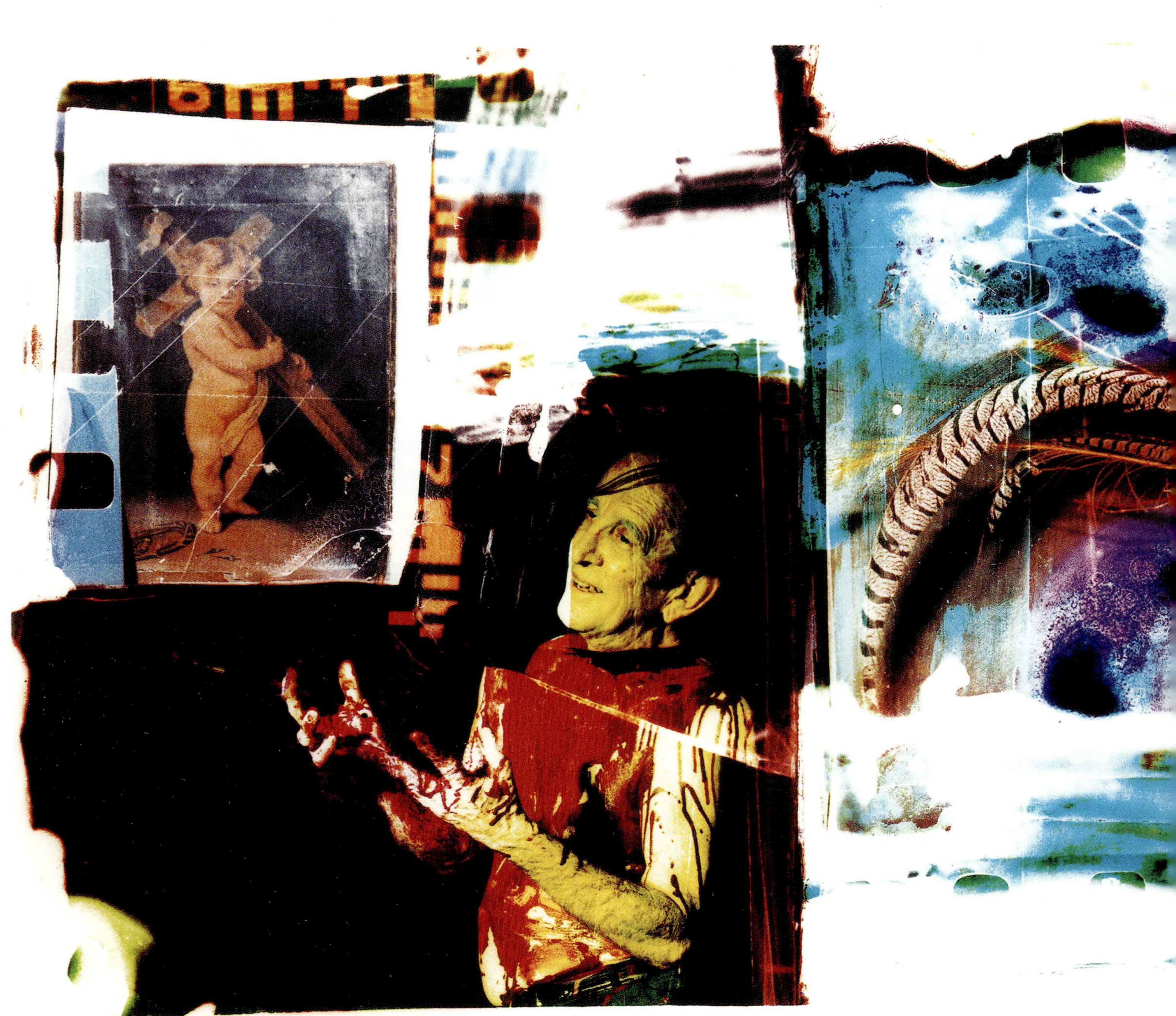

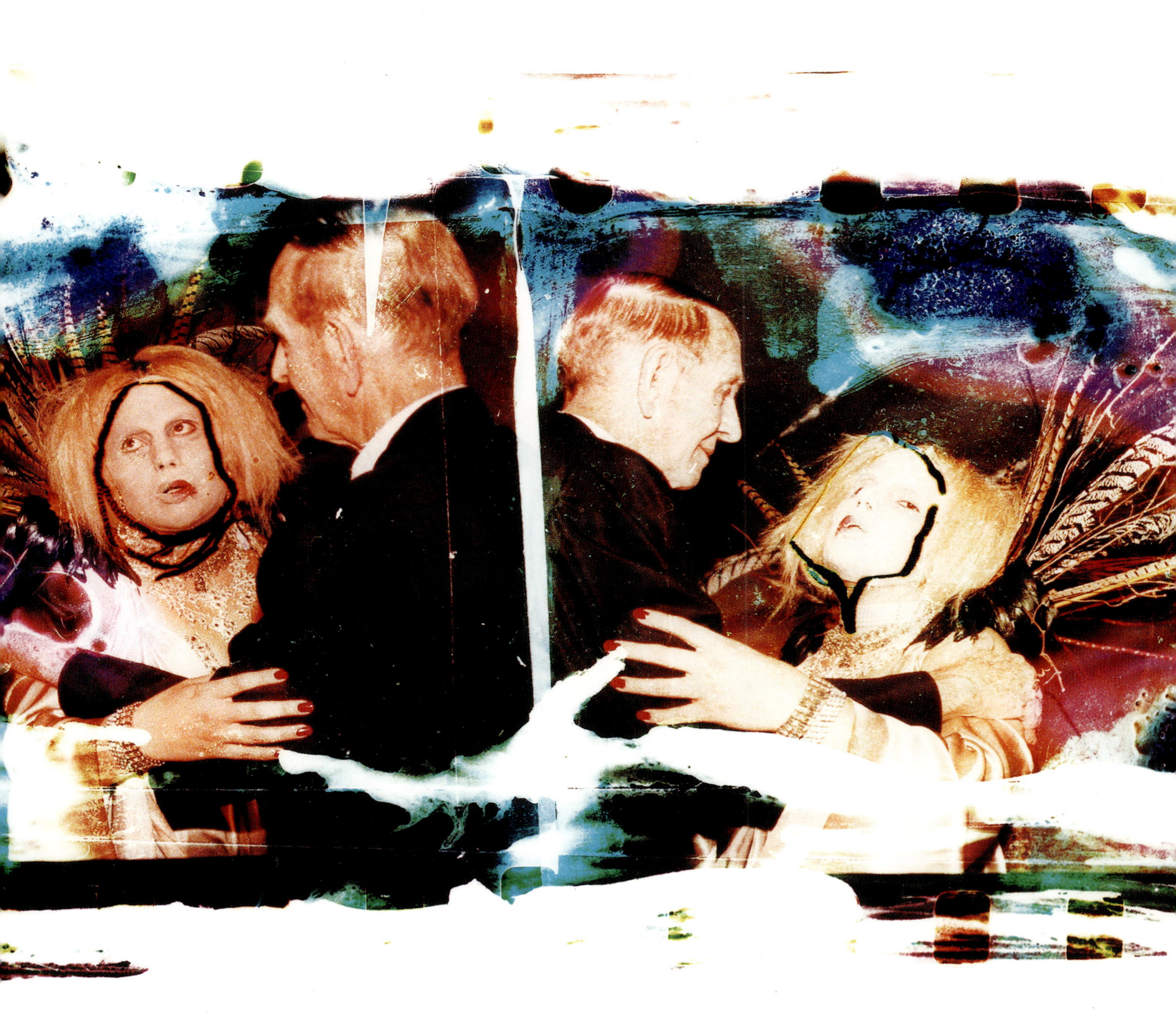

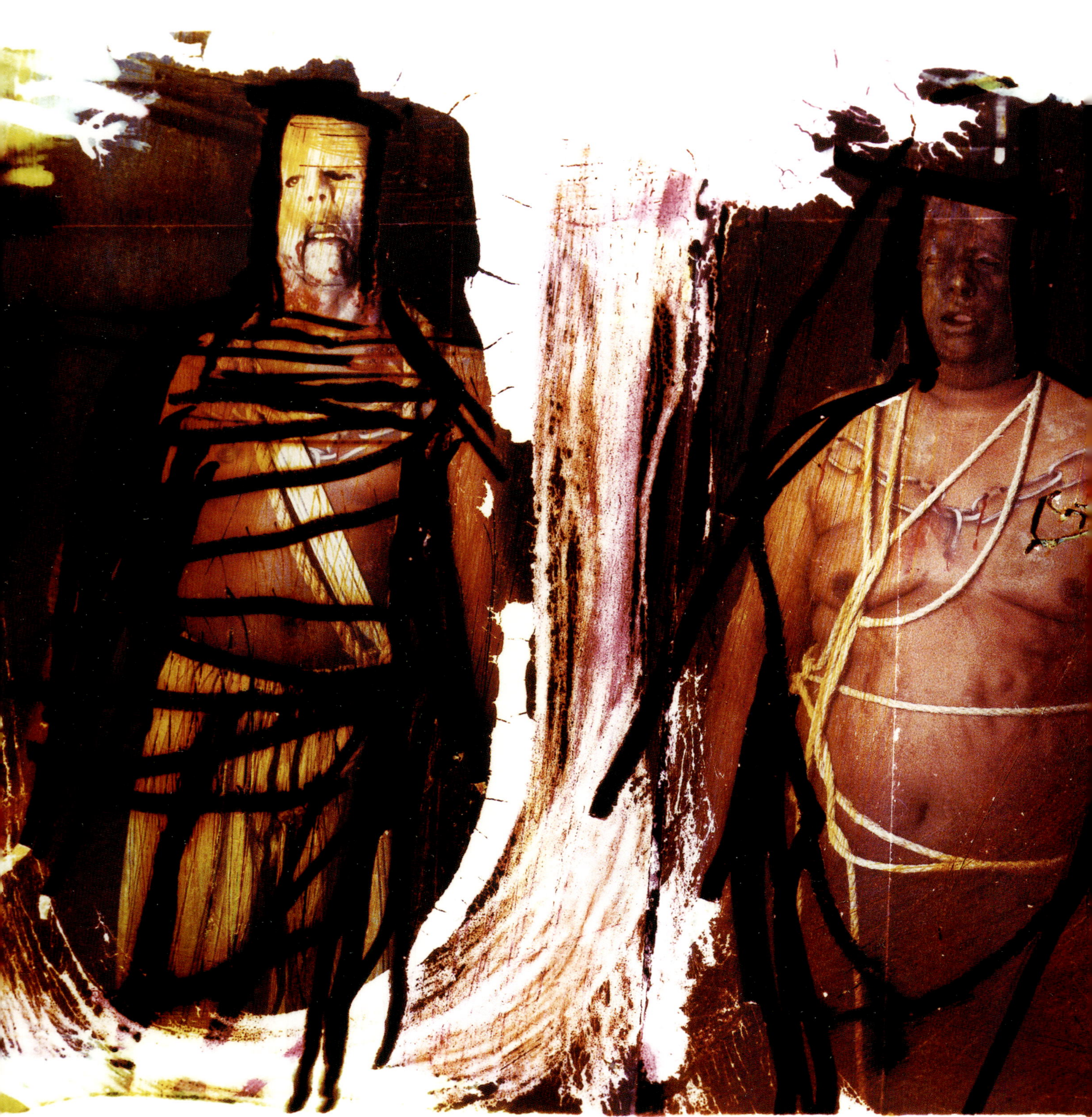

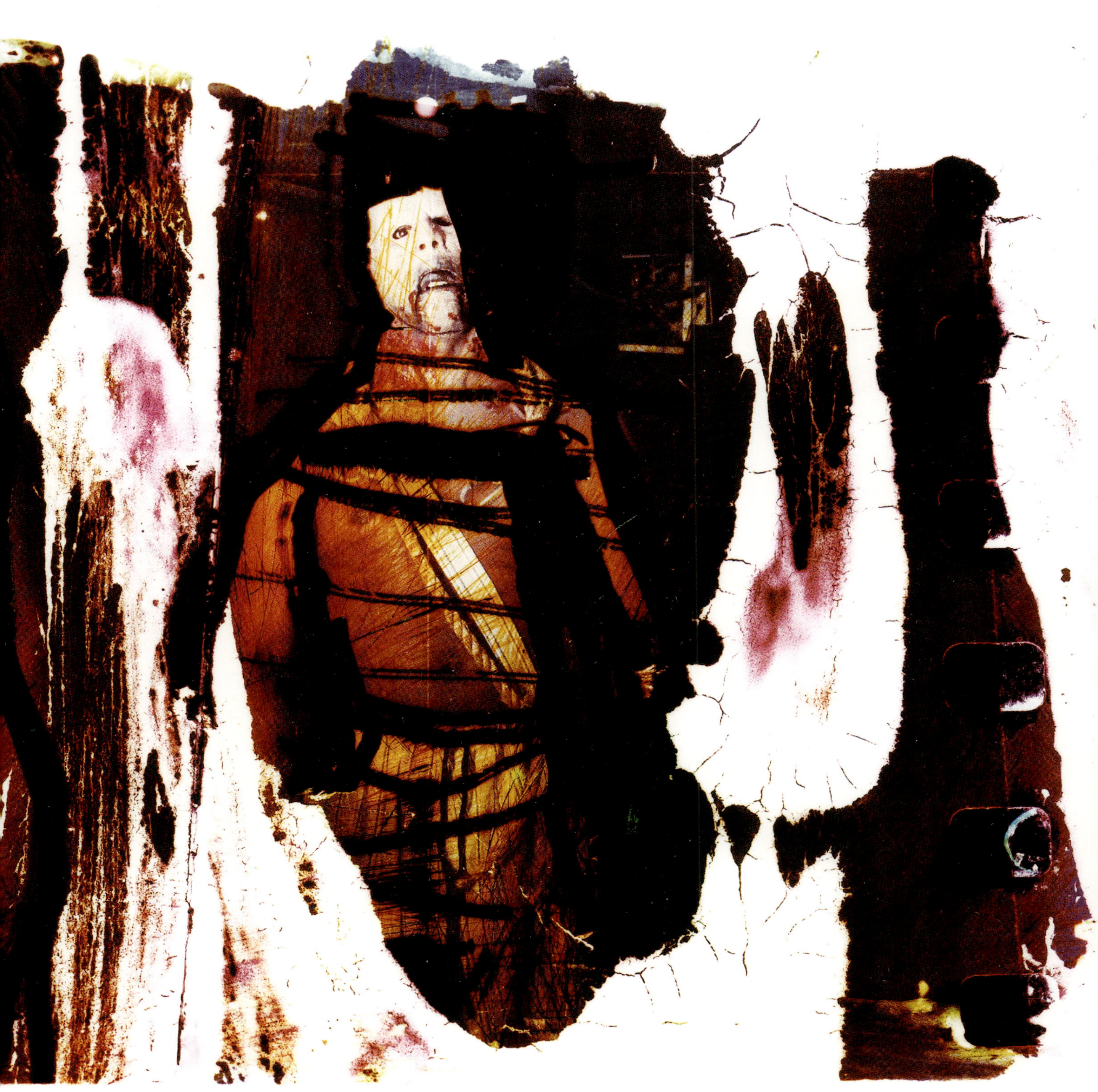

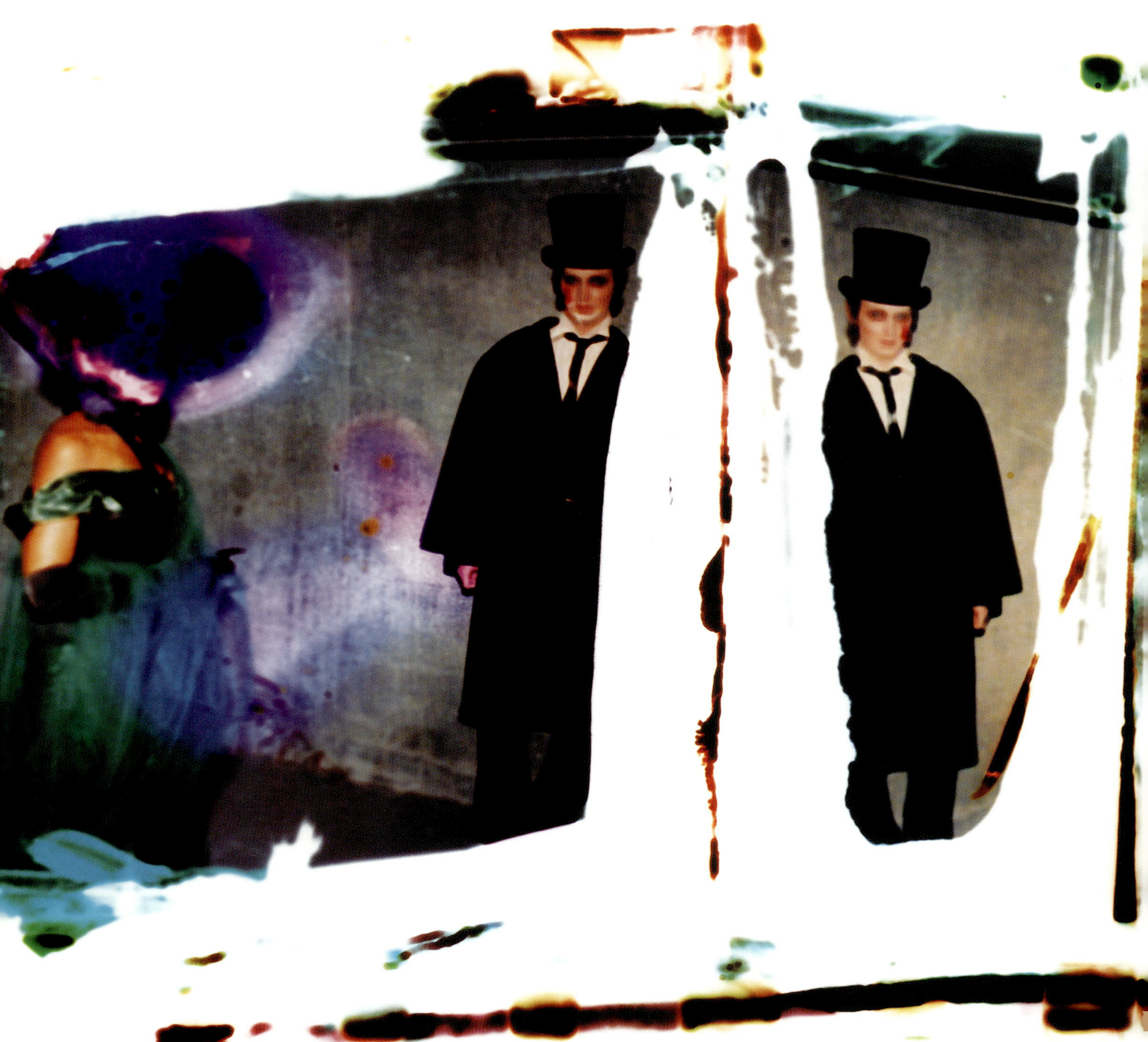

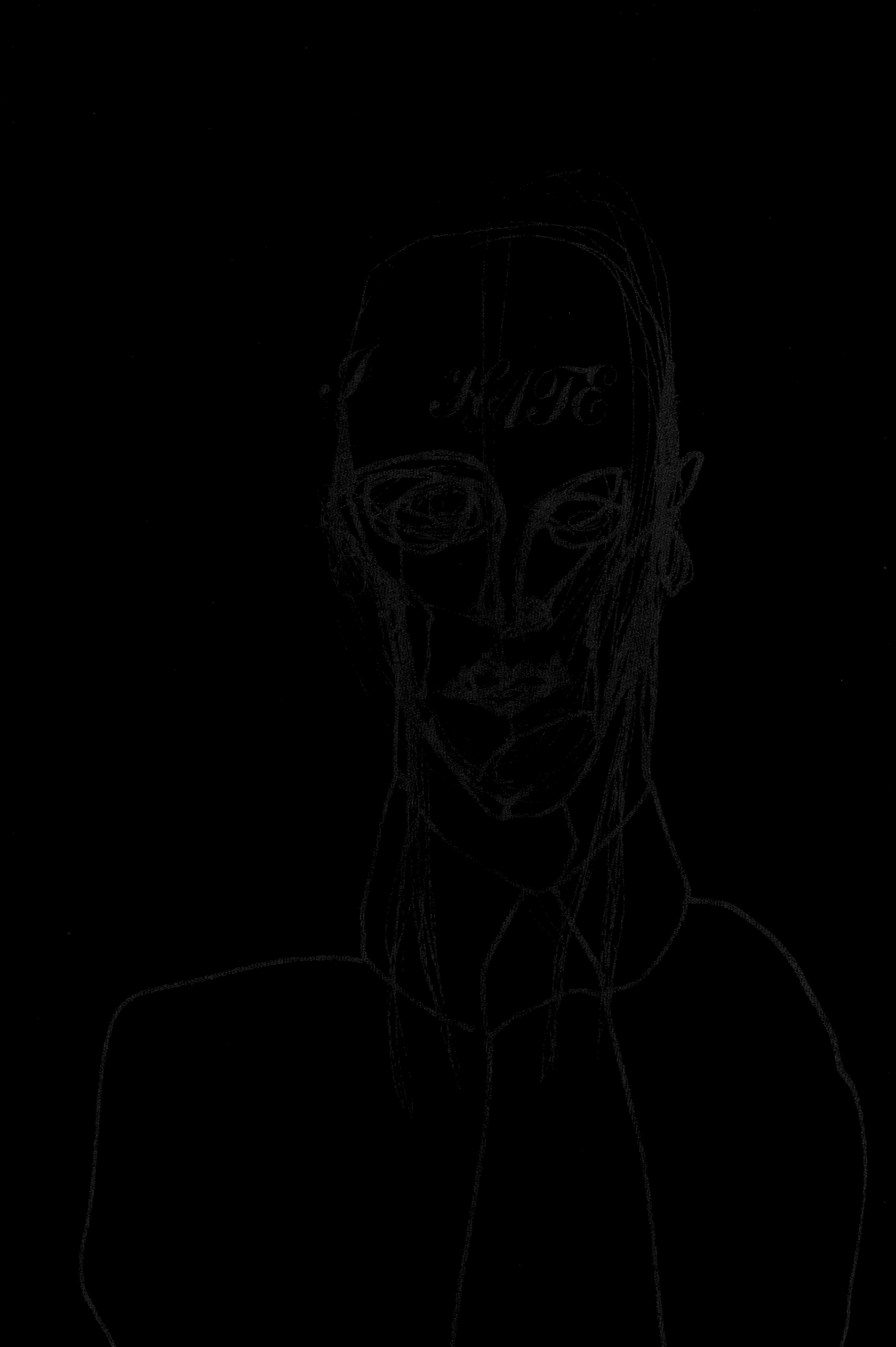

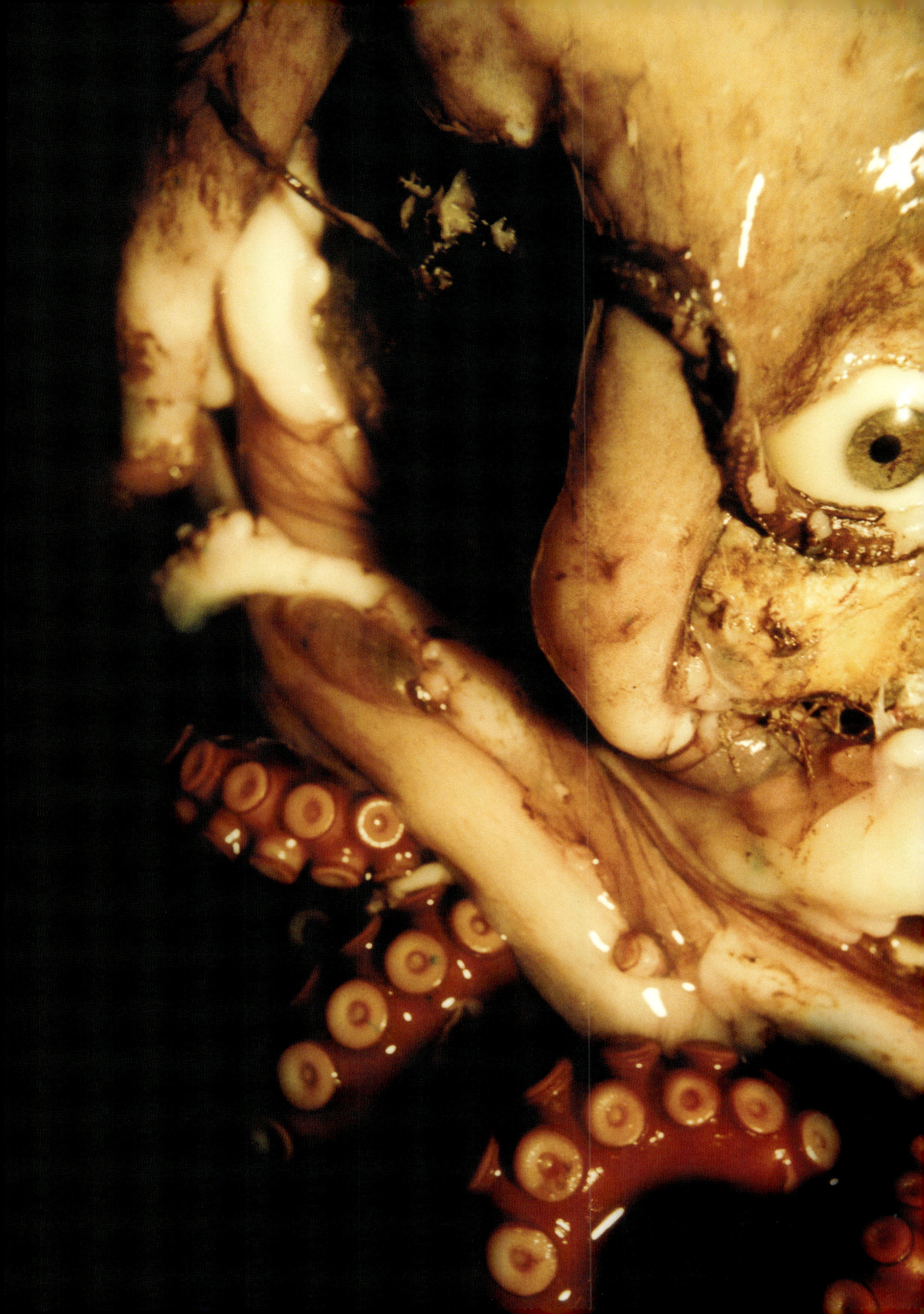

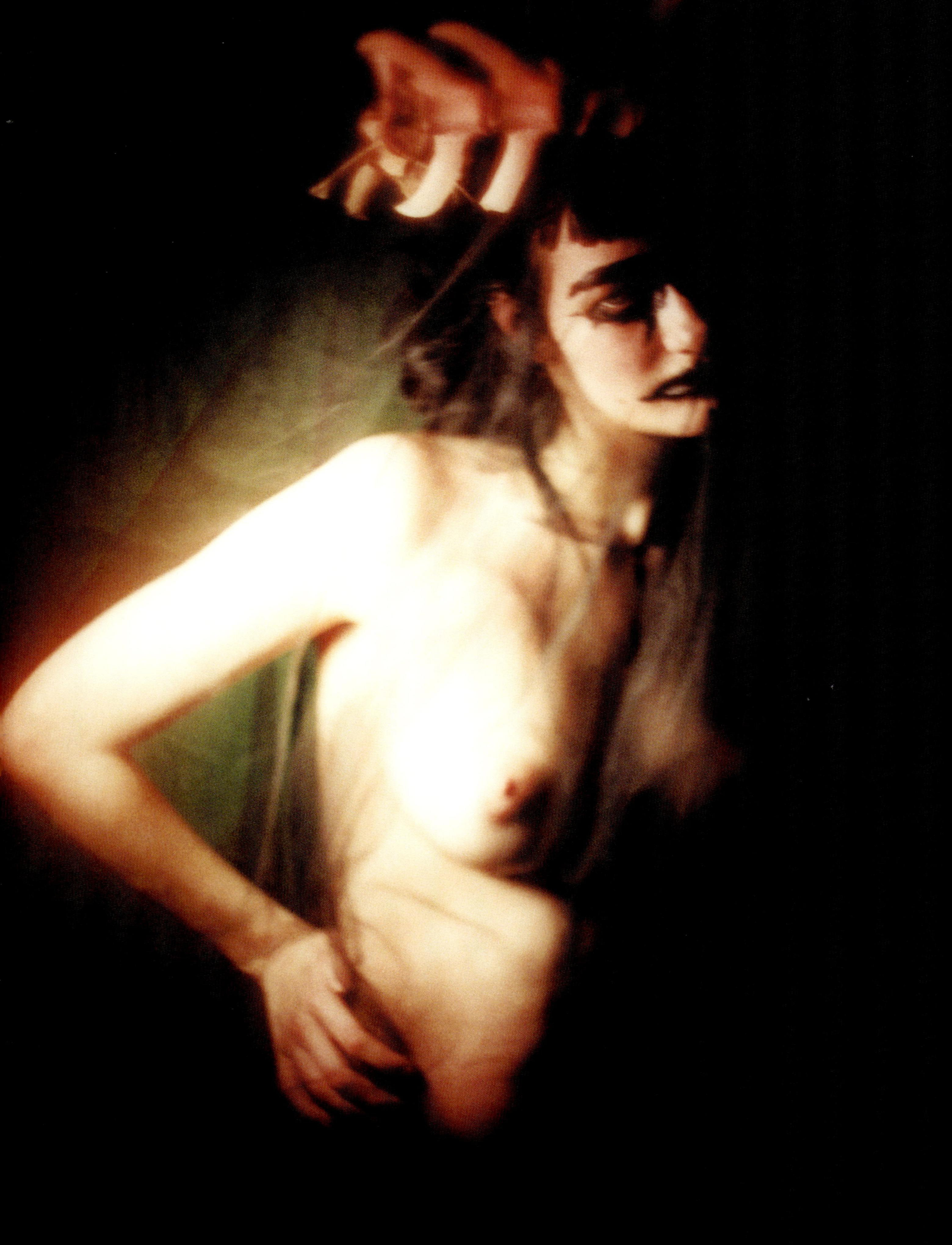

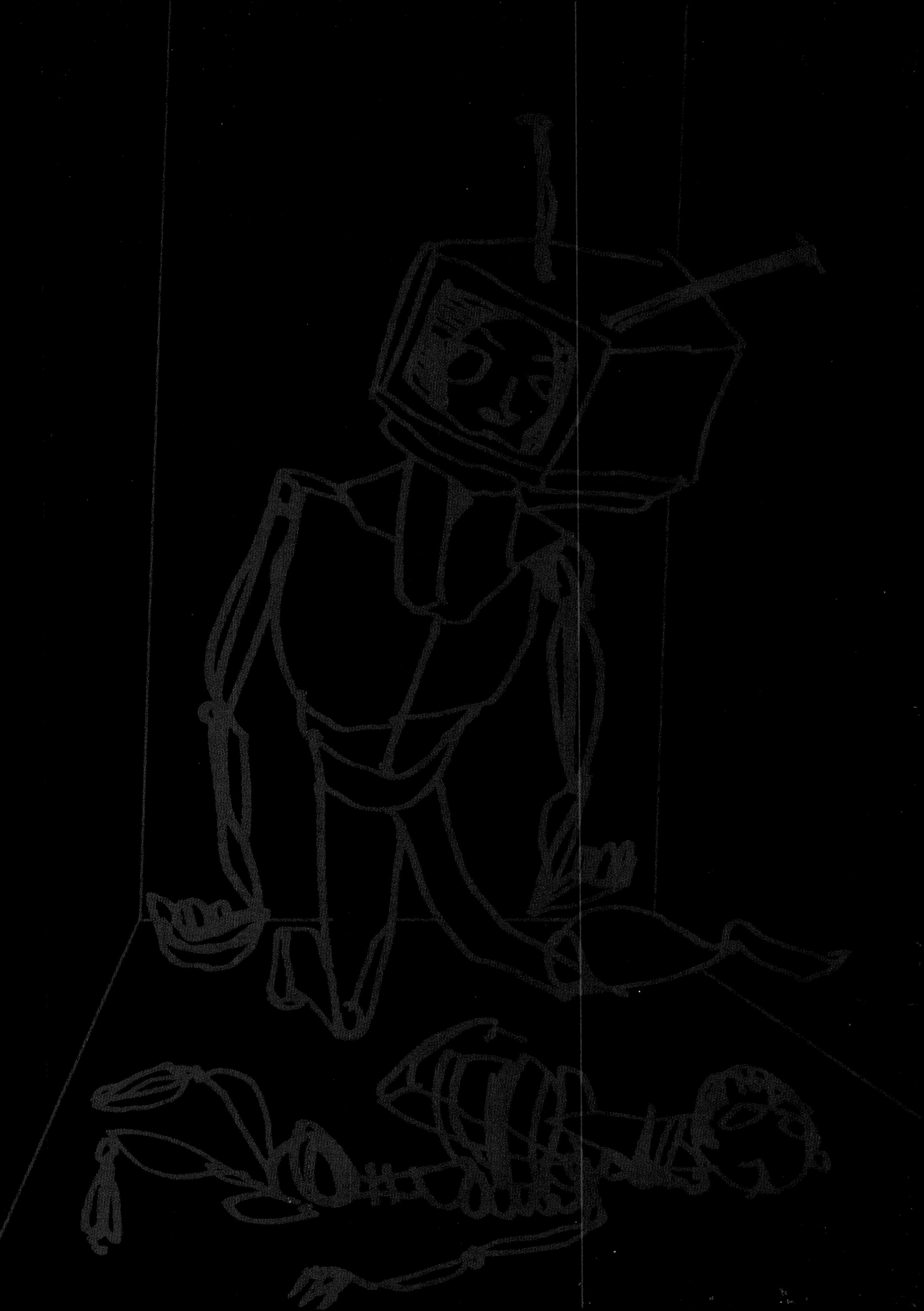

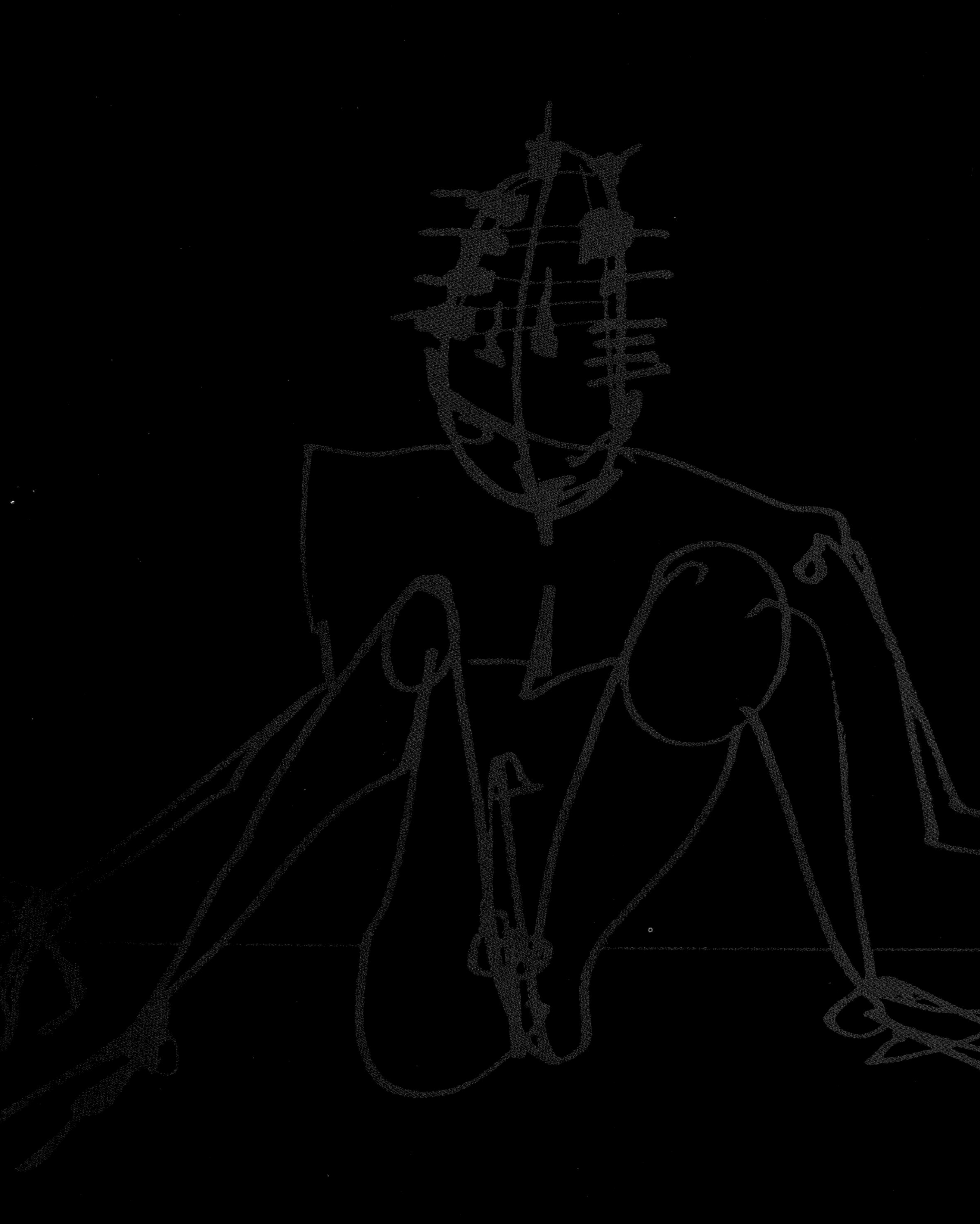

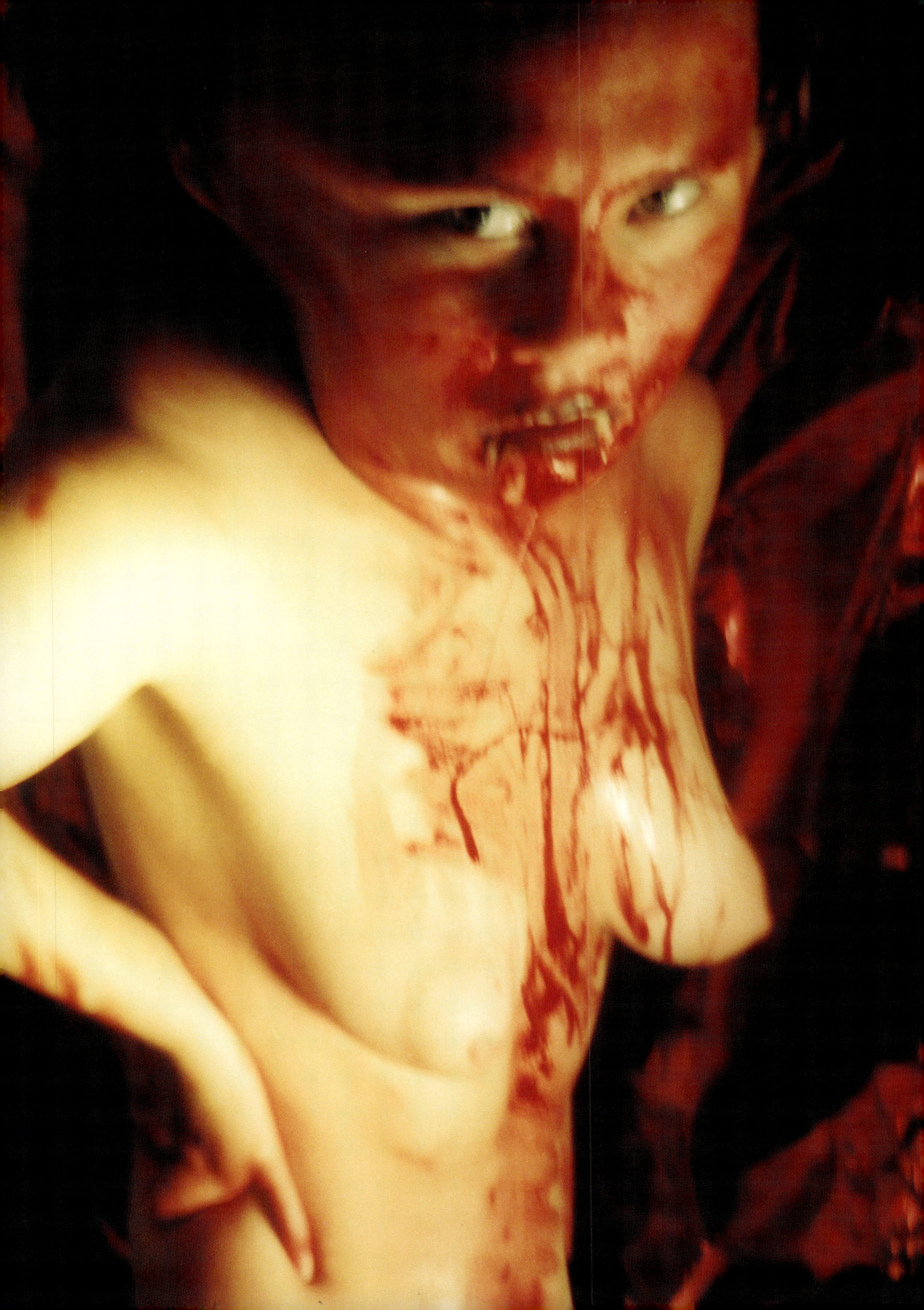

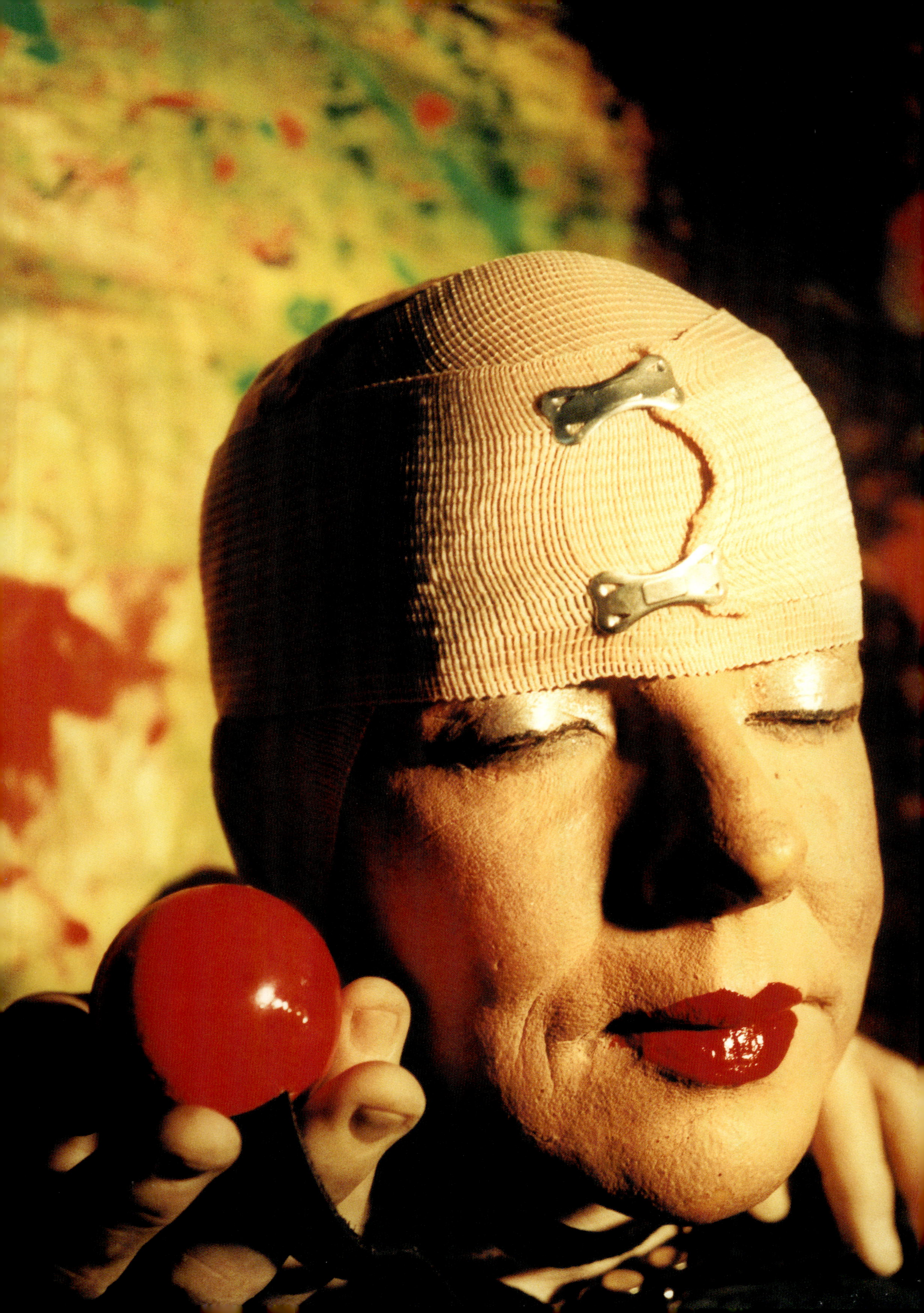

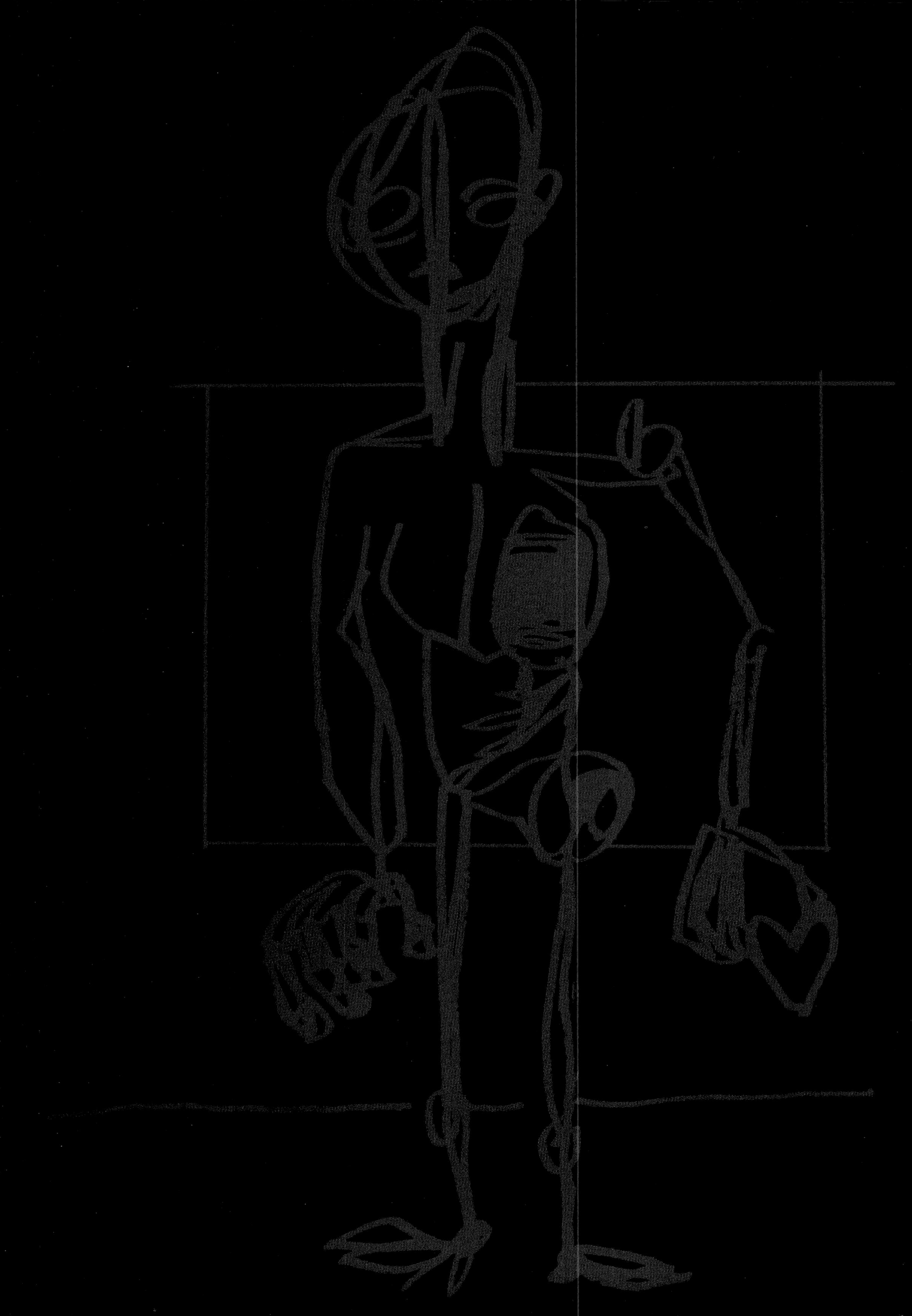

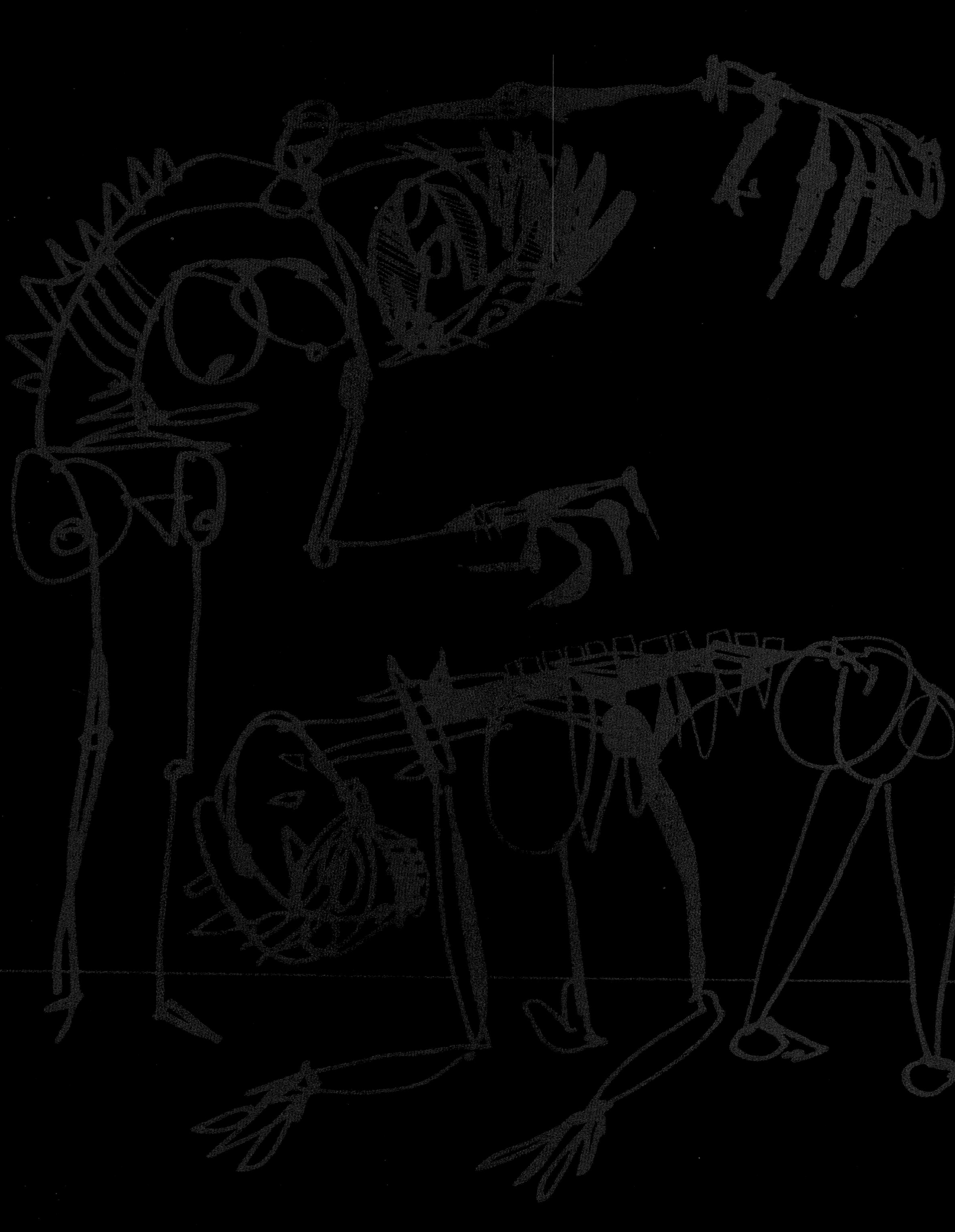

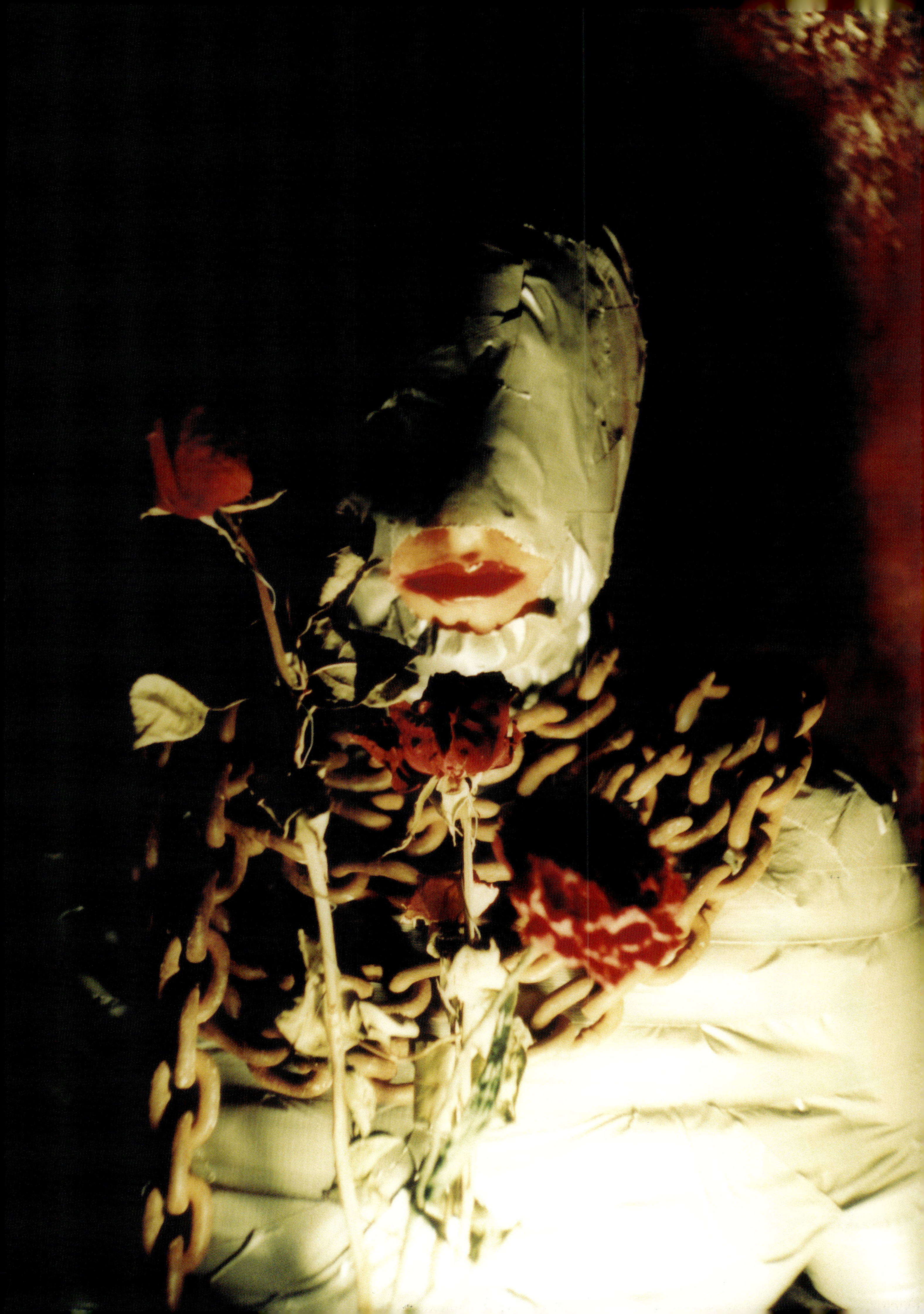

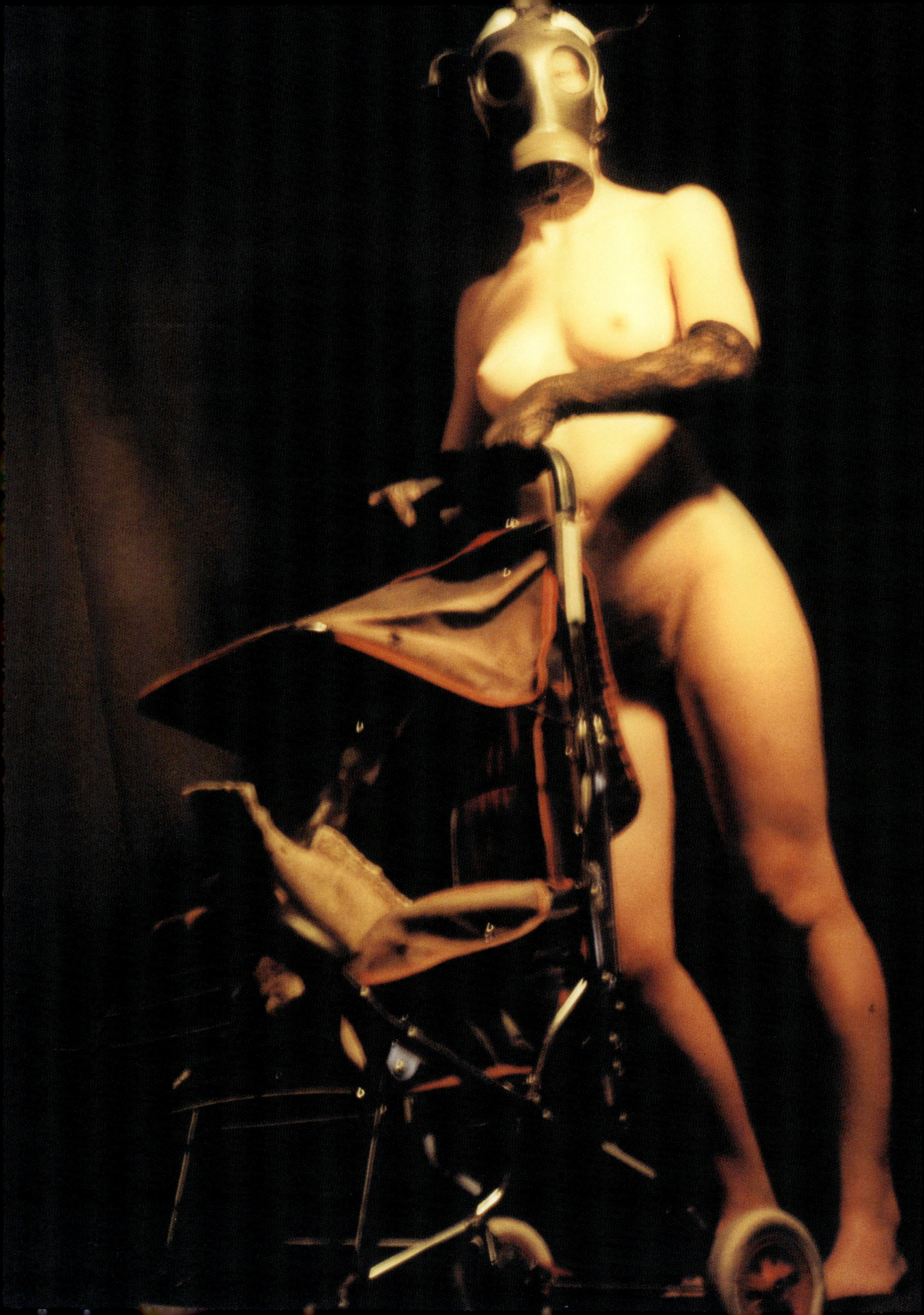

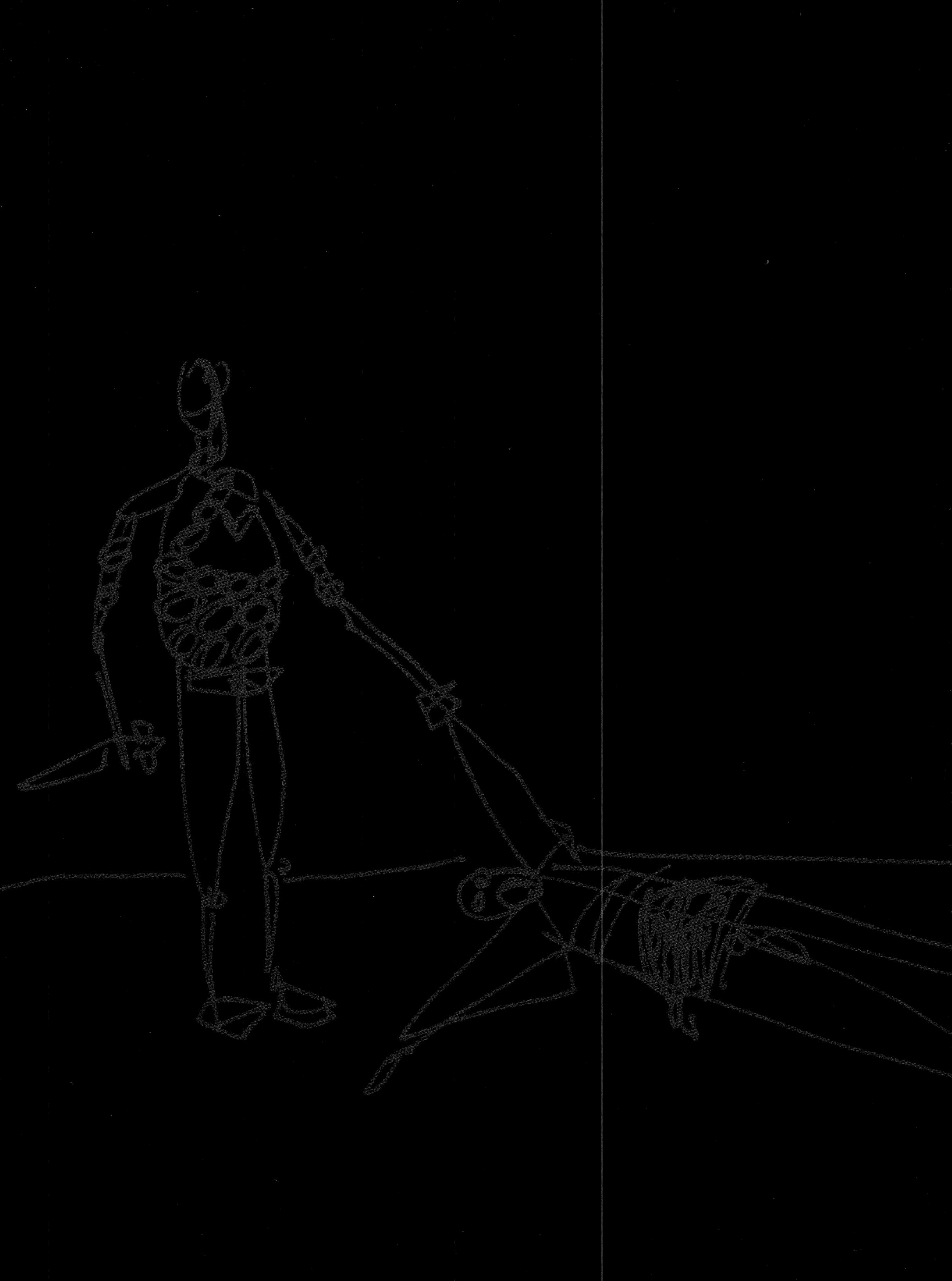

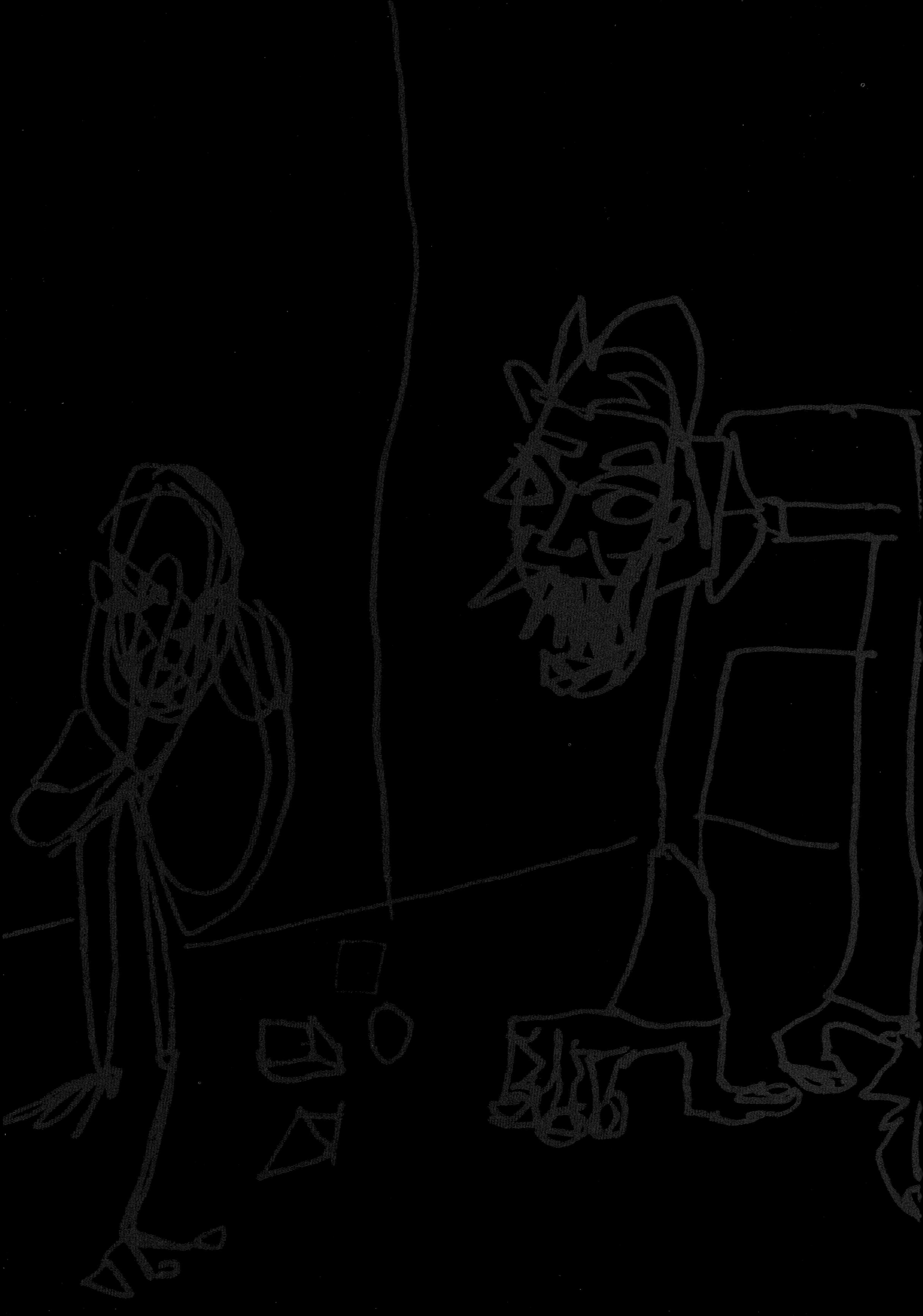

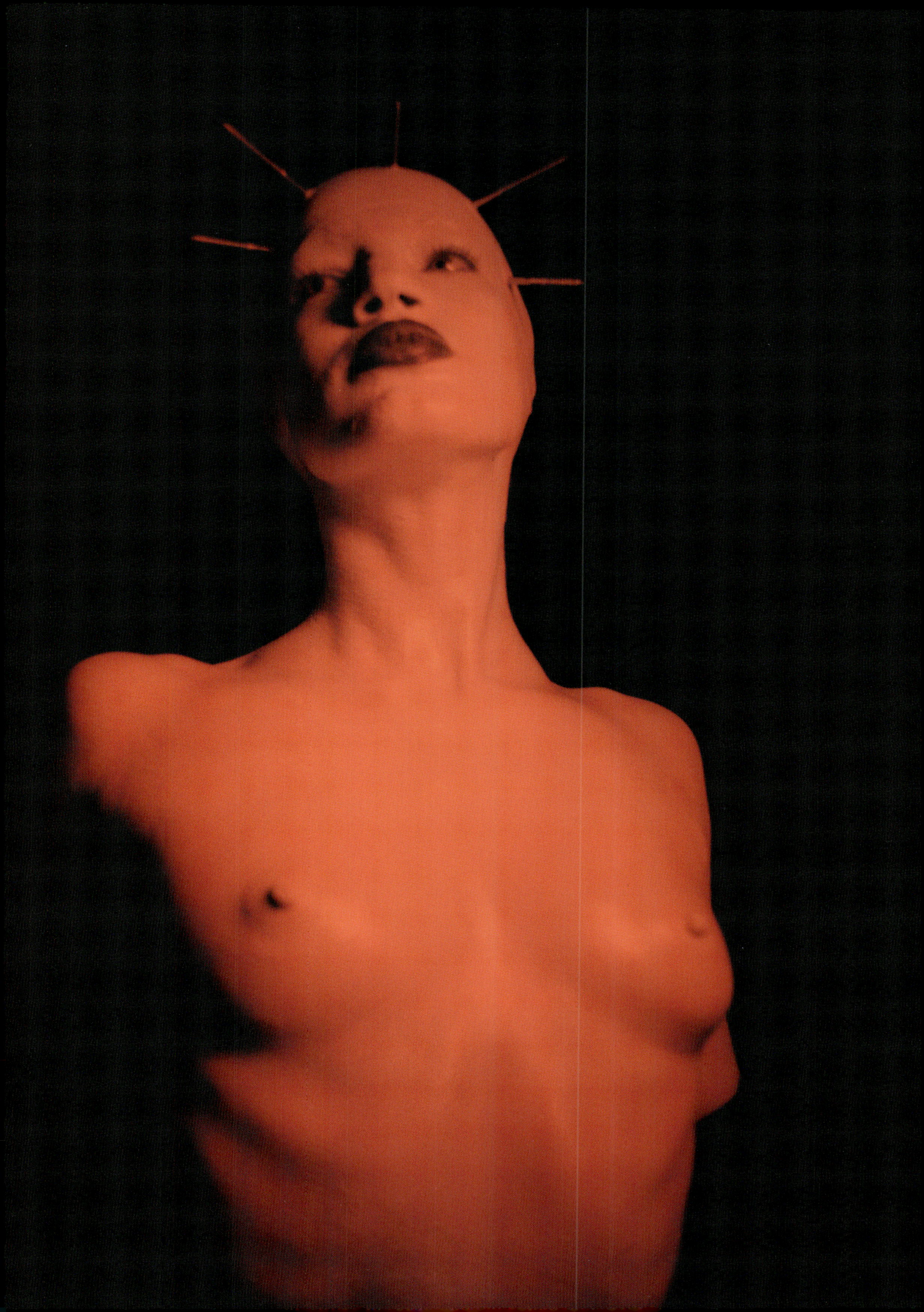

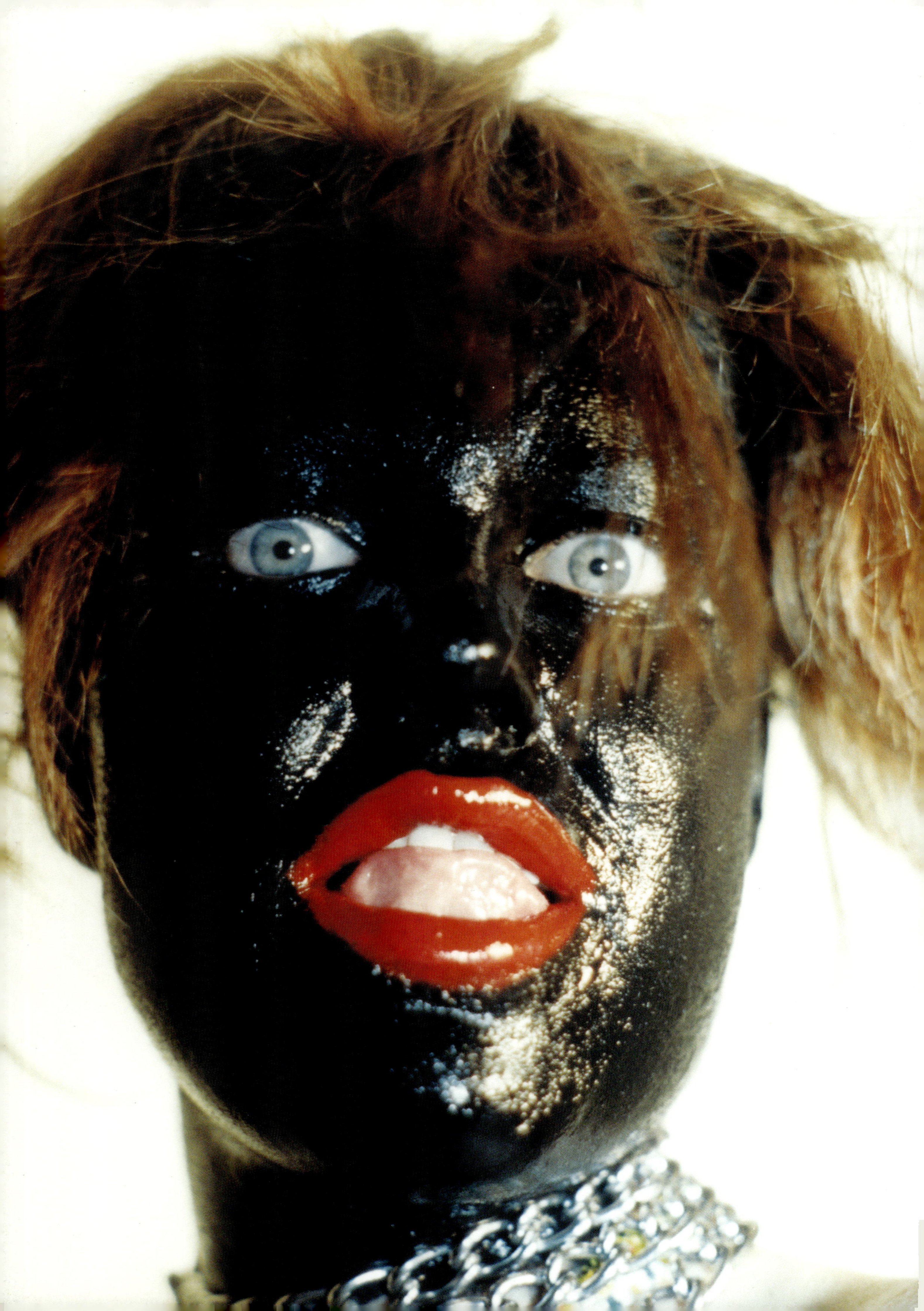

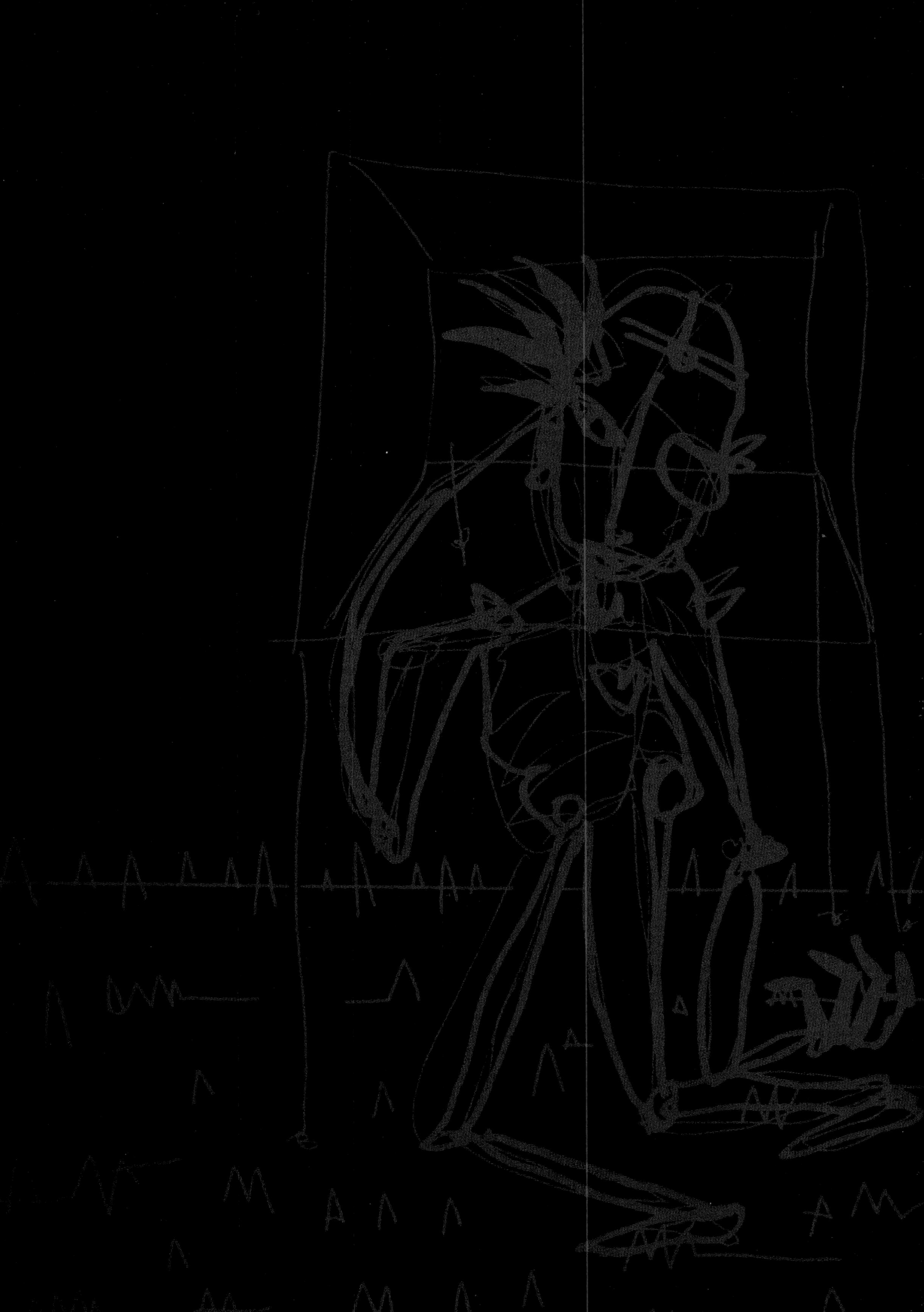

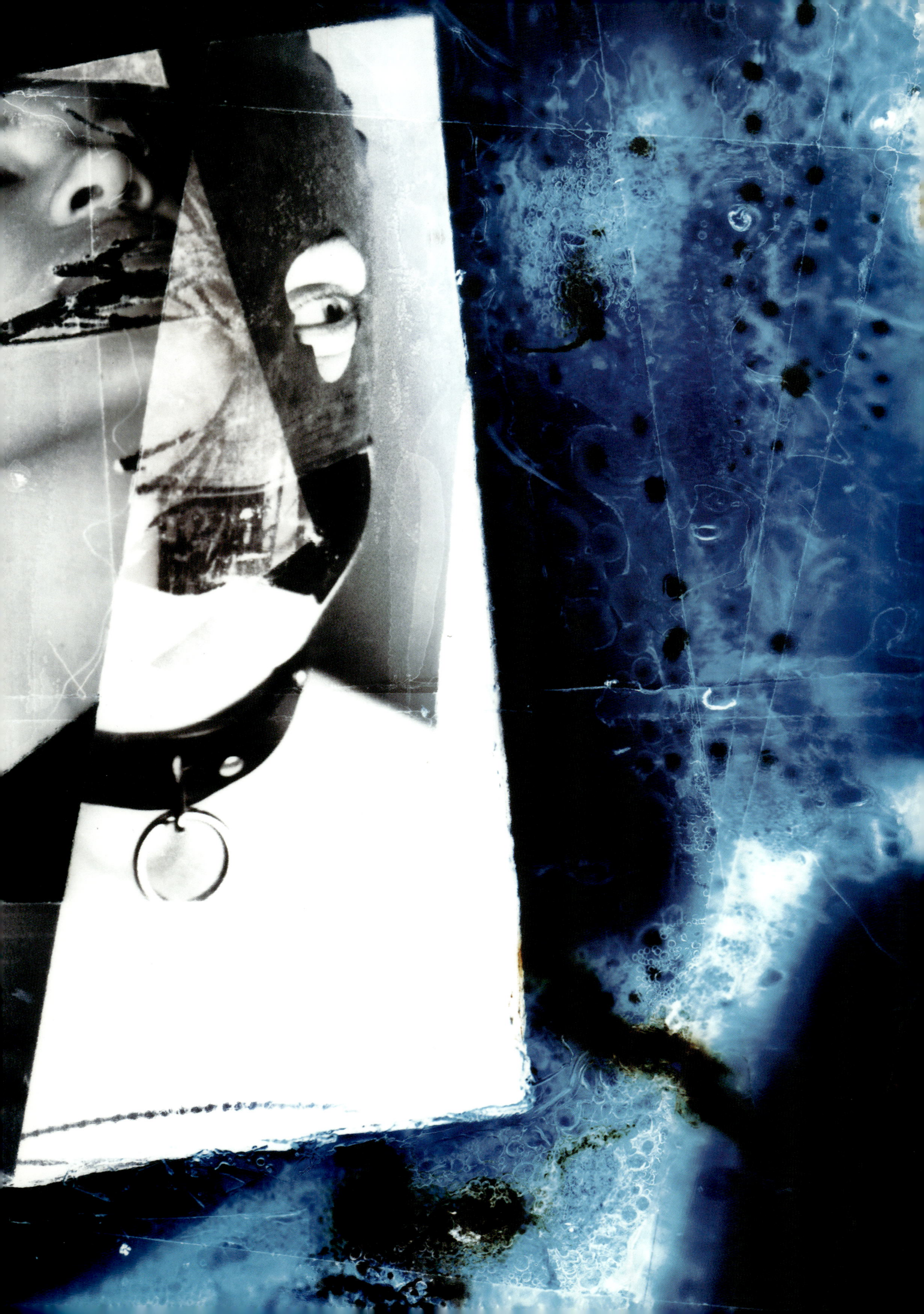

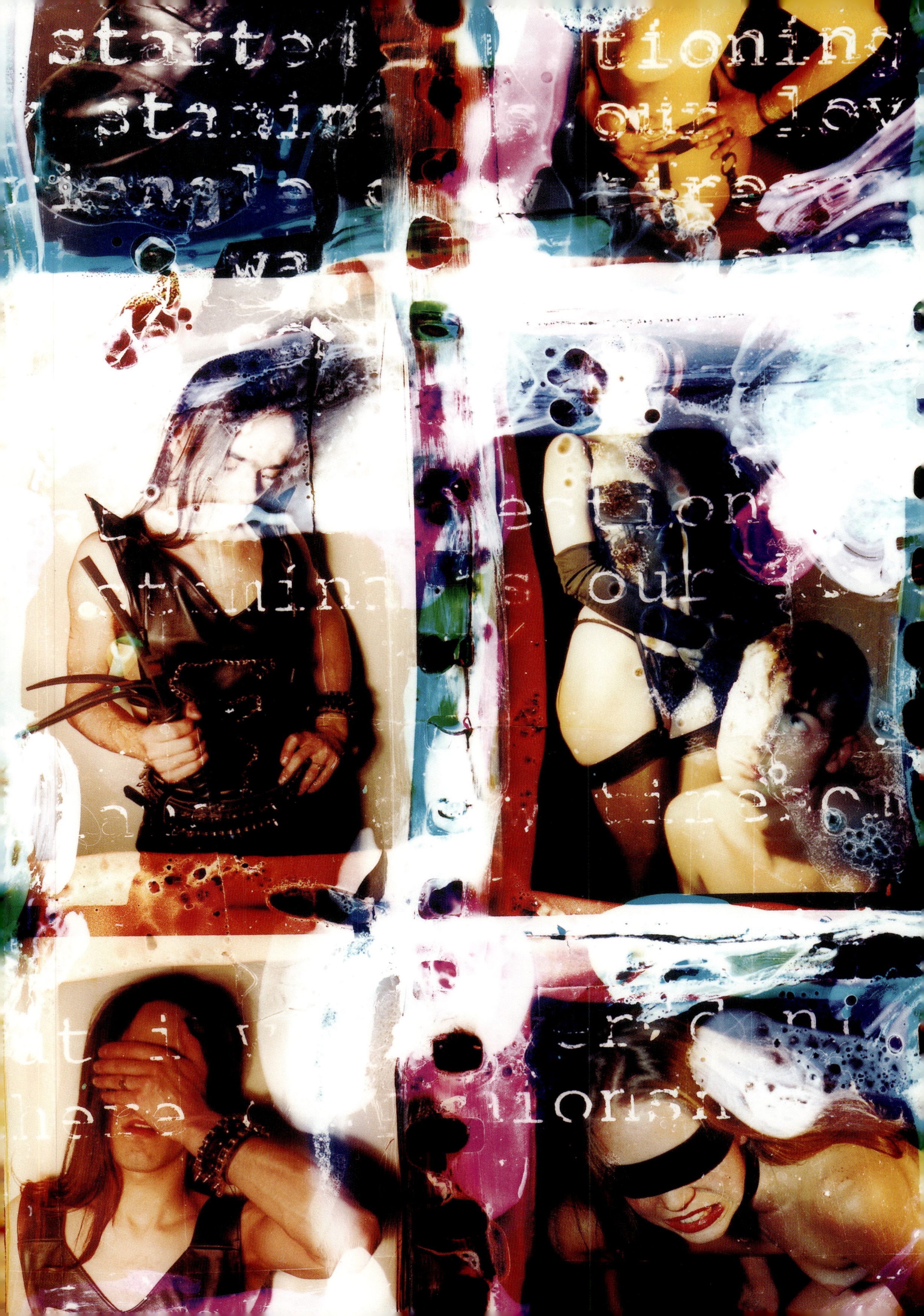
started
tioning

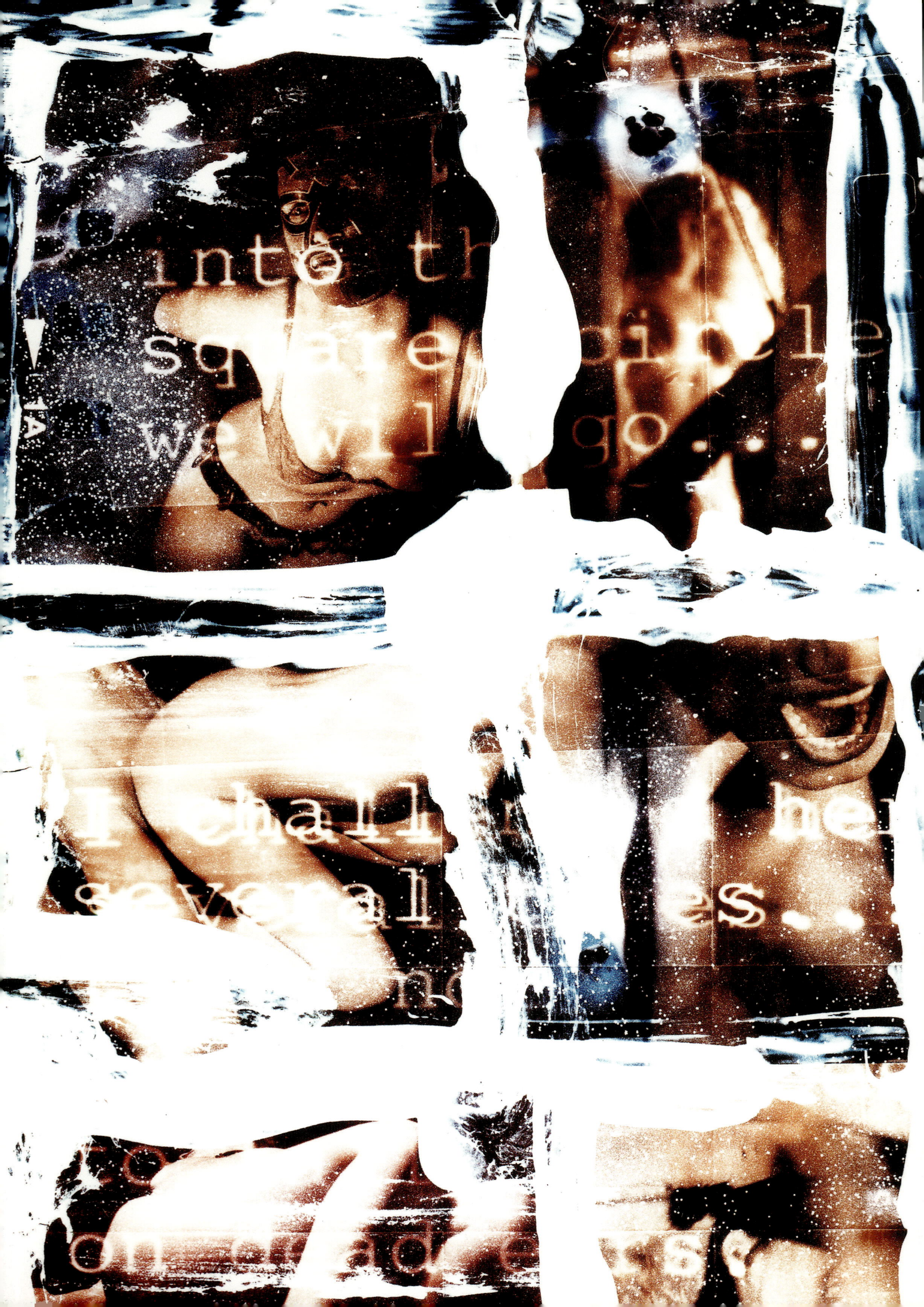
into th
square
we wil
go...
I shall
he
several
es...
on dead

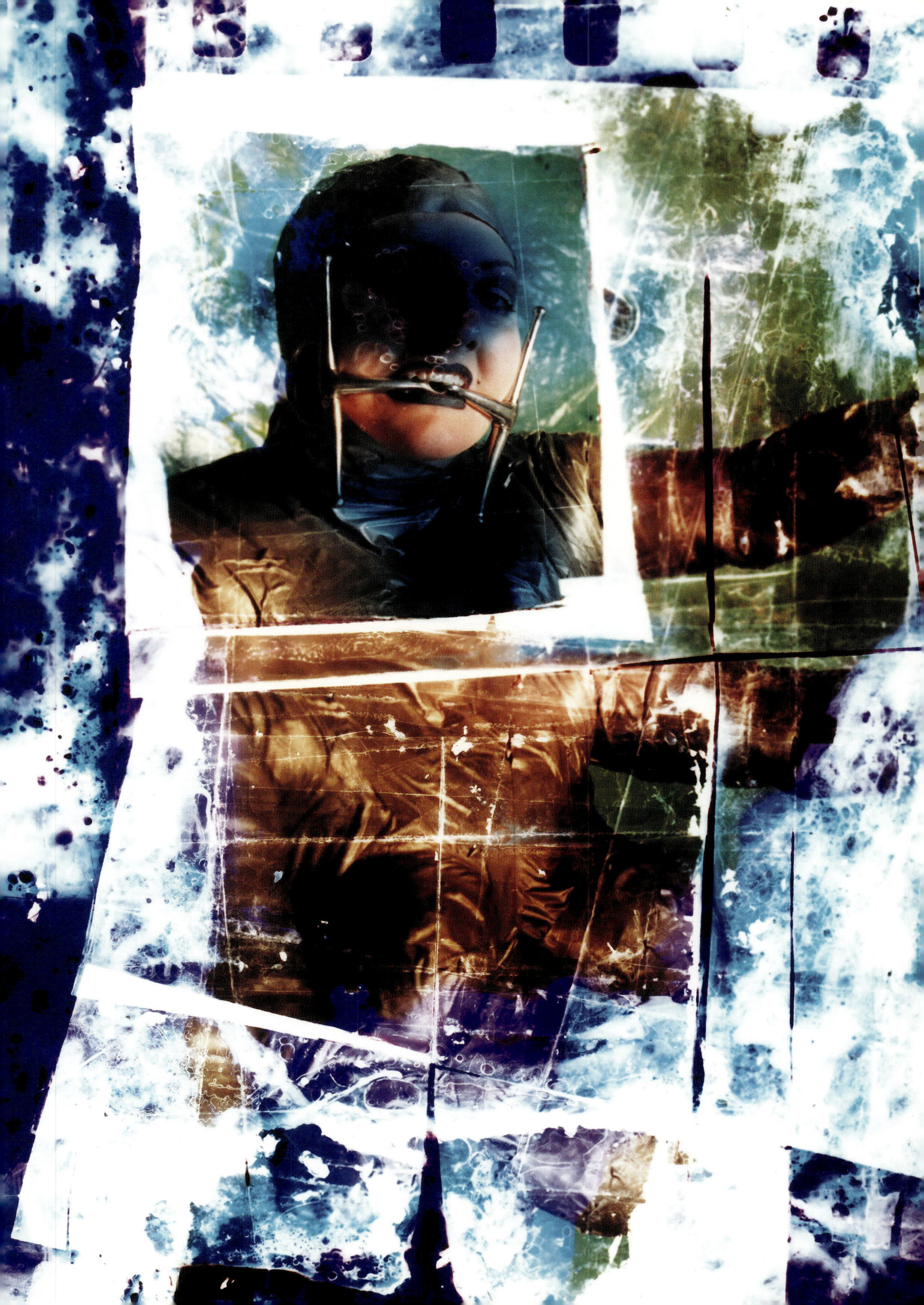

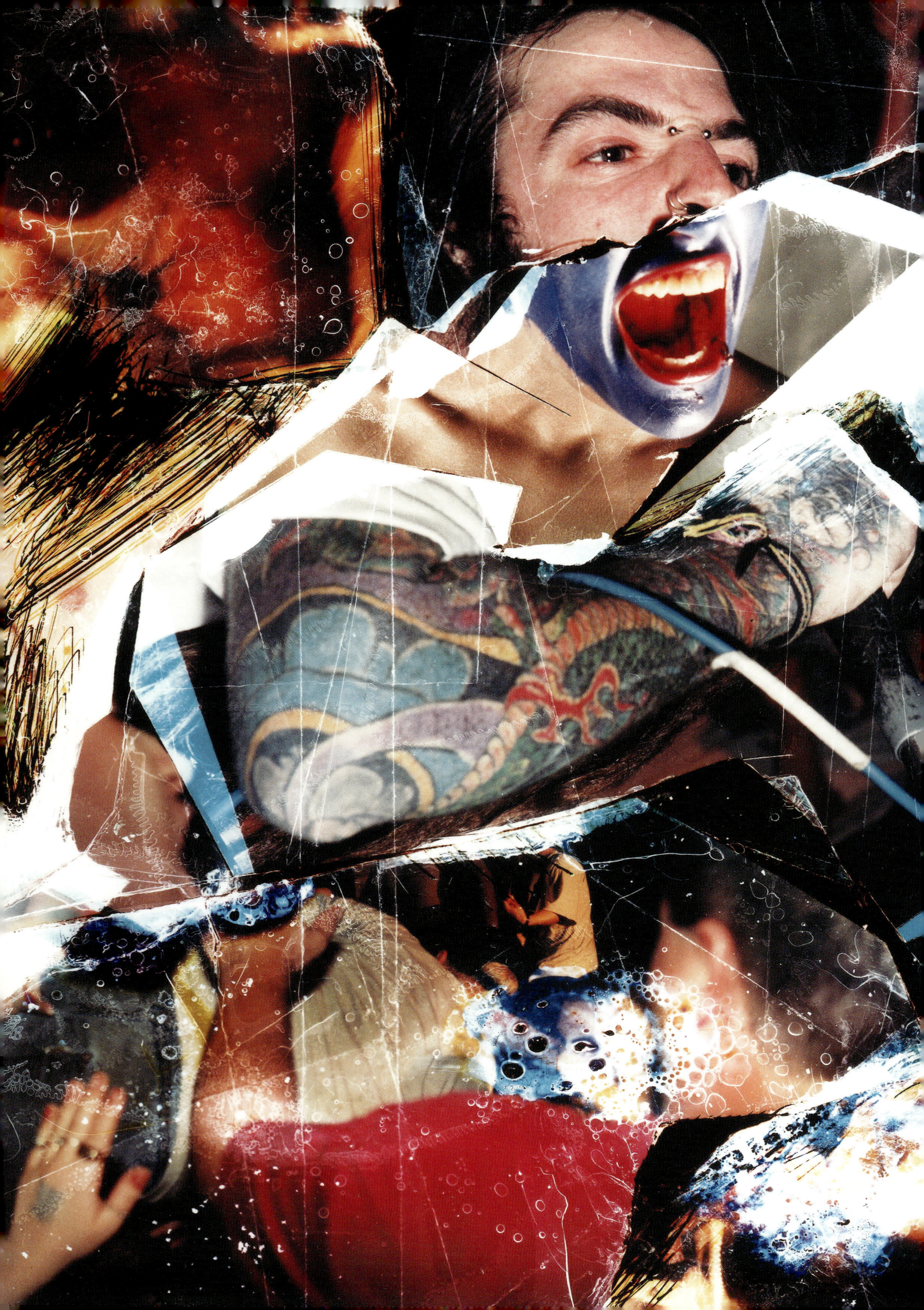

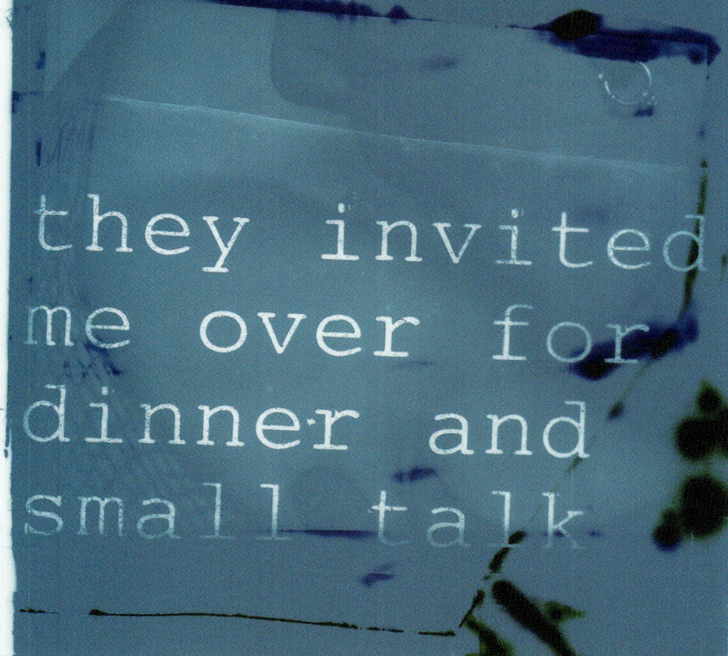

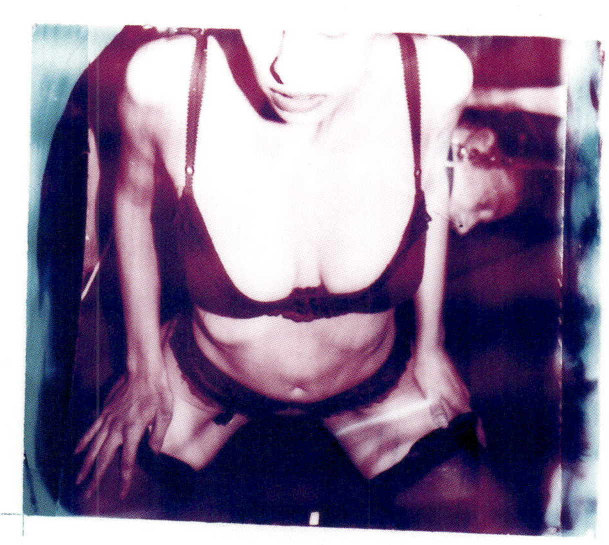

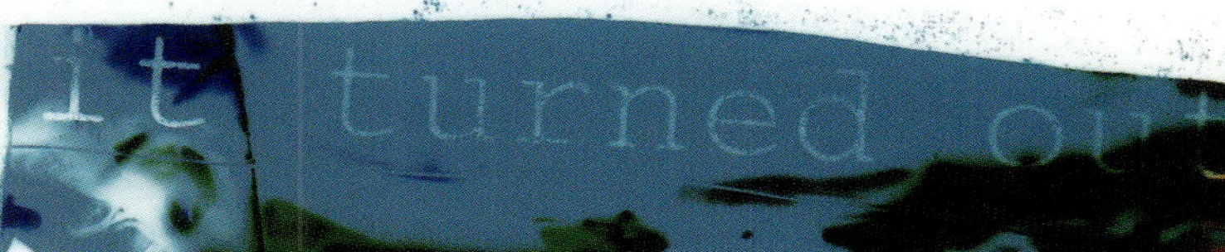

we had
nothing to say

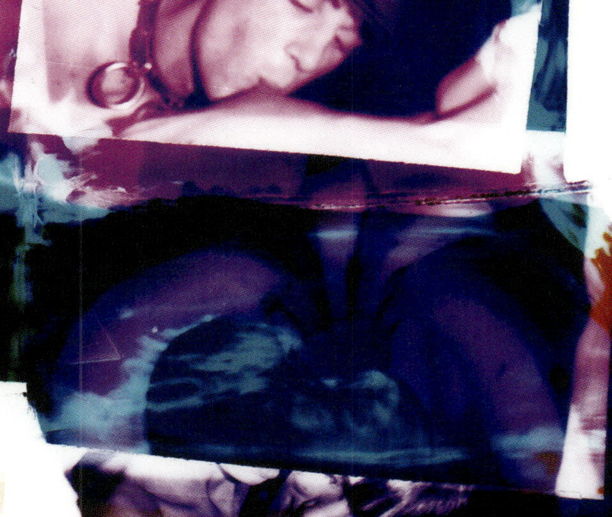

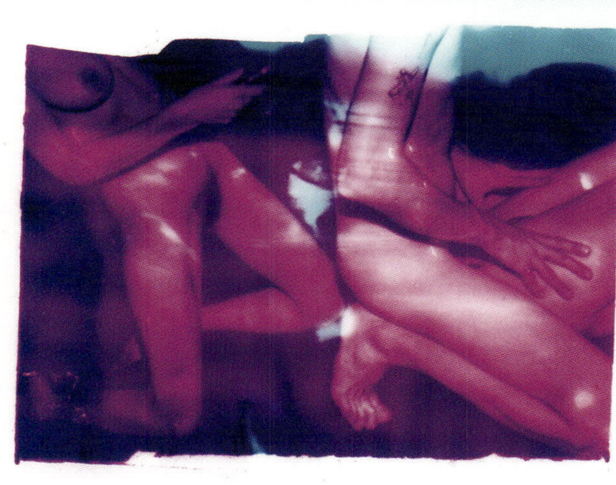

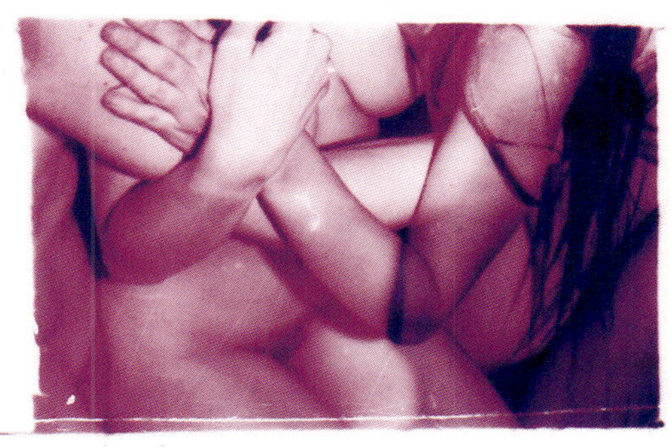

but the dinner was good

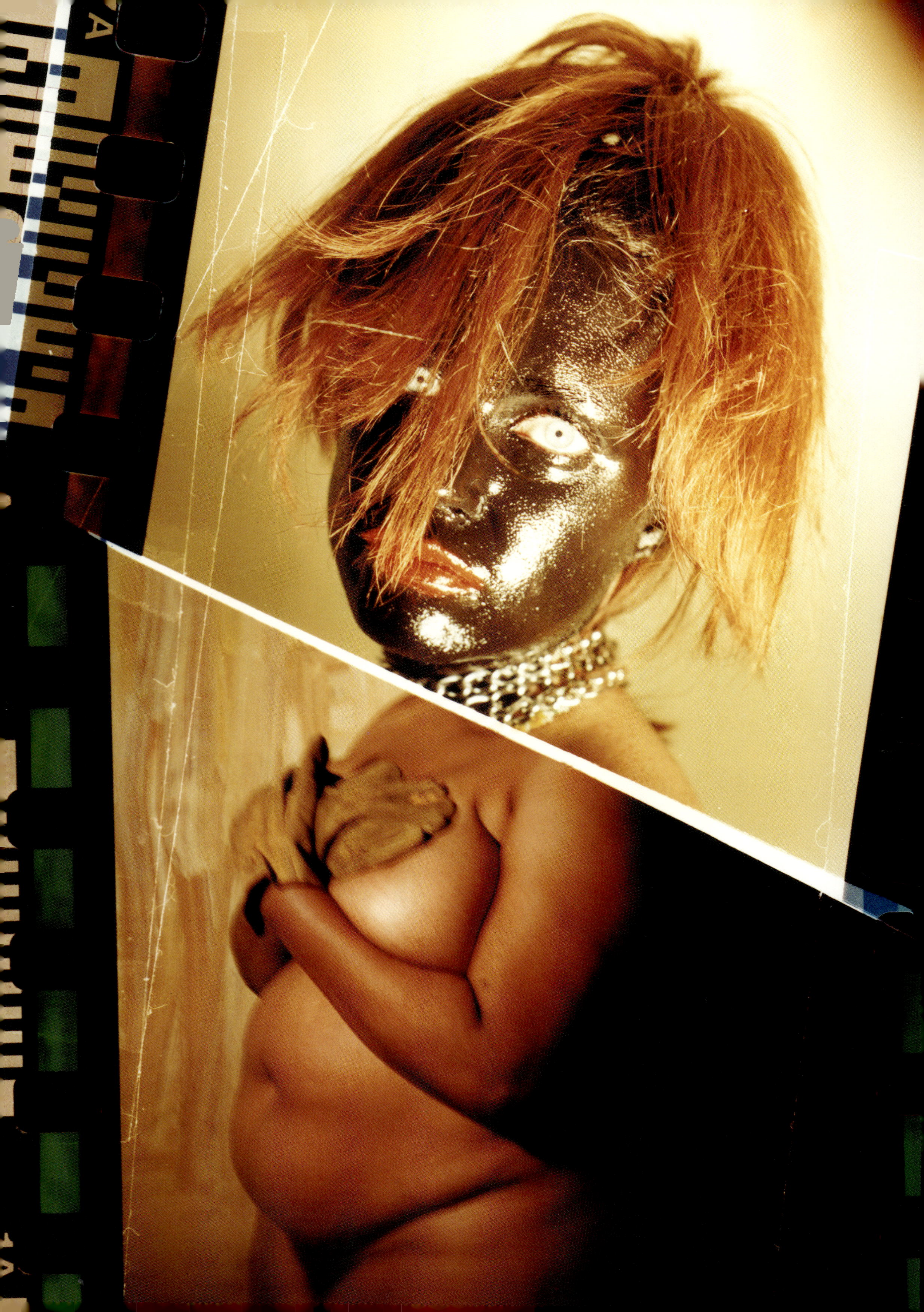

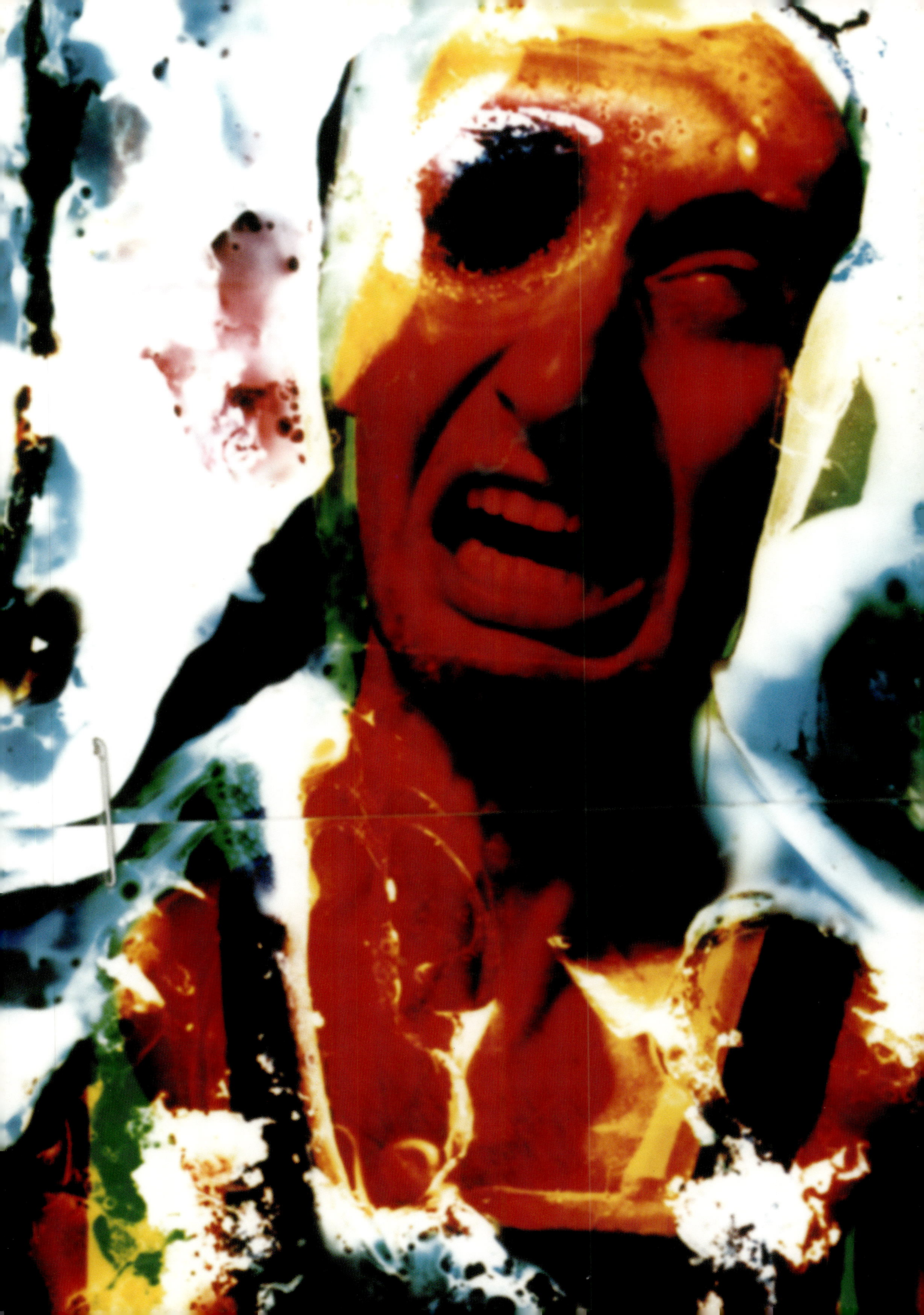

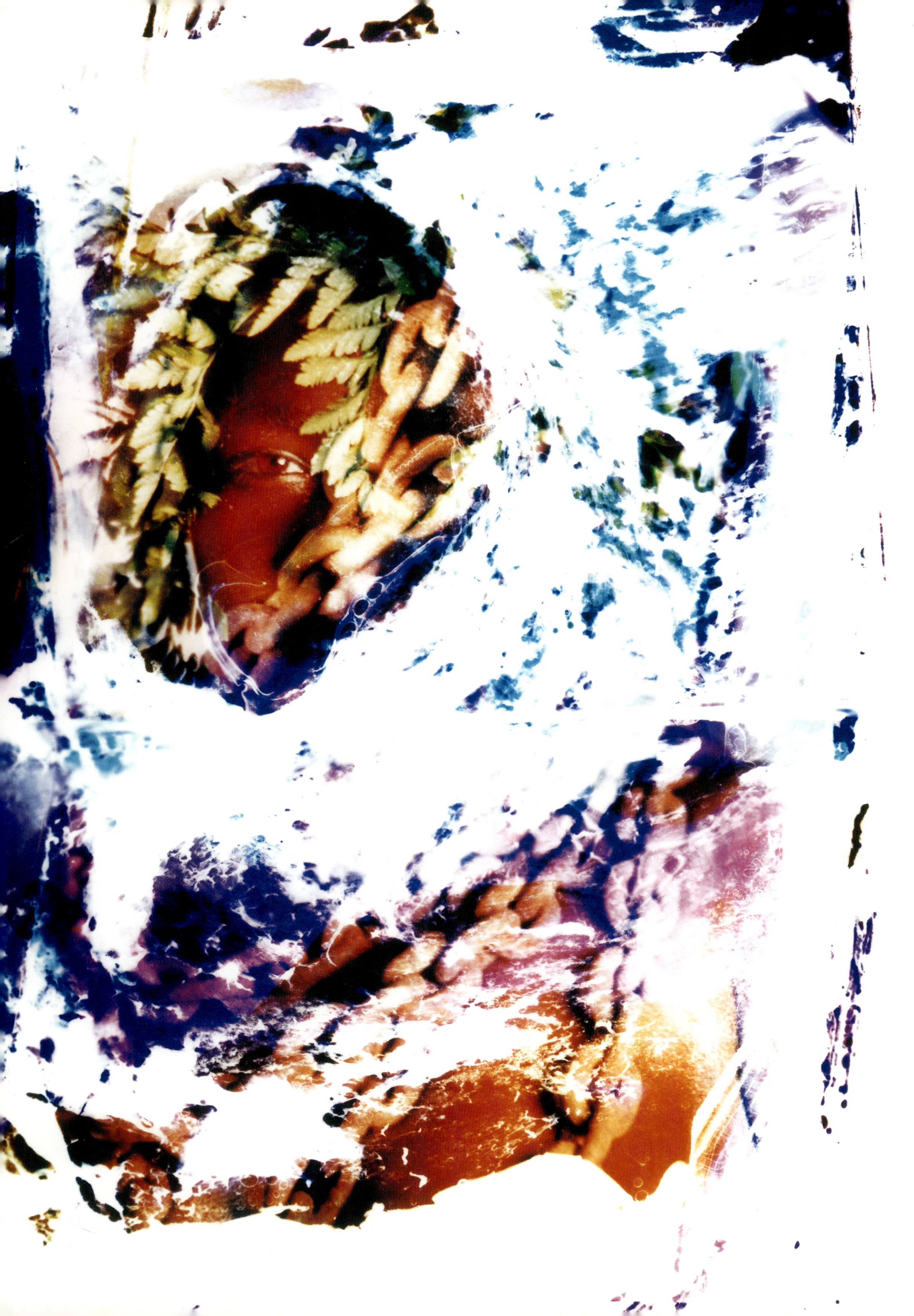

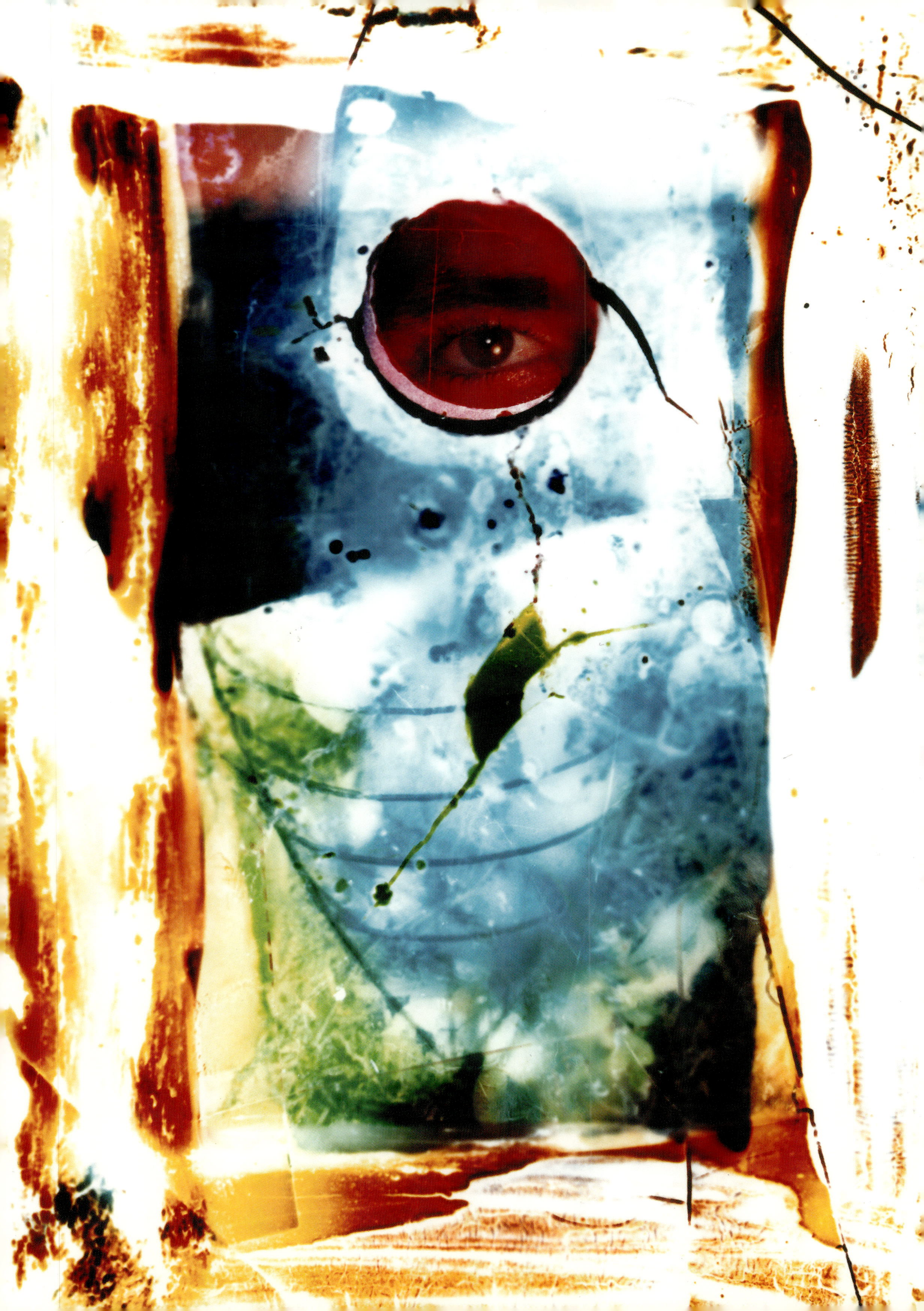

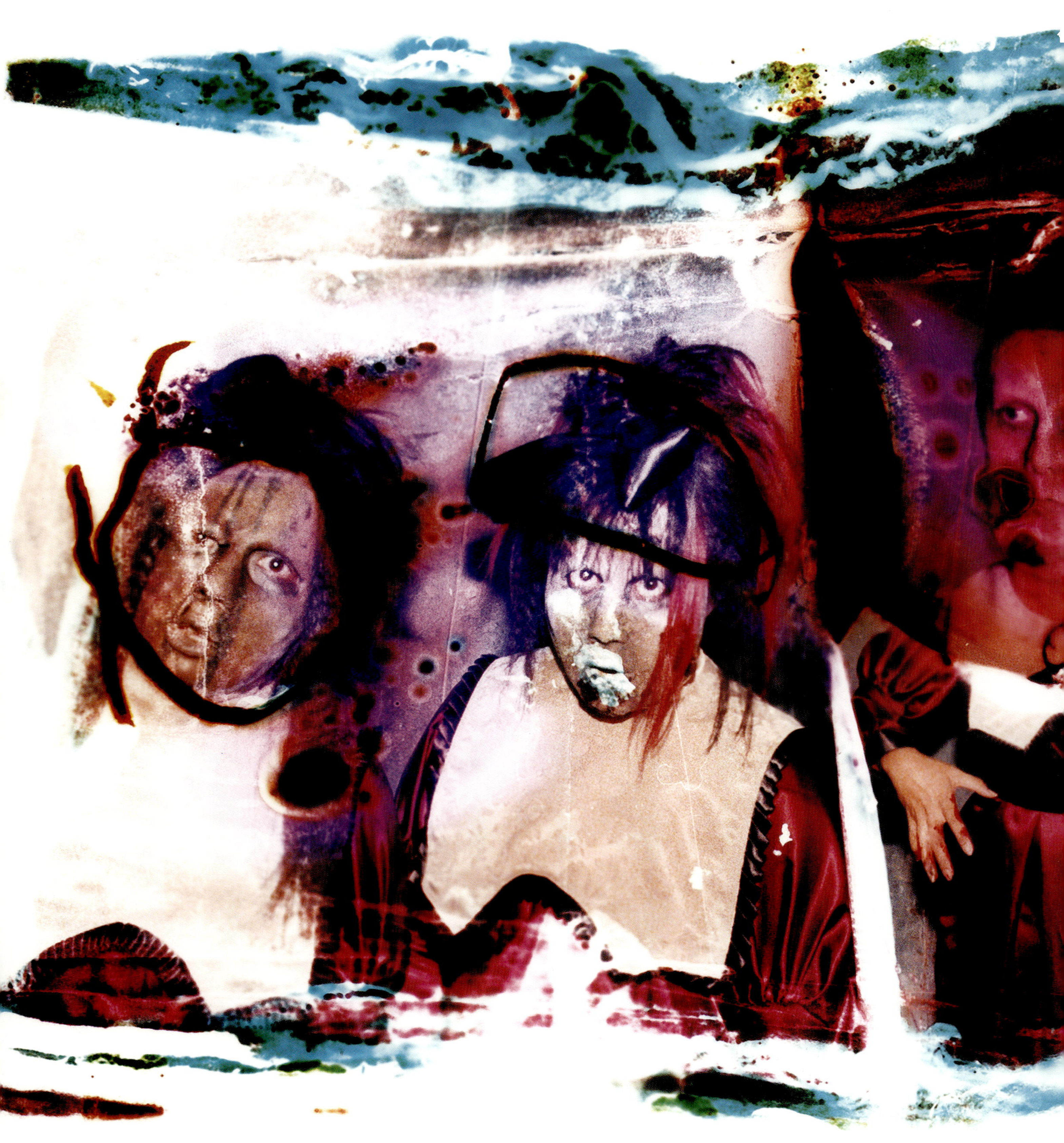

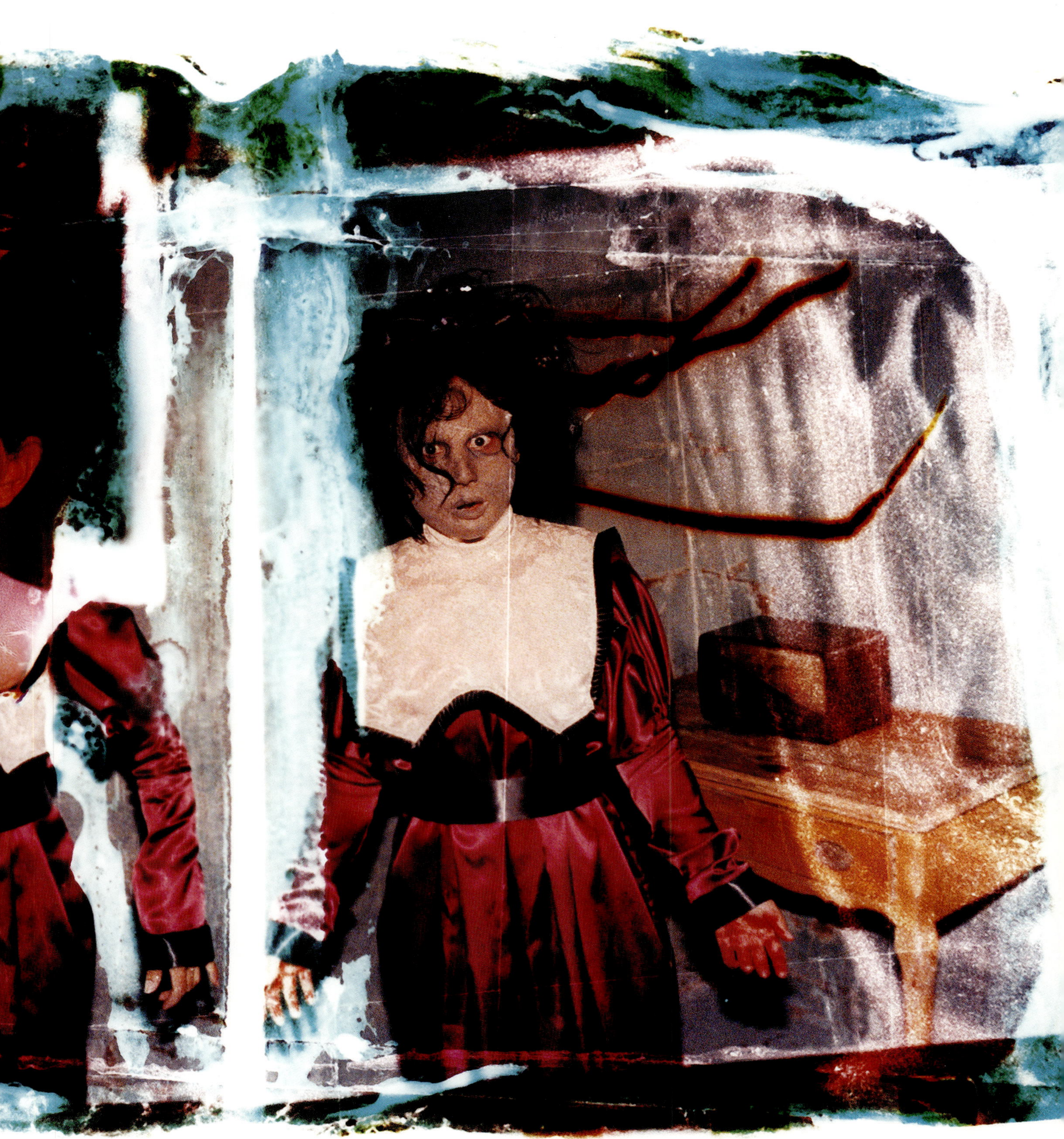

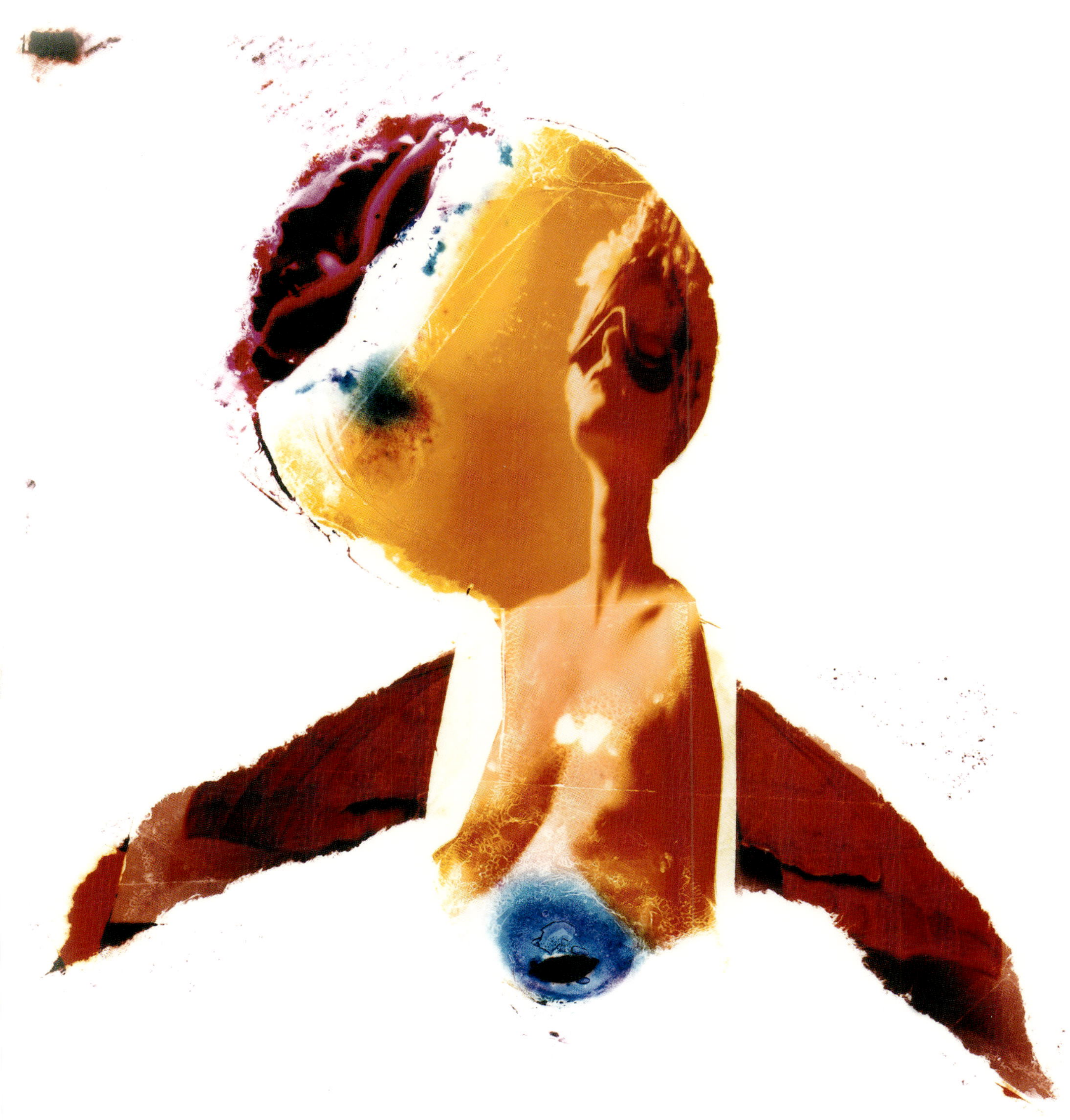

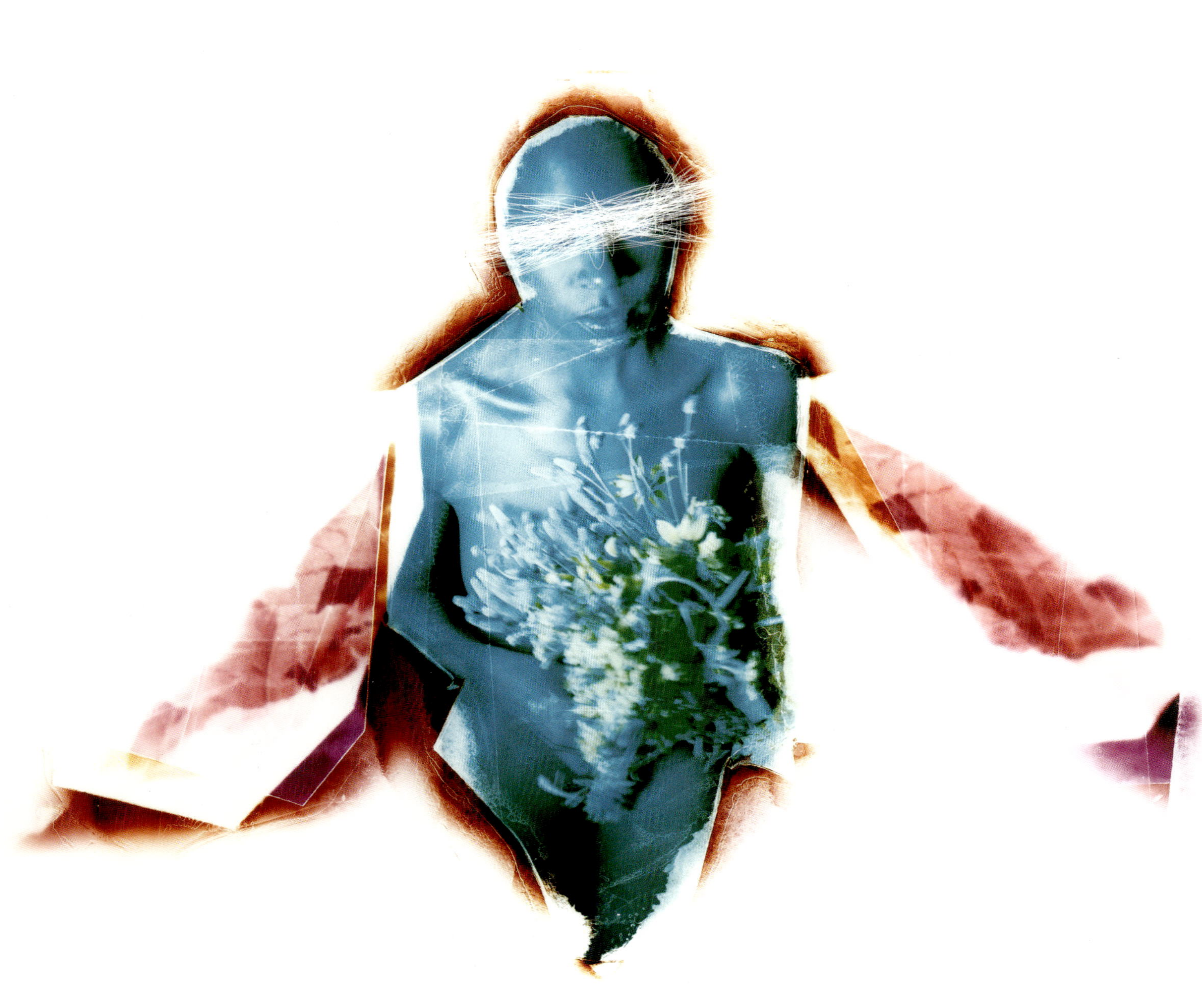

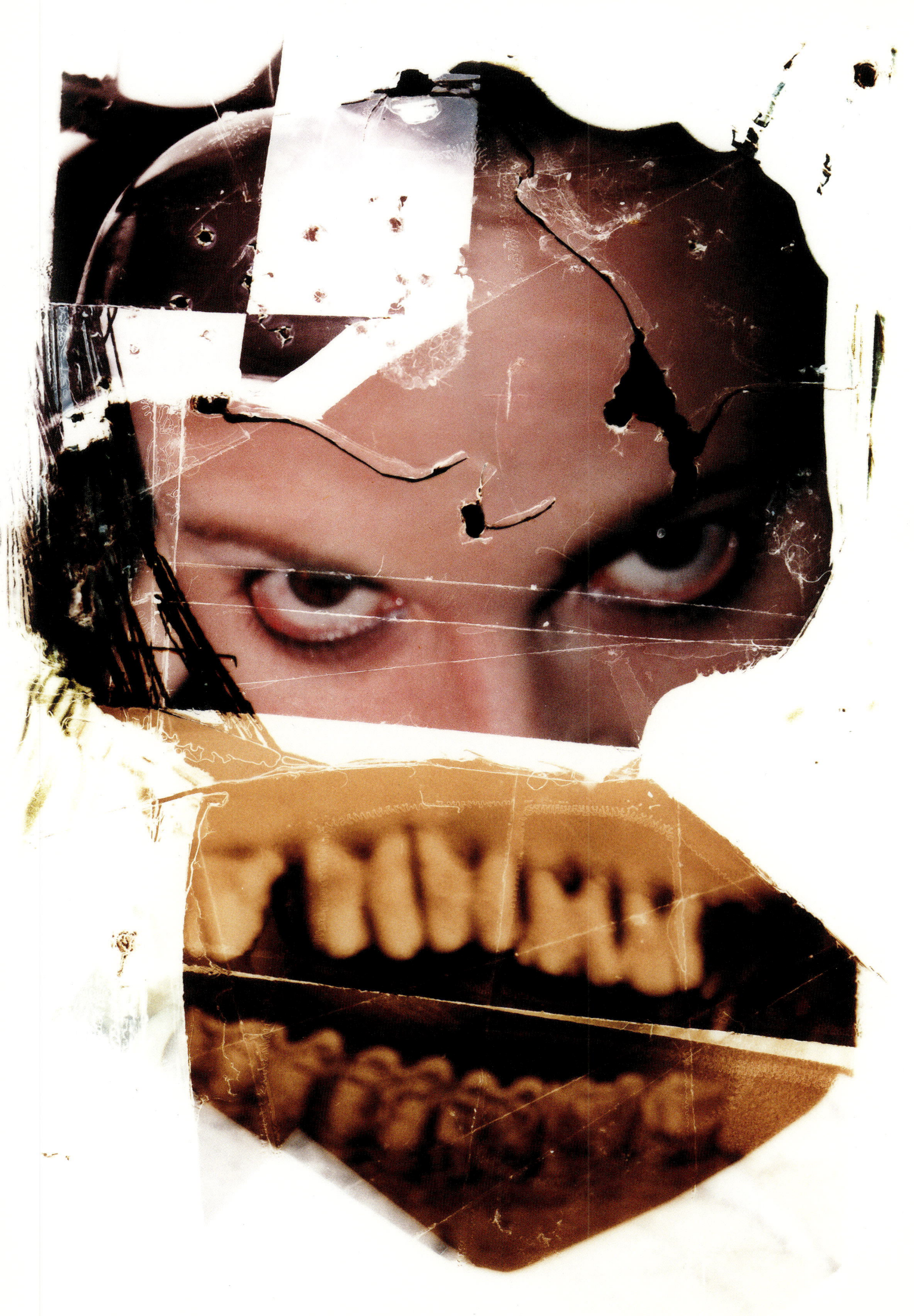

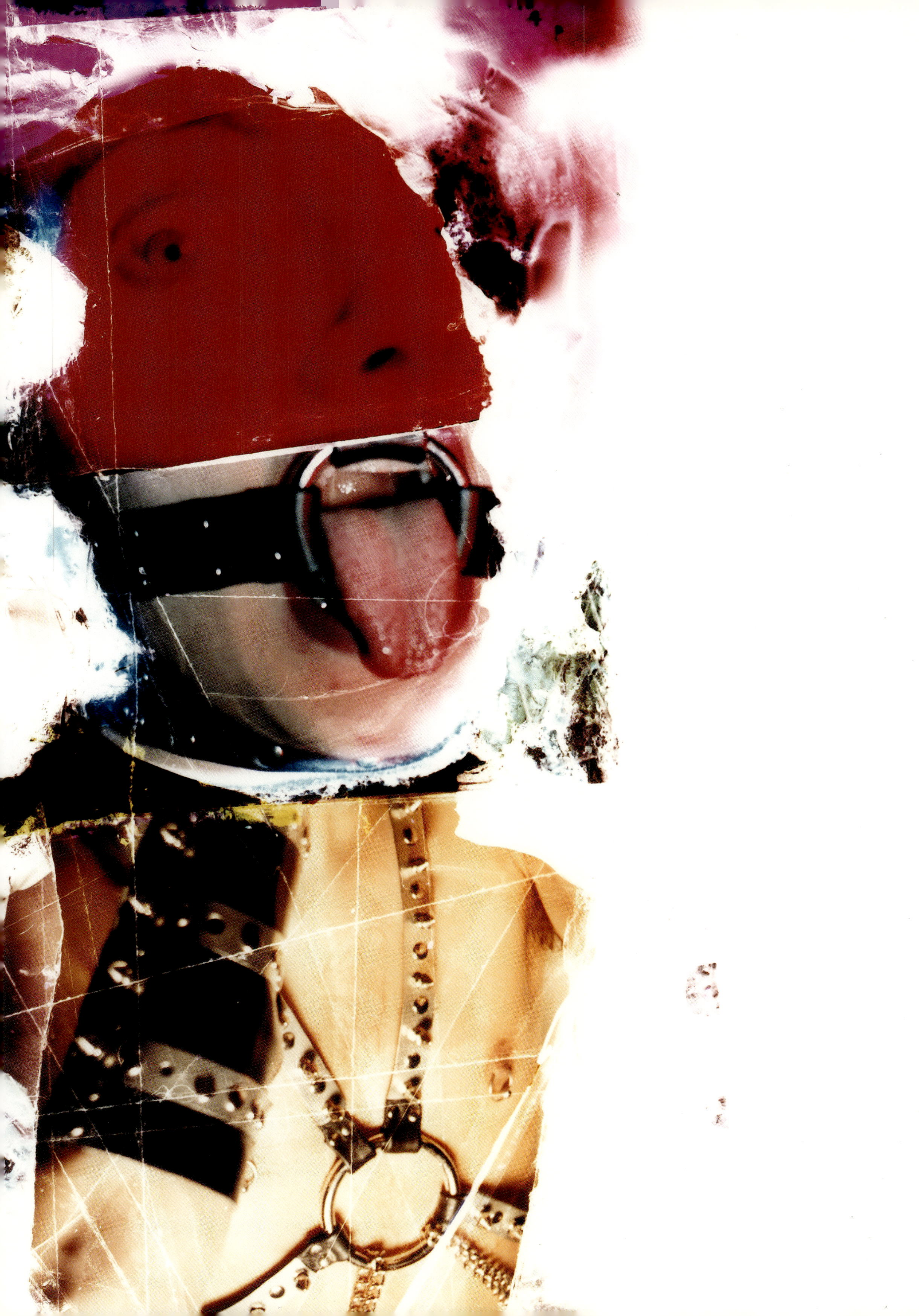

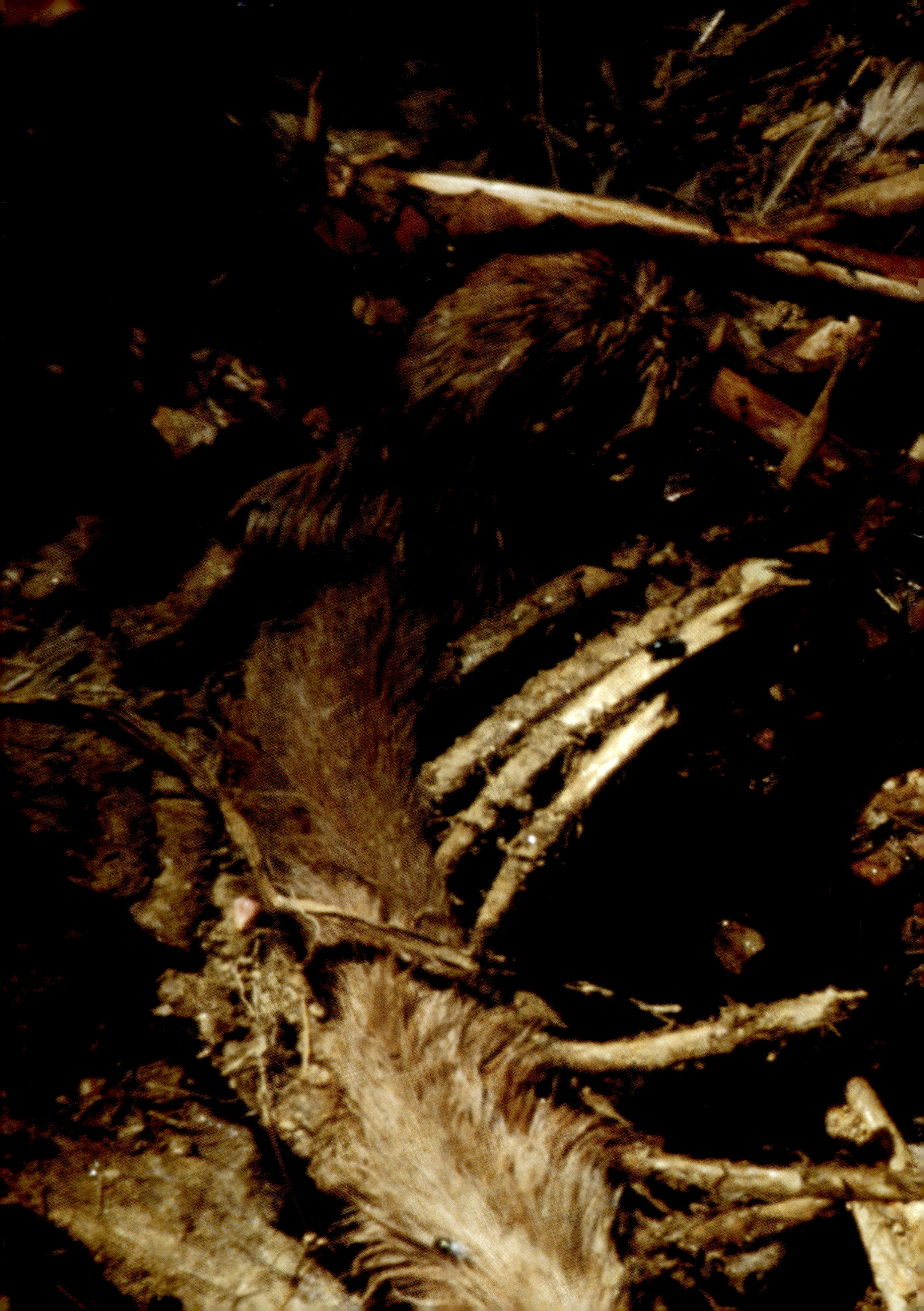

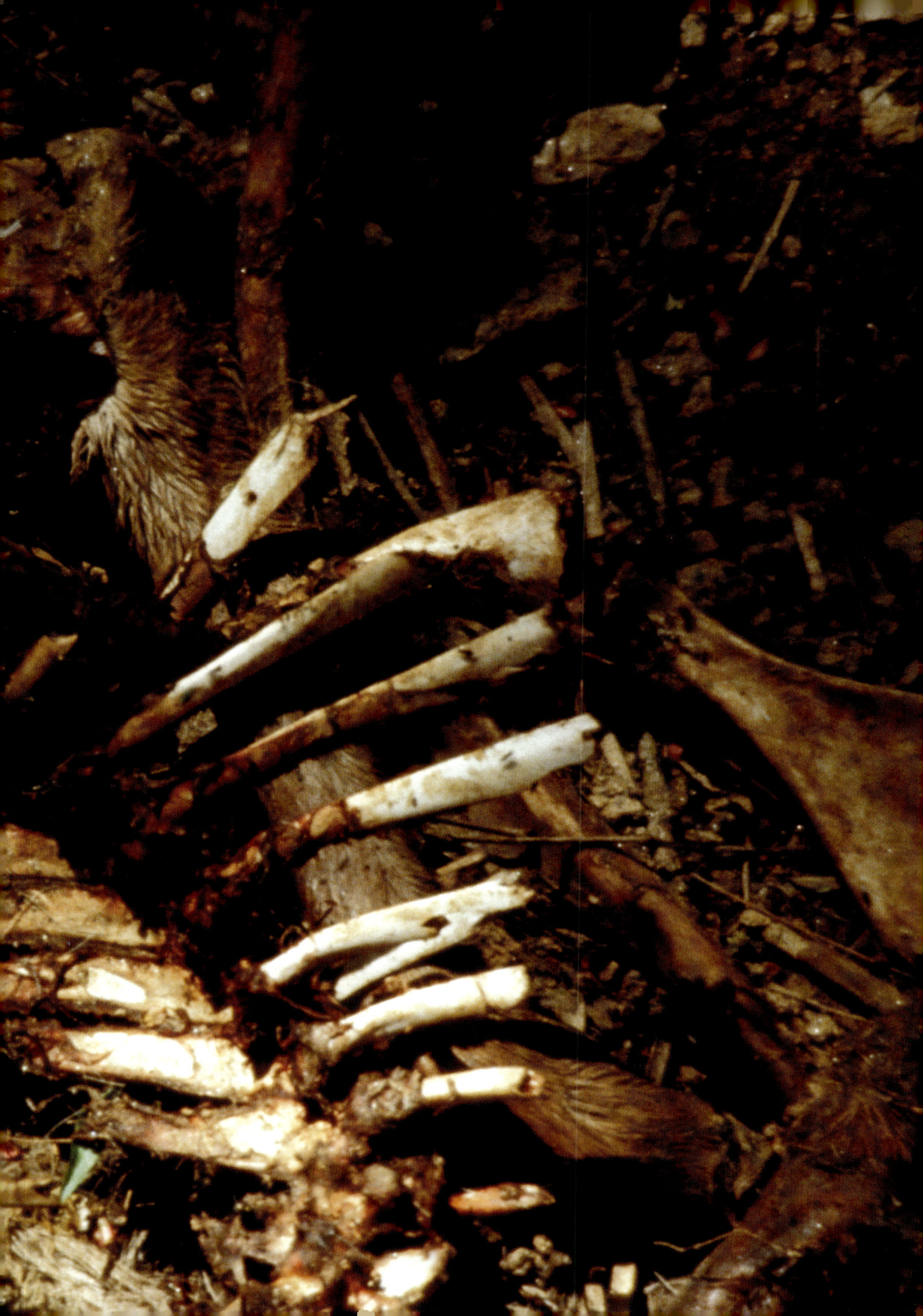

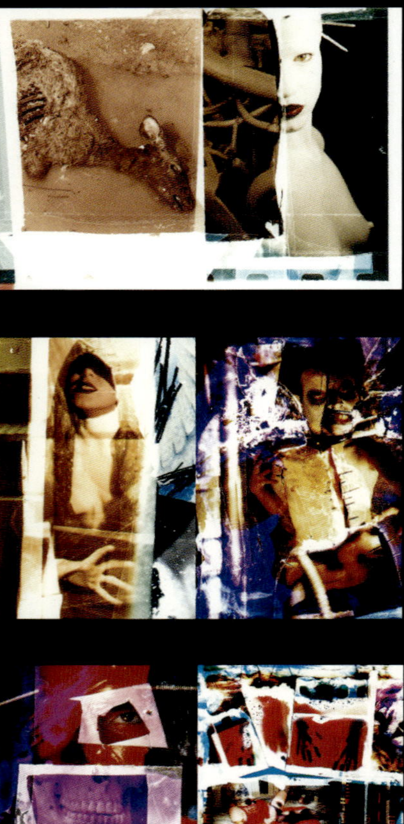

18-19. Pandora's box

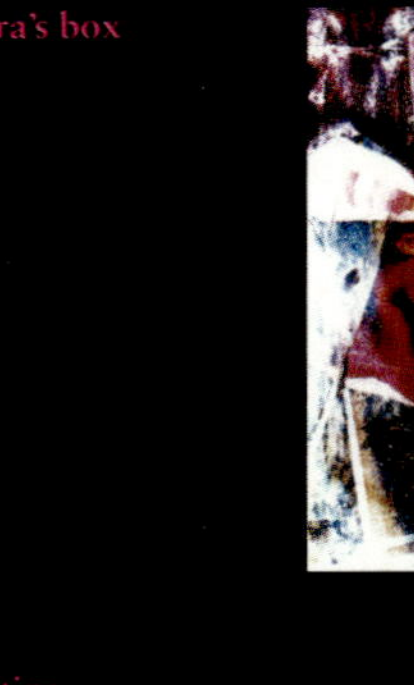

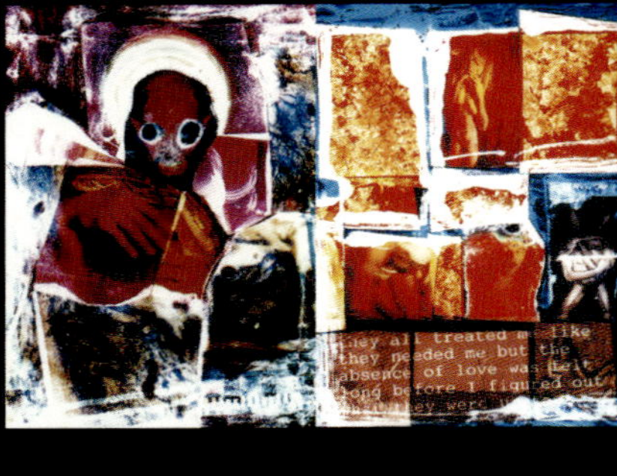

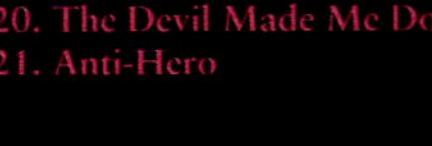

20. The Devil Made Me Do It
21. Anti-Hero

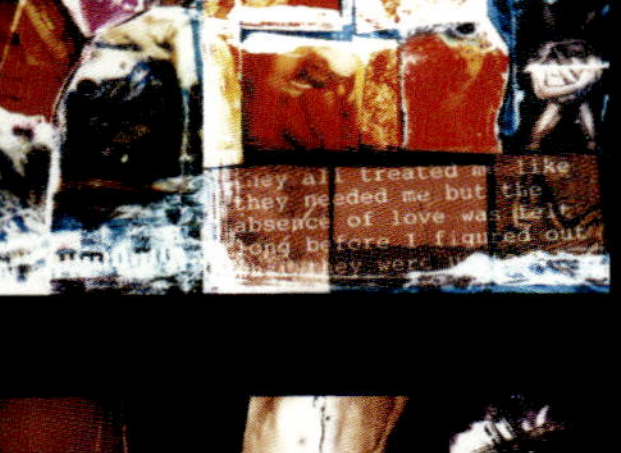

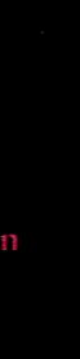

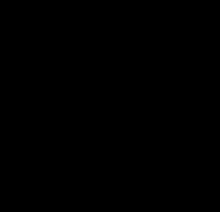

22. House Sitting
23. Electric Frankenstein

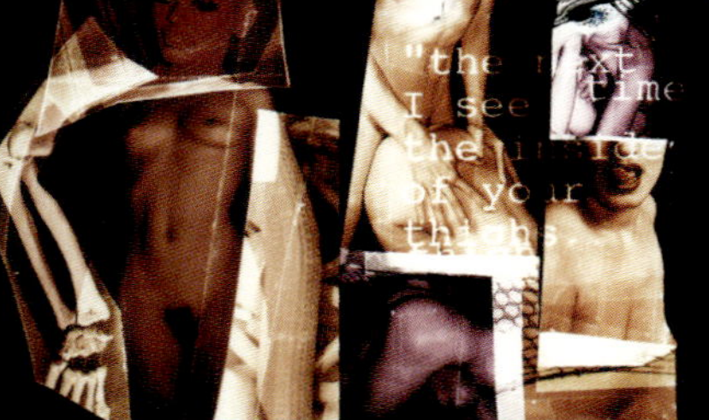

24. Anorexia
25. The Next Time I See
the Inside of Your Thighs

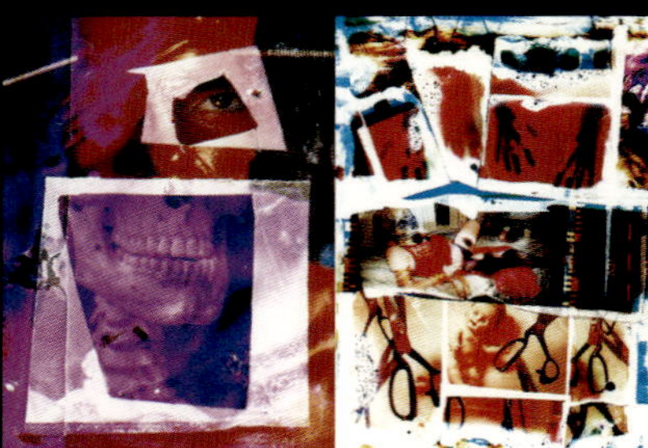

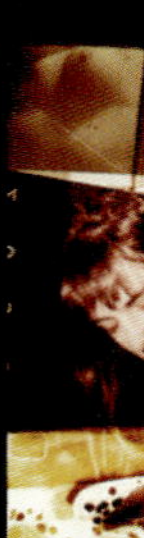

26. Trauma Test #1
27. Scissor Fight With My Wife

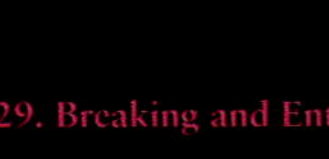

28-29. Breaking and Entering

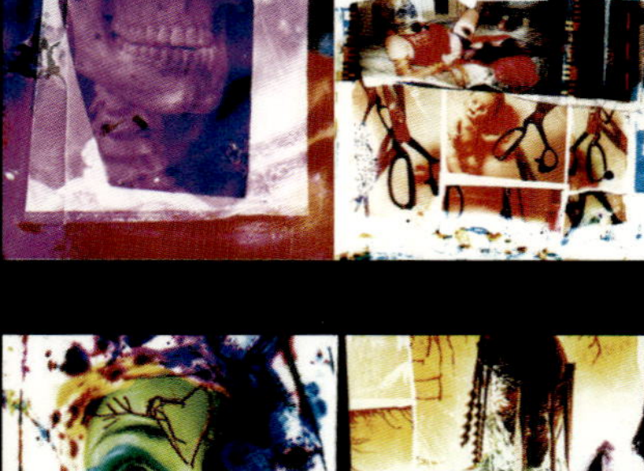

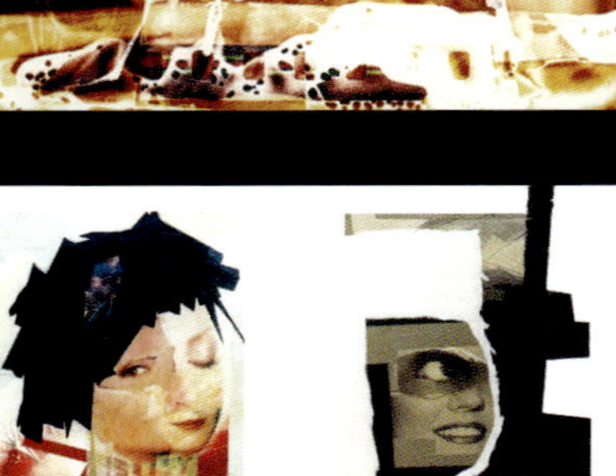

30. Love Letters
31. Jesus is Goth

32. Throat Sprockets Test #1
33. One-Eyed Bitch

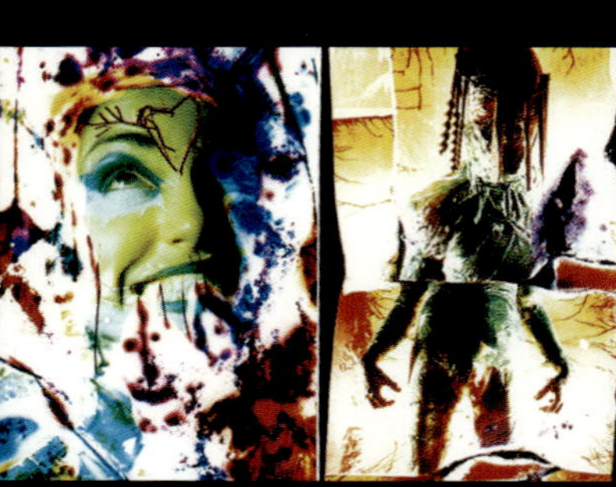

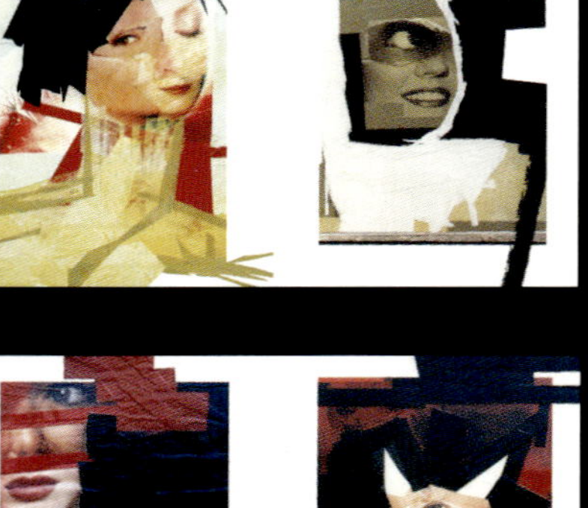

34. The Devil
35. Sinatra

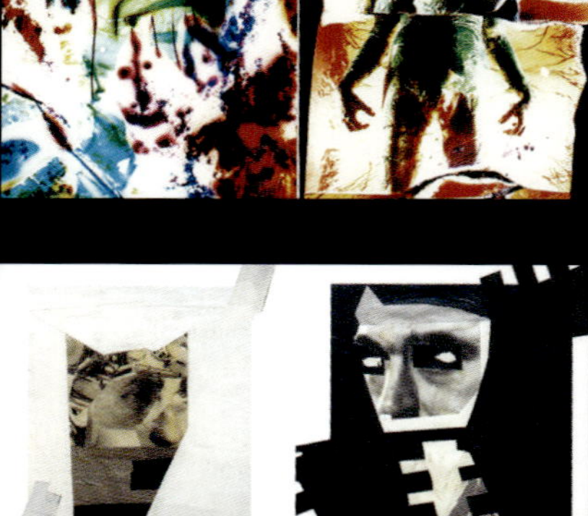

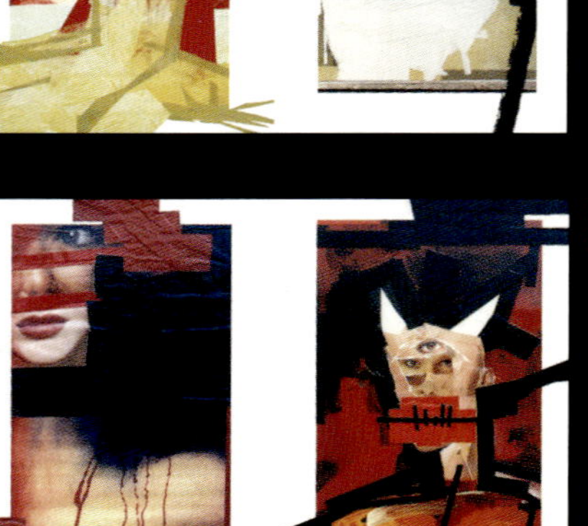

36. Cages
37. The One that Started it All

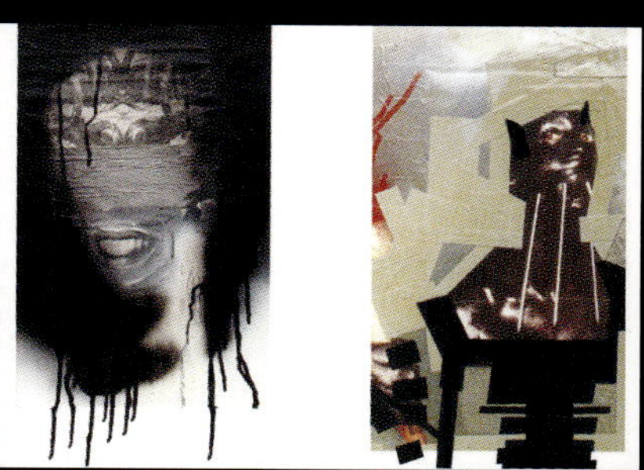

38. Angel
39. Slave State Hammer Test #1

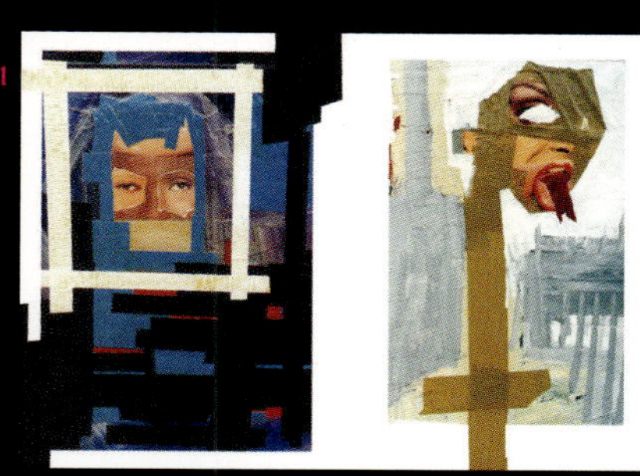

40. Man in a Box
41. You Speak with a Forked Tongue

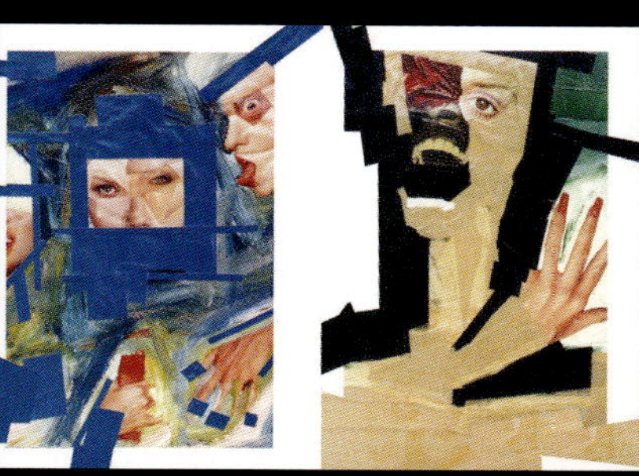

42. The 3 Graces
43. Fax Me

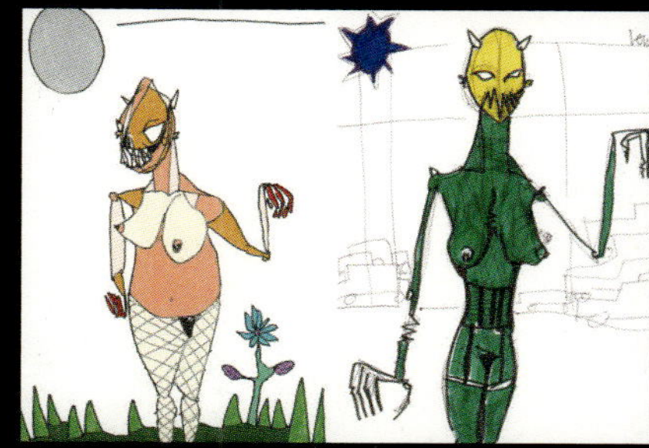

44. Pregnant Skull Test
45. Enemy Planet Sketch

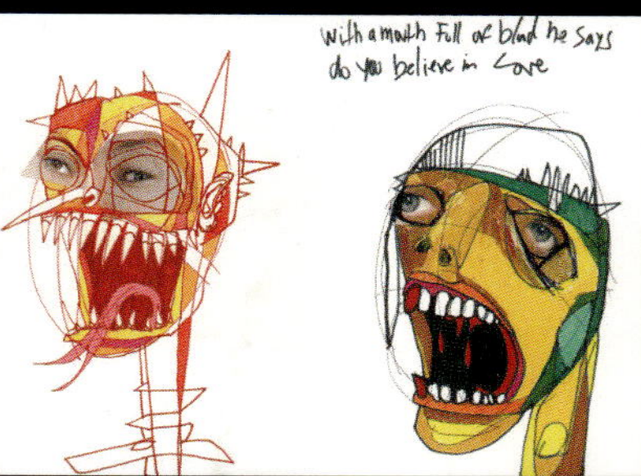

46. Ragin' Skeleton
47. Vampire Sketch

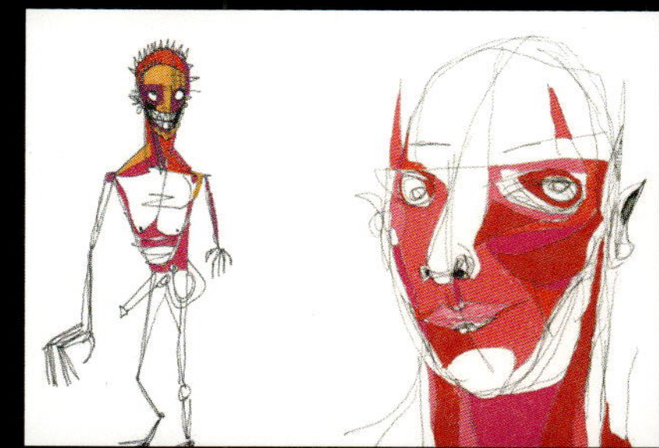

48. Untitled Sketch
49. Untitled Sketch

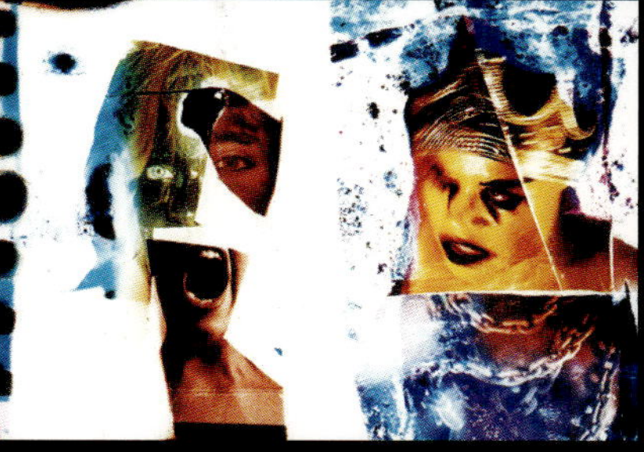

50. She Picasso
51. Queen Misery

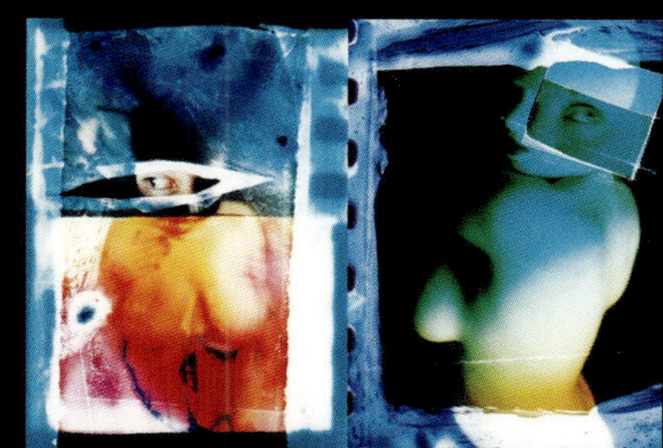

52. The Fear of Commitment
53. Reach Around

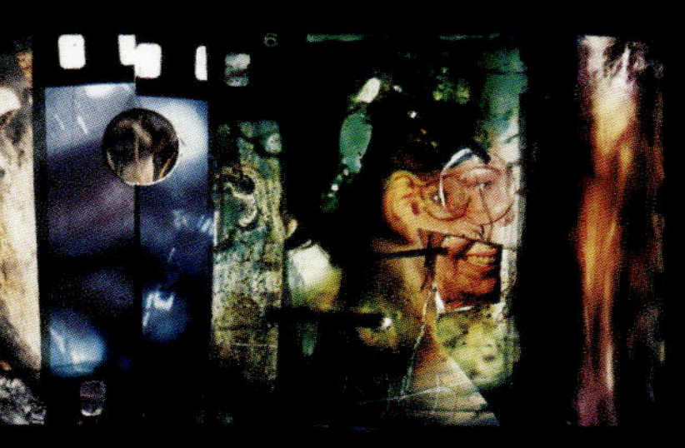

54-55. White Girl in an SUV

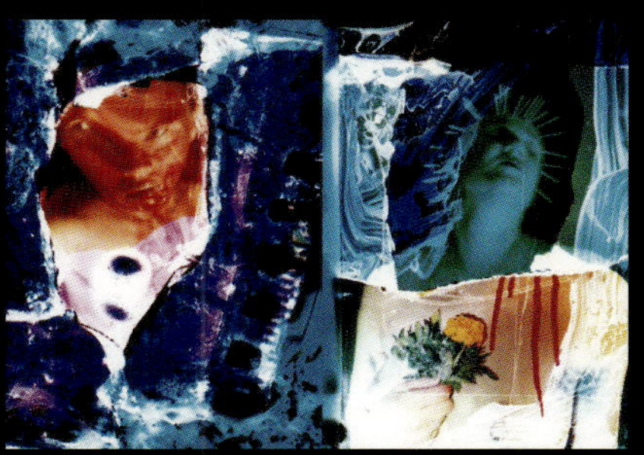

56. Princess Fell
57. When Liberty Fails

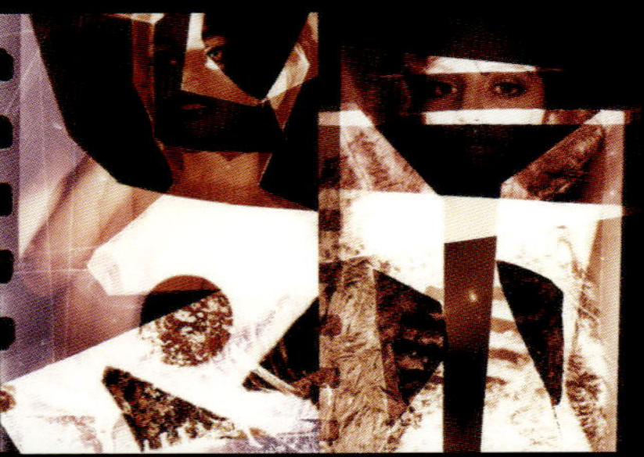

58. Bulimia
59. Bulimia #2

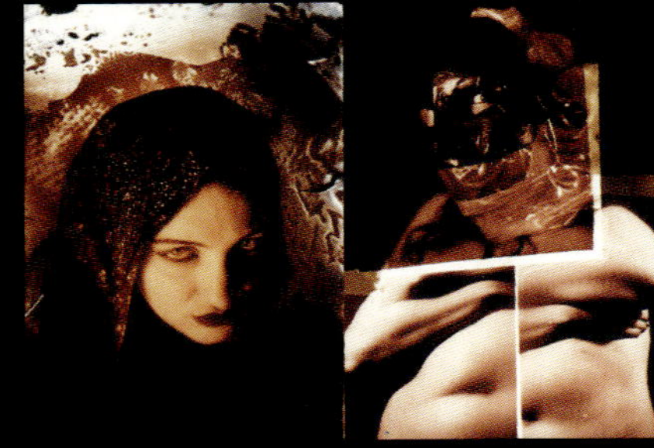

62-63. Adam and Eve

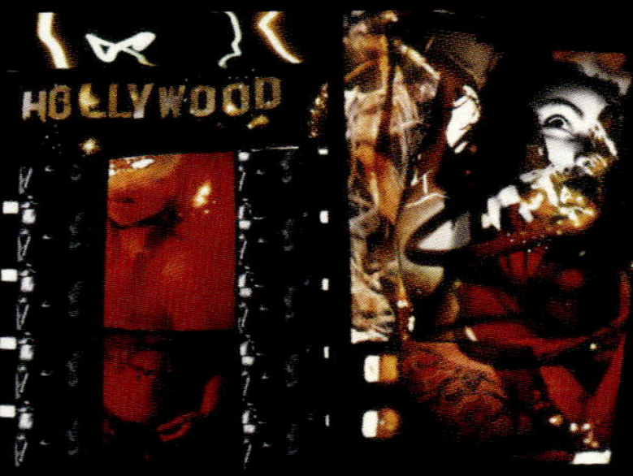

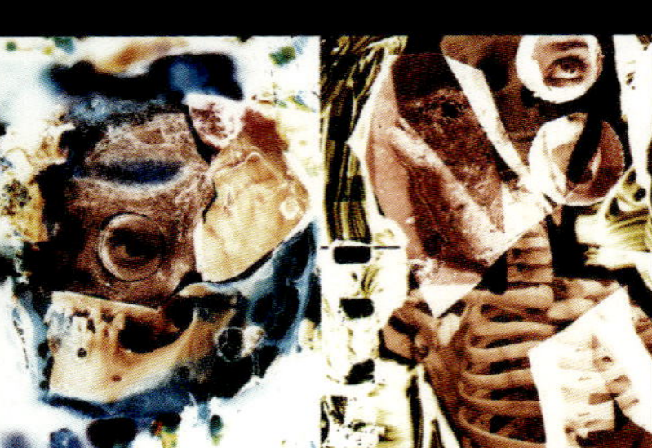

66. Pig Destroyer
67. Gravedigger

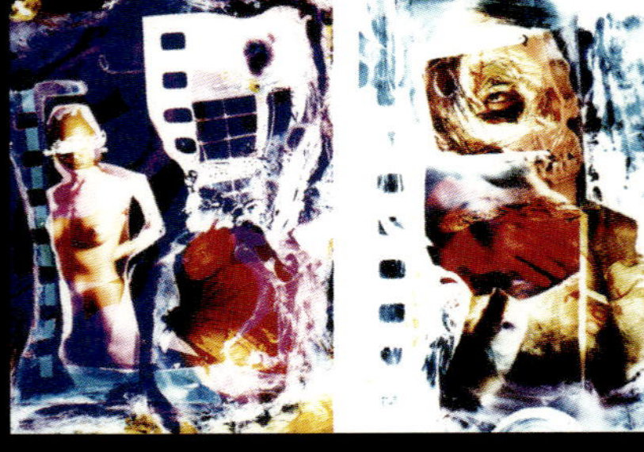

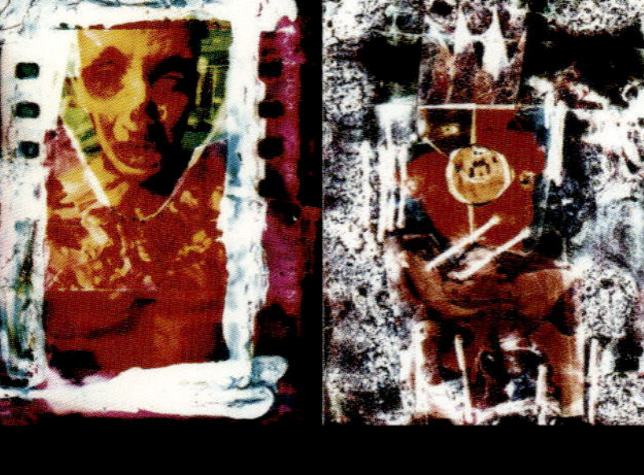

70. The Devil Within
71. Corpse Grinder

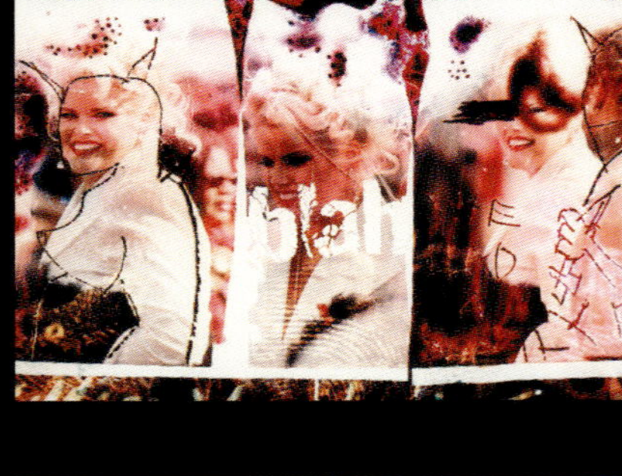

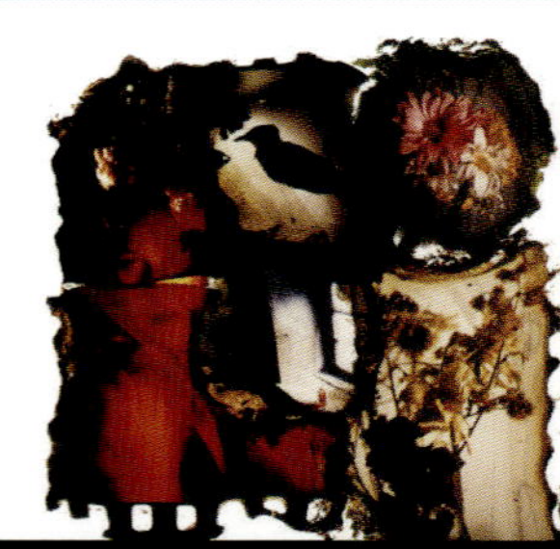

74-75. They Are Playing
Your Song

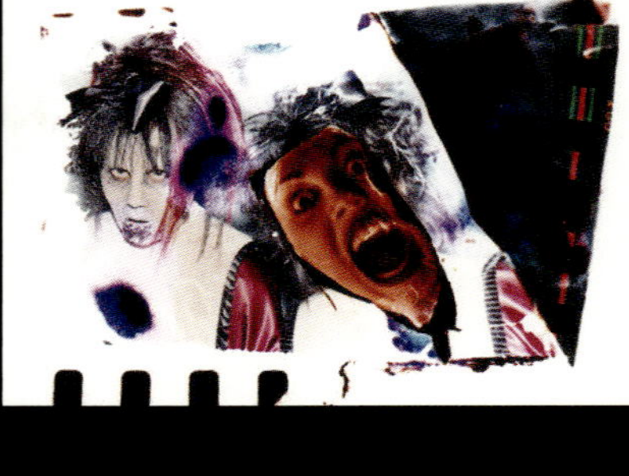

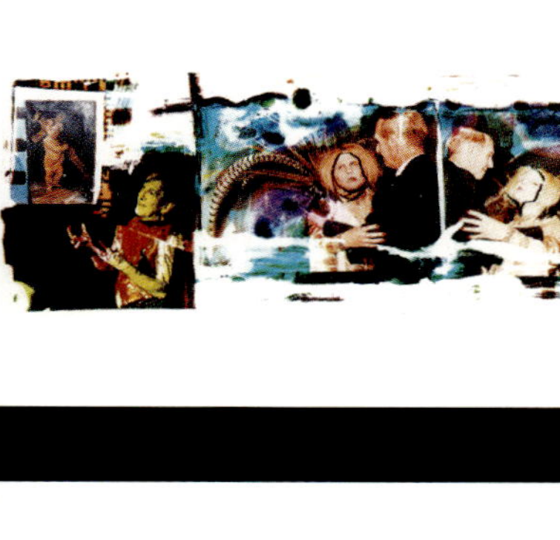

78-79. The Murder of
the Wife

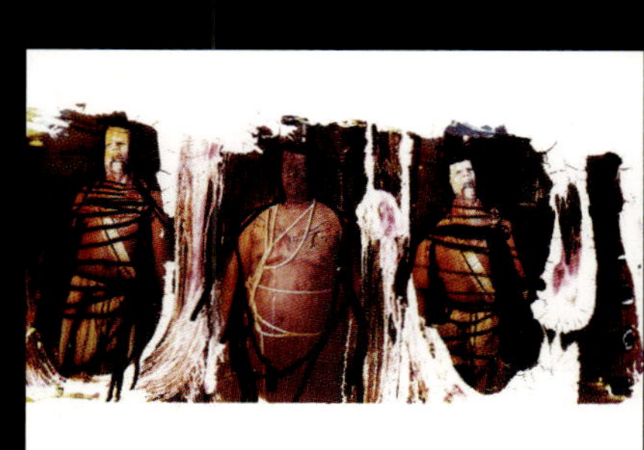

80-81. Slave State A

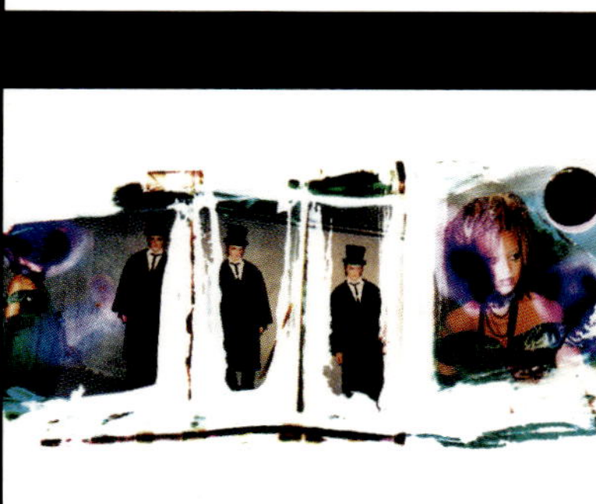

82-83. The Necromancers
1 & 2

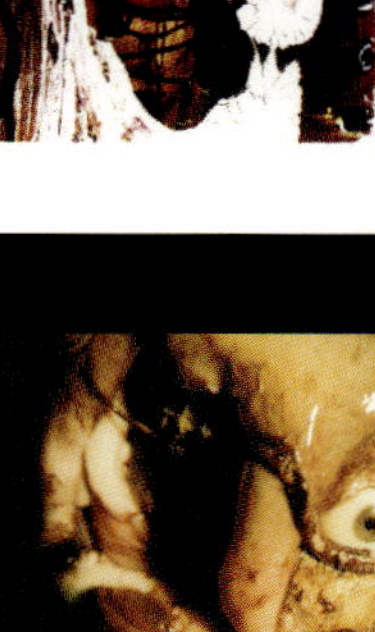

84. Untitled Sketch
85. The Making of
a Monster

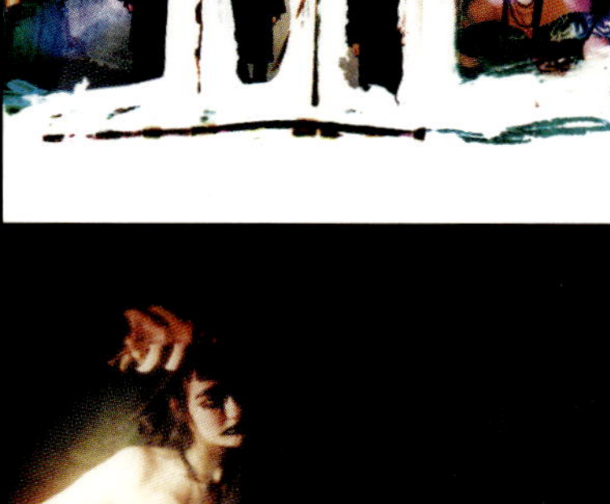

86. Swamp Witch
87. Untitled Sketch

88. Untitled Sketch
89. The Hollows of
the Womb

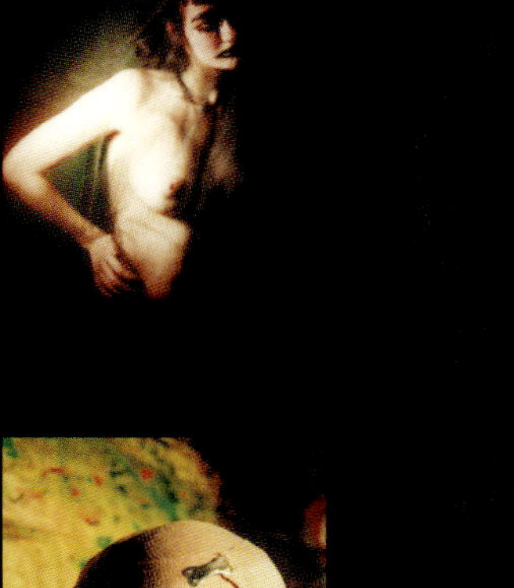

90. Headless Still Life
91. Untitled Sketch

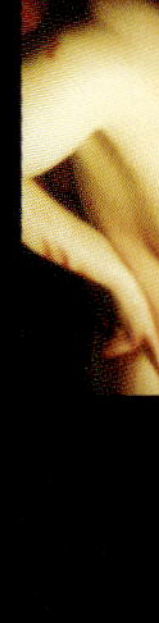

92. Untitled Sketch
93. Kept

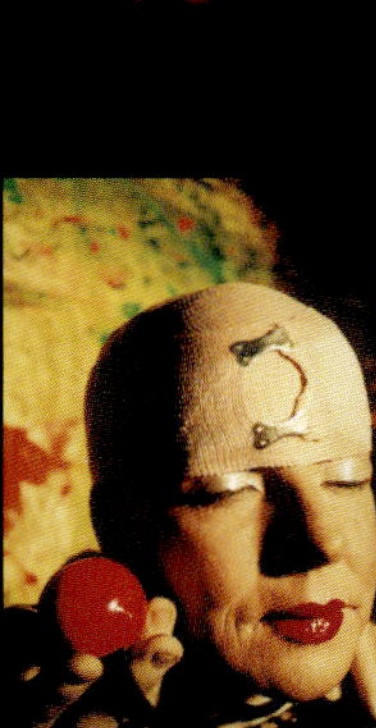

94. Gallery Shopping During
the Apocalypse
95. Untitled Sketch

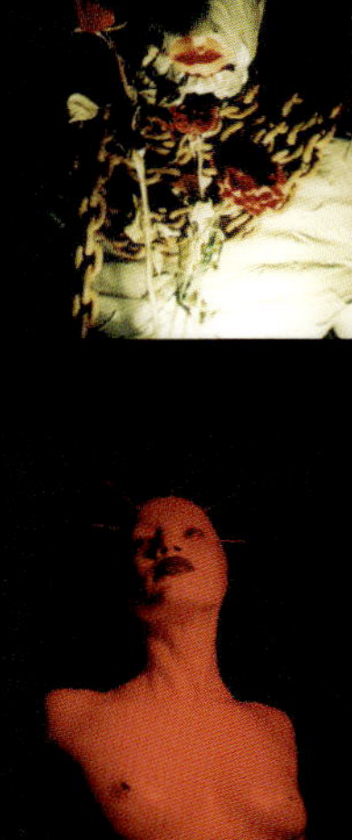

96. Untitled Sketch
97. Pandora SOLO

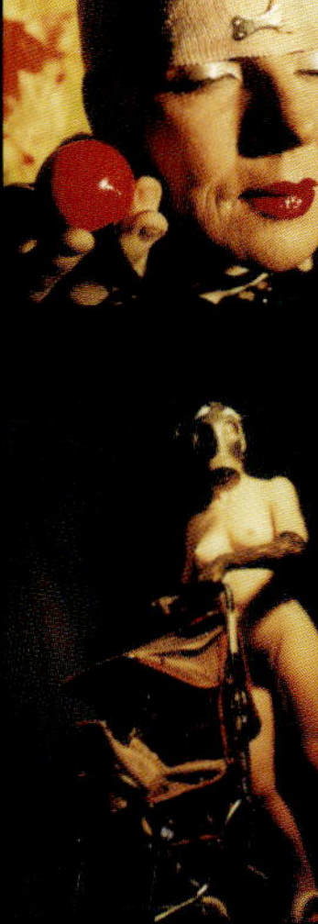

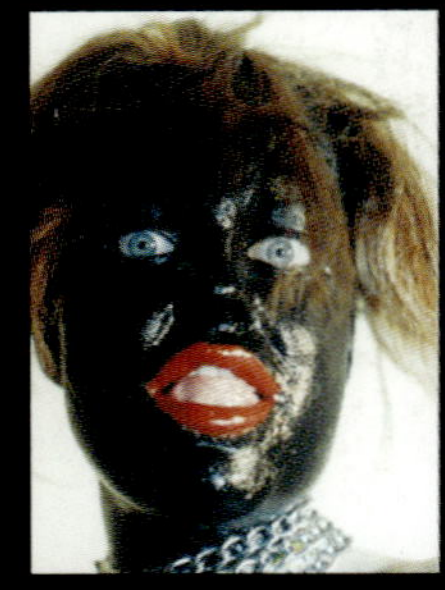

98. Jocking My Style
99. Untitled sketch

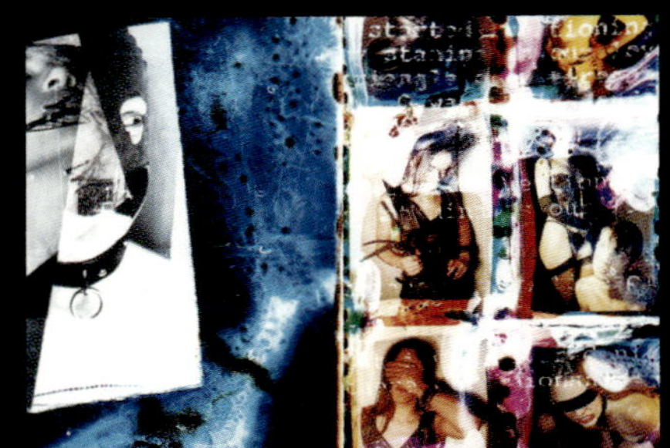

100. 2 Face
101. Lovers' Quarrel

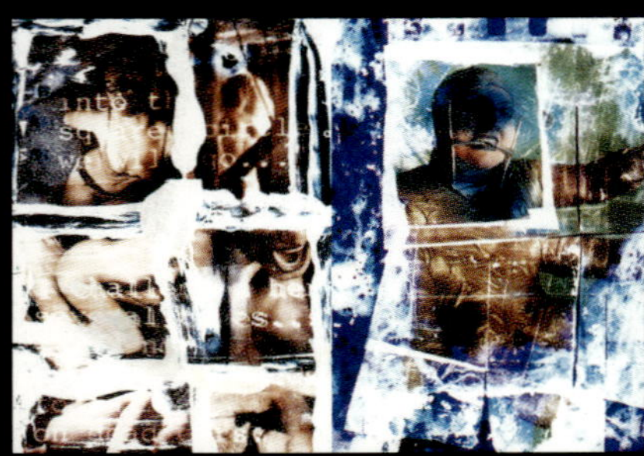

102. Into the Squared Circle
103. Mummy

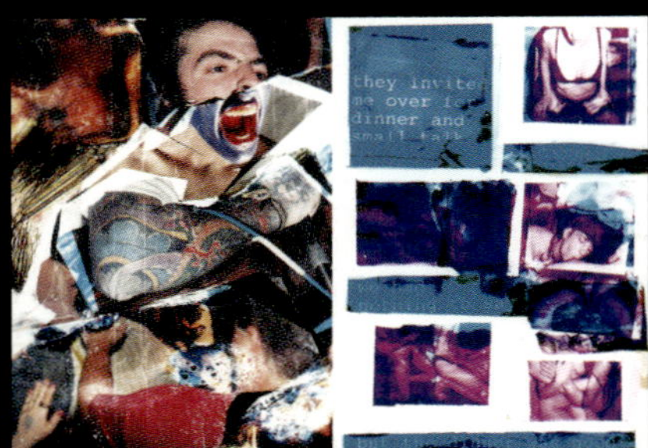

104. Speaking in Tongues
105. Dinner for 3

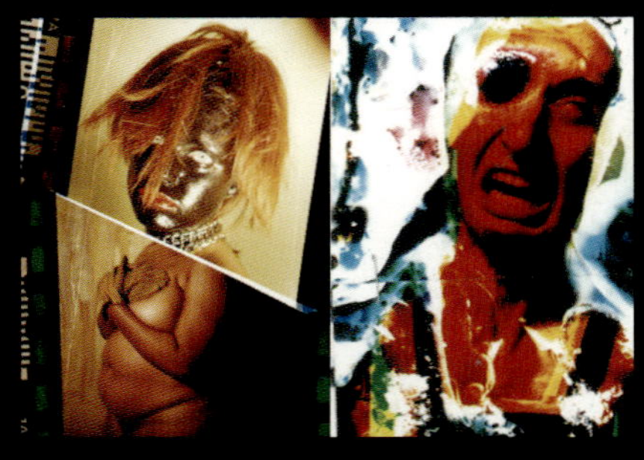

106. Without Guilt
107. Enraged Test #2

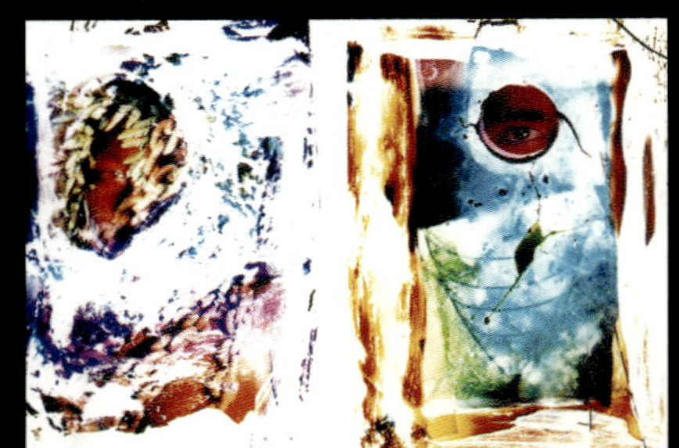

108. Slave Trader
109. Van Gogh Envy

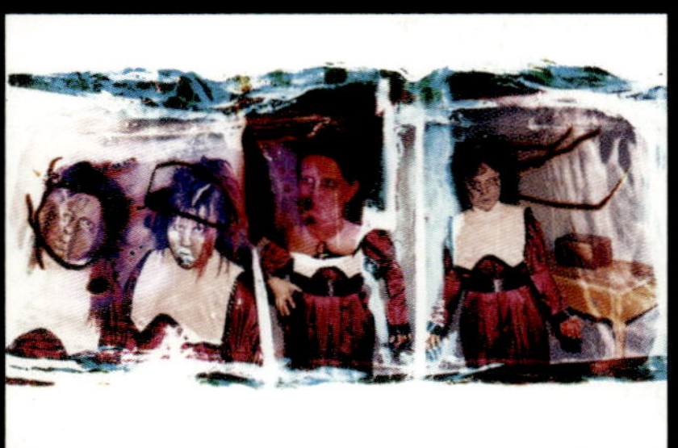

110-111. The Daughter and Zombies 1, 2, & 3

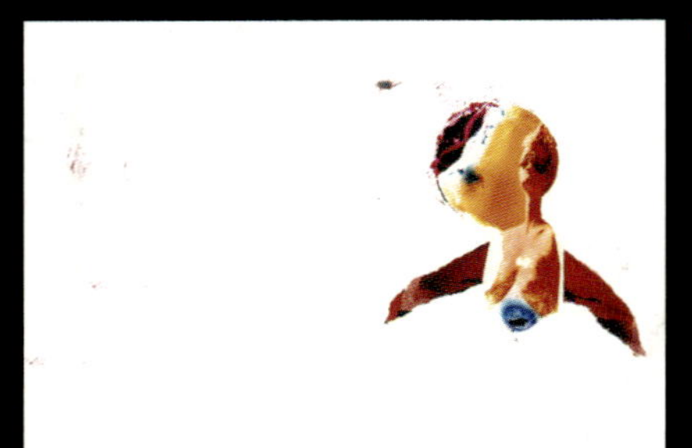

112-113. Icarus Flight Test

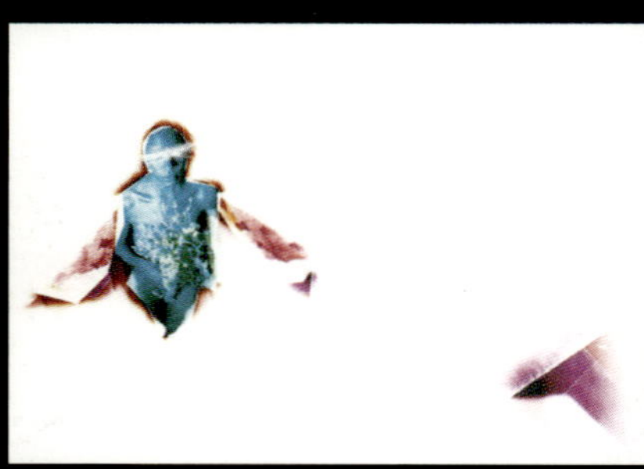

114-115. Wasp

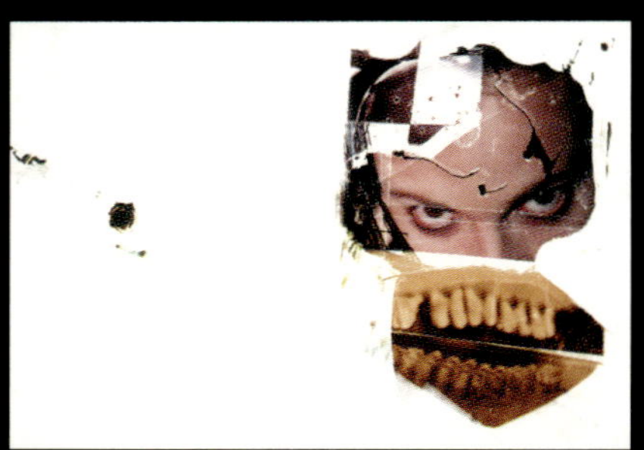

116-117. Crynology Test

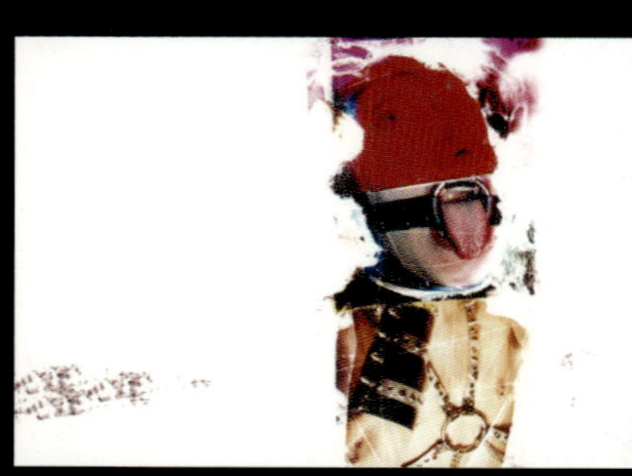

118-119. Spazmatic Masochist

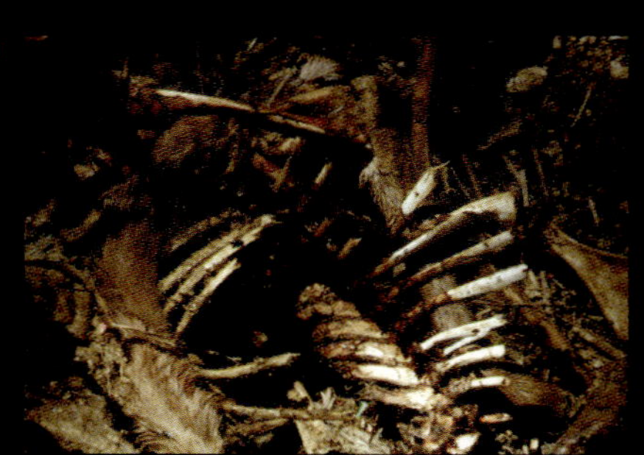

120-121. A Walk in the Park

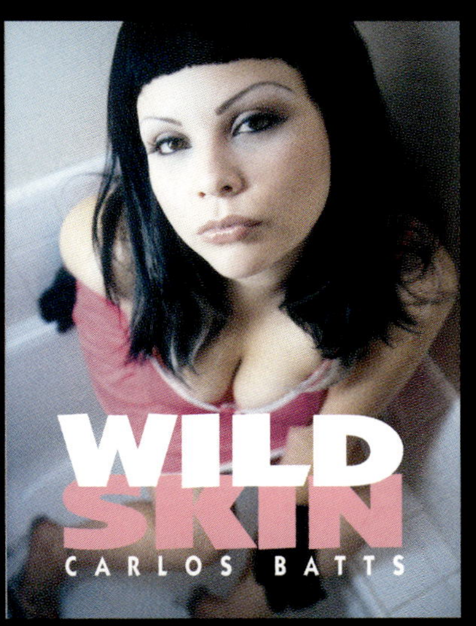
WILD
SKIN
CARLOS BATTS

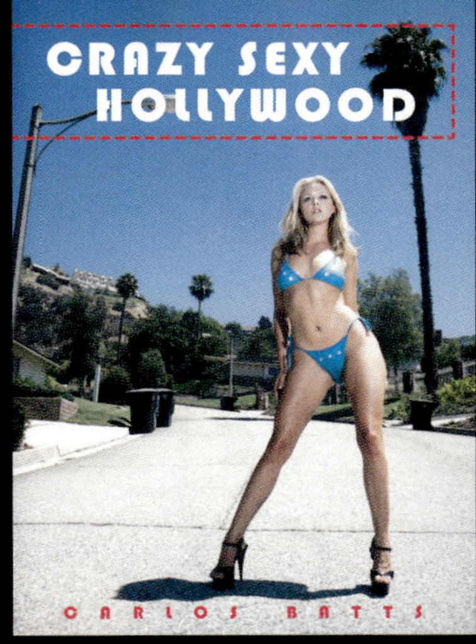
CRAZY SEXY
HOLLYWOOD
CARLOS BATTS

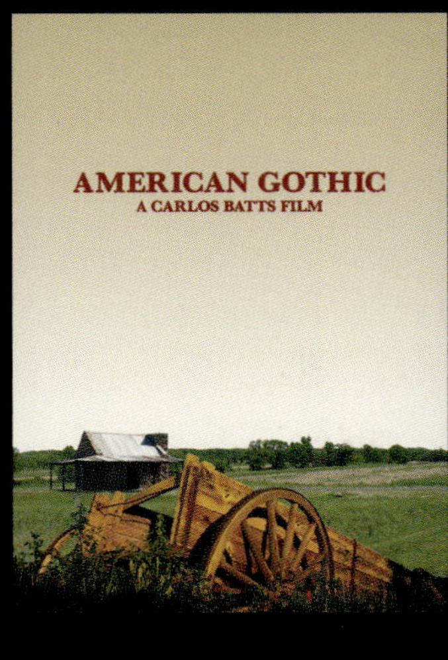
AMERICAN GOTHIC
A CARLOS BATTS FILM

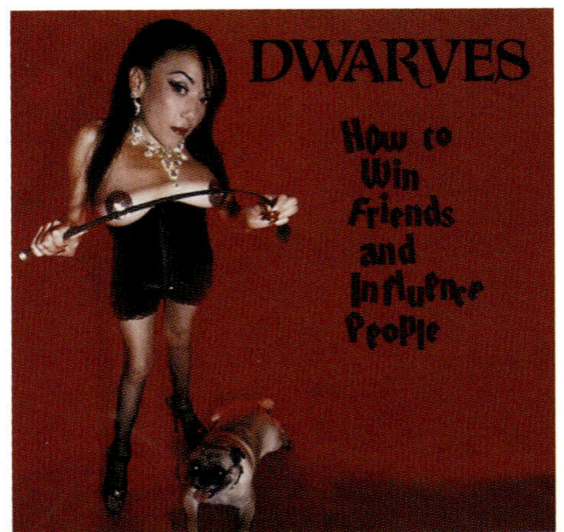
DWARVES
How to Win Friends and Influence People

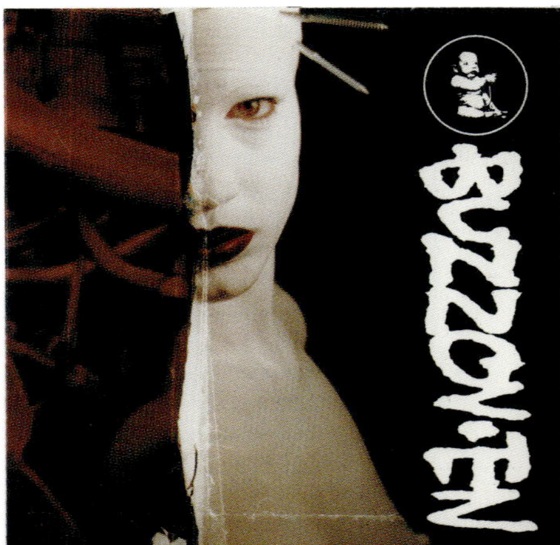
BUZZOV•EN

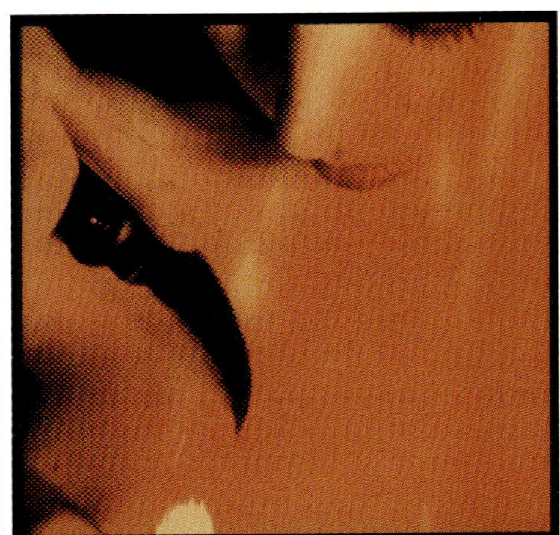

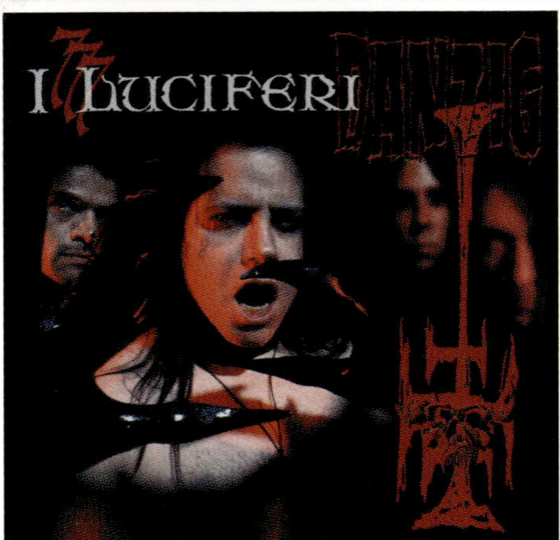
I LUCIFERI
DANZIG

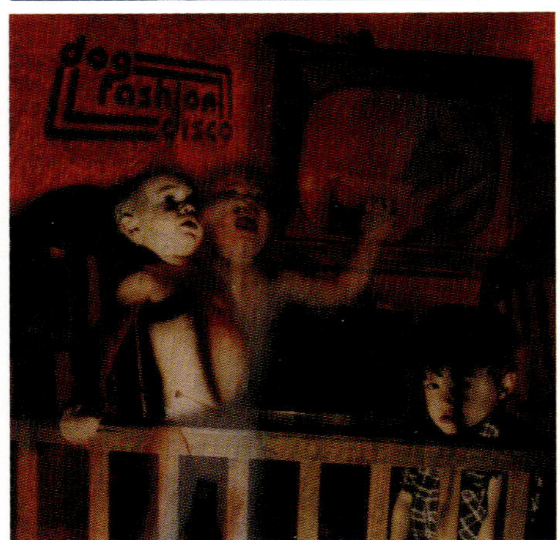
dog fashion disco

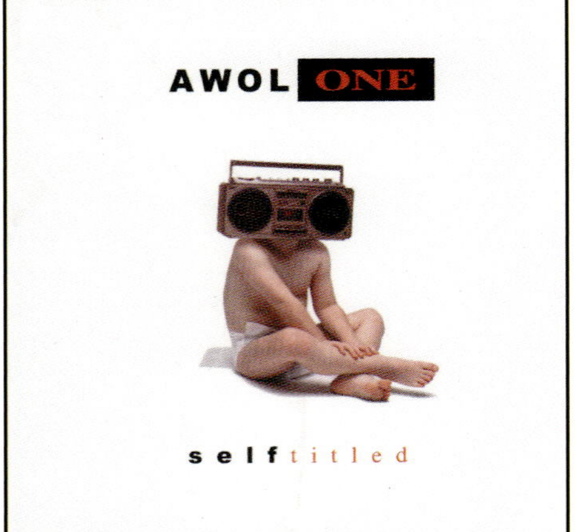
AWOL ONE
selftitled

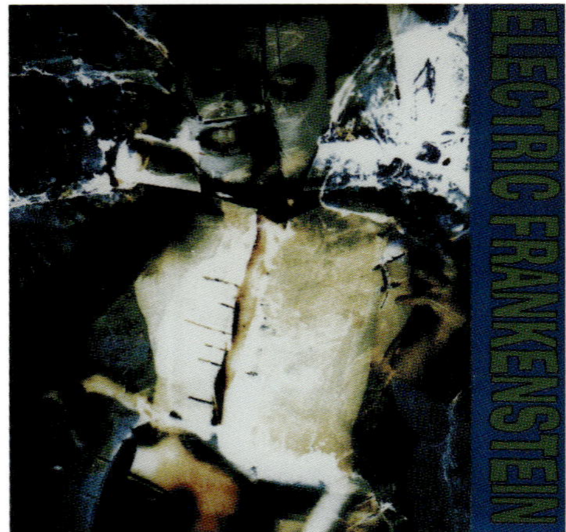
ELECTRIC FRANKENSTEIN

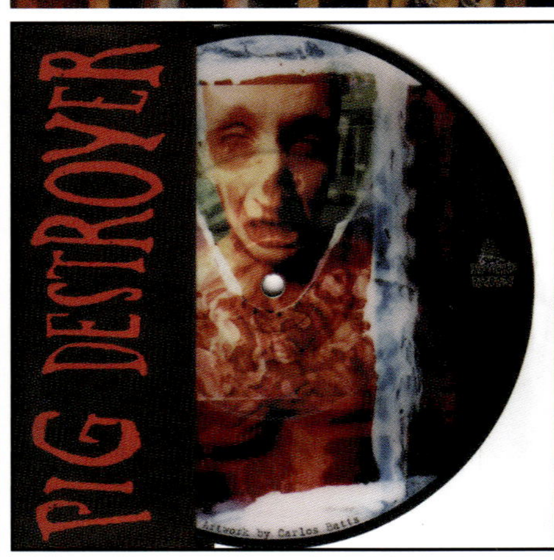
PIG DESTROYER
Artwork by Carlos Batts

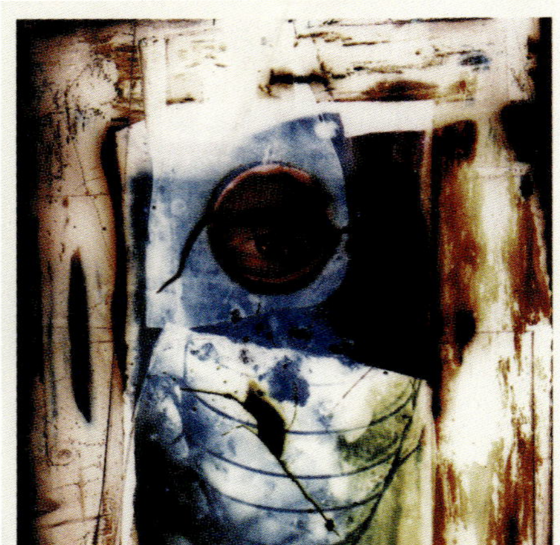

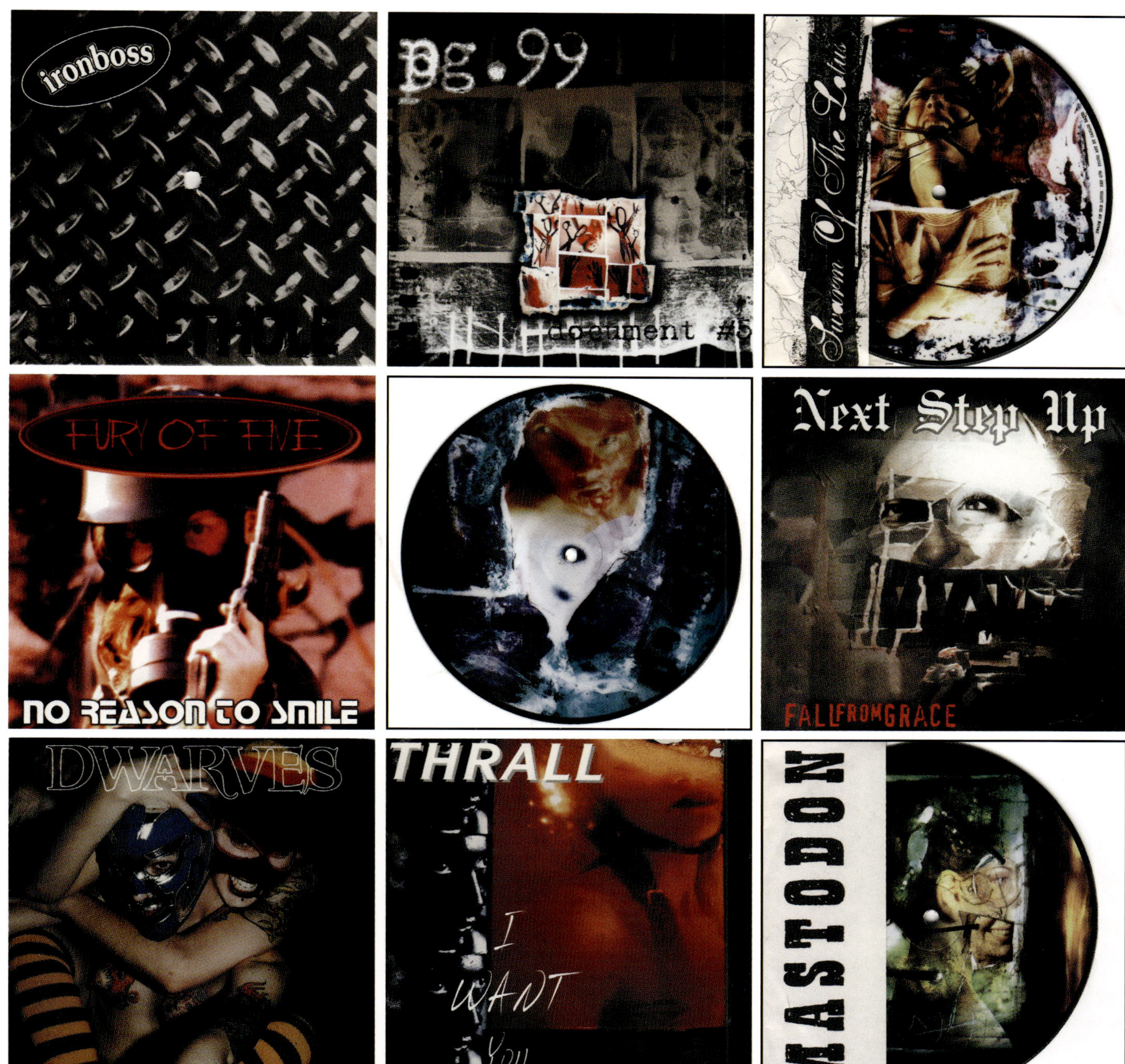

ironboss
pg.99
document #5
Swarm Of The Lotus
FURY OF FIVE
NO REASON TO SMILE
Next Step Up
FALLFROMGRACE
DWARVES
THRALL
I WANT YOU
MASTODON

American Gothic CD track listing

Mastodon Thank You For This
(taken from their Reptilian Records picture disc single)

Pg.99 Skinpack
(taken from the CD *Document #5* on Reptilian Records)

Swarm of the Lotus Ichabod
(taken from their Reptilian Records picture disc single)

Pig Destroyer Blonde Prostitute
(taken from their Reptilian Records picture disc single)

Daybreak Black Box
(taken from their Reptilian Records picture disc single)

Agoraphobic Nosebleed Lashings for the Old
(taken from their Reptilian Records picture disc single)

Dog Fashion Disco Day of the Dead
(taken from the *Day of the Dead* EP on Outerloop Recordings)

Radiation 4 Tick.Tock.Tick
(taken from the CD *Wonderland* on Abacus Recordings)

Buzzoven Useless
(taken from their Reptilian Records single)